*This book is personally
signed by the author*

GENTLEMAN JOLE AND THE RED QUEEN

BOOKS by LOIS McMASTER BUJOLD

The Vorkosigan Saga:

Shards of Honor • Barrayar
The Warrior's Apprentice • The Vor Game
Cetaganda • Borders of Infinity
Brothers in Arms • Mirror Dance
Memory • Komarr
A Civil Campaign • Diplomatic Immunity
Captain Vorpatril's Alliance • Cryoburn
Gentleman Jole and the Red Queen

Falling Free • Ethan of Athos

Omnibus Editions:

Cordelia's Honor • Young Miles
Miles, Mystery & Mayhem • Miles Errant
Miles, Mutants & Microbes • Miles in Love

The Chalion Series:

The Curse of Chalion • Paladin of Souls
The Hallowed Hunt

The Sharing Knife Tetrology:

Volume 1: Beguilement • Volume 2: Legacy
Volume 3: Passage • Volume 4: Horizon

The Spirit Ring

ALSO AVAILABLE FROM BAEN BOOKS

The Vorkosigan Companion, edited by
Lillian Stewart Carl and John Helfers

GENTLEMAN JOLE AND THE RED QUEEN

LOIS McMASTER BUJOLD

GENTLEMAN JOLE AND THE RED QUEEN

This is a work of fiction. All the characters and events portrayed in this book are fictional, and any resemblance to real people or incidents is purely coincidental.

A Baen Books Original

Baen Publishing Enterprises
P.O. Box 1403
Riverdale, NY 10471
www.baen.com

ISBN: 978-1-4767-8178-5

Cover Art by Ron Miller.
Frontispiece illustration by Dave Seeley.

First printing, February 2016

Distributed by Simon & Schuster
1230 Avenue of the Americas
New York, NY 10020

Library of Congress Cataloging-in-Publication Data

Names: Bujold, Lois McMaster, author.
Title: Gentleman Jole and the Red Queen / Lois McMaster Bujold.
Description: Riverdale, NY : Baen, [2016] | ?2015 | Series: Vorkosigan saga
Identifiers: LCCN 2015039675 | ISBN 9781476781228 (hardcover)
Subjects: LCSH: Vorkosigan, Miles (Fictitious character)—Fiction. | Life on
    other planets—Fiction. | BISAC: FICTION / Science Fiction / Space Opera.
    | FICTION / Science Fiction / Adventure. | FICTION / Science Fiction /
    General. | GSAFD: Science fiction. | Fantasy fiction.
Classification: LCC PS3552.U397 G46 2016 | DDC 813/.54—dc23 LC record available
at http://lccn.loc.gov/2015039675

10 9 8 7 6 5 4 3 2 1

Pages by Joy Freeman (www.pagesbyjoy.com)
Printed in the United States of America

In memory of Dr. Martha Bartter

GENTLEMAN JOLE AND THE RED QUEEN

Chapter One

It was a good day on the military transfer station orbiting the planet Sergyar. The Vicereine was coming home.

As he entered the station's Command-and-Control room, Admiral Jole's eye swept the main tactics display, humming and colorful above its holo-table. The map of his territory—albeit presently set to the distorted scale of human interests within Sergyar's system, and not the astrographic reality, which would leave everything invisible and put humans firmly in their place as a faint smear on the surface of a speck. A G-star burning tame and pleasant at this distance; its necklace of half-a-dozen planets and their circling moons; the colony world itself turning below the station. Of more critical strategic interest, the four wormhole jump points that were its gateways to the greater galactic nexus, and their attendant military and civilian stations—two highly active with a stream of commercial traffic and scheduled tight-beam relays, leading to the jump routes back to the rest of the Barrayaran Empire and on to its nearest neighbor on this side, currently peaceful Escobar; one accessing a long and uneconomical backdoor route to the Nexus; the last leading, as far as forty years of exploration had found, nowhere.

Jole wondered at what point in the past double-handful of years he'd started carrying the whole map and everything moving through it in his head at once. He'd used to consider his mentor's ability to do so as something bordering on the supernatural, although the late Aral Vorkosigan had done it routinely for an entire three-system empire, and not just its smallest third. Time, it seemed, had gifted Jole easily with what earnest study had found hard. Good. Because time bloody *owed* him, for all that it had taken away.

It was quiet this morning in the C-and-C room, most of the techs bored at their stations, the ventilation laden with the usual scents of electronics, recycled air, and overcooked coffee. He moved to the one station that was brightly lit, letting his hand press the shoulder of the traffic controller, *stay on task*. The man nodded and returned his attention to the pair of ships coming in.

The Vicereine's jump-pinnace was nearly identical to that of a fleet admiral, small and swift, bristling more with communications equipment than weapons. Its escort, a fast courier, could keep up, but was scarcely better armed; they traveled together more for safety in case of technical emergencies than any other sort. None this trip, thankfully. Jole watched with what he knew was perfectly pointless anxiety as they maneuvered into their docking clamps. No pilot would want to make a clumsy docking under *those* calm gray eyes.

His newest aide popped up at his elbow. "The honor guard reports ready, sir."

"Thank you, Lieutenant Vorinnis. We'll go over now."

He motioned her into his wake as he exited C-and-C and made for the Vicereine's docking bay. Kaya Vorinnis was far from the first of the techs, medtechs, and troops from the greatly expanded Imperial Service Women's Auxiliary to be assigned to Sergyar command, nor the first to be assigned directly to his office. But the Vicereine would approve, which was a charming thought, though Cordelia would doubtless also make some less-charming remark about how her natal Beta Colony and a like list of advanced planets had boasted fully-gender-integrated space services since forever. Personally, Jole was relieved that he only had to supervise the women during working hours, and that their off-duty arrangements here on-station and on the downside base were the direct responsibility of a rather maternal and very efficient ISWA colonel.

"I've never seen Vicereine Vorkosigan in person," Vorinnis confided to him. "Only in vids." Jole was reminded not to let his long stride quicken unduly, though the lieutenant's breath-lessness might be as much due to incipient heroine-worship, not misplaced in Jole's view.

"Oh? I thought you were a relative of Count Vorinnis. Had you not spent much time in Vorbarr Sultana?"

"Not that closely related, sir. I've only met the count twice. And most of my time in the capital was spent running around Ops. I was put on Admin track pretty directly." Her light sigh was easy to interpret, having the identical content to those of her male predecessors: *Not ship duty, dammit.*

"Well, take heart. I was put through a seven-year rotation in the capital as a military secretary and aide, but I still caught three tours on trade fleet escort duty afterward." The most active and far-flung space-based duty an Imperial officer could aspire to during peacetime, culminating in his one and only ship captaincy, traded in due course for this Sergyar patch.

"Yes, but that was aide to *Regent Vorkosigan* himself!"

"He was down to Prime Minister Vorkosigan, by then." Jole permitted himself a brief lip twitch. "I'm not *that* old." And just kept his mouth from adding, "...young lady!" It wasn't merely Vorinnis's height, or lack of it, that made her look twelve in his eyes, or her gender; her recent male counterparts were no better. "Although, by whatever irony, my one stint in an active theater of war *was* as his secretary, when I followed him to the Hegen Hub. Not that we knew it was going to end up a shooting war when that trip started."

"Were you ever under fire?"

"Well, yes. There is no rear echelon on a flagship. Since the Emperor was also aboard by that point, it was fortunate that our shields never failed." Two decades ago, now. And what a top-secret cockup that entire episode had been, which, glued throughout to Ex-Regent Prime Minister Admiral Count Vorkosigan's shoulder, Jole had witnessed at the closest possible range from first to last. His Hegen Hub war stories had always had to be among his most thoroughly edited.

"I guess you've known Vicereine Vorkosigan just as long, then?"

"Nearly exactly, yes. It's been…" He had to calculate it in his head, and the sum took him aback. "Twenty-three years, almost."

"I'm almost twenty-three," Vorinnis offered, in a tone of earnest helpfulness.

"Ah," Jole managed. He was rescued from any further fall into this surreal time warp by their arrival at Docking Bay Nine.

The dozen men of the honor guard braced, and Jole returned salutes punctiliously while running his eye over their turnout. Everything shipshape and shiny, good. He duly complimented the sergeant in charge and turned to take up a parade rest in strategic view of the personnel flex tube, just locking on under the competent and very attentive supervision of the bay tech. Exiting a null-gee flex tube into the grav field of a station or ship was seldom a graceful or dignified process, but the first three persons out were reasonably practiced: a ship's officer, one of the Vicereine's ImpSec guards, and Armsman Rykov, the only one of the new Count Vorkosigan's personal retainers seconded to his mother, in her other hat as Dowager Countess. The first man attended to mechanics, the second made a visual and electronic scan of the docking bay for unscheduled human hazards, and the third turned to assist his liege lady. Vorinnis tried to stand on tiptoe and to attention simultaneously, which didn't quite work, but she dropped from Jole's awareness as the last figure cleared the tube in a smooth swing and flowed to her feet with the aid of her armsman's proffered hands.

Everyone snapped to attention as the color sergeant piped her aboard. Admiral Jole saluted, and said formally, "Vicereine Vorkosigan. Welcome back. I trust your journey was uneventful."

"Thank you, Admiral, and so it was," she returned, equally formally. "It's good to be back."

He made a quick initial assay of her. She looked a trifle jump-lagged, but nothing like the frightening dead-gray bleakness that had haunted her features when she'd returned alone almost three years ago from her husband's state funeral. Not that Jole himself had been in much better form, at the time. The colonists of Sergyar had been entirely uncertain if they were going to get their Vicereine back at all, that trip, or if some stranger-lord would be appointed in her place. But she was wearing colors again now, if subdued ones, Komarran-style trousers and jacket, and her unmistakable smile had warmed to something better than room temperature. She was still keeping her tousled red-gray hair cut short; the fine bones of her face held out, like a rampart that had never fallen.

Her left hand, down at her side, gripped what appeared to be a small cryofreezer case. Lieutenant Vorinnis, like any good admiral's assistant, advanced upon it. "May I take your luggage, Your Excellency?"

Cordelia cried, sharply and unexpectedly, "No!" twitching the case away. At Jole's eyebrow-lift, she seemed to catch herself up, and continued more smoothly, "No, thank you, Lieutenant. I'll carry this one. And my armsman will see to the rest." She cast a quick head-tilt toward the girl, and a plea of a look Jole's way.

He took the hint. "Vicereine, may I introduce my new aide, Lieutenant Kaya Vorinnis. Just assigned—she arrived a few weeks after you left." Cordelia had departed six weeks ago to present the Sergyaran Viceroy's Annual Report to Emperor Gregor in person, and incidentally catch a little of Winterfair Season with her family back on Barrayar. Jole hoped that had been refreshing rather than exhausting, although having met the Vorkosigan offspring, he suspected it had been both.

"How do you do, Lieutenant? I hope you will find Sergyar an interesting rotation. Ah—any relation to the young count?"

"Not close, ma'am," Vorinnis replied, an answer Jole suspected she was tired of offering, but she did it without grimacing here.

The Vicereine turned and delivered a few well-practiced words of thanks to the honor guard. Their sergeant returned the traditional, "Ma'am, yes, ma'am!" proudly on their behalf, and marched them out again. Cordelia watched them go, then turned with a sigh to take Jole's arm proffered in escort.

She shook her head. "Really, Oliver, do you have to do this every time I transit? All I'm going to do is walk from the docking bay to the shuttle hatch. Those poor boys could have slept in."

"We never did less for the Viceroy. It's an honor for them as well as for you, you know."

"Aral was your war hero. Several times over."

The corners of Jole's mouth twitched up. "And you're not?" He added in curiosity, "What's in the box? Not a severed head—again—I trust?" It seemed too small for that, fortunately.

Cordelia's gray eyes glinted. "Now, now, Oliver. Bring home one dismembered body part, *once*, mind you, *once*, and people get twitchy about checking your luggage ever after." Her smile grew wry. "But that we can *joke* about that now...ah, well."

Lieutenant Vorinnis, trailing, looked vaguely appalled, though whether at the famous historical incident that had ended the Pretender's War, a disturbing number of years before her birth, or her superiors' attitude to it, Jole was not sure.

Jole said, "Do you want to take a break, Cordelia, before catching your downside leg? I don't know what meal schedule you're on, but we can provide." The entire Barrayaran Imperial fleet, and by extension this station, kept Vorbarr Sultana time, which unfortunately did not mesh with that of the colonial capital below, as the two planets had, among other things, different day lengths. Not that *the same time* on two different sides of a wormhole jump, let alone a string of them, had any but an arbitrary congruence. "Your shuttle will await your convenience, I promise you."

Cordelia shook her head in regret. "I switched to Kareenburg time when we made Sergyaran space a day ago. I *think* my next meal is lunch, though I'll find out when we land. But no, thank you, Oliver, not this round. I'm eager to get home." Her grip on the freezer case tightened.

"I hope we'll be able to catch up more thoroughly soon."

"Oh, count on it. When do you next cycle down to base?"

"End of the week."

Her eyes narrowed in some unconfided calculation. "Ye-es. That might just about do. My secretary will be in touch, then."

"Right-oh." Jole accepted this affably, hiding his disappointment. News from Barrayar arrived hourly by tightbeam. *Stories from home* arrived with returning visitors, more erratically. Could a man be homesick for a *voice*? A light, particular voice, still laced with a broad Betan accent forty-plus years after pledging and proving allegiance to an alien Imperium?

All too soon, they arrived at the shuttle hatch. Jole had inspected the vessel personally not an hour ago. The pilot reported at the ready. Jole stood aside with Cordelia, stealing a few more minutes together as her luggage was trundled aboard.

"You're traveling lighter, these days."

She smiled. "Aral was *used* to moving an army. I prefer simpler logistics." She glanced toward the shuttle hatch, as if anxious to be boarding. "Any forest fires downside that I haven't heard about by tightbeam?"

"None that have penetrated the stratosphere." Their traditional dividing line for their respective responsibilities. Cordelia rode herd on some two million colonists on behalf of Emperor Gregor; Jole suspected that a good half of them would be at her for attention the moment her foot touched the soil. At least he could make sure that no new troubles dropped on her from above. "Take care of yourself down there. Or at least let your staff do so." Jole exchanged a conspiratorial glance with Armsman Rykov, who acted more-or-less as the Vicereine's household seneschal, and who nodded endorsement of this notion.

Cordelia just smiled. "See you soon, Oliver."

And off she goes. And goes and goes, like any Vorkosigan. Jole shook his head.

He waited till he heard the docking clamps release, then turned away.

Vorinnis, pacing him, inquired, "Were you there, sir, when she brought back the Pretender's head?"

"I was *eight*, Lieutenant." He tried to rub the amusement off his mouth, and recover his expected admiral's gravity. "I grew up in one of the westernmost districts—it had no military shuttleport, so we weren't a high-value target for either side. I mainly remember the war as everyone trying to carry on normally, but all the adults being awash in fear and fantastic rumors. The Lord Regent had made away with the boy emperor, he was brainwashed by Betan spies, worse slanders...Everyone believed that Lady Vorkosigan had been sent on that commando raid by her husband, but the truth, I later learned, was a deal more complicated." And not all his to tell, Jole was reminded. "We meet fairly frequently in the course of business here on Sergyar—you may get a chance to try to get her to decant some of *her* war stories." Although upon reflection, Jole wasn't sure of the advisability of introducing a keen young officer to Vorkosigan notions of initiative. Metaphors about fighting fire with gasoline rose to his mind.

He grinned and returned to Command-and-Control, there to keep the Vicereine's shuttle in view till its safe touchdown was confirmed.

The Sergyaran afternoon was luminous, on the restaurant terrace overlooking what Cordelia could no longer call the encampment, nor even the village, but surely the *city* even by galactic standards. The terrace's perch above a sharp drop-off on the hillside lent a pleasant illusion of looking out into a gulf of light. When the server, seating her at her reserved corner table, inquired if ma'am wanted the polarizing awning raised, Cordelia answered simply, "Not yet," and waved him off. She sat back and lifted her face to the warmth, closing her eyes and letting its caress soothe her. And tried not to think how long it had been since any more palpable caress had done so. *Three years next month*, the too-busy part of her brain that she could not shut off supplied.

As an anodyne, she reopened her eyes to her surroundings. The two tables closest to hers were empty by arrangement, except for her plainclothes ImpSec bodyguard who already sat at the farther one, not-sipping iced tea and looking around as well. *Situational awareness*, right. Her over forty years as a subject and servant of the Barrayaran Empire had included all too many *situations*; for today, she was willing to default to *I have people for that*. Except that the fellow looked *so* young; she felt as though she should be watching out for him, maternally. She must never offend his dignity by letting on, she supposed.

She sucked in a long breath of the soft air, as if she might so draw its lightness into the darker hollows of her heart. The server brought two water glasses. She was only a few sips into hers when the figure she had been awaiting appeared through the building's door, glanced around, spied her, lifted a hand in greeting, and strode her way. Her bodyguard, watching this progress and taking in her guest's civilian garb, visibly restrained himself from standing and saluting the man as he passed by, although they did exchange acknowledging nods.

When Cordelia had first met Lieutenant Oliver Perrin Jole, back when he was, what—twenty-seven?—she had not hesitated to describe him as *gorgeous*. Tall, blond, lean, chiseled features—oh my, the *cheekbones*—blue eyes alive with earnest intelligence. More diffident, back then. After two decades and some change—and changes—Admiral Jole was still tall and straight, if more solid in both build and demeanor. The bright blondness of his hair was a trifle tarnished with gray, the clear eyes framed with what were really quite fetching crow's feet, and he had grown into a quiet, firm self-confidence. Still with those unfair cheekbones and eyelashes, though. She smiled a little, permitting herself this private moment of delicate enjoyment, before he arrived to bow over her hand and seat himself.

"Vicereine."

"Just Cordelia, today, Oliver. Unless you want me to start *admiraling* you."

He shook his head. "I get enough of that at work." But his curious smile grew more crooked. "And there was only ever the one true admiral, among us. My last promotion always felt a touch surreal, when I was in his company."

"You're a true admiral. The Emperor said so. And the Viceroy advised."

"I shan't argue."

"Good, because it would be a few years—and a great deal of work—too late."

Jole chuckled, twitched his long fingers at her in surrender of the point, if no other sort, and took up the menu. He tilted his head. "You're looking less tired, at least. That's good."

Cordelia had no doubt that she'd looked downright hagged often enough in their late scramble for their new balance. She ran a hand through her close-cropped red-roan hair, curling in its usual feral fashion around her head. "I'm feeling less tired." She grimaced. "I sometimes go for whole hours at a time without thinking of him, now. Last week, there was a whole day."

He nodded in, she was sure, complete understanding.

Cordelia wondered how to begin. *We haven't seen enough of each other these past three years* was not really true. The Admiral of the Sergyaran Fleet had moved smoothly into his tasks as the military right arm of the lone Vicereine of Sergyar—just as for the joint Viceroy and Vicereine formerly. He'd been accepted by the colony planet on his own considerable merits even when his mentor's immense shadow silently backing him was removed by that—could she call it untimely?—that immense death. Vicereine Vorkosigan and Admiral Jole had adjusted to the new patterns of their respective jobs, working around that aching absence, tightening the public stitches over that wound. Briefings, inspections,

diplomatic duties, petitions, advice given and listened to, arguments with budget committees both in tandem and, a few times,
in opposition—their workload After Aral was scarcely changed
in substance or rhythm from their workload Before. And, slowly,
the civic scar had healed, though it still twinged now and then.

The inmost wounds . . . they'd scarcely touched, or touched
upon, in mutual mercy perhaps. She would never count Oliver as
less bereaved than herself just because his grief was more circum-
spectly hidden—though she had more than once, as she forced
herself through what had seemed the endless gauntlet of public
ceremonies befalling the Viceregal Widow, envied him its privacy.

It was only their former intimacy that seemed taken away,
buried with its nexus point. Like two planets left to wander when
their mutual sun vanished. It was time, perhaps, for a renewed
source of gravity and light.

The server returned, and she was spared from her further inter-
nal . . . dithering, yes, she was dithering, by the minor distractions
of placing their orders. When they were alone again, Oliver relieved
her of her quandary by remarking, "If this is to be a working lunch,
someone was behindhand in supplying me with the agenda."

"Not work, no, but I do have an agenda," she confessed.
"Personal and private, which is why I invited you here on our
so-called day off." She wondered what signals he'd read in her
invitation that brought him here in comfortable-if-flattering civvies, instead of his uniform. He'd always been alert to nuance,
an invaluable trait back when he'd first been assigned as Prime
Minister Vorkosigan's military secretary in the hothouse political
atmosphere of the Imperial capital back on Barrayar. *We are far
from Vorbarr Sultana. And I'm glad of it.*

She took a sip of water, and the plunge. "Have you heard
anything about the new replicator center we opened downtown?"

"I . . . not *per se*, no. I am aware that your public health
efforts continue." He blinked at her in his most amiable I-am-
not-following-you-but-I'm-still-listening look.

"My mother back on Beta Colony helped me headhunt an

exceptional team of Betan reproductive experts to staff it, on five-year contracts. They're teaching Sergyaran medtechs in the clinic, as well as serving the public. By the end of their terms, we expect to be able to hive off several daughter clinics to the newer colonial towns. And, if we're lucky, maybe seduce a few of the Betans into staying on."

Jole, unmarried and unlikely to be so, smiled and shrugged. "I'm actually old enough to remember when that was new and controversial technology, back on Barrayar. The younger officers coming on take it for granted, and not just the Komarran-born ones, or the ISWA girls."

The server arrived with their wine—a light, fruity, well-chilled white, produced right here on this planet, yes!—and she fortified herself with a sip before continuing forthrightly. "In this case, the public good is also a personal one. As, um, Aral may never have mentioned to you, and I don't recall I ever did either, during one of the dodgier times of Aral's regency—before you came on board—we took the precaution of privately sequestering gametes from each of us. Frozen sperm from him, frozen eggs from me." Over thirty-five years ago, that had been.

Oliver's steely blond brows rose. "He told me once that he was infertile, after the soltoxin attack."

"For natural conceptions, probably. Low sperm count, lots of cellular damage accumulated over his lifetime. But—technology. You only need one good gamete, if you can sort it."

"Huh."

"For reasons more political than either biological or techno-logical, we never went back to that bank. But Aral made sure in his will that the samples' ownership was mine absolutely, after his death. On this trip home for Winterfair and the annual Viceroy's Report, I pulled them all. And brought them back to Sergyar with me. Those were what was in that freezer case I was—well, sitting on more like a mother hen than you knew."

Oliver sat up, abruptly interested. "Posthumous children for Aral? *Can* you?"

"That's what I needed the top Betan experts to determine. As it turns out, the answer is yes."

"Huh! Now that Miles is Count Vorkosigan in his own right, with a son of his own, I suppose another son—brother?—would not present an inheritance issue...Uh—would they be legitimate, under Barrayaran law?"

Her elder son Miles, Cordelia considered wryly, was only eight years younger than Jole. "I actually plan to sidestep all those issues by conceiving only daughters. This takes advantage of one of the peculiarities of Barrayaran inheritance law in that they will all be, without question, mine alone. They will bear the very prole surname of Naismith. No claim on the Vorkosigan's District or Vorkosigan estates. Nor vice versa."

Oliver pursed his lips, frowning. "Aral...would have wanted to support them. To say the least."

"I have been, and will be, setting aside the rather comfortable widow's jointure due me as Dowager Countess Vorkosigan for that purpose. Since I have both my salary as Vicereine, at least for a while longer, and my own personal investments, mostly here on Sergyar, to support a private household quite adequately."

"A while?" said Jole at once, pouncing upon a key point and looking alarmed. As she might have known he would.

"I never planned to remain as Vicereine till I died in harness," she said gently. *As Aral did*, she did not say aloud. "I'm a Betan. I expect to live to a hundred and twenty or more. I have fed about as much of my life to Barrayar as I wish to. It's time..." She drained her wineglass; Jole politely poured her more. "They say that a person should not make major life decisions or changes for at least a year after bereavement, due to having their brains scrambled, to the truth of which I can testify, except I'd make it two years."

Jole nodded bleak agreement.

"I've been thinking about this from the night we buried him at Vorkosigan Surleau." The night she'd cut all her waist-length hair, which Aral had always loved, nearly to the roots to lay in the burning brazier. Because the usual sacrificial lock had seemed absurdly inadequate. Not one of her fellow mourners had said a word in protest, nor asked one in question. She'd never worn it longer than its current finger-length, thereafter. "It will be three years next month. I think...this is what I truly want, and if I'm going to, it's time. Betan or no, I am not getting any younger."

"A person would take you for fifty," offered Jole. His own age, very nearly. He actually meant it; he wasn't just flattering her. *Barrayarans.*

"Only a Barrayaran. A galactic would know better." She considered *seventy-six*. It...made no sense. Except that sometime in the past three years, she had switched from counting her years not up from birth, but back from death—a grab-bag of time not growing, but shrinking, *use it or lose it.*

The server arrived with their vat-chicken-and-strawberry salads and fancy breads, giving her a moment to muster her next push. Jole, to his credit, had not asked, *Why are you telling me all this?* but had taken it in as a simple—well, maybe not that simple—confidence from a friend. And by no means an unwelcome one. She took another sip of wine. Then a gulp of wine. She set down her glass.

"We didn't have a large number of eggs to work with, once the substandard ones were filtered out. I took my share of damage over the years, too. But I think I can get as many as six girls, altogether."

Jole huffed a laugh. "Well, Sergyar needs women."

"And men. There were also a very few ova which might still be healthy as...I suppose you could say, enucleated eggshells. They will carry my mitochondrial DNA, anyway. And such enucleated ova are exactly what are used to host the same-sex IVF crosses."

Jole stopped in mid-chew and stared at her, blue eyes going wide. His quickness of mind had always been one of his more endearing traits, she reflected.

"If you like—and you can take as long as you need to think about it—I would donate to you some of those enucleated eggs, and genetic material from Aral, and you could...you and Aral could have a son or sons of your own. I mention sons for legal, not biological reasons. With an X chromosome from Aral and a Y chromosome from yourself, the offspring would be unassailably legally yours. With no damned bloody lethal Vor hung on the front of their names, either."

Jole swallowed his belated bite with the aid of a large gulp of his own wine. "This...sounds insane. At first blush."

He *was* blushing a trifle, actually. Interesting. On him, of course, it looked good. But then, it always had. *All the way down*, as she recalled, and suppressed a smile. "On Beta Colony, it would be routine. Or Escobar, or Earth, or any of the advanced planets." The normal planets, as Cordelia thought of them. "Or even Komarr, for heaven's sake. This biotech trick was worked out *centuries* ago."

"Yes, but not for us, not for..." He hesitated.

Not for Barrayar, did he mean to say? Or...*not for me?*

Instead he said, "So is this waste not, want not?"

"Just *want*."

"How many...how many such eggs?"

"Four. Which does not guarantee four live births, I hope you realize. Or, in fact, any. But it's four genetic lottery tickets, anyway."

"How long have you been thinking about this, um...extraordinary offer?" He was still staring at her wide-eyed. "Did you already have it in mind when you docked, the other day?"

"No, only since my conference with Dr. Tan, three days ago. We were discussing what to do with the leftovers, which was the one question I'd never anticipated. He suggested I donate the eggshells to the clinic, which could use them, and if this doesn't interest you, I probably will. But then I had a better idea." She'd hardly slept that night, thinking about it. And then she'd given up on running in circles inside her head trying to second-guess herself, and just invited Oliver to lunch.

"I'd never thought—I'd given up all thought—of ever having children, you know," he said. "There was my career, there was

Aral, there was...what we three had. Which was more than I'd ever dreamed of having."

"Yes. I'd thought you insufficiently imaginative." She took a fortifying crunch of chicken salad. "Not to mention insufficiently greedy in the extreme."

"How could I ever take care of..." he began, then cut himself off.

"Plenty of time to think about the practical details," Cordelia assured him. "I just wanted to put the idea into your head."

Oliver made a hair-clutching gesture, not quite jesting. "And explode it? You always did have that little sadistic streak, Cordelia."

"Now, Oliver. *Assertive*, perhaps. As you may recall."

From the way he choked on his next swallow of wine, he did. *Good.* But the next words out of his mouth were, unexpectedly, "Everard Piotr Jole?"

Good grief, he's naming them already! Well...she'd had her hypothetical girls named for a year. *Wow, this pitch went fast.* Fortunately, there was a certain amount of time built-in for second thoughts, and the cascade of worrying that she knew from experience would follow. "We're on Sergyar, here. Not bound to tradition. You could choose any names you liked. I'm going to name my first girl Aurelia Kosigan Naismith. They're all going to be named Kosigan Naismith, actually. Except the Kosigan will be an actual middle name, no hyphens or anything." *Or prefixes.* "I'm not sure they'll thank me, later."

"What, um...what does your son Miles think of this? Or his clone-brother Mark, for that matter?"

"I haven't discussed it with them yet. Nor do I intend to, till after the fact. I won't say, *Not Miles's business*, but I will say, *Not his decision.*"

"Did you—or Aral—ever tell him about us? Does he know? I was never quite sure. That is, if he knew and accepted me, or if he just didn't know."

And the grueling state funeral, which had been the last time Oliver and her sons had crossed paths in person, had been no place to bring it up. "Ha. No. Speaking of exploding heads, Aral always spared Miles that. I never much agreed with that choice, but I have to admit it was simpler."

He nodded relieved acceptance.

She regarded him a moment, and added, deliberately, "Aral was always so very proud of you. I hope you know that."

His breath caught, and he looked away. Swallowed. Nodded shortly. It took him another few breaths, but he recovered his train of thought: "When you started to tell me about this, I thought perhaps you were going to ask me to stand as godfather or something—what's that Betan term, co-parent?"

"A co-parent is legally, and usually genetically, the same as a parent—a godfather is more like the orphan's legal guardian in the event of parental death. And yes, I'm going to have to give thought to my new will. Fortunately, I have access to the best lawyers on the planet. And so will you, in the event."

"Aral Kosigan Jole...?" he muttered, as if he hadn't heard this, though she knew he had.

"No one would blink," she assured him. "Or Oliver Jole, Junior, or anything you like."

"How could I...explain their mother? Or their lack of a mother?"

"Anonymously donated eggs purchased from the gamete bank, perfectly standard. Which isn't even untrue. You hit fifty, and suddenly decided to have a child for your midlife crisis instead of a shiny red lightflyer, whatever."

He swiped a hand through his tarnished gold hair, and laughed uncertainly. "I am beginning to think *you* are my midlife crisis, Cordelia."

She shrugged, amused. "Shall I apologize?"

"Never." The best smile tugged up his lips, despite his dismay.

No—they hadn't seen enough of each other these past three years, had they. They'd merely swept past each other often. She and Oliver had both been running like hell for their work and other duties, frequently on different planets, or on opposite ends of a gravity well, and the last thing the widowed Vicereine, under intense scrutiny in her new solo position, possessed was any personal privacy. She envied Aral his cool former command of his privacy, in retrospect. And how his cloak of loyalties had stretched to cover them all.

She dug a card out of her pocket, scribbled a note on the back, and handed it across. "This is the doctor to see, if you decide to stop in at the rep center and leave a donation. My key Betan man, Dr. Tan. He's been fully apprised. In your own time, Mister Jole."

Jole took it gingerly, and read it closely. "I see." His long fingers placed it in his shirt pocket with care, touching it again as if to make sure. "This is an astounding gift. I would never have thought of it."

"So I concluded." She scrubbed her lips with her napkin. "Well, think about it now."

"I doubt I'll be able to think about anything else." His smile tilted. "Thank you for not dropping this on me in the middle of a working day, by the way."

She cast him a ghost of a salute.

His eyes grew warmer, intent upon her. "Huh . . . This makes it the second time that my life has been turned upside-down and sent in directions I'd never even imagined by a Vorkosigan. I might have known."

"The first being, ah, when Aral fell in love with you?"

"Say, fell in love on me. It was like being hit by a falling building. Not a building falling over—a building falling from the sky."

She grinned back. "I am familiar with the sensation." She regarded him in reminded curiosity. "Aral talked to me about nearly everything—I was his only safe repository for that part of himself, till you came along—but he was always a bit cagey about how you two got started. The empire was at peace, Miles was safely locked up in the Academy, political tensions were at an all-time low—not that *that* lasted—I go off to visit my mother on Beta Colony leaving him in no worse straits than another of his unrequited silent crushes. I come back to find you two up and running and poor Illyan having a meltdown—it was like talking him in off a ledge." Aral's utterly loyal security chief had never come closer to, if not weeping with relief, at least cracking an expression, to find in her not an outraged spouse, but an unruffled ally. *I knew Aral was bisexual when I married him. And he knew I was Betan. Melodrama was never an option, Illyan.* "The only surprise was how you two ever got past all your Barrayaran inhibitions in the first place." Not that she and Aral hadn't discussed Oliver in *theory.*

A flash of old amusement crossed Jole's always-expressive face. "Well—I'm afraid you'd think it was all more Barrayaran than Betan. It doubtless involved a lot less *talking,* which I cannot regret. The standard for declassification is still fifty years, isn't it? That sounds about right to me."

Cordelia snickered. "Never mind, then."

Jole cocked his head in turn. "Did he have that many, er, silent crushes? Before me?"

"I ought to make you trade"—Jole made his own *never mind, then,* gesture, and Cordelia smiled—"but I'll have pity. No, for all that the capital was awash with handsome officers, he more appreciated them as a man would a good sunset or a fine horse, abstractly. Intelligent officers, he recruited whenever he could, and if they happened to intersect the first set, well and good. Officers of extraordinary character—were always thinner on the ground. All three in one package—"

Jole made another fending gesture, which Cordelia brushed aside. "Oh, behave. The first time he ever saw you it was to pin that medal on you, wasn't it? He'd already studied the reports of the orbital accident, in detail—he always did, for those honors—and all your prior records. If nothing else, you'd just saved the Emperor the trouble of replacing about a hundred very expensively trained men." No wonder that Aral had recruited Jole as nearly on the spot as the paperwork and his physicians permitted. The *other* recruitment had come rather later.

Jole grimaced. "That always felt strange, to be cited for a set of actions I could barely remember. The hypoxia was cutting in badly by then. Not to mention the blood loss, I suppose. Or so my ImpMil physicians suggested, later. I could only think—but what if I had to do it again, and couldn't remember *how*?" His lips twisted up in belated amusement. "God, I was young, wasn't I?"

"You were as old as you'd ever been. As were we all, I suppose." After a moment, she added curiously, "Had you thought you were monosexual, before Aral?"

He shrugged. "If one doesn't count experiments at age fourteen. I'd dated women, as much as my career up till then permitted, which wasn't much. But things never quite clicked. After Aral, I thought I knew why." He glanced up through those lashes at her. "I was quite terrified of you, at first. Thought my head was going to end up in a sack."

"Yes, it took some time to talk you down, too."

"And I found out what the Countess's famous *Betan* conversations were all about. I'd never thought of myself as a naïve backcountry boy, till then."

Cordelia chuckled. "On Beta Colony, we'd have had *earrings* for it. We could have bought them in any jewelry shop."

"Ha. Remind me to tell you about the Betan herm merchanter I once met when I was out on my third escort tour. Without your tutoring, I'd have missed...well, an extraordinary week." He looked, for just a second, salaciously cheerful in his apparently fond memory. It wasn't a look she'd surprised on him for quite some time. It was no mystery why they'd both been getting through on zombie-pilot, these past three years; but she wondered when it had become a *habit*.

"I'm glad you were over your, er, shyness by the time you came to us again on Sergyar."

"The extra years and the captaincy under my belt probably helped."

"Something had, certainly." She bent her head, ambiguously but amiably. Silence fell between them, not unduly strained.

He twisted the stem of his wineglass; looked up at her directly. "This isn't going to be easy, is it. Or simple."

"It never has before; I have no idea why it should start now."

His laugh was low, but real.

They lingered only a little longer, reverting to talking shop—Chaos Colony made sure that they never ran out of shop—and then rose together. He did not offer his arm, although he might have done so here unexceptionably enough, and she did not walk too close. He helped her into her groundcar, brought round to the front; as it pulled away she twisted and studied him through the canopy, striding off to his own vehicle. He did wheel and give her a bemused little wave as her car turned into the street. His hand, falling again, touched his breast pocket in passing.

Cordelia was conscious of a twinge of frustration on Oliver's behalf, mostly because he never seemed to muster it for himself. Dammit, if there was ever a man who *deserved* to be loved... But if he'd made any connections since Aral's death, he hadn't confided them to her, not that he was under any obligation to do so. Her attempts at Barrayaran-style matchmaking had been extremely hit-or-miss over her lifetime, or she'd be tempted to try to help him somehow. There were valid reasons, she recognized ruefully, why Aral might have avoided her aid back when wooing Oliver. But Oliver was...complicated. *Which was why I broached this to him in the first place*, she reminded herself.

His tall, solitary figure was lost to her sight as her car rounded the next corner.

Chapter Two

Jole arrived twenty minutes early for his appointment with Dr. Tan at the rep center, and then couldn't make himself step inside. He walked up and down the side street, instead.

Kareenburg actually *had* side streets now, some thirty-five or forty years, depending on how one counted it, after its founding. Barrayar's first imprint on its new colony world had been a military base and shuttleport half-sheltered by a volcanic mountain that had blown out its side in some ancient cataclysm, standing sentinel with a string of sisters upon a wide plain. The pictures Jole had seen of earliest Kareenburg depicted a mud street lined with repurposed, and in some cases doubtless stolen, old military field shelters, as the base slowly upgraded from its first primitive incarnation. Like any up-sprung village serving a fortress on Old Earth or on Barrayar going back to the Time of Isolation, it had run heavily to such services as bars and brothels, but with the arrival of the first legitimate civilian colonists and a string of Imperial viceroys, government functions had slowly taken over the space, and the livelier aspects of the settlement had relocated.

Historical redaction had cut in with amazing speed, and those grubby early days were well on their way to being rewritten mainly as a setting for romantic adventure stories.

The hottest local political argument at the moment, and for the last ten years, was the transfer of the capital to some more selectively chosen region of the continent or one of the five others, resisted fiercely by those with major speculative investments in the present site. The Vicereine had dozens of scientific surveys on her side in favor of relocation, but Jole suspected she might be fighting one of her few losing battles with inertia and human nature. In the meanwhile, the racket of new construction extended and entrenched the proto-city in all directions.

These ruminations brought Jole around again to the doors of what the sign proclaimed as *Kareenburg Reproductive and Obstetrical Services*. *Kayross* for short, the intimidating polysyllables tamed and made friendly by the nickname. The building was not one of the old field shelters, but instead purpose-built, in a utilitarian mode that spoke of constrained budgets, as a clinic—if not *this* clinic, which had taken over the premises more recently.

I can do this. I can do anything. Hadn't Aral Vorkosigan taught him that? Jole took a breath and pushed inside.

. . . But, as he stepped into the queue at the reception counter, he was nonetheless glad he was wearing his anonymous casual civvies, and not his rank-heavy undress greens. Not that Imperial uniforms were an unusual sight on Kareenburg's streets. There were several people in line ahead of him—another man, a woman, and a couple, whose heads all swung around to observe him in turn—and he wasn't sure whether to be glad he had company, or to wish them all to oblivion. They were all sent to wait on uncomfortable-looking seats lining the side of the room, but when Jole stated his name, the receptionist jumped up, saying in a far-too-carrying voice, "Oh, yes, Admiral Jole! The Vicereine told us to expect you. Dr. Tan is right this way," and ushered him through a door into a short corridor, which had the faint chemical-and-disinfectant smell of every med clinic he'd ever unhappily encountered. So maybe it was some visceral memory of old pain and injury that was making him edgy? No, probably not.

She led him first into a room containing several comconsole desks, half of them manned by intent staffers and displaying dauntingly dense data readouts, or gaudy tangles that he guessed were molecular maps. The various colors and cuts of lab coats might proclaim different functions, ranks, and responsibilities, just as Imperial uniforms and insignia did, but this wasn't a code to which he had the key. And there were a lot more personal touches—plants, toys, holocubes, souvenirs. The clothing under the coats was anything but uniform, including a couple of young people wearing what were clearly Betan sarongs and sandals, though it was less clear if they were actually Betans. The coffee mugs, at least, were familiar.

The receptionist delivered him to the desk of a slight, dark-haired young man in a light blue coat that went to his knees, though he was wearing Sergyaran-style trousers and a shirt underneath.

"Dr. Tan, Admiral Jole is here."

"Ah, excellent! Just a sec..." He flung up a finger and finished whatever he had been about at his comconsole, shut down the baffling display of vibrant light lines, then stood up to offer Jole a firm handshake and a smile. The receptionist flitted away.

Dr. Tan *was* tan, and very healthy-looking, though his features were hard to map to any particular Earth ancestry—unlike Barrayar's population, lost and isolated for six hundred years and only rediscovered a century ago, the Betans had been using gene cleaning and rearranging for generations, which meant anyone's ancestors could be anything. "How do you do, Admiral? Welcome to Kayross. I'm so glad you came in. Any friend of the Vicereine's is a friend of ours, I assure you!"

Jole was a bit disoriented by that familiar Betan accent coming out of such an unfamiliar mouth, but he managed the handshake and suitable greetings. He tried not to let the accent sway him—he was here to make his own judgments... Or had he already decided, and all this going-through-the-motions was for what audience, exactly?

"Vicereine Vorkosigan said you would have questions, and that I was to answer them all. Would you care to start with a short tour?"

"Uh . . . yes, actually. Please. The only rep center I've ever been in wasn't up and running yet." That had been at a dedication ceremony in the Vorkosigan's District capital of Hassadar, back on Barrayar, which then-Prime Minister Vorkosigan, and therefore his aide, had attended in public support of his wife's manifold medical projects there.

Tan led him off to get suited up in some disposable paper garments, and then ushered him through the double doors at the end of the corridor. There, Jole found himself in a brightly lit clinical laboratory—busy lab benches cluttered with equipment under filtering vent hoods, a dozen absorbed techs bent over scanner stations. It reminded him a little of his tactics room, except that no one here seemed in the least bored. All the meticulously moving hands were smooth and gloved and steady.

The work stations on the first bench, featuring some especially rapt techs, were devoted to what Jole thought was the heart of the matter, fertilization. A couple of tightly temperature-controlled storage chambers held the culture dishes with early cell divisions. The lab stations on next bench over were devoted to what Dr. Tan dubbed *quality control*, gene scanning and repair. A second bank of warming cupboards continued the next stage of closely observed development, and then a last bench was devoted to implanting the ratified embryos and their placentas in the uterine replicators that would house them for the next nine months.

Through the next door, Tan relieved his guest of his crinkly paper overalls and hat, and guided him through a series of chambers devoted to the banks of replicators themselves, stacked five high. Panels of readouts monitored their progress. Pleasant music alternated with assorted natural sounds over speakers hidden somewhere. Individual jacks allowed soft, piped-in recordings of parental voices, speaking or reading. Jole found it creepily cheerful. Or cheerfully creepy, he wasn't sure which. He reminded himself that all those arrayed containers held individual people's—or couples'—most ardent hopes for the future. The next generation of Sergyarans. In fifteen years, all those disturbing biological blobs would be out on Kareenburg's streets, wearing strange fashions, listening to annoying music, and disagreeing politically with their beleaguered parents. In twenty-five years, they'd be taking on tasks that he couldn't presently imagine, though he guessed a few would be right back here working in this rep center, or its successor. Or offering up their own gametes for what the Vicereine dubbed *the genetic lottery.*

Could his own children be among them?

Why, yes, they could.

"Can conceptions—babies—ever get mixed up?" There were *stories* about such mishaps... Many of them passed along, Cordelia had pointed out, by people with irrational objections to the rep centers.

Dr. Tan smiled at him in a pained fashion. "Our techs are extremely conscientious, but to soothe the doubts of the, shall we say, biologically less educated, the genetics of any infant can be checked against that of its parents with a few cheek swabs and three minutes on the scanner at the time they take delivery. Or at any prior time, actually, amniocentesis being a trivial procedure with a replicator. The service is offered for free—or rather, included at no extra charge." He added after a moment, "We get that question a lot, from you Barrayarans. The Vicereine once told me to point out that our error rate is provably statistically lower than that of the natural method, but the late Viceroy advised me that it might not be taken in good part."

"I see," said Jole. He tried to come up with a few more suitably technical questions that would redeem his Barrayaran IQ in this man's eyes. Jole enjoyed Sergyar's sprinkling of galactic immigrants, on the whole, but he had to admit that they could sometimes also be remarkably annoying. He managed not to blurt out his own history as a natural, un-gene-cleaned body birth, in attempted proof of what, he could not say.

The fact came up shortly, however, when Dr. Tan took him back out to another room off the reception area, and left him to get on with an unmanned station that took his medical history in exhaustive detail. Jole was able to speed up this tedious process by plugging in his military medical records, which, after checking over to remove anything still classified, he'd stored on his wristcom for the purpose last night. This program was used to dealing with the arcana of Barrayaran military records, fortunately—quite a few veterans from the base chose to muster out here, or to come back later. Had Cordelia supplied Aral's? Yes, she must have, when she'd done her own. No one asked Jole for it, anyway, when Tan came back to rescue him.

"Any more questions? Are you ready for the next step?" Tan inquired jovially.

Jole searched his mouth with his tongue for an answer without finding one; in any case, Tan didn't wait, but motioned his VIP visitor along after him. He dodged aside to pick up some objects Jole could not quite make out, then brought him to another closed, blank door, labeled *Paternity Room*, with a sliding slot bearing the words *un/occupied*. A magnetized flip label read *Clean* on one side and *Do Not Disturb* on the other, to which Tan flipped it.

"Here is your sample jar," Tan announced, handing it across, "properly labeled as you see. The fluid inside will keep your semen alive and healthy until it can be processed. Check the label for accuracy, please."

Jole squinted and found his name and numbers duly recorded on the side. "Right...correct, that is."

"In the event of, so to speak, shyness, you will find a number of aids inside. I can also issue you a single-dose aphrodisiac nasal spray. We used to put them out in a basket, but they kept disappearing, so we had to go to rationing—my apologies." Tan held out a small ampoule.

Somewhat hypnotized by now, Jole warily accepted it. Tan opened the door and ushered him inside.

"Take all the time you need. Come find me personally when

you're done," Tan told him, his tones brightly encouraging. The door shut, leaving Jole alone in the quiet, dimly lit little room. He heard the slight scrape of the slot-label sliding to *occupied*.

The chamber contained a comfortable-looking armchair, a straight chair, and a narrow cot with a fitted sheet. A shelf offered a line-up of sex toys, most of which Jole had encountered less depressingly in other contexts, all with little paper ribbons around them proclaiming their sterilized state. The room also contained a holovid player—a quick check of the contents found a number of titles Jole recognized from barracks and shipboard life, plus a few that seemed highly unlikely to ever have played to that audience. Which made him wonder, just for a moment, what equivalents were passed around in the ISWA barracks, and if there were any of the women he dared to ask. Not Vorinnis, anyway. Maybe the colonel, if they ever got drunk enough together. The vid also offered an array of slide shows of beautiful young women, a few of beautiful young men, one of beautiful young herms, one of rather eye-grabbing beautiful young obese ladies, and others that became increasingly more otherly—this *had* been programmed by the galactic crew. A few more collections of images were downright repulsive, and a couple were simply incomprehensible, though Jole considered himself a traveled man. What none of them seemed, just at the moment, was arousing in any way. He shut the machine off.

I've been doing this since I was thirteen. It shouldn't be hard. Which, in fact, it wasn't—he'd never been more limp in his life.

He sat down on the edge of the cot, examined the instructions on the collection jar, and considered the nasal spray. It seemed like cheating, letting down the side, unbecoming to a manly, virile Imperial officer. Did he get any slack for being almost fifty?

This had to be the most un-erotic, not to mention unromantic, place he'd ever been in. What kind of bizarre irony was it, that it should also be the one to fulfill the main biological purpose of his ever having had a sexuality in the first place?

I could have done this when I was twenty... But he'd added thirty years of exposure to hard radiation, biological hazards, and chemical toxins atop them, here and there in his varied military career. God knew what insults his gonads had accumulated, starting with the space accident that had put him in hospital at ImpMil in his twenties. Jole also recalled, in an ancient untethered scrap of memory from his training days, some fellows who'd been working with experimental microwave weaponry making jokes about fathering only girls...Even if he were in the most traditional relationship imaginable, he'd still want to be doing it this way. Surely *no preventable defects or diseases* was the foremost birthday gift any father could give to his firstborn son... er, hypothetical child.

Hell with this. His own brain, his mind and memories, were surely stocked with all the images he could ever need.

He considered Aral. Surely there was a treasure-house of the most erotic memory imaginable. The range of things the man had been willing to try...And it would be weirdly appropriate, somehow. That beloved face laughed at him from the past, hugely amused at his present contretemps, but was too-quickly overlain with the cold, clay, empty version last viewed under glass in a chilled coffin, so wrong...and if he followed those worn thoughts down the spiral any farther, he'd end up weeping, not wanking. No.

Giving up, he broke the seal on the nasal spray and thrust it up each nostril in turn. The mist was cold and odorless, and appeared to do nothing. Now what?

Unbidden, a memory popped into his head of Cordelia, striding down an upstairs hallway of Vorkosigan House wearing only a towel, slung around her hips like a Betan sarong. Himself, tumbling out of a doorway in a panic. What emergency had it been, a fire alarm? Bomb threat...? He couldn't recall. He did remember the towel, oh yes. She'd worn her bare skin like space armor. Some armsman or servant had, sadly, soon handed her another towel. Suppose, instead of adding a towel, one were taken away...? That...was suddenly more interesting.

It seemed wrong to star her so in his mind-theater, but dammit, it was her fault that he was in this position in the first place. She could just put up with it.

She wore the long, swinging red hair of Aral's wife in the memory-scrap, though. Perhaps...he could picture her with it cut short. Short and curling. Yes, that felt better. And he could do without the Vorkosigan House fire drill of excited servants and armsmen, and, for that matter, without Vorkosigan House. This left his composite Cordelia standing in a blank whiteness. She raised her eyebrows at him, *Surely you can do better than this, kiddo...*

Yes, he could. He imagined his little sailboat, the first one he had owned on Sergyar, out on the local lake where he'd used to launch it. Out in the middle, far from any shore. Angled sunlight. Wind dead calm, because he had better things to wrestle with than the sails and tiller, just now. Cordelia sat on the forward bench and grinned at him, and unfolded the towel to sit upon. Oh, and no wristcoms on either of them. They'd left those ashore. Neither his office nor hers could reach them.

What else? She might like some chilled white wine; he handed her a glass, and she tilted it up. "Excellent," she pronounced, and she was certainly a shrewd judge. She looked up at him, intensely amused. She tossed her towel, and a few others, down in the center of the boat, neatly lined up along the keel, because she had a keen appreciation of the rules of physics as applied to small boats, and most everything else. She plunked herself atop them in that downright way she had of moving, the despair of her Barrayaran social arbiter friend, Lady Alys. Cordelia stretched herself to the light like a cat, and her face was free of strain or grief. "Oliver," she breathed, and the syllables of his name were warm in her mouth. She extended a sturdy arm above her bare torso, and her hand turned imperiously over. "Come here," she commanded throatily...

৩১০   ৩১০   ৩১০

Twenty minutes later, Jole emerged from the little room with his jar in his hand, lid screwed down tight. He blinked in the bright light, checked his fly, and trod off to find Dr. Tan. He didn't *feel* drunk. His walk—he tested it against the lines of the cheap floor tiles—was perfectly straight. But he felt simultaneously disembodied, and wholly in his body, a walking contradiction. *No wonder they have to ration that stuff.*

Tan greeted him with a pleased "Ah!" when Jole located him again at his desk. He took the jar and set it down without ceremony.

"When, ah...can I find out if I made the grade?" Jole asked.

"I'll put it in right away, and call you personally with the report...perhaps not today, but no later than tomorrow morning?"

Jole made sure the physician had his personal comcode.

"I expect it will be fine," Tan assured whatever look was on his face—Jole tried for blander. "Three hundred million to four are pretty good odds, after all." Tan hesitated. "About the leftovers—the clinic has a small but steady demand for high-grade high-achieving male gametes. You certainly meet all the criteria for physical health and intelligence and so on, despite your age. Would you care to donate the excess to our catalog? Anonymously, of course." Tan blinked amiably. "I rather think your face would sell."

Jole flinched. Well, Cordelia had warned him about this part of the conversation, in a way, hadn't she? "My face is not that anonymous, on Sergyar. I...let's get through the evaluation first, eh?"

"Very well. But do think about it, Admiral." Tan abandoned his office to walk Jole all the way to the front door, a sign of something.

Jole stood once more in the sunlit side street, feeling as though he'd just been put through a wormhole jump. Backwards. He contemplated the prospect of his lightflyer uneasily. He should have asked Tan how long it took that mist-drug to clear the system, but he wasn't going back inside now. He felt clearheaded, but that could be an illusion. Perhaps a walk around would help metabolize it, like other inebriants. He turned and made for the main street, a block off.

It occurred to him, belatedly, that Cordelia had several times mentioned that she was a replicator birth herself, back on high-tech

Beta Colony. That meant that her father, then-Lieutenant Miles Mark Naismith of the Betan Astronomical Survey, had once been through an experience very like the one Jole had just endured. And her mother the female equivalent, Jole supposed, though the women's version seemed more simply medical. More invasive, as he dimly understood it, but at least they didn't have to dragoon their libidos into cooperation. Did that make it better, or worse? On the other hand, they'd got Cordelia out of the deal, in the end. That...had worked out well.

Anyway, Jole himself was still at the gathering-data stage, really. The final decision would not be made till tomorrow, or much farther in the future if he chose to have his sample frozen. He had not hit any point of no return yet.

He passed a young colonial family on the sidewalk; she pushed a stroller with a cranky toddler, he bore a chest pack holding a sleeping infant, its slack little hands limp on his shirt. Jole wondered briefly what was the point of avoiding carrying children around during the nine months of gestation, and then turning around and lugging them like this when they'd escaped into the wild and were even *heavier*, but it seemed something that humans liked to do, because they kept doing it. He tried to imagine himself in the young father's place. Could that be his child? *Grandchild*, a dry part of his brain noted. *Shut up.*

He stepped aside around an elderly gentleman idly waiting for his dog to finish what dogs did at a lamppost. A dog. Maybe a dog would be simpler, saner...easier to explain. Many famous senior officers in history had sported famous pets/mounts/mistresses/plants...well, perhaps not plants. Although there was a certain cadre of fellows, after their twenty or twice-twenty years of service were up, who threw themselves into gardening. The more flamboyant live accessories seemed to be part of the mystique or public relations of command. Jole had always traveled lighter.

A few blocks of walking brought him out of Kareenburg's central business area, and he found himself staring across the street to the so-called Viceroy's Palace. The name was misleading—it was actually a low, rambling house. Surrounded, true, by a remarkable garden, gift of the Vicereine's even more remarkable daughter-in-law, which was growing up lushly these days to lend color and privacy, or the illusion of it. The old, hand-painted sign still hung by the gate.

The original Viceroy's Palace had been a relocated field shelter, much to the dismay of the first Viceroy. His unhappy successors had made do with several field shelters, stuck together in assorted arrays. These had at length been followed by a semi-fortified pre-fabricated dwelling of remarkable ugliness. The present Vicereine, in the first year of her and her husband's reign, had ordered it knocked flat and the site cleared, and started over with a saner and far more elegant design. The barracks at the back of the premises, which had housed Count Vorkosigan's personal arms-men during his tenure, were now converted to various Viceregal offices; the sole remaining armsman lived in the main house with a few other principal servants.

On impulse, Jole crossed the street and presented himself to the lone gate guard—another reduction from Aral's day. The premises' current security was thinner and much more discreet. Jole didn't mind the second, but wasn't so sure he approved of the first.

The gate guard, who knew him well, saluted. "Admiral Jole, sir."

"Afternoon, Fox. Is Her Excellency home to visitors?"

"I'm sure she's at home to you, sir. Go on in."

Jole strolled on up the curving drive. He almost turned around again when he spotted the array of parked vehicles, many of them with diplomatic stickers from the assorted planetary consulates based in Kareenburg, that marked some kind of dip-lomatic meeting—ah, yes, the welcoming reception for the new Escobaran consul was this afternoon, wasn't it. Jole had dumped the task of representing the Sergyaran military forces upon his downside base commander, to give the two men a chance to get acquainted in a less fraught setting before they had to sort out some inevitable contretemps involving, to choose an unfortunately unhypothetical example, off-duty soldiers with too much to drink and galactic tourists insufficiently briefed on the fine points of Barrayaran culture. Far better that they should first meet in the Vicereine's garden than in a hospital or, worse, the Kareenburg municipal guard's morgue. These elegant soirees had more than one practical function.

Perversely, being blocked from a chance to talk with Cordelia heightened his anxiety to do so. He continued on the walkway around the house, noting one security man in uniform and another pretending to weed, who made note of him with nods of greeting in turn, till the familiar murmur of voices and clink of glassware guided him to the patio and terrace that flowed out into the garden. Perhaps a hundred well-dressed people were scattered about, clutching little plates and talking. He hesitated on the fringe. Happily, Cordelia was in sight, wearing something light and flowing for the balmy afternoon, and her glance found him after only a moment. She immediately detached herself from the half-dozen people clustered around her and made her way to his side.

"Oliver," she said warmly. "How did your visit to the rep center go?"

"Mission accomplished, ma'am," he told her with a mock, but not mocking, salute. Her brows flicked up in pleased surprise. "I... we need to talk, but obviously not now."

"This thing is winding down, actually. If you can hang on for about half an hour, I should be able to start getting rid of them. Or you could come back later."

He had work on his schedule for this evening, unfortunately. "I'm not in uniform," he said in doubt.

"Oh, let these paranoid galactics experience a nonthreatening Barrayaran officer for a change. It will widen their world-views."

"That seems counterproductive, somehow. The whole *point* of having us all Imperially out here is to make our wormhole jump-points uninviting to the uninvited."

She grinned. "You look fine. Go do the pretty. I know you

know how." She strolled away, and several persons with agendas hidden or otherwise bee-lined for her.

Jole felt himself falling with the ease of long practice back into diplomatic-aide mode. He did check in first with his base commander, General Haines, who was properly attired in full dress greens, looking suitably broad and wall-like. The tall boots would be hot and sweaty, Jole was sure.

"Ah, Oliver, you're here!" said the general. "Didn't think you could make it. Is there anything afoot?" And, hopefully, "Can I leave now?"

"No and no. I'm just dropping by." He glanced around the party, which had reached a relaxed and tipsy stage. "What did you think of the new Escobaran consul?"

"Seems sensible enough, if young. At least he only has one sex, thank God."

Jole followed Haines's eye to the familiar, androgynous figure of the Betan consul, now chatting with the Vicereine. Consul Vermillion was a Betan hermaphrodite, one of that planet's bio-engineered, double-sexed... you couldn't call them a species, nor a race... Jole settled on *minority*. If the herm's assignment here had been intended as a cultural challenge to the local Barrayarans, it had fallen flat under the Vicereine's amused eye. Quite a few of the consulate personnel in Kareenburg were young diplomats on the make; if they didn't screw up on Sergyar, they had a shot at a more prestigious—and less forgiving—embassy posting in Vorbarr Sultana. The Vicereine had confided to Jole that she thought Consul Vermillion might very well be the next Betan ambassador to present portfolio to Emperor Gregor, a notion that made her eyes glint in an appealing but slightly alarming fashion.

A server paused to offer Jole a drink on a tray. "Your usual, sir?"

"Thank you, Frieda." Jole took a sip. Fizzy water, ice, and whatever mixer was available in the bar to give it a camouflaging color—he had been trained not to drink alcohol in any place that might offer diplomatic ambush back in his days as aide to the Prime Minister, and the habit had stuck.

"Ah, your Vorinnis girl is around here somewhere—there she is." General Haines nodded to a short figure in ISWA dress greens, which entailed skirts which were, Jole understood, not as uncomfortable in this heat as trousers and boots. She stood awkwardly on the other side of the garden gripping an untasted drink. "I had to explain to her that a last-minute personal invitation from the Vicereine did, actually, outrank her afternoon's filing."

"Good. They only met in passing the other day. Did you present her yet?"

"A while ago. She seemed a tad tongue-tied."

"Well, Cordelia will get her over that in due course. See she gets home to base as well, please; I have an, uh...unscheduled conference scheduled with the Vicereine after this."

Haines nodded, giving the girl a calculating glance. "How's she working out for you?"

Jole shrugged. "All right so far. She's keen, and it's clear she picked up a little Vorbarr Sultana polish on her last rotation—or maybe that's her Vor blood talking, there." He hesitated, considering. "When it comes to divvying up resources and personnel, Sergyar command has always been third in line for everything."

Haines sighed. "I've figured that out."

"Komarr command always gets first pick, on the theory that they'll be the hot seat if there is one, and Home Fleet is a close second. They arm-wrestle all the time over the best men. We get what's left. What's left, it turns out, are a lot of the best *women*. Send us more, I'd say." He added after a prudent moment, "No, you can't filch this one."

Haines snorted, but gave up mentally filling his vacant org chart. Jole gave him a cordial nod and moved off, stalking-horse fashion, to give anyone who wanted a shot at him their chance. It was frequently the fastest way to find what he was looking for, provided that he was looking for trouble.

"Ah, Admiral Jole!" a voice hailed him. Jole fixed an affable smile on his face and turned.

The incumbent civilian mayor of Kareenburg and one of his

councilman stirrup-riders approached him. Observing this, his two front-running opponents in the upcoming civic elections also closed in. They all gave each other wary, familiar nods.

"So glad to have caught you," said Mayor Yerkes. "Tell me, is the rumor true that you plan to close the base next year?"

"Certainly not, sir," said Jole. "I don't know how these stories get started—do you?"

Yerkes ignored this slight conversational speed bump. "The activity among the civilian contractors must indicate *something*."

"It's no secret that His Imperial Majesty has granted permission to open a second base," said Jole smoothly, thinking, *Now that the General Staff has finally fought the appropriation through the Council of Counts.* Possibly the closest most of them had come to a shooting war in Vorbarr Sultana for some years. "A single downside base has always been insufficient for defensive depth, not only in case of attack, but in the event of a natural disaster. The late Viceroy Vorkosigan had urged this expansion practically from the moment he set foot on Sergyar. You may be certain his widow will see his vision realized."

"Yes, but where?" put in Madame Moreau.

"That issue is still being discussed." Actually, it was down to a coin toss between Gridgrad or New Hassadar. Personally, Jole hankered for both, but he wasn't going to get them—certainly not simultaneously. The choice of final site was still a secret closely held, to limit the burst of financial speculation that would inevitably follow its disclosure.

"You *must* know more."

"I wouldn't say that, ma'am."

Mayor Yerkes gave him a look of amused frustration. Moreau and her co-challenger, Kuznetsov, just looked frustrated. In assorted ways, Kareenburg's downside military base was still the largest economic entity in the area, though now being edged out by the expanding government offices and the busy civilian shuttleport acting as entrepôt for the steady stream of new colonists. In any case, after a few more probing questions, the trio coasted off to test their luck with Haines. A futile effort, but Jole couldn't blame them for trying.

Lieutenant Vorinnis, who had spotted him just before he'd been surrounded by the anxious mayoral candidates, angled over to him. "Sir. General Haines said I should accompany him, sir . . . ?"

"Quite right, Lieutenant."

The girl visibly relaxed. Jole inquired lightly, "So, what did you think of the Vicereine, now you've had a chance to exchange a few more words?"

"She wasn't as scary as I thought." Though Vorinnis said this as if she were still unsure. "I know she's a grandmother, but she doesn't seem very . . . grandmotherish. As if she's ignoring the categories."

Jole smiled. "She's always done that," he conceded. "But you should have met her before . . ." *Before half her light was extinguished.*

"Not much chance of that, sir."

"No, I suppose not." He glanced out over the top of her dress beret. "Heads-up; we're about to get Cetagandans." She wheeled to follow his nod.

Despite his ghem-lord status, the Cetagandan consul in Kareenburg conformed to local, casual styles—shirt and trousers which, while doubtless comfortable, somehow managed to look about five times more expensive than what anyone else wore. His cultural attaché was unfortunately stuck, like Haines, in dress unsuitable for the sunny afternoon, dark with a heavy over-robe. Also ghem, he came complete with his clan's formal face paint: blue and green swirls slashed with gold in an ornate pattern, giving him a vaguely subaqueous air. A lesser ghem in a lesser venue would usually make do these days with a small colored decal on the cheekbone, as, indeed, the consul himself had, appropriately to his garb. The overdressed attaché was either a nervous novice, or had been oddly unadvised by his superiors. The consul, who'd finally noted Jole's arrival, spoke a word in his subordinate's ear and guided him in Jole's direction.

As the two ghem lords sidled around the other guests toward him, Jole ran a mental review of the current disposition of everything moving upside, but as of the morning report all was quiet and routine. The multi-jump wormhole link to the nearest of the Cetagandan Empire's eight primary worlds, Rho Ceta, had its terminus on the route between Komarr and Sergyar, closer to the former; therefore in a position to cut the route and the Barrayaran Empire off from Sergyar and everything that lay beyond it on that side. Which was why Komarr command held the jump-points militarily for several empty systems in, handing off about three-fourths of the way to the Rho Cetan command doing the same for their side.

The last overtly hostile move in force that the Cetagandans had made in that quarter had been over forty years ago, in the second year of Aral's regency for the young Emperor Gregor. On the heels of Vordarian's Pretendership—an attempted palace coup on Barrayar that had nearly brought down Aral's shaky new government—Cetaganda had sought to wrest away conquered Komarr and newly discovered Sergyar from Barrayaran hands. The attack force never made it through the chain of jump-points doggedly held by the Barrayaran Admiral Kanzian, soon backed in turn by reinforcements led by Aral himself. Aral had then returned home to an awkward combination of a hero's welcome and a local uprising on Komarr.

According to Aral, it had been the Cetagandan plan for all three events to occur simultaneously. Such a pile-up might have overwhelmed even him, but the Pretendership had ended abruptly many months before anyone could have predicted, and the restive Komarrans, whose agenda hadn't actually included exchanging a Barrayaran occupation for a Cetagandan one despite their willingness to accept aid, had been divided and laggard. So Aral had been able to take on his crises one at a time instead of all together. It had made for a hellish few years, Jole gathered. But Cetaganda hadn't tried again through *that* route.

And Aral and Cordelia's private tragedy of their soltoxin-crippled young son Miles had been running along in constant counterpoint with all of that, Jole realized anew. His own prospect of parenthood made this a less distanced and more disturbing thought.

"Ah, Admiral Jole, how good to see you here," said the Cetagandan consul, a minor lord by the name of ghem Navitt. "May I take this opportunity to present to you our new cultural attaché, Mikos ghem Soren?"

Jole exchanged greetings with the young consulate officer, who eyed his casual civilian dress in faint doubt, delicately conveyed by some slant of posture. Jole introduced Lieutenant Vorinnis in turn, who regarded the tall ghem lord with the stiff dubiousness of a cat told off to make friends with a dog. Ghem Soren's precisely gradated half-bow in return was almost as dubious. The Cetagandan military service also had a women's auxiliary, with long-running traditions of its own, but they were almost all commoners, un-gene-modified Cetagandans.

The Vor were a warrior caste, historically. The ghem were that as well, but had a more complex social genesis, as half-commoner half-haut in-betweeners—better than the one but never good enough to be the other. This endogenous inferiority complex tended to make the ghem touchingly twitchy about status. The Vor as a class had their own traumas, in Jole's opinion mostly self-inflicted, but covert fears of genetic mediocrity were not usually among them.

The face paint and Cetagandan gene-mods would have made ghem Soren's age hard for a Barrayaran eye to judge, but Jole had the advantage of an ImpSec dossier forwarded last week, standard evaluation for all such postings. The attaché was thirty, young for his position among the long-lived Cetagandans. On the make? *Silly question.* If he was a ghem lord and breathing, he was ambitious.

"Welcome to Sergyar, Lord ghem Soren. I trust you will find it an enjoyable posting."

"Thank you, sir. My only regret is that I was assigned too late to meet the legendary Admiral Vorkosigan."

Jole nodded shortly. "It was a privilege to know him."

"Your Emperor must sorely miss him, and his strategic expertise."

And hadn't Jole had *this* probing conversation a hundred times before, with assorted galactic observers in the wake of Aral's death. "Missing him, truly, but not his expertise. He was a great teacher as well as a great man, and fostered many younger Barrayarans in his vision and skills. He was my professional mentor for over twenty years, so I can testify to this from personal experience." *Decode* that, *you Cetagandan puppy. There are damn few officers in the Service more steeped in Aral's training than me, and I'm sitting guard on your wormhole outlet, right. Don't even* think *of trying anything.* Jole went on smoothly, "And, of course, I still enjoy the benefit of Vicereine Vorkosigan's wide experience and wisdom. We work together very closely. You may find your tour here on Sergyar under her aegis to be edifying in many unexpected ways."

"I shall hope so, sir." Ghem Soren glanced around. "Her garden is nearly worthy of the work of our ghem ladies."

It's better, ghem-boy, and you know it. The Cetagandans made art as much an arena of genetic competition as sport—or war. "So kind of you to say so. It is certainly one of her delights. By all means, tell her just that. It will amuse her no end." Jole extended a faux-helpful finger. "Ah—I'm afraid your face paint is running, my lord. The heat here is not kind to formal attire. You may wish to duck into the lav and adjust it before she sees it, though of course the Vicereine would never say a *word*..."

The young ghem, to Jole's amusement, flinched and raised a hand to his gaudy face. Vorinnis's eyes widened just slightly, though she suppressed any other expression. The consul, spying the Vicereine across the garden temporarily unsurrounded, more adroitly closed out the conversation with a few stock diplomatic phrases, and towed his newbie subordinate away.

Vorinnis remarked, "I'd never met a ghem-lord face-to-face before, not in full colors. Though I saw a few on the streets in Vorbarr Sultana, around the embassy quarter."

Jole smiled. "Small, helpful criticisms delivered in a tone of sweet concern usually serve to counter the worst of their inbred obnoxiousness."

"Saw that, sir."

He added, after a moment's reflection, "If no such happy opportunity presents itself, praising the superiority of the haut, which no ghem will ever be, can be made to serve almost as well."

They both watched obliquely as ghem Soren sidled discreetly into the garden's guest lav, a kiosk whose mundane function was camouflaged by a well-placed riot of plants and vines. Vorinnis's lip curled slightly. "Would mentioning Barrayaran victories over the ghem also work?"

"If done subtly. Subtlety counts. In Admiral Vorkosigan's train, of course, we never had to say it out loud."

"Can't get much more subtle than that, I guess."

"It certainly worked, in its day." *Though we'll have to find something else from now on.*

Vor women were not historically warriors, despite a thousand songs and tales of young women disguising themselves as boys and following their brothers/lovers/husbands/vengeful hearts into battle. Some of the stories were even true, uncovered in the hospital or morgue tents of the day. The end of the Time of Isolation and the introduction of galactic-style induction physicals had put paid to that era. But Vor women were more usually praised as the mothers of warriors.

Not that this didn't sometimes entail war as well, as left-at-home Vor ladies were compelled to heroically defend the keep, or tragically fail to. There had been a famous Countess Vorinnis from the heart of the Bloody Centuries who'd mocked her besiegers, who were holding her children hostage, by standing on the battlements, flipping up her skirts, and bending over to shout down through her spread knees for them to do their worst, as they could see she could get more children where those had come from! The siege had failed and the children had survived, but Jole couldn't help reflecting that the family dynamics of that generation must have been boggling to witness, from a safe distance. One of these days, he would have to ask the present Vorinnis if she was a direct descendant.

The party herd was finally thinning out. *Yes! Everyone leave, dammit! I want the Vicereine now!* Jole sent Vorinnis back to Haines, sipped another fake cocktail, and tried not to jitter while waiting for his chance.

Chapter Three

The diplomatic reception seemed to drag on unduly, but at last Cordelia was able to hand over the task of gently expelling the more inebriated lesser guests to her personal assistants, and the cleanup to her very competent house staff, and motion Oliver after her. When he'd appeared so unexpectedly, hesitating on the walkway, he'd looked as tall and cool as ever, but a faint panicked light in his blue eyes had put her oddly in mind of a cat that had just had an inadvertent ride in a dryer. She led off into the garden to her favorite private nook, made a visual check for displaced diplomats, and flung herself down on the comfortable chaise, kicking off her shoes and letting out her breath with a whoosh. "Glad that's over. Oh, my feet."

Smiling, Oliver seated himself in the nearby wicker chair. "I remember how Aral used to rub them for you, after these ordeals."

"Yeah," she sighed, resting for a moment in a memory that didn't hurt *too* much. She looked up in sudden hope, but he didn't follow this observation with, say, an offer to do the same. She sat up, crossed her legs, and rubbed her own feet, instead.

She continued, "I saw you making the rounds—thanks. How was your hit count, this party? Should we search your pockets for hotel room keys, love notes on napkins, or ladies' underwear?" In his days as Aral's handsome aide, the receptacles of his uniform had been a source of several interesting surprises after similar events, even when he'd sworn that no one had come close enough to touch him.

"It was only mystery lingerie the once," he protested in amused indignation. But added after a moment's reflection, "All right, twice, but it was in a bar on Tau Ceti and we were all drunk. Both a permanent puzzle—you'd think they'd at least have thought to write their comcode on the crotch or something. Did they expect me to search for them like Cinderella?" He mimed holding up a pair of slender undies, with a look of canine hope.

Cordelia emitted a peal of laughter. It felt good. "Or send ImpSec to do it for you."

"ImpSec actually did get handed anything I couldn't certainly identify. I sometimes imagined I might uncover a glamorous Cetagandan spy hatching a dastardly plot, but it never turned out to be that interesting."

Cordelia rubbed the grin from her mouth. "Oh, well." She sat back again. "So, how did you get along with Dr. Tan?"

He shrugged. "He was very civil. And enthusiastic. And appallingly Betan."

"Was that a good point or a bad point?"

"Just a point, I think. It was...a stranger experience than I'd expected." He seemed about to say more, but then shook his head and visibly changed tacks. "I left him with what he persisted in calling my *sample*. As if my gonads were a bakery case. The next step, if my gametes don't all turn out to be croakers...well, the next step is coming up very quickly."

"Do you know what it will be?"

"More or less. That is, I know the question, but not the answer. I have to decide whether to freeze my sample now, and push everything off for later, or go ahead with the fertilizations.

freeze all the zygotes—embryos?—whichever, or start one of them. Or more than one, I suppose."

"Miles, when he was contemplating this technology for my future grandchildren, wanted to start twelve at once and do them all in one efficient batch. Like growing his own platoon, I gather. I offered to take turns with Ekaterin holding his head under water till he had a better idea, but as it turned out, she didn't need my help. Wonderful girl, my daughter-in-law. I still don't know what he did to deserve her."

Oliver chuckled. "From what I've seen of Miles, I can just picture that. But no, no Jole platoons. Or squads, even."

"You could hire help. I'm certainly planning to."

"I'll have to, presumably. I don't see how else... You're not starting all six of your girls at once, are you?"

"No, no! Though I have been studying up on optimum family age distributions. As nearly as I can tell, there isn't one. Or there are several, depending on what one wants."

"When will you decide?"

"I already have, at least step one. I told Tan to go ahead with all six fertilizations. That's in process—done, actually. Another few days to finish the cross-checks against genetic defects, and effect any necessary repairs, and then five will go into the freezer and the sixth into the oven, so to speak. And nine months from now, Aurelia will be... my problem." Her lips curved up. "It's a little frightening, but really, she can't possibly be more of a challenge than Miles was."

Oliver nodded in wry acknowledgment of this. "The more I learn about your first year on Barrayar, the more amazed I am that you stayed."

"I'd burnt my Betan bridges pretty thoroughly at the time, right after the Escobar war. But yes. In less than, what, the course of eighteen months, I'd met Aral—*here*, right on this planet, which *I'd* discovered, and which would be a Betan daughter colony right now if your fellows hadn't got here a year earlier—helped him put down a military mutiny, escaped, got sent right back into the war *against* Barrayar, been a POW, went home, *left* home—fled it, I suppose. Found Aral, married him, both of us planning nothing more strenuous than to be retired in the backcountry and raise a pack of kids. And I very stupidly plunged into my one and only pregnancy. Then Emperor Ezar tossed him—both of us—into the damned regency. Then the first assassination attempt—did I ever tell you about that one? Sonic grenade, missed. And the second—which didn't—the soltoxin gas grenade disaster. Then the emergency C-section, and Miles plunked into a scrounged uterine replicator by an utterly inexperienced surgeon—I swear that man was more scared than I was—and then the Pretender's War, and all *that* mess. We finally decanted Miles in the spring, so damaged, poor tyke, and of course old Count Piotr went off like another grenade in that horrible fight about it with Aral, which ended with them not speaking for the next five years, and . . . and that was my first year on Barrayar, yes. No wonder I was exhausted." She leaned her head back against the cushion and exhaled noisily. "But that was my secret evil selfish plan, when I came to Aral. We were going to have six kids together. It would have been terribly antisocial on Beta, with its strict population controls. He was always . . . Aral always knew, of course. That that had been my dream, shattered by events. And regretted that he couldn't—give me what I'd given up so much to obtain. That was why we froze the gametes, when we had a breather."

"He'd always planned to give you more children, then."

"Say rather, hoped. We'd both pretty much given up on planning, by then. It never worked out." She blinked. "Still didn't. And yet . . . here we are. Forty years late. But *here*, by damn." She scrubbed a hand through her unruly hair. "So what do you want? Really want, not just think is most prudent. Or worse, think is what *I* want."

"I think . . ." Oliver hesitated once more, then went on, "I think I want to place my genetic bet, as you put it. Go ahead with the assemblage and the fertilizations, all of them."

"Stake your claim on the future?"

"Or at least get past to the next stage of fretting. I'm already tired of this one. Or if it turns out not to work—" He broke off that sentence partway.

Did he mean to say, *Be done with it*? "You still wouldn't be done with choosing. Since you'd have the option of purchasing some other enucleated eggshells. Or there are a couple of alternate techniques for assembling zygotes, a bit trickier."

He rubbed a hand over his brow. "Hadn't thought of that. This keeps getting more tangled."

"Not indefinitely. If nothing else, the arrival of actual children replaces theory with practice. And time to fret with...lack of time to breathe, sometimes."

"The voice of experience?"

"A database of one does not give me infinite expertise, alas. A fact that ought to give me pause, but I'm *done* waiting for this."

Light footsteps; Frieda poked her head around the shrubbery. "Do you need anything, milady? Sir?"

Cordelia considered. "A real drink, I think. Not the apple juice and water. Glass of the white, if it's not all put away by now. Oliver?"

"My usual, thank you, Frieda." The servant nodded and went off. At Cordelia's raised brows he added, "Still on duty tonight. Or I'd like nothing better than to sit here with you and get sotted till midnight. Unfortunately, that only gives the *illusion* of solving one's problems."

She said apologetically, "Didn't mean to give you a problem, Oliver. Meant to give you a gift."

He snorted. "You knew precisely what you were doing."

She scratched her neck and grimaced. "Which actually does bring me to the next thing. If you tell Tan to go ahead with the fertilizations, next thing you do, before you so much as set foot in a shuttle again for your next upside rotation, is sit down and do the next-of-kin directive. Or destruction directive. Tan will give you the right forms—the clinic keeps them on file for every zygote in their possession."

"The...what directive?"

"Zygotes are different legal entities than gametes. Gametes are property, part of your own body that happens to no longer be in it. Zygotes are a lawsuit waiting to happen. Inheritance issues, you know. From the moment of fertilization, even if you choose to freeze them all but *especially* if you choose to start one in a replicator, somebody needs to know where your kids, or potential kids, will end up if you go up in a ball of light, or, or slip in the shower, or whatever."

Oliver frowned. "That's right. You told me once that your own father died in a shuttle accident. Not an example chosen at random, Cordelia?"

She shrugged. "I still ride shuttles."

"I...um. No, I hadn't got that far in my thinking, I confess. Whom did you select? Miles, I expect?"

"By default, yes. But also by design. I'm not totally happy with it—if I'd wanted my girls to be raised on Barrayar, I'd be doing this there, not here. I should add—if you were to fail to make a proper directive, their default guardian would be whoever is your next-of-kin. Which is who?"

He looked rather taken aback. "My mother, I suppose. Or my eldest brother."

"Can you picture them raising your orphaned children?"

"Mine? Maybe. At a stretch. Aral's..." His face twisted up in a hard-to-interpret grimace. "If I'd had a traditional Barrayaran marriage, with children, I suppose I must have—well, wait, no. There might have been my hypothetical wife's family to fall back on. Um."

Cordelia rubbed her eyes with the heels of her hands. "Let me ask you another question, then. Where do—did you—think your career is going in the next ten years? Where are *you* going?"

His brows flicked up. He said in a cautious voice, "Do I take from all this that you mean to retire on Sergyar? Stay here as a permanent colonist?"

"It *is* my planet...You understand, all of this is new thinking, since my life was cleaved in half three years ago. Before...

before, I'd planned to go back to Barrayar, to the Vorkosigan's District with Aral when he retired at last, to a medically supported, galactic-style very old age. His father, leathery old bastard that he was, lived into his late nineties with less help. Somehow in my head I thought Aral, with his new heart and all, would certainly do better. A hundred and ten at least. And then, one goddamn burst intracranial artery later, I was twenty-six years ahead of myself." She shrugged sharply. "Plans. Never any good."

His hand went out to her, but fell back. "Yeah."

He was quiet for a long time; Frieda came back, distributed the drinks, and left them again, glancing curiously over her shoulder.

"My twice-twenty years is coming up in a decade," he began again at last. "I'd never planned to go for a three-times-twenty. I was going to start to think about my retirement, my second career, whatever, in, oh, another six or seven years, maybe. *Where* I would be, then . . . well, I'm in the Service. It's not all up to me. As you have just pointed out, even being alive tomorrow is not up to me."

She looked away. "Aral once spoke of offering you a job in his district, after we went home. Actually, your pick of several. He had plans, you see."

"Ah." Oliver took a swallow of his non-drink. "I expect I could have gone for that." He continued after a moment, "I've no strong personal ties on Barrayar. My family and I were close enough before I left for the Academy at age eighteen, but since then we've all grown further and further apart. My home town was always enough for them. It . . . wasn't, for me. My father died—you remember—just before I was assigned to Sergyar. My mother has lived with my sister for years. My district has developed—last time I was back, everything I remembered fondly from my childhood was changed, built over. Gone. Sergyar . . . is starting to look pretty good to me, really." His clear glance flicked up to her. "Would you be willing to stand godmother to me in this? Because . . . at least they'd be with their half-siblings. Slightly more than half-siblings."

"Entirely willing," she assured him. "Note that the center'll want a few more in-case-of options, in descending order of choice, so your family needn't be excluded altogether."

"Can one revise the directive, later?"

"Oh, yes. They suggest you review it yearly."

"Hm. Sensible enough."

She sipped more wine, put down her glass on the little table, drummed her fingers on the chaise arm. "If you were to—if you ever decide to—muster out on Sergyar, would you be willing to make that reciprocal?"

His eyes flashed up at her, startled. "What, before Miles?"

"Before Barrayar, at least."

His lips pursed. "But . . . you'd be dead. I can't—that's not—I have trouble imagining that." Except, by the troubled look on his face, he was. He blinked suddenly. "Wait. You're not just talking frozen embryos here, are you."

"Not after next week, no."

He blew out his breath. "That is possibly the most terrifying responsibility anyone has ever offered me. Not excepting ship command or being the last man standing between the Prime Minister and anything coming at him." He blinked some more. "Pretty damned flattering, Cordelia. Are you in your right mind?"

She smiled crookedly. "Who knows? That's a hypothetical for now, note."

"Noted. But still . . ." He didn't say still *what*.

He did glance at his chrono, and scowled. "Blast. I have to get moving. I still have to go back to base and change. Who knew when I signed up for the space service that I would spend so much time arm-wrestling with contractors? Concrete by the kiloton. But my shuttles have to have somewhere to land." He drained his drink and stood looking down at her, somewhat limply draped on the chaise. "Cordelia . . ." He hesitated.

"Hm?"

He seemed to swallow. Blurted, "Would you like to go sailing again sometime?"

She sat up, surprised. Aral had taught him to sail, back in his twenties, and to enjoy the sport. She had actually preferred sailing with Oliver, as she'd been less likely to end up having an unscheduled swim due to a certain person's addiction to pushing his envelopes. The memory made her catch her breath, and blink rapidly. "I haven't been out on the water since…forever. I'd love it. I think I could clear my schedule, yes." She paused, confused. "Wait. Didn't you say you'd sold your boat last year?"

"I'll find something. If you can pry out the time."

"For this, I'll pry it out with a chisel. Sounds delightful. Excellent, in fact." She wallowed around on the chaise and held out her hand. "Help me up," she commanded.

A funny look crossed his face, but he leaned over, grabbed her hand, and civilly heaved. She found her feet, and her shoes, and walked him back to the house, where they parted company. *You that way; we this way.* But not for long, she reflected comfortably.

It was another three days before Jole had time to catch up with the Vicereine. He lured her out to the base with an offer of dinner at the officers' mess, no special treat, and a chance to avoid Komarrans bearing pitches, which evidently was. At any rate, as he led her across the back shuttle runway toward the base's far side, both of them squinting in the slanting sun, she was still going on about it.

"Anything that would affect my patch?" he inquired of this complaint, as they trudged across the edge of the tarmac. In the distance, the mountain's gouged-out side wavered in the reflected heat.

"Not directly. It's the usual—they want to institute extra planetary voting shares for persons making special material or investment contributions to the advancement of the colony, just like at home in their domes. Persons, coincidentally, who mostly would happen to be themselves. My counter-suggestion that we just grant everyone ten inalienable voting shares by moving the

decimal point over was nixed by my advisors on the grounds
that I would be perceived as mocking them. Which I would be.
I would prefer to derail any move on a referendum before it gets
rolling, though."

"Surely allowing a referendum would be safe. Everyone who
is not them would vote against it, right?"

"Possibly not. Enough optimistic people might be swayed by
the statistically unlikely idea that *they* could be among the few
to benefit to go along with it. Face it, one doesn't up stakes and
travel out to Sergyar to take on the work involved here without
a certain innate optimism." She amended as they strolled along,
"Except for the Old Russian speakers, who are naturally gloomy
at all times, as nearly as I can tell."

Jole's lips curled up. "I think I can promise you that the
subjects of your nascent local democracy experiments will not
pursue you onto my Imperial base."

"You lie, but I don't care . . ." She stared, nonplussed, as they
arrived at their destination and stopped.

"And what do you see here, Cordelia?" Jole gestured broadly
around at the two-meter-high stacks of sacks confronting them.
The stacks sat in turn on pallets arrayed out for dozens of meters
in all directions, like a large-scale model of some geological
feature, badlands dotted with mesas and channeled by ravines,
except more regular. Zigzagging semi-randomly, Jole led her to
the center of the maze.

"Many, many bags of stuff. Not belonging to me, I point out
prudently."

"Delivered by the contractor months early—that should have
been our first clue—"

"A contractor, *early*? Really? Already your tale begins to
resemble some drunken hallucination."

He nodded glumly. "Although I haven't started drinking yet.
It *was* to be the plas mixer for the new runways on the second
base, at—is it decided yet?"

"Gridgrad." She wrinkled her nose. "The residents may want

to give that village a new name after this hits, but that, happily, will not be my problem. Unless they try to name it after Aral and make me come out and give another damned speech."

A good near-equatorial location, like Kareenburg, to the net energy benefit of shuttles striking for orbit. Jole was satisfied. At least with that aspect. The fact that the site was a tenth of the way around the planet... "And yet we are far from Gridgrad. Both in terms of time and distance. The earliest projection for starting the dig on the runway foundation was at least another year. Year and a half, realistically."

"And yet, I am failing to see the problem. The matrix mix would have had to be hauled from here to there sometime, yes?" She poked doubtfully at a bulging bag. "Unless someone starts a new materials manufacturing plant at Gridgrad awfully soon, which is not a proposal that has yet crossed my desk. Though I expect one will, in due course."

Jole shook his head. "The latest high-tech materials innovation, this. Very strong when set, yet resilient under repeated massive impacts, such as landing shuttles. Allowing the engineers to use half the volume and weight, and therefore cost, even at a higher price per ton. Per thousand-ton, for this sort of application."

She raised her brows at him, in standard Cordelia-challenge. "It's plascrete. Lasts for centuries, right? And it's not as if you're suffering for storage space. You have square kilometers of empty base, if you want them, Imperially reserved for future barracks and runways. Though I should probably warn you, some Kareenburg developers are already starting to eye them covetously."

"Lasts only after it's mixed and set." Jole made another broad gesture. "The terms you are missing are 'latest,' 'high-tech,' and 'innovation.' The ingredients of the old-style plascrete are indeed remarkably durable. *This* crap, however, while lovely when fresh, undergoes chemical deterioration if not mixed with its activator and placed by its best-by date. Which is less than a year from now. How long the manufacturer had this sitting around in their yard is anyone's guess, but it's been a while."

"Plascrete with planned obsolescence," she said, in a tone of wry admiration. "Who knew?"

"Not, unfortunately, the quartermaster officer who let it onto the base last week. Rattled, perhaps, by all the delivery vehicles blocking the main gate, he signed off on the loads without running them past the engineers. The first problem being, of course, that it was not supposed to be delivered *here* at all, but rather, at Gridgrad-to-be-disclosed."

"So they not only shift their dodgy stock, they duck a stiff extra delivery expense. Nice."

"*And* the base accounting department, who also didn't check with the engineers, but only came out and counted the sacks to be sure they matched the invoice, was seized with a burst of unprecedented efficiency and paid the bill."

"A recoverable glitch, surely. The misdelivery address alone should put you on solid legal ground. Make them come and take it back, and recoup your credit. Aral would have."

"*Aral* would have threatened to make them eat it—and made them believe him." Jole paused in brief retrospective envy of a command style that had always seemed beyond his touch, or at least his acting abilities. Aral's trick had been that it was no trick. "I already have. Well, not the eat-it part. They claim that such a move would bankrupt their business—leaving them unable to deliver next year. And no other vendor to replace them, not for those volumes. I sent one of my more forensically inclined procurement fellows to check out that assertion, and he claims that it's true."

Cordelia's brow wrinkled. "Those fellows—Plas-Dan, isn't it?—you'd think they'd know better than to piss in the bucket they're trying to drink from."

Jole grinned at Aral's old plaint about politics. *Not* one of his public utterances, to Jole's regret. "You would, yet here we are. And—civilian colonists. Belonging, therefore, to you—Your Excellency. A word in your private ear, as it were." His thoughts veered a bit—her private ears nestled coyly in her wild hair, when he studied them from this distance. Different somehow from when she'd worn her hair long, weighted down by its own mass or aristocratically bound back and adorned with live flowers.

Her face twisted up in expressive dismay. "Dammit, I knew you lied.... Do you want me to look into Plas-Dan, see if I can turn up some better handle on them?"

"It's worth a go. Without endangering next year's supply of plascrete, if you please."

"Right-oh..." She scowled around at their fortress of moldering solitude. "Is this why you brought me out here, sort of a do-it-yourself cone-of-silence without the cone-of-silence alerting everyone that we were talking secrets? Not that it wasn't a pleasant-enough walk."

The afternoon was warmer than the one of her garden party, the air even brighter, as the sun slanted gold. Did her feet hurt, after him making her march out to the far backside of the base? He glanced at her shoes, which seemed sensible enough. For about the eleventh time since then, he regretted not volunteering to rub her toes when they had been so invitingly bared to him, but he had still been off-balance from his trip to the rep center, and what would she have thought of so arrogant an offer, anyway? That had been *Aral's* place.

"Yes...no. Not only that," he admitted. *Not that at all.* Was Plas-Dan merely convenient camouflage, the first he could grab off the shelf? Although setting Cordelia on them did seem the next logical step. "I had an unrelated personal addendum."

She leaned against the stack, crossed her arms under her breasts, and smiled at him. "You always have claim on my ear for those."

He took a breath. "After we talked the other day, I went ahead and ordered Tan to complete the fertilizations."

"Congratulations! You're almost a father, then. I'm guessing you went with freezing the zygotes, till you work through your career decisions, though?"

"Yes, in fact. Anyway, that's what I told Tan when he called with the update this morning. It wasn't that. It was...one of the four didn't make it, Tan said. Normal attrition for this stage, he said."

She hesitated, then gave a conceding nod. "I'd started out with twenty eggs, brought from Barrayar. Half of them failed, for one subtle reason or another. Biology at that micro-level is trickier than most people realize. And more cruel."

And his added one more to that loss. *Will you always be ahead of me, Cordelia?* "Yes, Tan was very willing to explain all the details, boiled down for the layperson, I gather. Molecular biology never having been my forte. It wasn't the mechanics. It was..."

She waited, still leaning relaxed against the shadowed sack-wall but, he thought, keenly alert. *In your own time, Mister Jole.*

He stared down at his regulation shoes. "Two weeks ago, none of this was even part of my mental furniture in any way. One week ago, I was simply...unnerved, I guess. Boggled. But that quartet of shadow-sons took root in my mind so fast. I was thinking, only the one. And then we'd see. Then two, because there's this assumption that a boy ought to have a brother, although I'm not so sure mine appreciated me. And then, but what if...How can I be, already by today, how could I be..." He trailed off, not so much tongue-tied as baffled by his own churning thoughts.

"Mourning for a lost dream-child?"

He nodded. "Something like that." It wasn't what he'd expected of himself. When he'd blurted to Tan to begin, some part of his mind had been arguing—hoping?—that they might all fail, and then this test would be over. Resetting his life to zero. Ending the suspense. *Soonest begun, soonest done.* But then, when he'd been handed a part of that dark wish...had he any right to call it *grief*? He glanced up at her. "And no one on this world I could talk with about it except you. Which is really why we are out here. To tell you the truth." *Finally.*

She sucked on her lower lip, and scuffed her shod toe in the red dirt. "You know, Oliver...I wonder if you aren't being ambushed by your own habits a bit, here. None of this is anything illegal, or immoral, or scandalous, or anything but good for the future of Sergyar. Or likely to bring an Imperial government crashing down. That painstaking discretion is all from the past, now, along with the reasons for it. You went down to the rep center and bought a donated egg or three. Lots of people do. You can talk about it with anyone, really."

"Easier said than done, and you know why."

"If you're wincing at the thought of criticism from people with their heads still stuck in the Time of Isolation, or more fundamental places—even though the T-oh-I was over before any of them were born—well... if you want to play *What would Aral do?* you know he'd have said *Publish and be damned*, or choicer words." She blinked thoughtfully. "Grant you, that attitude always terrified his younger advisors, once he finally got old enough to have younger advisors. The older men, who remembered what he'd been like raging around Vorbarr Sultana in that bad patch in his twenties after his first wife died so brutally... would have been unsurprised at anything. But of course, the youngsters didn't talk to the old sticks if they could possibly avoid it, so they mostly never had their illusions shattered." He wondered if she was thinking of her son Miles. She looked up, her gray eyes urgent and earnest. "Oliver, you are *all right*. This is all right. This is the new Sergyar, not the old Barrayar. No one is going to try to assassinate anyone over it in a fit of vicarious outrage, really."

"And yet even *you* say, *anonymously donated egg*."

Her smile slid sideways. "Well... no reason to go actively hunting for trouble, either, eh?"

He had to laugh a little.

"Try it," she challenged, absurdly forthright as usual. "Next time you're all gossiping around the water cooler, or whatever you fellows do on base or upside. *For my fiftieth birthday, I've decided to have a son*, or whatever. All right, maybe the younger lads won't understand, but most of the older officers are parents themselves. You may find out you've joined a club you never knew existed. Ask them for advice—*that'll* win them over in a hurry."

That last was a convincing argument, to be sure. But he managed, austerely, "Soldiers of the Imperium do not gossip. We just exchange mission-critical information."

She snickered. "Right. All your fellows gossip like washerwomen."

He grinned back, his heart lightened, though he could not say exactly how. "Except with more bragging and lies, pretty much, yeah."

He became aware that he was standing very close to her, in the cool-warm shade of the concealing sack-walls, his arm out propping him almost over her. When at this rare range it always vaguely surprised him to rediscover that, though a tallish woman, she was shorter than himself. The air was very quiet, not even the distant boom or whine of one of the orbital shuttles taking off or landing. They might have been a hundred kilometers away from anyone, out in the rugged volcanic hills somewhere. Picnicking, perhaps. Now, there was an idea for a weekend retreat...

The scents trapped on the still air teased his senses—light sweat, her hair, the perfume of her soap, the dry dust of the plascrete. He became conscious of her lips, as she regarded him with a quizzical half smile, face tipped up, and that she had gone quite still, and what did *that* mean? He also became aware that a certain witless part of his body was earnestly suggesting that backing up the Vicereine to a wall of plascrete sacks and doing her standing would be a delightful addition to both their afternoons.

Hell you say. I'm not putting you in charge of anything to do with the Vicereine ever.

How long did that bloody Betan nasal spray *last*, anyway?

He shook himself out of his temporary hypnosis and took an abrupt step backward. Did she just catch her breath? He had to, though he trusted he concealed it. "Well!" he said brightly. "Supper, Your Excellency?"

She did not, immediately, push off from the wall. Her chin tucked. Her smile didn't thin, exactly, it just became a little stiffer—the *nice* smile she used for the holovids, not for him. "If you say so, Oliver. Lead on."

He almost offered her his arm, but hesitated too long; she was already striding off. He followed.

I have to find a boat. Somehow.

As they walked back toward the building housing the officers' mess, Cordelia suppressed a scowl. She had been very nearly certain Oliver had been about to kiss her. And she had been very nearly certain that she would like it. She had before, on certain special occasions...

Don't be stupid, woman. You know he prefers men. She'd known that for decades.

Do I? In that case, why hadn't he found himself one, in the past three years? Not in those first few shell-shocked months, no. But she knew that he collected passes from both sexes—and the rare visiting herm—she'd seen that both back in their Vorbarr Sultana period, and since he'd been assigned to Sergyar Command. Oliver had been awkward at ducking them in his first days, absorbed in learning his new tasks as the overworked aide to one of the most high-powered men on the planet, and then there had followed that amusing period when he'd been so caught up in Aral that barely anyone else seemed to register. But in time, he'd become as deft at giving off silent *don't try me* vibes as any virtuously faithful Vor matron. As had she, she supposed, but given that she was Aral's wife, very few men who weren't obviously insane had ever bothered her with unwanted advances. Although her own social obliviousness had doubtless also helped smooth things over. Any whose futile hopes she could not depress herself, she could send ImpSec to hand on a clue to. Word like that got around.

Which suggested that she, too, might be out of practice at this sort of thing, except that she had never been in practice in the first place. She'd been thirty-three years old, a Betan Astronomical Survey commander, in a situation as unconducive to romance as any she could imagine, when Aral had, *ha*, fallen in love on her—her lips curved up again at the memory of Oliver's extremely apt turn of phrase, melting her urge to scowl—and her life had never been the same again.

She considered Oliver's confidence—the real one, not the Plas-Dan smokescreen. He was, she realized belatedly, trying to process a sort of technological miscarriage, without the words or even the concepts for it. No way to package the experience for himself at all. Would it help if she suggested he name the lost zygote? Volunteer to aid him in burning a Barrayaran death-offering? Or would that be too intrusive? Offensive? Or just incomprehensible? No, not that—she had not mistaken the bewildered pain in his voice. Maybe just being his good listener was enough. The one friend he could talk to. *Damn. I meant to give you a gift of joy, not . . . this.*

The base officers' mess was divided into two sections, an efficient cafeteria downstairs for the people in a hurry, and a somewhat less utilitarian dining room upstairs, with wide windows looking out over the shuttleport. The food all came out of the same kitchen, merely being plated and served more nicely up here. She and Aral had eaten many working meals with the military staff in this mess, when colony concerns had taken them onto the base, usually in one of the smaller private rooms off either end of the main one. Today Oliver simply guided her to a table by the windows. Heads turned as they passed. The service was instantly attentive, certainly. Happily, the enlisted server was one of the older hands, undaunted by his Admiral and the Vicereine.

Discussions of what were, Cordelia suspected, only going to be the first of several thousand other practical issues involving the impact of the new base carried them through the salad and the main course. Oliver was clearly amused by her not-at-all secret hope that the boost to the Gridgrad settlement by this huge infusion of military money and construction people would shift the center of colonization away from Kareenburg's *why-for-the-love-of-logic* semi-desert ecosystem—not to mention the active tectonic boundary and not-actually-dead volcanoes—to the much more salubrious, well-watered, and geologically stable zone around Gridgrad.

"This place was never picked for a colony site in the first place," she argued. "It was picked because the caves in what is now Mount Thera made a dandy cache to hide an invasion fleet's worth of supplies from people like, well, passing Betan Astronomical Survey vessels, while the old war party scraped together that insanely stupid Escobar conquest scheme. Grant you, the caves did work exactly as hoped, I'll give old Emperor Ezar's bloodthirsty cutthroats that much credit."

Oliver held up his hands palm-out in nondisagreement—he'd heard this rant from her before. A motion by the table that was not their server bearing dessert caught her eye, and she stopped in mid-spate to look around. Oliver's aide, Lieutenant Vorinnis, presented herself, and Cordelia's heart caught with the fear that it might be some crisis, soothed when the girl offered a hesitant, even hangdog, salute.

"Admiral Jole, sir. Good evening, Your Excellency." A respectful motion in Cordelia's direction that was neither salute nor bow nor curtsey—more of a bob. "My apologies for interrupting"—a glance at their empty plates indicated hope that she was not too ill-timed—"but I received this...this thing, and I didn't know what to do with it. I showed it to Colonel Martin, but she didn't know either, so she said I should ask you, sir, because you'd probably know all about this kind of stuff. And someone said they saw you come up here, and—well, here."

She thrust out her hand, holding a stiff, colored-paper envelope in a style Cordelia recognized, but hadn't expected to see in this place. Oliver, too, recognized it, his brows rising as he took it for closer examination. "Well, well. What have we here, Lieutenant?"

"I *think* it says it's an invitation to a party at the Cetagandan consulate. Although the wording's a little...oblique. From Lord ghem Soren. Supposedly." She said this in a voice of gruff suspicion.

"Well, that it is. Addressed to you personally, I see, no mistake there. Hand-calligraphed, too, as is right and proper for a rising young ghem. Someone made him practice, once. Assuming he didn't panic and pay someone more expert to do the task for him, which would be considered terribly déclassé if he were caught at it. Paper hand-made, good touch, though doubtless purchased." He ran the card extracted from within delicately under his nose, and sniffed.

Cordelia sat back, beginning to be amused. "What else can you determine?"

"Cinnamon, rose, and gardenia, I think. Not terribly subtle, but perhaps he was making allowances for the recipient, which suggests a certain effort at diplomatic courtesy. Or perhaps even straightforwardness, perish the thought. See what you make of it, Cordelia." He handed the card and its envelope across to her.

"A fellow shouldn't be drenching letters in perfume, should he?" asked Vorinnis uneasily. "Or are all their consulate invitations like that?"

"You've heard of the language of flowers, Lieutenant?" asked Cordelia.

The girl's rather straight and thick eyebrows lowered. "Wasn't that some Time of Isolation custom? Different flowers would have different meanings. Red roses for love, white lilies for grief, that sort of cra—thing?"

"That's right," said Oliver. "Well, Cetagandan ghem culture, when it's at home, doesn't just stop at flowers. Objects, artistic choices and their juxtapositions, flowers—naturally—scents, you name it. All convey coded messages."

"Should I take this to Base Security, then? I wondered."

"Ah—coded *social* messages, usually," Oliver clarified. "The things the ghem say with plasma cannons tend to be more direct. I'm sure it pains their sense of aesthetics."

"Oh. Aesthetics," said Vorinnis. Her tone conveyed uncoded dubiousness.

Oliver went on, "So the elements you need to observe to deconstruct this will be the choices of paper, ink, the particular style of the calligraphy, wording—extra points for obscure poetic references—the method of delivery—which was what, by the way?"

"I think somebody handed it in at the gate, and it went by base mail after that."

"I see."

The girl craned her neck at the paper still in Cordelia's hand. "So what *does* it say? Convey."

"Well, to start with, it is in the correct form, which indicates some baseline of respect, personal or professional," Oliver began.

"Or a basic ability to follow the instructions in an etiquette manual," Cordelia put in. "Which is not a point against the boy, mind you."

She handed it back across, and Oliver turned it over once more. He said, "The paper itself is relatively neutral, the colors of envelope and card blend pleasingly enough, so there is no covert hostility. Calligraphy style is formal, not familiar, but not official. The scents, however . . . heh."

"What?" Vorinnis did not *quite* wail.

Cordelia put in, "Cinnamon for warmth, which is supposed to give a hint how to construe the other odors blended in. Roses—for once, even the Cetagandans follow the old Earth traditions—love, lust, or friendship, depending on the color of the rose."

"How can you tell the *color* of a rose from its *scent*?" said Vorinnis.

"Cetagandans can," said Oliver. "So can a lot of other people, with a little training. It's not a superpower."

"And—oh, dear, I forget gardenia. Oliver? Help us out."

"Hope," he intoned, blue eyes crinkling just a tiny bit, though he kept his face perfectly straight. "Lord ghem Soren is asking you for a date, Lieutenant. He hopes you will accept." He handed the papers back to the girl.

She accepted them, her face scrunching up in unfeigned bewilderment. "Good grief, *why*?"

Cordelia's brow wrinkled at this. It didn't sound as though it boded well for either the ghem lord or the Vor lieutenant. She wasn't sure whether to wince or sit back and watch the show. For now, she sat back.

"Well, the ghem are very competitive," said Oliver. "I know very little of this one yet, but as a general rule you may guess that he either wants to show you up, or show you off."

Vorinnis's face stayed scrunched. "I'm not sure I follow that, sir."

Oliver rubbed his lips, meditatively. "Alternatively, I observe that a cultural attaché is often an unofficial spy. What slicker way to keep tabs on the competition's boss than to date his secretary?"

Vorinnis drew herself up in offense. "Sir! I would never!"

"I didn't suggest that you would, Lieutenant."

"That could cut both ways, of course," Cordelia put in. "Is there any disinformation you want to feed the Cetagandan consulate this week, Oliver?"

The lieutenant grew less stiff, considering this wrinkle.

"Not especially. You?"

"Not offhand. I'd have to think about it."

"But what should I do about this, sir?" said Vorinnis, waving her ... prospective love letter? Bait? Cetagandans, not to mention run-of-the-mill, un-gene-modified humans, could also *lie* with flowers, after all.

"We are not at war with Cetaganda, nor even, at the moment, in an especially tense diplomatic phase."

Not by Oliver's standards, certainly, Cordelia reflected.

"I'd say you are free to accept or decline as you wish, Lieutenant."

"Although should you wish to decline in an especially cutting fashion, I'm sure Admiral Jole can direct you to some useful reference materials," Cordelia put in.

"Oh, there's an entire manual for military support staff to diplomatic outposts in the Cetagandan Empire, to which I call your attention just as general background reading, Lieutenant. Although I don't recommend trying that route unless one is expert. Shows far too flattering an interest, you see." He added after a moment, "Also, it's very long and detailed."

"Have you read it, sir?"

"I had to nearly memorize the damned thing, when I became aide to the Prime Minister. It ended up being relevant much sooner than I'd anticipated. Hegen Hub War, after all."

"I see, sir." Vorinnis was getting a very thoughtful look, under her lowering brows. "So you're saying this could be, um...career development? Know your enemy?"

"Admiral Vorkosigan's motto might as well have been *Know Everything*. No one could, but in his train, it wasn't for lack of trying. I've brought the obvious cautions to your attention, and I expect you understand them. I think you can manage the rest."

"Sir. Uh, thank you, sir. Ma'am. For your time." She returned an uncertain, if faintly bucked-up, smile, and a parting salute, and trailed away, turning her letter over once more.

Cordelia removed her hand from her mouth as soon as she could decently contain her grin. "Oliver, you were *encouraging* that poor girl."

"Hey, that's my job as a mentor. Alternatively, I might have been having mercy on that poor sod of a ghem lord."

"I am not at all sure that aiming a Vorinnis at him qualifies as a merciful gesture."

"Well, presumably, we will find out. At least, I hope she debriefs to me, later."

"I want all the gossip if she does. Oh, my."

"Should we meet by the town fountain with scrub brushes?"

"I'll bring my dirty laundry if you'll bring yours."

He made an amused face. "I am not following that metaphor out any farther, thanks." Fortunately, the arrival of dessert relieved him of the necessity. But he glanced up toward where the girl had gone, and his slight smile became a slight snicker.

"Share the joke?" prodded Cordelia.

"Her redolent letter just reminded me of an Aral-story. Oh, God, should I tell this one? I may be the only living witness."

"And if you drop dead, it'll vanish out of the historical record? Tell, Oliver." It couldn't be one of the hard ones, if it was making him smirk like that.

"Tell you, maybe. I can't imagine sharing it with Vorinnis. Or anyone else, really." He swallowed a bite of sherbet. "Right, so...in the aftermath of the Hegen Hub war, we spent a good deal of time stuck up in Vervain orbit. While young Gregor was downside wooing the Vervani to such good effect, Aral and I were sorting through the details—beating out the six-way cease-and-desist-fire and peace agreements. There was this one obnoxious Cetagandan envoy who seemed to imagine they could still jerk us around *even though they had just lost*. They would send all these hand-calligraphed notes, very formal and faux-respectful, which of course some poor sod then had to transcribe—"

"That sod being yourself?"

"Frequently, yes. For the, ah, hotter ones, at least. So we had a spate of these, each one smellier than the last—up to twelve scents at once, we had to send them down to the lab for chemical analysis to be sure, sometimes—most of which, if interpreted in the correct order, which for some reason he didn't think we could do, worked out to assorted deadly insults. Aral was getting more and more impatient with this ghem ass, and as I was trying to decode the most recent, he finally said, 'Just give me the damned thing,' twitched it out of my hands, and took it into the lav. Where he proceeded to amend it with, er, his own personal scent mark."

Cordelia muffled a cackle with her napkin, turning it into a dainty choke. "I *see*." And she could, oh, she just could. *Pissed off*, indeed.

"'They shouldn't have any difficulty interpreting *this* reply,' he said. And stuffed it back into its envelope as-was and had me hand-carry it back to the Cetagandan flagship. The envoy's expression as he figured it out was one of the joys of my young life to date. I could just *see* his face drain, even under all the paint."

"Oh, my. And then what happened?"

"Envoy didn't say a word. But evidently, Aral was right about them taking the point. That twit vanished out of the delegation, and our next missive was much more conciliatory. And, er, odorless."

"You're right, I never heard this one."

"Oh, that exchange *so* didn't go into the official records. On either side, as far as I know. *I* thought it was perfect, although I suppose you had to have been there for all the aggravating lead-up to really understand the full impact. It did bring home to me that Aral was a man who would do *anything* for Barrayar. Without limit."

"That . . . is true."

"Aral wasn't the least ashamed of the gesture—it certainly worked to put the wind up the Cetas—but I do think he was a little ashamed of losing his temper, later."

"Ah, yes. He had a thing about that." *Aral-stories*, Cordelia thought. Slowly, that massive, complex presence was being reduced to Aral-stories. "I hate having to give public speeches about him," she sighed. "Each neat little squared-up box of words, with all the messy bits cut off because they don't fit, seems to make him smaller and simpler. Turning the man that was into the icon that they want."

"Maybe the icon that they need?"

She shook her head. "I think they'd be better off to get used to dealing with the truth, myself."

He grimaced. "There were a lot of silences that seemed a burden to me at the time . . ."

She nodded understanding of what he was not saying.

"—but damn if I'm not glad I don't have to give those speeches."

"Aye."

Chapter Four

Jole's next morning was spent locked down in one of what looked to be an endless string of confidential meetings going over assorted contractors' bids on the construction of the new base. Budget and Logistics did the initial triage, but all final approvals had to be run past Haines and Jole, with the B&L officers jockeying for their favorites. Sergyar Command's B&L departmental needs and those of the Emperor were normally fairly congruent, but not always, and Jole had to remind himself now and then, as voices rose and the highlighted numbers were presented again in *brighter colors*, which side he was on.

As they broke for a late lunch, he and Haines walked over to the officers' mess together. Crossing the main quadrangle, Haines shaded his eyes and frowned at the distant mesa of plascrete pallets. "Have you managed to get any further with those Plas-Dan bastards?" he inquired.

"The Vicereine has promised to sic some of her forensic accounting people on it. Depending on what she can come up with and how fast—I'm hoping for early next week—we should be able to devise *something* useful. In the long run, we need plascrete more than vengeance."

Haines grunted disconsolate concurrence. "Sucks some days, to have all these boys with guns and not be allowed to shoot anybody. It could be so *cathartic*."

Jole could only snort agreement.

On the whole, Jole liked Fyodor Haines. The general had been assigned here only two years ago, and had so far proved the plodder type of officer, counting down the bare handful of years left to his twice-twenty—which meant, in the main, that everything got done on time and without unnecessary fuss. Vastly preferable for his actual peacetime duties than the thwarted-warrior type, which—an understandable antipathy to civilian contractors aside—Haines wasn't.

Haines's domestic life was currently in some mysterious disarray; his wife of many years had stayed back on Barrayar when he'd been posted to Sergyar, ostensibly to care for aged and ailing parents, possibly due to having reached some abrupt breaking point about moving *one more time* to follow the drum. His two older sons were now in college, one on Barrayar, one on Komarr, which accounted for his current austere lifestyle and most of his pay, but his daughter had been shipped out to Sergyar a few months back to join her father. Jole was uncertain if this constituted a promissory note that his wife would soon follow, or if young Frederica Haines had been seconded as a marital spy. If the latter, her mother's suspicions were unjust; if Haines's stolid allegiance to his marriage oath didn't keep him from attempting some adulterous liaison, his aversion to emotional uproar certainly would.

As they cleared the cafeteria line and seized a small table by the windows, Haines said, "On another subject entirely, I have been commissioned as a scout."

"Oh?" Jole unfolded his paper napkin and contemplated his limp sandwich. But the regulation stew and the stiffly clotted pasta had been even less enticing, on this subtropical day.

"Seems your officer corps is conspiring to throw you a surprise birthday party for your fiftieth. I could get behind the party idea, but I suggested you might not care so much for the surprise aspect."

"That's pretty much correct," Jole agreed. Although a part of him could not help being secretly touched, even if the conspirators' main motivation was a transparent desire to get drunk and set off fireworks. It was like the inverse of a mutiny. "I'm actually not wild about either part. I was planning to ignore the day, myself. All those getting-older jokes."

"Been there, done that," Haines, half-a-dozen years older than Jole, said without sympathy.

Jole's brow wrinkled. "It seems a few months early to be planning any such thing."

"Some of their notions seemed a touch grandiose. They wanted lead time."

"Bored, are they? I bet I could find them some more work."

Haines's lips twitched. "The advantage of letting them set up something on base, besides the convenience, would be control. With Base Security in charge of the collateral damage, rather than the Kareenburg Municipal Guard."

"The advantage of letting them set up something fifty kilometers out in the desert would be that they couldn't burn anything down."

"The catering would be less handy."

"Consider it a field exercise?"

"Mm, maybe," said Haines, judging by his narrowed eyes, drawn by this vision.

"Kayburg Guard would have to be notified anyway," Jole pointed out. "Given that the boys and girls will want to bring dates. Call it joint maneuvers. If you imply you're considering downtown Kayburg as an alternate venue, they'll fall all over themselves to help you set up out in the country instead."

Haines chuckled. "I like the way you think sometimes, Oliver. Remind me not to get crosswise to you in a debate." He took a ruminative bite of stew, and added, "And families. Haul out the wives and families to the picnic, for ballast."

"Good thinking."

"You could bring a date."

The party idea took on a sudden new charm. "I could ask Vicereine Vorkosigan."

Haines pursed his lips judiciously. "Not what I would call a date, but that would set a tone, for sure."

It might at that, although possibly not the sedate one Haines was clearly hankering for. But then, Haines didn't know Cordelia very well.

"It wouldn't settle any bets, though," Haines added a bit morosely.

Jole didn't bother to pretend not to understand. "What, betting whether I'd show up with a woman or a man?" His tone grew a trifle biting. "I see a way we could collude to clean up on that one. I could ask Consul Vermillion, and we could wax them all."

Haines held up a contrite hand. "No business of mine, except that people *ask* me. As if I'd know!"

"I . . . did not realize that," Jole conceded. Although he didn't see how he had anything to apologize for. *Because I don't have anything in the first place?*

Pared to its essentials, the Barrayaran officer corps favored heterosexual marital stability in its senior members mainly to cut down on the potential for ambient personal dramas slopping over into work, as they tended to do. But any nonstandard-issue personal life that supplied one's superior officers with zero drama would do just as well, in Jole's view. And it was a view he'd let be known, certainly. With an emphasis on the zero-drama part, because he'd thought that could stand to be underscored.

"I may be sorry I asked, but what are the current rumors about my personal life?" *Or lack of one.*

Haines shrugged. "They call you the dog who does nothing in the nighttime."

"Come again?"

"Don't look at me! I was told it's a literary reference. Which probably accounts for it making no damn sense." Haines scowled in retrospective suspicion. "A touch Cetagandan, if you ask me."

"I see." Well, that could have been worse. The trouble with giving rumor nothing to chew on was that it freed it to make up *anything*. "Welcome to the fishbowl, Admiral Jole. Though it's not as bad here as at Komarr Command. Or Home Fleet, God help 'em." He'd *aspired* to Komarr Command once, the hot seat of the empire. And just where, in his last few years, had what had once been a driving youthful ambition drained away? Could it be that he was...*content*, here on Sergyar?

"That is happily true," Haines agreed.

Jole considered the general. Fyodor was pretty level-headed, an experienced father, and a good sample of an average officer. And he knew how to be closed-mouthed. As a test subject, as Cordelia would no doubt put it, he could be nearly ideal. Jole tried the sentence once, secretly inside his mouth, for practice. And then quelled his doubts—his panic?—and let it fly: "Actually, for my fiftieth birthday, I was thinking of having a son."

Haines's eyebrows went up, but he did not, for example, fall off his not-very-comfortable cafeteria chair or have any other such overreaction. "Don't you have a few preliminaries to get through first? Or have you managed to smuggle them past all your interested observers?"

"Not as many as one would think. The Vicereine"—*yes, hide behind Cordelia's skirts*—"has been pitching the virtues of that new rep center downtown. It seems all you have to do is walk in, present yourself, and buy a donated egg. All right, you do have to jump through a few hoops to prove yourself a, er, qualified purchaser. But it skips a lot of the other difficult middle steps."

"Dating, courtship, weddings? In-laws?" Haines's mouth twisted up. "Seems like cheating, really."

"Galactics—I'm told—do it." *All the time* was probably not technically correct.

"Well, galactics," said Haines vaguely.

"I admit, when I picture the scenario, I keep seeing a boy of about, oh, seven. Age of reason and all that. One I could talk to, and do things with. I'm not sure how you get from the single-cell stage to that one, though."

Haines shrugged. "Having an infant aboard is no holiday, but any man who can learn to field-strip a weapon can learn to change a damn nappie. Just handle the kid gently but firmly, like an unexploded bomb. You wonder how some of those whiners would have dealt with the old horse cavalry days—manure by the metric ton, back then. I've no patience with a man who's afraid to get his hands dirty. And at least babies more-or-less stay where you put them, at that age. Now, toddlers... suicidal maniacs, the lot of 'em, boy or girl. I'm so glad *that* stage is over." He took a firm swallow of his iced tea. "I don't know why you don't have a mate—of whatever flavor—Oliver, and it's no business of mine, but I will tell you, parenting is a team sport. You need backup, reserves. I admit, back when, it was more my wife's family and the other base women trading favors than me, depending on where we were. But that does seem to me the one big flaw in your battle plan."

"The Vicereine claims one can hire help."

Haines snorted. "On Sergyar? Have you tried to hire *anyone* on Sergyar lately?"

"About a hundred contractors?"

Haines waved a conceding hand. "Point. But it doesn't get any easier scaled down." His eyes narrowed. "I've suggested to Freddie that she get a part-time job of some kind. She thinks it's because I'm too cheap to give her an allowance, but *I* think it might help keep her too busy to get into trouble. Except what would she do with the money? Like giving ammunition to a drunk. Babies are just a challenge. *Teenagers* are a nightmare. Look ahead, Oliver."

"I... think I might do better taking it one step at a time."

"Mm, that's the way you do have to take it. Maybe fortunately." Haines added after a moment, "I don't deny I have mixed feelings about those replicator centers, but I have to admit, I'd prefer it for my daughter. Just think. She'd never have to date a boy at *all*." He paused in apparent contemplation of this attractive state of theoretical affairs, or non-affairs.

"I'd think you were in an excellent position to intimidate suitors."

"But everyone knows I'm not allowed to *use* the plasma cannons for personal purposes."

Jole choked a laugh around his last mouthful of sandwich. "Besides, she's only, what—fifteen?"

"A fact I have let be known, but I'm not sure it helps." Haines sighed. "Horrible age, fifteen. Part of the time she's still my little princess, Da's Cadette, and then, with no warning—it's like some hostile alien life-form takes over her brain. One minute it's all puppies and ribbons, the next—the female werewolf!" Haines made claws of his hands and mimed a snarl, possibly the most expression Jole had ever seen the man display. "The bathroom is a war zone right now. Last week she had half her friends and the Cetagandan consul's son in there, learning how to apply ghem face-paint patterns."

"That seems . . . cultural," Jole offered, in some attempted consolation.

"Eh, I suppose you'd think so. But when I made her clean it up after, *perfectly reasonably*, you'd think I was Mad Yuri come to life again."

"Er . . . can't you requisition a place with two bathrooms?"

"Base housing is crammed right now. I'd have to make some other officer's family trade down."

"Pull rank?"

"Mm, but that would also entail pulling rank on his wife, which would have, shall we say, proliferating consequences. Base wives have their own, what d'you call it—the Vicereine would probably say, culture. I'd call it an insurgency network. Cross them at your peril." He added after a moment, "I did put myself on the waiting list, though."

"That's very conscientious."

Haines shrugged. "Choose your ground, they say." He opined after another brooding moment, "The only trouble with those uterine replicators is that they don't do *enough*. Twenty! Why can't some Betan boffin come up with one that keeps 'em in there till they're twenty? I swear it would sell." He sucked down the last of his iced tea, and crunched the ice.

As they walked back across the quadrangle for the afternoon rematch with B&L, Jole reflected that Cordelia seemed to be right about the secret parents' club. He'd gained more insight into his general in the past hour than in fifty prior work-focused committee meetings. That Haines seemed willing to regard Jole as a... provisional prospective member?—seemed curiously encouraging. Though perhaps it was merely a case of misery-loves-company? Other people's children had been a topic supremely uninteresting to Jole before now. He sensed those horizons shifting within his mind, opening up new vistas. Some of them were a little alarming.

Barrayar's warships did not carry families, and its far-flung stations, principally charged with protecting vital and potentially disputed wormholes, did not encourage dependents to occupy expensive upside residence. Military families therefore tended to collect in just such downside shuttleport support bases as were Haines's patch. In his upside career, Jole had mostly dealt with such issues at a distance, as distractions to his techs and troops in their tasks. It was possible the ground general might have more to teach the space admiral than Jole would at first have thought.

He was also getting a better sense of why Cordelia had been so insistent about those next-of-kin forms. Barrayaran history was full of details about what Aral had been doing during the first few years of the regency, which were also the first few years of his marriage—yet except for the shock of her cutting short the Pretender's War by cutting short the Pretender, it was mostly silent about Cordelia. But what she'd mainly been occupied with had been infant Miles, during a period when it had been medically uncertain if the child would live. When she'd sent Aral off, for example, to that lethal slugging match for the Rho Cetan-route wormholes that was later dubbed the Third Cetagandan War, she'd been left to go it alone, still a stranger-sojourner on her adopted world—her father-in-law Count Piotr being more hazard than help at that point. What would that whole time have been like for Aral if there *hadn't* been a Cordelia to entrust his beloved boy to?

Jole suspected that Miles might not have been the only casualty.

One expected the advent of children to rearrange one's future. No one had told Jole that they could also rearrange one's *past*. It seemed an extraordinary reach to have, for a set of boys who weren't even blastospheres yet. He shook his head and followed Haines into the Admin building.

ぐ    ぐ    ぐ

A few days later, Jole powered down his personal lightflyer on the pavement in front of the Viceroy's Palace and slid out. Before he could step toward the front door, though, it opened partway, and Cordelia slipped through in a vaguely furtive manner. She was dressed for the backcountry in a sage-green T-shirt, sturdy tan trousers, and boots, and carried a canvas satchel. She waved at him and hurried over; he opened the passenger-side door and saw her safely within, then returned to the pilot's seat.

"Away, fly away, before somebody else catches up to me with *Just one more thing, Your Excellency . . . !*"

"At your command, Vicereine." Jole grinned and popped them into the air. "Where are we headed on our mystery errand, might I ask?"

"Mount Rosemont. I have the exact coordinates for when we get closer."

Jole nodded and dutifully banked the lightflyer around. Mount Rosemont lay about two hundred kilometers to the southeast, and was the largest and most spectacular volcanic mountain of the scattered chain anchored by Kareenburg's hollowed-out peak. One didn't need coordinates to find it; even at this modest altitude he could see it, a broad and symmetrical shape on the horizon, its snowcapped top glowing like a beacon in the westering light of late afternoon.

"Thank you *so much* for the lift," Cordelia added. "I really wanted some company for this errand. And not just to hold the vidcam."

He was to hold a vidcam? Curious. "I thought you had plenty of company. Rykov, the ImpSec crew, your entire staff...?" In fact, she usually needed to be quite firm to successfully shed them.

She grimaced. "Not the right kind of company."

"And I am?" Heartening notion.

She nodded, and leaned her head against the seatback in a gesture not, he thought, entirely of physical weariness. Kareenburg rapidly fell away behind them, and the outlying settlements strung along the watercourses passed as well. All signs of invading humanity soon vanished into the level red scrublands of the semi-desert.

"So...what's in the satchel?" he tried, when she did not at once go on.

She grunted an almost-laugh, and burrowed her hand inside to lift out a sealed plastic bag containing about a kilogram of...?

"Sand," she answered his raised eyebrows.

"Sand?"

"Betan sand. It arrived here by jump-transit a couple of days ago, but this is the first I've been able to break away." She added after a second, "Have you had your dinner yet? I didn't think to ask." Which suggested just what part of her packed schedule she'd sacrificed to create this break.

"No, but I have ration bars in the boot along with the medkit, if we don't get back in time for a civilized meal." And if they did, might he persuade her to join him? Somewhere better than the officers' mess, not that Kareenburg offered any wide array of choices.

She chuckled. "You would. Always prepared, Oliver. I suppose it's habit by now."

"Pretty much," he conceded. "So. Sergyar has sand." In a bewildering array of types and grades, judging by his recent experiences with the contractors. "Why are we importing it from Beta Colony?"

"It was sent." She sighed. "I know you know something about how Aral and I first met, right here on Sergyar? Except it wasn't named Sergyar yet. In my Survey log it was only an alphanumeric string and a stunning discovery."

He nodded in a way that he hoped would not discourage her from going on. Jole had heard the tale several times, from Aral and from her, somewhat differently remembered; he never tired of the repeats, though, since some odd new detail seemed to pop up in every version. Not quite *How I met your mother*, but still personally riveting.

Aral's version opened with him standing guard on the invasion-supply cache as captain of his old cruiser the *General Vorkraft*, in distant exile from Barrayaran HQ, Aral's career being in deep political eclipse just then. He'd taken his ship on a scheduled patrol out through the short chain of wormholes leading toward Escobar, then returned to his orbital watch only to find that a Betan Astronomical Survey vessel had slipped in by another route and blithely set up shop while his back was turned. His attempt to peacefully, if firmly, intern the interloping Betans had been thoroughly botched by a group of politically motivated mutineers, who'd seized the opportunity to stage their coup when Aral had led a team downside to capture the Betan survey party led by Cordelia. Things had gone rapidly to hell thereafter, in both versions, though Cordelia's usually included the most cutting editorial asides. How the pair of them, equally if differently abandoned by the ships they'd commanded, had teamed up to recapture the *General Vorkraft* and save Aral's life and subsequent spectacular career was a legend by now. And, like most legends, distorted in the public retelling.

"My second-in-command, Reg Rosemont, was shot dead in that first melee—nerve disruptor, he never had a chance. I always think of him as the first casualty of the Barrayar-Escobar War. Well, him and Truth."

Truth is always War's first victim, the old saying went. And Jole had reason to suspect that was . . . truer than usual, for that particular war. He nodded.

"Burying him before we left our Survey campsite was practically the first task Aral and I ever shared. Reg was our xeno-geologist—I think I told you that once—brilliant fellow. God, the waste of it all. Anyway, when we were officially slotting in names to go along with the grid numbers for all the mountains last year, I held out for renaming HJ-21 after him. It seemed . . . I don't know. Something. I sure as hell wasn't going to let them name anything else after Prince Serg."

"Mm," said Jole. Vorbarr Sultana politics had been a snake pit in Serg's era, for all that the crown prince had died heroically—and, it seemed, luckily for the empire—at Escobar. Jole had once remarked to Aral that he was glad his own career hadn't come along till much later. Aral had just said, *So am I.*

"So, I told the Barrayaran Embassy on Beta to pass that news along to whatever surviving family of Reg's they could locate, which they dutifully did. In consequence, a couple of days ago, this"—she lifted the satchel—"turned up in the Palace mail, along with a letter from Reg's sister. I think I met her once . . . twice? She was apparently the only family member who still remembered him much. Forty-five years ago, after all. There being no plans to disinter poor Reg and ship his remains to Beta, she thought this might be the next best thing—bring a little Betan soil to him. She asked me to put it on his grave. I thought we could get a vid of me doing so, and send it back to her." She frowned down at the satchel in her lap, reverting to her old Betan Survey mode by adding, "It's been sterilized for microorganisms, of course."

"And she taps the Vicereine of Sergyar for this?"

"No, she taps Reg's old commanding officer, I think."

"That's . . . nearly Barrayaran. Betan feudal ties?"

"Something like. Or whatever one can get, out of a generally uncaring and forgetful world."

An updraft from a warm patch of ground below lifted the flyer with a lurch. Jole overrode the correctors before they dropped the flyer and its passengers back to the set course with undue jaw-clopping haste. Rising with the thermal was a faint, spiraling cloud: a flock of tiny radials, each one no bigger than a fingertip, shimmering like the soap bubbles they resembled. Unfortunately, as they splattered noisily against the canopy of a flyer plowing through them at several hundred kilometers an hour, they popped less like soap and more like snot. Jole grimaced and turned on the canopy sonics; the slime slithered away to the sides and was blown off.

This species of radial occupied somewhat the niche of parasitic insects, being blood-sucking biters of the local fauna; but being also very slow moving, they were easy for humans to brush away from their skin. Slapping them in place was not recommended, as the ensuing residue was more corrosive than the original bite would have been. He would have to hose down his lightflyer promptly when they got back to Kareenburg. "Gah!"

Cordelia grinned sideways at him. "I admit, I do not love those things myself. But I'd rather run into the little ones than the big ones."

Which had an alarming tendency to not so much squash as explode. "Really. Any side bets as to which Sergyaran species will be the first to go extinct under their new human management?"

"No takers, I'm afraid." She added after a reflective moment, "People petition for plasma arcs to defend themselves, but really, that's overkill. Not at all sporting, either. You can take one of those big suckers out with a burning stick." She added after another moment, "If you don't object to setting your hair on fire." And, after a longer, more meditative pause, "Or one can use a laser pointer."

Jole bit back a smile. "Laser pointer? Really? How would you know this, Cordelia?"

"It was an experiment," she returned, a bit primly.

"In biology, or sport?"

"Mm, some of both. I was doing the biology. Aral was considering the sporting aspects. Granted, he didn't love the bloated little vampires either."

The ground was starting to rise below them, changing from scrubland to scattered forest to solid forest as the altitude wrung more water out of the air. Cordelia supplied the exact coordinates, and the lightflyer beat upslope and partway around the mountain to a level where the forest began to again grow patchy and stunted, this time from the night chill of the heights.

"Have you been up here before? I mean, since that first time," Jole inquired, looking for a safe landing zone in the spot that Cordelia and his nav system agreed looked about right. There was a nasty steep ravine to avoid, and uneven sloping ground, and lightflyer-grabbing branches from what passed for the Sergyaran version of trees. They shared the same generally fractal design as both Old Earth and Barrayaran trees, anyway, tending here to muted gray-green color schemes.

"Once, soon after we were assigned to Sergyar. We came up and burned a Barrayaran death-offering, by way of propitiation to whatever gods or ghosts haunt this place. The marker was still there all right back then . . . thirteen years ago, I suppose. But the ground could have subsided or shifted since, or animals, or . . . well, we'll see."

"Hm." Glad he wasn't trying to do this after dark, Jole found an opening and eased the lightflyer down to a reasonably level landing. He checked his sidearm—a mere stunner, but sufficient to drop most of Sergyar's more hazardous wildlife without further argument—and joined Cordelia in the undergrowth. She peered around and began walking back and forth; she was soon puffing in the thin air. Not being entirely sure of what signs she was seeking, Jole followed along, sparing a look-round for the sake of wider situational awareness. The place seemed profoundly peaceful.

"Ah," said Cordelia at last. She stopped before what was plainly a standard-issue Barrayaran military grave marker from three or four decades back, the corrosion-proof metal deeply incised with Rosemont's full name, rank, numbers and dates. It had been part-camouflaged by a few saplings crowding it, taller than Jole. Cordelia scowled at them, then unshipped her own sidearm—a more robust plasma arc—set it to narrow beam, and unceremoniously nipped them off at ground level and tossed them out of the way. She then set the arc to wide beam, low power, and circled the marker, clearing a broader patch in a controlled burn. It looked darkly tidy when she finished, as if the grave had been tended all along.

She pulled a vidcam from one of her trouser pockets and handed it to Jole. "I guess I'll wing this. Be sure to get a good close-up of the marker, and some pans around at the view. If we flub, we can do it again, although . . . well, I'll try not to flub." Taking the bag of sand in her hands, she took up a stance by the marker and lifted her chin, her face settling into that tilted expression one took on when recording a message to a person invisible except in the mind's eye. Jole fiddled with the viewfinder—why did they have to make the controls so tiny these days?—and then nodded for her to begin.

"Hello, Jaceta. As you can see, I received your message and your gift safely." She held up the sandbag. "I'm standing here by Reg's grave at the three-thousand-meter level of Mount Rosemont." She paused while Jole moved in to get some good shots of the marker. "As you can also see, it is a very beautiful spot." No lie, that; he panned in turn up at the shoulders of the great peak looming in the middle distance, then slowly wheeled to take in the whole wide plain below. For good measure, he added a few close shots of the most attractive of the low-growing native plants nearby that had escaped Cordelia's cleanup. He returned the focus to her and motioned her to continue, which she did, producing a few kindly, flattering reminiscences of the deceased officer, and then slowly scattering the sand as if it were the seeds of some precious healing balm. She'd certainly had more than enough practice speaking at memorials these last three years.

Presumably concerned lest the ceremony seem too brusque, she went on with what he recognized as a modified version of her Sergyar sales pitch, which he illustrated with a few more pans around at the present lovely scene. If one had to die and be buried, it all seemed to imply, this spot on Sergyar was a fine and private place to do so. Jole couldn't disagree.

Cordelia's eyes were growing a little strained as she continued to push out words toward their unknown destination. Jole rolled a finger to indicate she could probably wind up now. She did so, in the end not giving some Betan quasi-military salute, but just bowing mutely over her hands placed palm-to-palm. Blessing? Apology? Jole cut the vid.

"Oh-God-I-am-so-tired-of-*death*," she declared in one unpent huff of breath, whether to the thin air or to him he was not quite sure. She unscrunched her eyes and smoothed her grimace, sighed, and trod over to collect the vidcam and stow it, plus the emptied plastic bag, in her satchel. "Hardly fair to Reg's sister to say so, I suppose. My own fault, for stirring up whatever memories she had. No good deed goes unpunished and all that."

He wanted to give her some more-substantial comfort in her reminded grief, or whatever this was, but physical intimacy was not the cure. They'd tried that once, in mutual desperation soon after Aral had gone, and it had ended in tears in all senses. She'd not seemed arousable, and his interest had soon flagged, weighted down by the distractions of the hour. It had been like two eunuchs trying to make love. (He wondered briefly how the bioengineered sexless Cetagandan ba made out, if at all. Did they even have anything like sex lives or drives?) In retrospect, he'd realized, he and Cordelia weren't as practiced as it might have seemed. They'd never really made love to each other; they'd made love to or for Aral simultaneously. The ghost between them had still been far too palpable. They'd both sheered off, in a spirit of forgiveness rather than recrimination, canning comfort-sex as a bad idea. *Or just badly timed...?*

He wondered what memories were passing before her eyes,

in this serene spot that had once hosted horrors. Something, for she stared a moment at the marker and said, "Huh! You know, you and Reg look—looked—something alike. Not in the shape of your face, but the height and the hair. His was light like yours. I wonder why I never noticed that before. I suppose... if he'd lived, he might look something like the way you do now." She squinted at him, as if trying a new face on his form the way one would swap out clothes on a sales-vid image. "He was about three years younger than me. Four decades younger, now, frozen in time that he is." She added after another moment, gazing down at the burned and sanded soil, "I expect he's just clean bones down there. We had nothing for a coffin, or even a shroud—we stole his clothes for the living."

How close had she been to her dead exec? Jole wondered. And if forty-five years could not supply recovery, what hope was there for him? "It's been a long time."

She scrubbed her hand through her curls in her typical impatient gesture. "We'd *burned* the hair once. It was all dead and buried well enough, till this damned sand thing brought it back up. I'm not sure there is any such thing as recovery; there's only forgetting. One just has to... keep forgetting till one slowly gets better at it."

Her echo of his thought briefly unnerved him. He said, "It's as if people have to die twice, that."

"Yeah," she said, and neither of them needed to say which people. She wandered over to Jole, and they strolled arm-in-arm around the glade for a few minutes, letting the beauty of the mountain seep in. She was not trembling, nor showing any other outward signs of old traumatic stress renewed. But her mouth was still tight.

"Will you pick a home site on a mountain, for the view, when you retire?" he asked, watching her look out over the vastness.

Her lips relaxed a little. "Not me. Miles is the one who is in love with mountains. He'd adore this spot. No, I want to be on the water, right on it. I have a plan... I ought to show you the place sometime, but we'd need at least a day away from Kayburg, maybe two."

"That sounds interesting," he encouraged this line of thought. A day or two away from work, together, at some less fraught task than this forced memorial, with time to talk; that could be... good. He refused to give it any more specific label. Keep it open. *What, for escape?* He was hardly going anywhere.

She smiled, as if shy to be making this confession. "Actually, it's more than a plan. I bought a stretch of shoreline some years back just as a bit of personal speculation, since I thought we'd be returning to Barrayar. Well, and because I'd fallen in love with it at first sight. It's on a lobe of this sort of leaf-shaped natural sea harbor on the east side of the second continent. Far from the capital, old or proposed."

Indeed, the very first settlements on that continent had been approved only a few years back. They could be no more than hardscrabble hamlets by now.

"I told myself it was prudently parental, because who knew where-all in the empire Miles's or Mark's kids will end up? One of them *might* want to move here... And then, well, plans changed. Everything changed. Things do that."

"Yeah." He gave her a cautious hug around the shoulders. Less self-consciously, he fancied, she rested her head against him for a moment. They still stood in angled sunlight at this altitude, but the plains below had gone formless and gray with the rising dusk.

Something dull orange glinted down there; a thin plume of smoke rose from the camouflaging shadows up into the light. "Huh. Is that a fire?"

Cordelia lifted her head and narrowed her eyes, too. "Seems to be. Brush fire? There are no settlements over that way." She corrected after a moment, "That are registered."

"Perhaps we ought to swing past and check it out." It was time they were moving on anyway. When the dusk climbed to this level, some of Sergyar's less-savory native creatures would be waking up and looking for breakfast. Mostly they didn't know what to make of humans, but there were a few evil-tempered brutes that would try anything, and if they spat it out or threw it up later, that wasn't much of a consolation to the mauled.

"Fire," Cordelia recited, in her most Betan tone, "is a natural part of the ecosystem. But yeah." She glanced in the direction of Kareenburg, its nimbus of lights visible at this distance even if its details were not. "It isn't that far out of our way."

By unspoken mutual agreement, they turned and made for the lightflyer.

Chapter Five

Full dark had fallen by the time their lightflyer approached the fading red-orange ring of the creeping brush fire. Cordelia craned her neck. The blaze had burned itself out beyond the lip of a low river valley, probably for lack of fuel, and seemed in process of suppression both up and downstream, due to the dampness of the vegetation in this tail-end of the rainy season. Parked partway up the riverbank, a scorched-looking aircar was... no longer on fire, apparently. At the center of the irregular semi-circle of destruction, a possible solution to the mystery presented itself: a small group of human figures cowering on a sandbar in midstream. The lightflyer swooped closer.

"Get some light on this, Oliver," Cordelia said, and he nodded and switched on his landing spots. Those individuals who were looking up shaded their eyes against the sudden glare. Cordelia counted six: one was waving at them frantically, another was trying to stop him; one sat on the sand with his head buried in his knees; one sturdy figure just stood spread-legged, staring up at them dourly. The other two... milled, Cordelia feared, although how only two people could create a mill was a bit of a puzzle. It looked like two females and four males, or rather—two girls, four boys. "It's a bunch of kids from Kayburg. Good grief, isn't that Freddie Haines down there?" She was the one glowering upward. "Maybe they're brats from the base. That would be your patch, Oliver."

Oliver's gaze, too, swept the scene below. "Isn't that lanky one Lon ghem Navitt, the Cetagandan consul's son? That makes this a diplomatic matter. Your patch, Cordelia."

"Oh, thanks," she muttered, but accepted the return-of-serve. "Can you land us on that sandbar?"

Oliver eyed the proposed landing site with disfavor. "Land, yes. Take off again—depends on how solid the footing proves."

"Well, it's not quicksand, or those kids would be up to their necks by now."

He grunted agreement and gingerly set the flyer down, as close as he could get to the middle of the bar and still be far enough away from the group to not squash anybody underneath. Touchdown was not quite the solid *thunk* one would prefer, but the flyer did not tilt precipitously, so it sufficed. *Any landing that you walk away from is a good one* the saying went, Cordelia was reminded.

They slid out of their respective sides of the flyer and closed ranks in front of it, starting toward the group. The boy who had been waving ran forward eagerly, only to skid to a halt and take several steps back as he recognized them. "It's the *Vicereine!*" he wailed, unflatteringly appalled.

The other girl grabbed Freddie Haines's arm in equal dismay. "And *Admiral Jole!*" Freddie gulped, but stood her ground.

Cordelia mentally ratcheted through a choice of several voices, and decided upon dryly ironic, as opposed to Crisp Command or Concerned Maternal. "So, what's all this, then?"

Freddie's female friend more-or-less pushed her forward, or at least ducked behind her. A couple of the others also looked toward her, silently drafting her as spokes-kid. By which Cordelia guessed that Freddie possessed the highest-ranking parent among the military brats here. Or that she was the ringleader. Or both, of course.

Freddie swallowed and found her voice. "We only wanted to show Lon how the vampire balloons blow up!"

The Cetagandan boy, looking undecided whether to speak or not, compromised by nodding. The larval form of the ghem, Cordelia reflected, was just as unprepossessing as anybody else's teenagers. At age fifteen, Lon had acquired nearly his full adult height, and his people ran to tall; the rest of his development still lagged behind. The general effect was of one of those primary-school science experiments where Bean Plant No. 3 was raised without enough light, growing long and thin and pale and barely able to stand upright.

The boy who was curled up with his face to his knees lifted it long enough to cry, in a voice of anguish, "My *mom's aircar!*"

Oliver broke in firmly. "First of all, is everybody here, and is anybody injured?"

Freddie braced herself under his cool eye. "Everyone present and accounted for, sir. We all waded out to the river when the fire...started." *All by itself*, this seemed to imply.

"Ant got a little scorched," volunteered the female friend, pointing to the boy crouched on the sand. "We *told* him it was too late to save anything!"

The picture slotted in rapidly. It had been an expedition to the backcountry for one of Sergyar's more exciting sights, at least if you were really, really bored: exploding radials. The biggest ones, party-balloon sized, clustered in the watercourses and came out in force on windless nights. The animals did not, of course, explode naturally.

Had this expedition been parentally authorized, or not? Cordelia's eye took in the sidearm holstered at Freddie's hip, a military-issue plasma arc, and decided *Not*. Anyway, six kids were never going to fit into the absence of a back seat in Oliver's lightflyer.

Several of the youths were wearing wristcoms. "Has anyone

called their parents yet?" Cordelia inquired. A telling silence fell. She sighed and raised her own wristcom to her lips.

Kayburg's municipal guard commander was home eating dinner, Cordelia discovered, which reminded her that she hadn't eaten hers yet, which made her quite cheerily ruthless about interrupting his. While Oliver hauled the burned boy around to the boot of his lightflyer for a visit with his first-aid kit, she explained the situation bluntly and succinctly, and extracted a promise of the immediate dispatch of a guard flyer big enough to carry the miscreants back to Kayburg for subsequent sorting and returning-to-senders, or at least to families. She added a roster of names and parental names, extracted against some resistance from their catch. A couple of the youths looked as if they might have held out against fast-penta, but with the application of a sufficiently cold vicereinal eyeball, their friends ratted them out soon enough. Siblings Anna and Ant-short-for-Antoine were base brats; the other two boys were Kayburg civilian offspring, and Lon ghem Navitt was of course in a class by himself, though sharing a classroom at the Kareenburg middle school with the rest of them, hence their association.

Oliver returned with the singed Ant, the boy's red face now glistening with a thick smear of pain-killing antibiotic gel, his blistered hands likewise anointed and wrapped in gauze. Oliver released him back into the concerned arms of his young comrades.

"Nothing too serious, but I'll bet it hurts like hell," Oliver murmured to Cordelia. "I gave him a shot of synergine to help calm him down. He was having a bit of a meltdown about the aircar, understandably."

"That should hold for now," she murmured back. "The municipal guard is sending a lift van to collect them. I'd expect them within the half-hour."

Oliver nodded in relief, and looked over the distraught little company once more. He grimaced and motioned Freddie aside.

Freddie Haines looked rather like her father, perhaps not entirely fortunately, though she was healthily robust and plump with thick dark hair. A trifle spotty, an affliction she would doubtless outgrow in due course. The few times Cordelia had glimpsed her heretofore, she'd seemed confident and not unduly shy for her age, but her current situation was enough to tax anyone's backbone. She kept hers straight, but Cordelia sensed the strain. Oliver, staring down at her, took a moment to compose his opening line. Freddie seemed to take the stretching silence for an ominous sign, and swallowed in anticipation.

"Is that your da's plasma arc?" he asked, quite mildly under the circumstances Cordelia thought, though Freddie wilted.

"Yes, sir," she managed.

"Did he give you permission to take it off base?"

"He said no one should go out into the backcountry unarmed, on account of the hexapeds," she returned.

Oliver allowed this ambiguous statement to hang in the air, palpably unaccepted. Freddie squirmed under that sardonic gaze, opened her mouth, closed it, and finally broke. "No, sir."

"I see."

A quick mental review of military sidearm regulations suggested that this took the girl well over the line from *unfortunate accident* to *illegal act*, complicated but not improved by her status as a minor. It wasn't exactly a bonus for Fyodor Haines, either.

"But it was good we had it!" she said, in a tone of desperate protest. "A couple of those big skatagators tried to come up on the island after us, and I fired it into the sand and scared them away!"

Oliver's eyebrows twitched, though he managed not to betray any other sign of unbending. The skatagators were low-slung, amphibious, and carnivorous native hexapeds that infested the rivers and did sometimes attack people, when their tiny brains were triggered by the right wrong motions. By the time their senses of taste and smell signaled *wrong prey*, it was usually pretty messy. A bright plasma-arc blast into the wet sand and the resultant steam explosion would have sent them scuttling back into the turbid water in a hurry, Cordelia had no doubt. Shooting one of the skatas instead would have been a bad move; the thrashing wounded animal or dead carcass would quickly have attracted more scavengers, including its cannibalistic brethren. She considered the familiar conundrum inherent in complimenting a child for doing something well in the course of what ought not to have been done at all, and kept her peace.

"You'd better give it to me," said Oliver, holding out his hand. "I'll undertake to return it to your father."

"Yes, Admiral Jole, sir." Freddie unbuckled the holster and handed the weapon across to its duly constituted Imperial authority.

Without the least outward sign of a man burying a hot potato, Oliver quietly made it disappear into the boot of his lightflyer. Cordelia wondered if the girl appreciated what he'd just done for her. Perhaps her da would point it out later. She couldn't decide if she longed to be a fly on the wall for that conversation or not. She gave Oliver a silent nod of approval as he rounded the lightflyer once more; he gave her a silent nod of acknowledgment.

In a very few minutes more, the municipal guard lift van arrived to clear the scene. They followed it back to town.

Fyodor Haines was the first parent to arrive, turning in to the parking lot behind the municipal guard's main station mere moments after Oliver had put down their lightflyer in a painted circle. Haines pulled up his groundcar beside them. The two men got out and greeted each other; Haines spared a semi-salute for his Vicereine.

"What the hell is this about, Oliver?" Haines asked in a worried voice. "They said none of the kids were hurt—is that right?"

Oliver gave a quick summation of events, glanced around to be sure they were still having a private moment, and handed back the plasma arc wrapped in its holster. Haines swore under his breath and made it vanish again into his car.

"Damn. Thank you. I didn't know she *had* that."

"Don't you keep your sidearms locked up, in quarters?"

"I always did when the boys were .young. I thought girls preferred, like, *dolls*." Haines, vexed, set his teeth.

"Freddie didn't strike me as the doll type," said Cordelia, "not that I've had much experience raising girls. But leaving aside the idiocy of what the kids were doing out there in the first place, she does seem to have kept her head rather well when things got out of hand on them."

Haines rubbed his mouth, taking in this paternal consolation. "Hm. We'll have to have words. Confine her to quarters for a week, at least."

"That seems fairly appropriate," Cordelia said cautiously.

"Yes, except they're *my* quarters." His face scrunched in dismay, presumably at the vision of a week of his evenings locked up in the exclusive company of a surly distraught teenager. "*Damn but I wish her mother would come out.*" He shook his head and trudged off for the back door of the guard station.

Cordelia and Oliver, too, went inside. At this point Cordelia figured her sole reason for still being there was to make sure Lon ghem Navitt made it back to his people without incident, so the two of them sat back out of the way while the rest of the variously upset parents trailed in to retrieve their erring offspring. Cordelia had the subliminal impression that the Kayburg guardsmen didn't get overly exercised about anything that didn't involve extracting actual dead bodies from hard-to-reach places, such as the insides of smashed lightflyers or sick skatagators. Nonetheless, they performed a pretty good Stern-And-Grim to put the wind up all concerned, and with luck spare themselves a repeat of this event. They only threatened, but did not invoke, any formal charges—it may have helped that one of the town boys was the son of a woman who clerked for the guard station.

Just as Cordelia was slipping over from seriously hungry to savagely starving, and starting to wonder if the Cetagandan consul was planning to leave his son overnight in jail for a life-lesson, the cultural attaché Lord ghem Soren arrived, in the same formal face paint and attire he'd worn to her garden party last week. He smelled of strange esters—perfumes, inebriants? in any case, not Barrayaran-style alcoholic beverages—and looked faintly harassed. The hand-off hit a snag when it was determined that he was not Lon's actual parent.

Cordelia intervened smoothly, assuring the dubious guard sergeant that as an officer of the consulate, ghem Soren constituted a legal authority sufficient to the purpose.

"Where are Lord and Lady ghem Navitt tonight, Lord ghem Soren?" Cordelia inquired easily.

"Hosting a moon-poetry party at the consulate, Your Excellency. An autumn observance at the Celestial Garden on Eta Ceta, which, uh, it is there now. Autumn. They couldn't leave the ceremony in the middle, so they sent me."

Did that mark ghem Soren as a trusted confidant, or low man on the duty roster? The latter, Cordelia decided, which simultaneously explained his otherwise after-hours aroma. Oliver looked enlightened and amused. Bean Plant No. 3 made no objection, seeming more relieved than disappointed at this substitution. In any case, the pair traipsed out again with as little further interaction with the local authorities as ghem Soren could manage.

It was now officially Bloody Late, and Cordelia still had a string of report files to read before her morning meetings. She let Oliver escort her up the main street with no more than the briefest detour through an all-night sandwich shop, one of the few places still open in downtown Kayburg on this dull midweek night. They walked on toward the Viceroy's Palace munching their sandwiches out of their wrappings. At the corner of the side street that led to Kayross, she balled up the paper in her hand, dropped it in a trash receptacle, and hesitated, staring down toward the half-lit facade of the replicator clinic.

Oliver followed her glance, and gave her a lopsided smile. "Did you want to stop in and see Aurelia?"

"They keep a night staff, but it isn't really visiting hours."

"I'm sure they'd make an exception for you."

"I'm sure they would, too. But I shouldn't impose. And there really isn't that much to see even on the magnifying monitor yet. People are pretty blobby at this stage."

Oliver wasn't buying her nonchalance. Was she that transparent, or was he just being Oliver? "You still want."

"Well . . . yes."

He turned her firmly leftward. "It's been a long day, and tomorrow is another one. Grab your treat while you can."

"Are you thinking of keeping me in a good mood for the sake of my oppressed subordinates?" She took his arm as they started off again.

"Maybe it's enlightened self-interest, then."

"Ha."

The medtech who came, after a few minutes, to the front door buzzer did indeed recognize her at once, and let them in without demur. He cross-checked the records and led them back through several doors to a freshly arrayed bank of replicators, sorting through to the right monitor. The light level was muted, the picture indeed tiny and blobby, like some low form of sea life.

Oliver peered dubiously over her shoulder. "So strange. And yet amazing." He glanced around as if wondering in what freezer his own future hopes were being stored. But he didn't quite muster the boldness to ask.

"Yes," she had to agree.

"You're smiling."

"Yes," she had to admit. Her smile crept wider, igniting a reflecting glint in Oliver's eyes. Even the medtech, when he let them out and locked the doors again, smiled back, as if infected by her compressed joy. Her weary stride widened to almost an Oliver-stretch as they turned up the main street once more.

At the Palace gate, Cordelia apologized for keeping him up past his bedtime and hers. "I didn't anticipate all the complications on that outing. I suppose one never does."

"If you anticipated them, they wouldn't be complications, eh?"

She laughed and bade him goodnight.

∽   ∽   ∽

Cordelia woke in the small hours, as she so often did these days, with an old memory floating up out of her dream fragments. An unvoiced *huh* of bemusement shook her.

She'd been in her twenties, eager to advance into her adult

life. Tops in her Survey classes, clumsy in her social interactions, she'd been thrilled to at last acquire her first real sexual partner. Their affair had been sporadically renewed as their duties in the Betan Astronomical Survey permitted, culminating in a several-month voyage as declared affiliates, sharing a cabin and junior-officer duties. They'd made plans for the future. Equals in love and life, she'd thought, till it came time to put in for the same promotion.

He would go first, they decided; she would take downside duties to raise their allotted two kids, and then it would be her turn. She applied for and took the desk job as planned, but somehow the declaration of co-parent status and the fertilizations were not forthcoming, though she'd had her egg extraction and signed up for her mandatory parenting course. But he'd had no time to attend to those details before he shipped out in his first captaincy; too many new duties to get atop of right now. It had seemed reasonable.

All ran to plan till he'd returned from that first voyage with a different woman in tow, a junior ensign and xeno-chemist uninterested in having children. *We just made a mistake, Cordelia,* he told her, as if correcting an error in her navigational math. *It's nobody's fault, really.*

Even if she'd been the scene-making type, she wouldn't have made protest in the public place he'd prudently chosen for this revelation, and she'd let him slither away, imagining his lie undetected. It wasn't as if she'd wanted him *back.* He'd gone on to a steady career in the B.A.S.—even, eventually, the two kids, with a partner a few down the line from either Cordelia or her replacement. And the next year, the captaincy of the *René Magritte* had opened up for her, a better ship than his if the truth be told, so, no harm done, right?

And two voyages after *that* she'd discovered this planet and Aral, and the rest was, very literally, history.

The tale of that duplicity was the first intimate secret about herself she'd shared with Aral, during their fraught trek here, in fair trade for one of his own, considerably more blood-soaked and lurid. Aral had come by his gift for the dramatic honestly, she had to concede, and she smiled to recollect how even at age eighty he could still electrify a room just by walking into it.

Which made, in retrospect, her Betan clot's betrayal the best thing he'd ever done for her. Was it too late to send him a thank-you note? She wondered if her face was as much of a blur in his mind by now as his was in hers. All that lingered of him was the picture of the pain, not even the pain itself, of that stab through the center of her soul. An image still strangely clear.

Catastrophic events had conspired against Aral's hopes to repair that old wound of hers, yet decades later he'd made sure to leave in her hands the means to do so herself, if she chose. Trust Aral to honor even a tacit promise grandly.

These weren't tales she could share with Oliver, she realized, at the moment or perhaps ever. He might take them the wrong way. In fact, they were of no use to anyone at all, not even to her, now were they? Sighing, she folded the memories back into herself, and turned over in the dark.

⚬ ⚬ ⚬

Jole arrived at his downside base office the next morning to find his aide neither late, nor hung-over.

"How was the party at the Cetagandan consulate last night, Lieutenant?" he asked her, as she presented him with a sacrificial offering of coffee. "Did you learn anything interesting?"

"Very odd." Vorinnis wrinkled her nose in distaste. "The food was...tricky. And then they passed around these things that you were supposed to sniff, but I only *pretended* to inhale." Jole gathered that this was less for the sake of virtue than of paranoia. "And then my so-called date went off and left me halfway through. I had to sit through about an hour and a half of this weird poetry recital all by myself. By the time Lord ghem Soren got back, he'd lost his turn at reciting, which made him all miffed and not much company."

Jole suppressed a smile. "Ah. I'm afraid that was not exactly his fault. Lon ghem Navitt was picked up with a group of his classmates by the Kayburg guard after an, er, self-inflicted accident out in the backcountry last night, and the guard wouldn't let the kids go till they had inconvenienced all the parents sufficiently to make their point. Ghem Soren was apparently told off by his boss to go collect the lad. For what it's worth, he didn't seem too happy with being assigned the detail."

"Oh." Vorinnis blinked, taking this in. She did not then inquire, *How do you know all this, sir?* Was he simply presumed to be omniscient? But she grew a shade less peeved. "Other than that, he mainly seemed to want to tell me all about his family tree. Did you know he had a Barrayaran ancestor? Ancestoress, I guess."

Jole raised his eyebrows. That tidbit had not been in the cursory ImpSec dossier he'd read on the fellow, though it had named a couple of unexceptionably Cetagandan-sounding parents from ghem Soren's planet of origin, a lesser satrap world which lay beyond the higher-status capital of Eta Ceta from Barrayar. "No, I didn't. Do tell."

"It seems his great-grandmother on his father's side was a Barrayaran collaborator during the Occupation, and got taken along with the family when the Cetagandans pulled out. I can't quite figure out if she was Vor or prole, or a servant or mistress or what, though he called her a third wife. Sounded like some kind of concubine to me."

"Mm, more than a servant, anyway. That's a status with official standing and rights, but her children would certainly be lower in rank than their senior half-siblings." Jole sipped coffee and considered his next leading question in this engaging debriefing. "And what sorts of things did he ask you about?"

"He wanted to know if I rode horses, back on Barrayar. He seemed to think all Vor did. I mean, all the time, to get around. And carriages."

"And, ah, did you ride? As a sport, of course." Aral had instructed him in horseback riding on those long-ago country weekends down at Vorkosigan Surleau, though they had both preferred the sailing. He'd apologized that he was not so expert a cavalryman as his late father General Count Piotr Vorkosigan had been, and sounded almost sorry that he could not gift Jole with this superior mentor; Simon Illyan had just muttered, *Count your blessings.*

"Not really, except a couple of times when I visited some cousins. My family lives in Ouest Higgat." The Vorinnis's District capital, that, and like most such cities a major political and commercial hub. "My father works in the District Bureau of Roads and Bridges. Mostly on the lightflyer traffic-control systems. He'd been an orbital-and-air traffic controller back when he was in the Service, which was how he got into that line. Mikos seemed sort of, I don't know, disappointed when I told him that."

"What, is our ghem lord a historical romantic?"

"Well, that's another explanation," she allowed.

"As opposed to . . . ?"

"He's a twit?" But her tone was by no means definitive.

"Mm," said Jole, declining to commit to an opinion on this point yet. "I wonder if this supposed connection to Barrayar is why his superiors assigned him to this post? Or if it was the other way around—exploring his roots?"

"I . . . we didn't get that far."

"I also wonder if that's why we find a ghem of his age and lord's rank on the civilian side. Did that little Barrayaran blot in his genetics bar him from the military brotherhood?"

"We didn't get that far, either. I wonder . . . if I shouldn't have been quite so short with him." She frowned in fresh doubt. "Maybe I should invite him back. To do something. Give him another chance."

Jole shrugged noncommittally. "Some innocuous outdoor activity, perhaps? Gives him an opportunity to amend his lapses without committing you to any implied, ah, implications." Although not, by preference, a night hunt for vampire balloons, despite the chance to demonstrate the Barrayaran cultural passion for fireworks; they were not in need of more brushfires. He bit back the impulse to pass on Cordelia's tip about the laser pointers. Although he rather thought that he would pay money to see the *Vicereine* deploy that technique.

Vorinnis's thick brows drew down. "I'll have to think about that, sir."

And then his coffee cup was empty and it was time to gather up the agendas and move on to the next materials-procurement meeting. Jole, glancing out the window at the light-drenched morning activities of the base, wondered how all his youthful dreams of military glory had come down to this. On the other hand, these current mundane labors might silently serve some future smoking sod who'd had glory dumped on him, who wouldn't have to spare a single frantic thought for *Where the hell can I land this thing?* Invisible victories, eh.

Aral, he thought, *would understand.*

ⅎⅎⅎ   ⅎⅎⅎ   ⅎⅎⅎ

It was late afternoon when Cordelia called him on his office comconsole. He hit the key that would signal *No Interruptions* to Lieutenant Vorinnis in the outer office, and leaned back in his station chair. The look on Cordelia's face over the vidplate was amicable enough, but her lips were compressed.

"What's afoot, Your Excellency?"

"Not a great deal, unfortunately. I received an interim report from my people on your Plas-Dan friends."

"Ah? Anything I can use?"

"I don't yet see how. They were able to trace the, I guess you could call it a life-history, of your mixer. It was an order that was cancelled in the middle of its production run last year when the customer switched to a cheaper product. Plas-Dan couldn't force them to take it, though they tried. So there it sat, a blockage in their overheated yard, till some bright soul figured out they could shift it onto you, solving the problem on their end. They think they've done nothing wrong. Or at least—alas—nothing *actionable.* We checked that out, too."

Jole grimaced. "At least not any kind of action we're allowed to take. Granted, suppliers have been foisting overpriced crap and spoiled goods onto their military customers since armies were invented. You would *think* they would be more cautious about who they were offending."

"Given that you and I between us are the biggest on-going customers on the planet, yes. There are, hm, things we can do back to them, down the line. Their trick seems short-sighted."

"We may be the biggest, but we aren't necessarily the most profitable. A lot of civilian projects are willing and able to out-bid us, or so I am lately told. If all of Plas-Dan's production is tied up with our large, low-margin orders, they can't squeeze in the plums." He hesitated. "Also, I can't help wondering if they're trying to sabotage the move to Gridgrad. Or at least delay it."

Cordelia tapped her lips, considering this. "Delay to what end?"

"The arrival of a new, more pliable viceroy?"

"Mm, but I haven't discussed my retirement plans with any-one but you. I don't see how anybody else could anticipate it."

That was . . . flattering. If also slightly alarming. "You still haven't told Gregor yet? Or Miles?"

"Gregor's heads-up will be next. Once Aurelia passes the one-month mark safely, I figured. Eight months should be plenty of time for him to look around for my replacement. Or a bit longer, maybe—there's room in the Palace for one baby, but I'd really like to be out of there before her first sister comes along. I don't think Gregor'll send me an idiot, do you? Nor some political remittance-man he just wants exiled from Vorbarr Sultana. Though he does need to corner a candidate both able *plus* willing."

Jole smiled a little, though the vision of having to work with some other civilian boss than Cordelia opened at his feet like an unexpected sinkhole in the road. He hadn't really thought ahead to that aspect, had he? "I think you may find it harder to let go than you imagine. You've had it your own way on Sergyar with very little Imperial oversight. I know the Komarran Imperial Councilor gets far closer attention."

"Well, Komarr." She shrugged. "Anyway, the point is, there is some wriggle-room in my nine-month goal. Maybe some time to break in the new viceroy, before I run?"

Historically, Jole thought, such changes-of-command were usually more sharp-cut, reflected and reinforced by the elaborate formal hand-off ceremonies. And for good reasons. "You might not have to linger. If you're on the same planet, they can always track you down for consults on the comconsole. You can run, but you can't hide."

Her lips twisted in new repugnance. "Hadn't thought about that. Oh, lord, do you imagine they'll still want *speeches*?"

He hid a laugh in a cough. "Probably. You'll just have to learn to say no, Cordelia."

"I say no to people all day long. They don't like it one bit."

"It's true you're at odds with a lot of the investment money and energy in Kareenburg, right now. You haven't made a secret of your long-term plans for the place."

She swiped her hands through her hair. "What part of 'Let's not site the planetary capital next to an active volcano' do they find *hard*? This place should be a *nature reserve*. All right, maybe a historical park, later on. But then when that damned mountain next goes off it'll only take out dozens or hundreds of people, not *millions*."

"I've never disagreed," he placated her. "I will be entirely willing to shift all of the downside Imperial Service headquarters and its economic impact to the new base—once it is built. An aim not aided by cost overruns before we even break ground, I must point out." Hell, they were still building *Gridgrad*. *Lack of infrastructure* was an understatement.

Cordelia wrinkled her nose in doubt. "Is this overrun likely to prove fatal?"

"Not…really. I expect we'll endure much worse before we're done, unavoidably. And I'm fairly sure Plas-Dan realizes that as well as we do. It's the sly *calculation* of this one that ticks me off." He scowled.

"Is there any way you can recycle that stuff into some earlier project? At least recover *some* of your costs. Or break ground early?" She gave a frugal housewifely sniff. "Build the runway right now?"

"I wish. It's not just materials, it's labor."

"You have an army. Of sorts."

"And we'll be using them, but untrained or trained-for-something-else grunt labor isn't as useful as one would think. You still need experienced people to supervise, and to drill the crews to keep them from killing each other with the machinery. *If you think safety is expensive, try pricing an accident,* as the sign says. And it's a multi-part puzzle much of which has to be assembled in strict order, and if a critical piece or person goes missing the whole parade grinds to a halt." He pursed his lips in reflection. "And this is a relatively forgiving project, if a large one, in a forgiving environment. All my career I've ridden in jumpships, *trusting* them. And their manufacturers. I'm glad I didn't know then what I know now. I'd have been paralyzed with terror."

This won a laugh from her. "An empire built by the lowest bidders? I suppose that explains much." She sighed. "I'm sorry I can't be more helpful. If I get any clever ideas, I'll let you know." She gave him a half-salute and cut the com.

He blew out his breath and sat back. He'd almost wished for some clever evil plot, which they could then engage to out-clever. It could be surprisingly hard to counter Plain Stupid. Even by heroic measures.

As he tapped open his calendar to make a note, his eye fell on a familiar date coming up next week, and his heart seemed to clench cold to half its size. *Three whole years already?* Of course Cordelia would have seen it coming too; of course she would not have mentioned it aloud. As far as he knew there weren't any further formal civic observances planned, thankfully. On that first mortal anniversary there had been a dedication and a speech, which he had attended in support of the widowed Vicereine, but they'd had no chance to get drunk together afterward. Last year, they'd been running on separate tracks—he'd been off on the scheduled inspection tour of the military wormhole stations out toward Escobar, she'd been downside dealing with the colony crisis *du jour*. There was no tradition for this, either public or private, between them. *That makes us free, doesn't it?*

Perhaps, on that day, he might try to take her sailing...? *No.* Not on that day. He wanted a day where forgetting was *possible.* This weekend? That might not be too close.

And just what exactly do you mean by sailing, *Oliver?* Half his mouth tried to smile. Comfort sex, they had once proved, was no comfort at all; they'd just distressed each other to breaking. And for all of the too-rare-in-retrospect extraordinary experiences they'd shared with Aral—the unholy *scheduling* they had required!—*sharing* Aral, had they ever really made love to each other? Had she ever once indicated that might be her desire? Had that strange, subliminal, never-spoken-aloud little distance she'd always kept even when they had touched skin-to-skin been for her sake, or his, or *his*?

And if he dared ask for more now, would he be putting their long friendship to the test, or to the torch? His lips quirked. No, that was too melodramatic for his downright Cordelia, wasn't it? She'd just say no, or, more probably, *No, thank you*, and if he was particularly unlucky that hour, treat him to one of her hilariously dreadful Betan-style psychological cold-packs for his bruises. His ridiculous sense of risk was not for the degree of danger, just for the weight of the bet.

He reached for his comconsole and tapped into his address file. He hadn't used this one for several years, but there it still was...his fingers seemed to move of their own accord, the assured, easy phrases falling from them quite as if his small, cold heart were not pushing into his throat.

Hello, Sergeant Penney. Do you still have your place, and do you still rent your boats? If so, I'd like to book an exclusive for this weekend, as I would have a special guest...

Chapter Six

Cordelia pressed her face eagerly to the aircar's canopy as Lake Serena swung into view. Serena was the smallest, shallowest, and most biologically interesting of the chain of lakes skipping sporadically down the long rift valley south of Kareenburg. The fact that it was only the third-closest to the town-and-base had preserved it from development so far, and she rather selfishly hoped would do so for a while yet. It reminded her of Sergyar as she had first seen it forty-five years ago, wide and empty and inviting, except, as it had turned out, for a few (hundred) biological booby-traps. She doubted the scattered colonists had found and sprung them all yet, though they were certainly working on it steadily. She considered a pitch for medical school grads on the neighboring Nexus worlds: *Come practice in beautiful Kareenburg, where you will never be bored! Or entirely sure what you're doing!* And didn't *that* go for everyone here, all the way to the top...

"This was a *good* idea," she said to Oliver, likewise craning his neck beside her, and he smiled a bit smugly.

"I was very glad to find Sergeant Penney was still out here.

I'd got rather out of touch with him, after I'd traded up for my second boat."

Oliver's second sailboat had been a larger craft, suitable for ferrying less nautically inclined—or more creakily aging—guests in comfort on the bigger lake closest to town. He'd scarcely had it out since Aral's death, and had finally sold it off to an enthusiastic civilian shuttle pilot who had spotted it gathering dust on its storage skid at the marina. Cordelia was glad for this renewed spurt of interest—getting outdoors was good for Oliver, not to mention getting away from a workload that would swallow him alive if he let it. He'd always been a detail-man, which was good up to a point—during that whole state-funeral circus, the five-ship cortege convoy had moved like clockwork under his personal command, and she'd have been ready to kiss his feet if she hadn't been so numb—but without someone around to order him to stop, she wasn't sure he ever would.

As the aircar banked, the homestead on the western shore peeked through Sergyar's version of trees, echoes of their Earth counterparts despite their distinct biochemistry. Penney's Place had started as a plank dock floating on old barrels and a jerry-built shack on a shady bluff above the water. A couple of larger and better shacks had not so much replaced as been added to them, marching up the shoreline like a hermit crab's abandoned shells to climax, for the moment, in a low rambling house with a wide verandah lovingly hand-built out of local materials; the latter marking the arrival of Ma Penney in the retired twenty-year-man's life. Camp cuisine had also taken a marked turn for the better about then, as Cordelia understood it. The couple now eked out a pleasant existence on Penney's modest pension, Ma Penney's garden, and holiday rentals of the old shacks and Penney's boats to unfussy Kareenburg proles willing to, mostly, do for themselves.

The man himself appeared around the side of his house as Armsman Rykov brought the aircar down for a neat landing on a graveled patch. Penney wore tattered shorts, worn sport shoes, and a deep tan scarified by a few old plague-worm marks; he waved amiably. He was a stocky man about ten years older than Oliver, and had been among the earlier settlers to make their passage by the shortcut of mustering out of the Service right from here. At the time Cordelia and Aral had first arrived thirteen years back, Penney was already an old Sergyar hand, working on his second shack, but Cordelia hadn't met him till after Oliver had found this place as a cheap and private slip to launch his sailboat. Foremost among Penney's many virtues, from Cordelia's point of view, had been his unruffled willingness to treat Oliver and his occasional incognito guests just like any other Kareenburg weekenders.

"How de' do, Adm'ral Oliver. Ma'am. Ryk. Long time no see," he greeted them as they clambered out of the aircar. Oliver and Cordelia received a retired-soldier salutelike gesture, the armsman a handclasp; those two had always rubbed along well, being of similar ages and service histories. There would probably be beer on the verandah, later, while Rykov's principals bobbed about on the lake, and a good long exchange of mission-critical information, bragging and lies optional.

After the necessary preliminaries including a visit to the privy and the ritual offer and refusal of food—they'd brought their own picnic—they strolled down toward the dock. Cordelia veered aside abruptly. "Good heavens, what's this lovely thing, Penney?"

It appeared to be a flawless crystal canoe, held up on sawhorses, but a tap on the hull gave the duller thump of some unbreakable plastic.

Penney smiled in satisfaction. "M' stepson brought it to us— latest thing, he says. Transparent hulls for see-through rides—fellow who makes them up in New Hassadar wants to branch out to different shapes, soon as he can work out the prototypes. That plastic has positive buoyancy, too, so's you can't sink it for trying. It's really popular with the guests—I mean to get a couple more soon, but he's backordered."

"Is it available today?"

Penney squinted out over the lake. "Maybe later? It's a mite windy for it now anyways. Good for your sail, though."

The wind was, indeed, picking up. Cordelia enjoyed its ruffle through her hair as they stepped down onto the creaking dock. Oliver frowned a little into the west, perhaps disappointed that it wasn't brisker; but this was nearly ideal for her, although she admitted Aral would have found it tame.

"Your old boat's held up well, Adm'ral," said Penney, as he and Rykov helped them into it. "It's proved good for my rentals—very stable, so the amateurs don't turn it turtle and make me have to go out and rescue them. I'm thinking of offering it to that New Hassadar fellow as a model for his next design, maybe get a trade."

"You've taken good care of her," said Oliver in return appreciation.

Rykov pointed sternly to the float-belts lying across the seat, and Cordelia and Oliver dutifully put them on. Part of the many little tacit deals she had worked out with her armsman over time; she would play safe, and he would stay out of her hair. Rykov at least had learned to be sensible about what was a risk and what wasn't, unlike the hyper-keen young ImpSec fellows Vorbarr Sultana kept sending out as the Vicereine's official security, whom she occasionally wanted to beat to death with their own rulebook. She'd had to pull rank quite *firmly* to keep them from tagging along today. *A private life.* What a concept. Well, that was coming, if she had her way. She could hardly wait.

The old moves came back to her as Oliver raised the mainsail and she tended to the jib, letting it luff till Penney and Rykov shoved them off far enough out for her to drop the centerboard. Then Oliver tightened up the boom and took the tiller, and she hitched down the jib-sail line to its cleat, and they were off, skimming over the water. "Perfect!" she called back to him as she took the front seat, facing rearward. The lake was lovely, the distant striated cliffs striking, but scenery in this direction was even better, improved still further when he slid off his shirt to bare his spacer-pale (though more, these days, just office-pale) skin to the sun. All right, so he wasn't twenty-seven anymore, but who was? And he'd never been *weedy*. It was good to see him looking so relaxed and happy, squinting into the light till the crow's-feet seemed to wink at her.

"Too bad we couldn't lose our wristcoms," he sighed, with a glance at his.

Cordelia held up her own. "I don't know about you, but I've set mine to 'volcanoes.'"

"What?" he laughed.

"I've trained my staff. I have five levels of interruptions, ranging from one, 'If you must know,' two, 'Diplomatic crisis,' then three, 'Has to involve emergency medical teams,' through four, 'Only in case of erupting volcanoes.'"

"What in the world is Level Five, then?"

"'Family,'" Cordelia intoned. "Although, since they are all quite a number of wormhole jumps away, I'm usually safe there."

"What level would you use for Emperor Gregor, then?"

"Oh, he's family, too."

"Ah. Yes. He would be."

As the wind heeled the boat over and they picked up speed, she grinned back at him, exhilarated, and moved her weight to the side for balance, secure in the knowledge that *Oliver* would not make her hang bodily out on some stupid little rope, toes curled around the thwart and spine rigid, with the black water skidding under her butt like racing pavement. There were a few things in these Sergyaran lakes one did *not* want to swim with.

Oliver made the hand-signal warning, *Coming about*, and together they shifted everything to take them on a heading out past the opposite promontory and into the widest section of the lake. *Clear sailing*, indeed. He offered her a turn on the tiller, which she took, while he stretched out in the prow and smiled sleepily at her, then stared up at the sail and the sky as if trying to read the future there. Or maybe he was just reverting to worrying about his billion tons of assorted troubles in orbit, which would not be so fine. Counterproductive, even.

After a while she glanced to the west and frowned, not liking the future she was seeing edging up over the kilometers-distant rift wall. "Those clouds look pretty dark. Was this predicted?"

"There's no front due. I checked." He roused himself to follow her glance. "Local pop-up thunderstorm, I think."

"Maybe it'll pass to the south."

"Eh..."

By mutual, unspoken assent, they switched to a course that would head them back past the peninsula toward Penney's Place. This involved a lot more tacking and scrambling about, as the breeze shifted unfavorably. They weren't *quite* back to shore when the wind whipped the water to whitecaps, the sky turned dark, and the cold rain began to pelt down in sheets. Oliver still brought the old boat into the dock under jib alone, perfectly aligned and without undue crashing. Penney and Rykov waited anxiously to receive the painter and tie ropes, and to help hoist the hooting Cordelia onto the slippery boards.

"We'll put 'em to dry in the sun later!" Penney yelled over the wind's bluster, helping Oliver wrestle down the sails. "This blow won't last. Sorry for the timing, though!"

"Aye!"

Boat secured, they scrambled up the flat stepping stones on the bank to the somewhat alarming shelter of the lashing trees, and then, more prudently as the next sheet of rain hit them, to the front porch of old Shack One.

Cordelia shivered, and Oliver glanced at her in concern. "Cold, Cordelia? You shouldn't be standing around wet."

"You could come up to the house," said Penney. Another sheet of rain blasted past, droplets ricocheting up onto the porch to brush their faces. He pursed his lips. "Or there's a fire laid on in the shack—it might warm up quicker."

"That sounds good," said Cordelia, thinking about how the influx of wet guests might discombobulate Ma Penney, who, as she recalled from their prior meetings, did not share her spouse's class-unconsciousness.

Oliver raised his brows and rubbed rainwater from his face.

"Good thinking!" he said, and promptly took over, bundling her inside, starting the fire in the fieldstone fireplace, and dispatching the already sodden Rykov for their picnic cooler. Even after all these years, it gave Cordelia a Betan frisson to be *burning wood for warmth*, but the orange flames flickered up cheerily in the damp shadows, and she edged near and held her chilled hands to the radiant heat.

Penney's first shack reminded Cordelia of many old cabins she had seen up in the Dendarii Mountains back in Aral's district, though its one room was, if possible, even smaller. In the architectural progression up the shoreline from primitive to rustic to backcountry-comfortable, it possibly qualified as primordial, its plank door secured with a rope latch, its windows made of old bottles stuck in frames. But its roof, thickly shingled with random sheets of scrap plastic and metal, kept the rain out. It was furnished, at the moment, only with a lone bed, a table doubling as a washstand, and a few rickety chairs. A line was coiled on one wall, obviously Penney's old clothes dryer. Oliver collected it and played it out past the fireplace to hook to the wall opposite, then put it to its intended use by flopping his wet shirt over it.

"You...?" he said, glancing at Cordelia.

Cordelia decided her sports bra qualified as a top by camping standards, and followed suit, or unsuit. She took off her squeaky wet deck shoes and sodden socks, as well, setting the first on the hearth and the latter over the line. Oliver nodded approval and imitated her.

A knock at the door heralded the return of Rykov with the cooler, and dry towels protected in plastic. He handed it all in, declining to stay; apparently the blow had interrupted his lunch up at the main house. Cordelia sent him back to his beer and company, and with luck some more dry towels from Ma Penney.

They pulled up the table and chairs in front of the fire and laid out sandwiches and fruit; a couple of thermoses even yielded a choice of hot coffee or tea. Oliver stretched his damp pale feet to the fire with a sigh of satisfaction. "This isn't so bad." He glanced across at her with a crooked smile. "Though not what I'd pictured, quite."

"The mandate for today is *Get away from Kareenburg*," said Cordelia. "Anything after that is gravy."

Thoughtfully, Oliver extended her another sandwich, which she took. He said, "Good to see you getting your appetite back. I thought you'd lost too much weight. After."

"Well...yes." Cordelia chomped. Oliver drummed his fingers on the table and cast her another thin smile. An unusual silence fell. He sighed again, though this one sounded less satisfied than tentative. Cordelia sipped tea, sluicing out her mouth with its pleasant astringency, and studied him. Always an aesthetic pleasure. But he seemed a trifle on edge, opening his mouth as if to speak, then closing it again. Cordelia tried to imagine anything whatsoever that Oliver couldn't say to her, after all these years, and came up blank. She essayed curiously, "What's on your mind, Oliver?"

He made a little throwaway gesture. "Well...to tell you the truth...you."

Her brows rose. "What have I done?"

"Nothing."

"Huh? Should I have?" Her mental review of tasks she might have left unaddressed was derailed by his firm headshake.

"Not at all."

She stared at him, nonplussed. He twisted uncomfortably in his wooden chair. She drank more tea. He drank more tea.

He rose to throw another log onto the fire, sat, and started again: "You haven't found anyone, after. I mean, on the personal side. For yourself. Lately, I mean. I know not earlier, you don't have to explain that to me."

I haven't what? It took her a moment to unravel this one. He meant a...lover, partner, bed-friend, spouse? Something in that general direction, anyway. "Oh. Good heavens, no. Never even thought about it. It's just not...never made it to my to-do list, no. And where would I find *time*?"

"There is that." He gave a conceding head-duck.

She blinked at him. "Yourself?"

"What? No!" He hesitated. "That is to say...not. Not been looking."

She frowned. "Would you like to?"

"I'd thought not. At first, you know." She nodded. He went on, "But lately...I've been thinking. New thoughts. You know."

She didn't know, but she was willing to try to catch up. After all, this was *Oliver*, whose happiness she certainly valued, possibly more than anyone's outside her own family. She ran a quick mental review, but she couldn't think of anyone that she'd noticed, young officers or diplomatic fellows or any worthy-enough man he'd be likely to run across in Kareenburg, who'd been doing the old flag-down-Oliver dance around him. Lately. Not that she'd been noticing a whole lot, lately. "That sounds good. That sounds like...recovery, actually." *The real kind.*

The head-tilt this time suggested this was a fresh thought, and not an entirely comfortable one. "Eh...maybe." His stare at her was becoming beseeching.

Sorry, my telepathy is on the fritz today, kiddo. Wait. Could it be that he feared she would think less of him for this desire to move on?

"Have you found someone who looks likely? Oliver, I think that would be a fine thing for you. But you don't have to ask me for *permission*, you know!" She sat up straight, considering. "And certainly, Aral—and if you have any such silly qualms, I'm telling you flat out right now—Aral would have wanted you to find happiness, too. He always did."

Among the many secret doubts Barrayar's Great Man had confided to her over the years, as he'd confided to no one else—because after a certain point of history, nobody'd wanted to let him down off the bloody pedestal they'd erected under him and allow him to be so scarily human as to admit doubts—was a fear that their intense and abiding relationship might have been impeding Oliver in some way, professionally or personally. That Aral had diverted him from some more proper or better destiny.

Well, better, anyway. Almost anything would have been more proper, by Barrayaran standards. *And many others*, she admitted ruefully. Betans generally wouldn't have blinked at the gender thing, but the age and rank disparity would have made them choke sand. She'd been pretty alarmed herself, at first.

A not-disagreeing head-jerk from Oliver; good, she wouldn't have to pound that bit of sense into him. But it was followed by another ambiguous hand wave that indicated she hadn't got to whatever was eating him even yet. There were many less entertaining ways to beguile a rainy hour than to play guessing games with Oliver about his emotions—and what *was* it about Barrayaran males that made them so, so, so . . . *Barrayaran* about such things?—but it would make it a lot easier if he would just be more *frank*.

So what was he trying to say? That he'd spotted a potential heartthrob, but it wasn't going well? How could it possibly not go well? Unless he'd set his eye on someone especially difficult, and he'd certainly experienced at least one life-model about how to manage the difficult. This was baffling.

She sat back, crossed her arms, pursed her lips, and studied him. His chin came up in unconscious response to the challenge, and what a fine chin it had always been. "You know, it occurs to me—belatedly—have you actually had any *practice* at seducing people?"

His eyes widened, then narrowed back down. "Certainly! I'm hardly asexual, Cordelia!"

"I didn't suggest that! You have to be one of the least asexual people I've ever met. Much to the puzzlement, I have no doubt, of those who have flung themselves so futilely at you over the years, poor sods. And odds." Definitely both odds and sods. "But I was thinking, rather—as opposed to just triaging people trying to seduce *you*?"

His mouth opened indignantly. Then closed. Then pressed closed. Then opened a cautious mite to murmur, "That's . . . an alternate view. I suppose it might, ah—did it look like that to you?"

"I saw one success, many misfires, and for the rest of the time, you were out of range on your trade-fleet convoy tours. Where I gather you were not needlessly monogamous?"

"Uh, no, but...I don't think I'm *picky*, but there were also many work considerations. Especially after I acquired my captaincy."

He would have been very conscientious about those, likely. And the shifting fleet duty did not lend itself to anything long term. "So—what is it that you'd *like* to have?"

He sat back and crossed his own arms. And rather bit out: "Vorkosigans. Apparently. Although it seems too narrow a taste to be evolutionarily likely."

She sighed. *I miss Aral bitterly, too.* "Can't fault you for that one. But what is it you would like that you can *have*? Or can you say?"

"I seem surprisingly unable to articulate it, today."

She waved a hand. "Well, then, let's try tackling the problem from the other end for a bit. Try imagining your ideal partner. Or fling, even. A fellow, I presume? Age, physical type, emotional style, anything? Name, rank, serial number...? I mean—this could be mission-critical information, you know."

He was beginning to be balefully amused by her, judging by the expression on his face, but he just shook his head as if in disbelief. Although he added, "You know...after Aral, I did think it was men, but I'd had girlfriends before that. Not many, but there were one or two I'd imagined might be my end-game. Other things happened instead. And then there was that herm. Remarkable person in its own right, Captain Thorne, but do you know—the best thing about that fling was that for one whole week, I could *stop worrying about my damned categories.*" He blinked and frowned, as if this were a sudden new realization.

"Do you think you're really bi, then? Like Aral?"

"I...it would make more sense than a kink for herms. It's not as if I went out looking for more, after that."

She tried another tack. "So...who was your first crush?"

This surprised a bark of laughter from him. "My *what*?"

"You mentioned kinks. Most people who have them, I mean really have them hardwired into their psyches, not just mild preferences, can identify their roots way back before puberty."

He made a hair-clutching gesture, though he was still laughing. "Oh, God. This is turning into another one of those *Betan* conversations, isn't it? Although I have to say, the herm was not so bad, as Betans went. Had the most *endless* fund of bizarre questions about Barrayar and Barrayarans, though."

"But I want to *help* you, Oliver! If I can," she amended. She couldn't help adding aside, "Although I really want to hear more about that herm, sometime."

"You just like salacious gossip."

She smiled sunnily at being so profoundly understood. "Yes, but there are so very few people I can have it *with*."

"I see." He swallowed his tilted grin, and more tea.

"First crush," she reminded him firmly.

"Aren't there dogs with grips on a subject like this? Terriers, wasn't it? What makes you think a man can even *remember* back that"—a slight hitch in his breath, a sudden weird look crossing his face—"far..."

"Do tell," she prodded, settling back and preparing to be entertained.

"Mugged in Memory Lane. How did you know? Yes. Back in my district primary school, when all the other boys in my classes were giggling in excruciating puppy love over the pretty girl in the third row, I always suffered—and I use that word with some precision—the most devastating crushes on my *teachers*." And added under his breath, "God, Oliver—who knew...?"

"Ah!" said Cordelia, feeling pleased. "I think I know about that one! An authority kink, Oliver. Or possibly a power kink." *Good grief, no wonder he went for Aral.* "That...makes all kinds of sense, in retrospect."

"To you, maybe."

"Male or female teachers?"

"Uh...both. Actually. Now I think on it. Which I haven't done. For years." He gave her an accusing look, as if it were her fault.

"Well, many kinks are orthogonal to gender. You do realize there are more than three categories, all on one axis, for human sexual preferences, don't you? I think you may just be suffering from a shortage of categories."

"And here I thought I was plagued with too damned many. More than one *axis*? How do your Betans chart that—with imaginary numbers?"

"Probably. I mean, I don't know that much about the professional sexuality therapists, but I do know they use some pretty complicated math. Anyway, I quite see that it gives you a built-in structural problem, as you rise in age and rank. At least with the kind of social and age pyramids Barrayar is running at present. You have fewer and fewer potentials in the shrinking pool of authorities above you. And if you aren't moved by subordinates...?"

He shook his head quite firmly, though whether in agreement or disbelief she wasn't just sure.

"Then that pretty much leaves you with the uninteresting, the unavailable, and the unappetizing. I mean, just passing the current General Staff, Council of Counts, and Council of Ministers under mental review, for example. Not to mention their dowager dragons." She made a face, thinking of some of the more repellent derelicts of time in that opinionated crew.

His eyes crinkled in amused horror, evidently envisioning some of the same strong personalities. "Nightmarish! I agree with you there."

She waved a didactic finger, growing firmer in her hypothesis and pleased with her own insight. She hadn't lost her touch, eh? "There is nothing *whatsoever* wrong with you, Oliver. You just happen to find yourself in a target-poor environment at the moment, is all."

"And yet the range is so short."

"What?"

He set down his cup firmly on the plank tabletop. He then stood up, walked around the table to her side, grasped her chin, turned her face up, and bent to kiss her.

"*Blurf*...?" said Cordelia, her eyes springing wide. At this distance, he was blurred and double, and anyway, as he deepened the kiss his blue eyes closed. She felt her own lids squeezing shut in response, as her lips parted. He tasted like sun and rain and tea and Oliver. He tasted really *good* . . .

When they broke for breath after a minute . . . or two . . . or three, he murmured, "Ah, so *this* is how Aral diverted all those Betan data-spates."

"I won't say you're wrong," she muttered back into his smile, and then there followed a few moments of reshuffling that somehow ended up with her on his lap, the rickety chair creaking ominously under its doubled load, and a better angle for exploration that did not risk doing anything bad to his back.

A few . . . some . . . more minutes of this, and her eye was drawn as if by magnetism to the tidy bed, made up just a couple of meters away. Oliver followed her glance.

"There happens to be a bed here, I see," Cordelia remarked.

"I see it, too. Noticed it first thing when we came in. Because an Imperial officer should always be observant."

"It would probably be more comfortable than this chair. Which is making strange squeaky noises." As was she, Cordelia supposed. "Not very wide, I admit."

"Wider than the bottom of the boat, though."

"Than what?"

"Never mind . . ."

The personnel transfer between vessels was accomplished without mishap, as Cordelia would have expected under Oliver's command. The old bed also made squeaky noises, as they settled on its edge, but did not wobble so precariously.

On his next breath-break, Oliver hesitated and said, "God, I am so out of practice. Shouldn't there be, like . . . three dates or something? For proper respect? Used to be. They keep changing the rules all the time. Damned kids."

Cordelia blinked blurrily. "There was the docking bay welcome. And the garden party. And dinner at the officers' mess. And sailing makes four, actually. Yeah, we're good. More than good."

"Ah. Very true." Brightening, he closed in once more.

"And besides, all my ImpSec duennas are a hundred kilometers away in Kareenburg. How often does that happen?"

"Never waste," wheezed Oliver, his mouth trailing down her neck, "a tactical opportunity."

"Damn straight."

But just before they abandoned the vertical for a better axis, Cordelia held up her hand and tapped her wristcom. Oliver gave her a dismayed look, but she shook her head.

"Rykov? Vorkosigan here. I'm diverting all my incoming calls to your wristcom." She waved out the recode on the little holographic display. "Got it?"

"Yes, milady," Rykov's surprised voice came back.

"If anyone below the level of *Volcano* wants me, tell them I will be in conference with Admiral Jole for, for some unspecified period of time. No interruptions, please."

"Right, milady. Understood."

She wondered if he did. An observant man, Rykov, like all of Aral's old sworn liegemen, but, like his brothers-in-arms, deeply discreet. They might need to have a long gossip later. Much later.

"Vorkosigan out," Cordelia gasped, as Oliver did something shivery to her ear with his endlessly talented lips. The kiss that followed this up was as delicious as ever.

"Oh, Oliver," she murmured when she had her breath back, a little while later. "My body thinks this is the best idea ever. My brain... is not so sure."

He nuzzled down the other side of her neck, and lower. "Is this to be a Betan ballot? My body votes with yours. My wits... well, call it two against one with one abstaining."

"Are you *asking* for a vicereinal veto?"

"You have the power, Your Excellentness." He hesitated, then rolled up on one elbow to search her face, his lips curved up, his eyes serious. "Though if this goes much further I'll have to step out to the back for a minute or two."

"Dark out there, in the rain. Cold."

"That's the idea, rather."

"And lonely."

"That, too."

"I'm talking myself into this, aren't I?"

"Mm."

"Mm what?"

"That was me not interrupting you."

She forced her smile back straight and declared, "I'm a grownup. We both are. We can *do* this."

"Memorably, yes."

She went still, and held a finger to his warm lips. "No. No memories. A new start."

He considered this a moment, nodded, drew breath, and said forthrightly, "How do you do, Cordelia? My name is Oliver. I should like very much to make love to you for the very first time right now, please."

Her lips twitched up. *Big goof—who knew?* She considered the bones of his face, the arch of his nose, those amazing sapphire eyes looking back at her in fathomless curiosity, the absolutely centered *Oliverness* of him, now, at this age, in this place. Where neither of them had ever been before.

"Yes," she breathed, and, "yes..."

The physicalities were as awkward and absurd as ever, but the *touch*, oh, she'd so missed touch, and why did, and, oh, "Oh... do more of that..."

"Aye-aye, ma'am," he mumbled around a mouthful of surprisingly sensitized breast.

And why, "...did we evolve all this bizarre behavior just to swap DNA? Or did the DNA evolve us? Sly molecule. But we hijack the program. Biological pirates." His mouth found a lower harbor; she...made a rather undignified noise, she was afraid. *Dignity need not apply, no, no position open for* you *here, move along.* "Ah! Ship *ahoy*, Admiral..."

He raised his head and eyed her. "Cordelia...you're thinking sideways again."

"Can't help it," she gasped. "You're doing a pretty good job of scrambling my neurons, you know."

The smile dipped out of sight. "Good," he said smugly. "I think I need more sideways in my life."

"Can supply."

"Right..."

The sun, sliding below the scattering clouds, had touched the horizon outside before they found need for any more words.

Chapter Seven

Jole woke early the next morning in the old bed with Cordelia
tucked up under his arm, bonelessly relaxed, her breath moving
slowly with a sound too dainty to be called snoring, quite. He
inhaled the warm smell of her hair, the slick of her skin, next
to his face on the pillow. *Elation*, he decided, was the name for
this emotion, excited and a little scared. In an infinite number
of ways, he was glad he wasn't a teenager anymore, but it was
heartening to still find that wild western boy, buried yet alive
down under his layers of age and experience.

Without the youthful insecurity, though. He was glad to
have lost *that* part. Yesterday had been *good*. Far better than his
first—in retrospect—highly impractical naughty nautical visions.
So often, reality disappointed imagination; not this time. It was
going to be all right. Or at least . . . all right for now. He kissed her
awake and set about proving to them both that yesterday hadn't
been a fluke. She was all sleepy little cat noises and welcoming
limbs, with the odd practical jink that was so utterly Cordelia.

Quite a good time later, she rolled off him, flopped down

with a thump, and muttered, "Hungry." He wanted to linger on in Shack Number One for, oh, the rest of the year, maybe. But their food cooler had only been stocked for a day, not this unplanned extension. Like an army in the Time of Isolation, this reduced them to scavenging for provisions from the nearby civilian population. Ma Penney, it turned out, was entirely prepared for this incursion, and they ended up picnicking on her front porch with boiled eggs, bread and butter, dried fruit, homemade coffeecakes, and strong, welcome tea with cream.

The morning was warm and windless, the surface of the lake like glass, mirroring the farther shore and the cloudless sky. One last sail before they departed was obviously off the menu. Far from being disappointed, Cordelia eagerly organized an excursion in that bizarre transparent canoe that had so caught her eye yesterday. Rykov and Penney helped them hoist it up off its sawhorses—it was surprisingly lightweight—and carry it to the water. As Rykov handed him down his paddle, Jole tried to read the armsman's opinion of this new turn in his widowed liege lady's life, but the man was typically expressionless. Which told its own tale, perhaps—if he'd *approved*, he might actually have smiled. It was not unknown for him to do so, now and then. On the other hand, if he'd seriously disapproved, there were a dozen ways he could have subtly interrupted or interfered before now. Rykov...well, Rykov was Cordelia's chain-of-command, not Jole's. She'd know how to handle him.

Cordelia had taken the rear seat, which gave her the best view through the hull and the task of steering. She aimed them left along the shore, up toward the quiet backwaters that headed this arm of the lake. Jole enjoyed the slowly moving shoreline, and the kiss of the sun on his face and through his thin shirt. A lone, red-furred hexaped drinking from the water raised its neckless head, froze, and stared at them, its four eyes unblinking. It clacked its triangular beak a few times, then scuttered away into the undergrowth. At the lake's shallow end, the strange-colored water plants hissed over the hull as they slid through them.

The little radials were out, floating about in iridescent clouds, a confetti-celebration of the morning.

"Oh, you have to see all this," said Cordelia, the first words she had spoken for a while. "Turn around and take a look."

Jole shipped his paddle, grasped the thwarts, and swung around with all the due care of a fully dressed man not wishing to convert his boat ride into a swim. The canoe was broad in the beam, however, and quite stable for its class. He stared down through the hull, and then, after a moment, slid to his knees for a closer view. And then to his hands and knees.

It was like being a bird looking down through an alien forest. He could count three ... six, eight different sorts of little creatures moving through the shading stems. Even more shapes than the round and six-limbed models familiar from dry land, and remarkable subtle colors, reds and blues, silvery and orange, in stripes and spots and chevrons. A larger ovoid slid past, then jerked aside; its ... meal? ... escaped in a gold flash and a cloud of bronze smoke, and Jole laughed half in surprise, half in delight. "What *are* all those things? What are they called?" And why, for all the times he'd skimmed over this very lake, had he never noticed them before?

"No idea. It's possible most of them don't even have names, yet. We still don't have enough people doing basic science surveys. Even after forty years, most of this planet is a mystery. What bio-people we have got are mostly tied up doing evaluations of the proposed settlement sites, looking for hazards. Finding 'em, too, sometimes. Though generally the first colonists do a bang-up job of that all on their own." Cordelia vented a particularly vicereinal sigh.

Jole grinned, still staring downward. "This is like looking through some magic mirror in a kids' story. It's like there's this whole other, secret Sergyar down there! That no one knows about!"

"Yep." Her voice was warm, pleased with his pleasure.

After a few more minutes of staring down, Jole waved his arm vaguely about. "Take us around. Let's see more."

"Aye-aye, Admiral."

She dipped her paddle, and more strange sights slid past.

His nose was nearly pressed to the plastic, now. A skatagator—a small one, no longer than his arm—scooted by just below him, close enough to have touched had this hull been the un-barrier it seemed. It bumped up curiously, or at least, reactively, against the keel, then drifted off. The canoe brought him silently over a bed of stones very near the shore, where the shapes and colors of the living things changed yet again, then on another long line through the water-forest; then, at last, out into a deeper channel, where the light fell away into mystery once more.

He sat up blinking as if from a trance, wondering when the back of his neck had acquired a prickle that was going to become a cheery red sunburn, later. Cordelia was smiling with all the fascination he had just bestowed on this surprise Sergyar, except that she was looking at *him*. "What?" he said.

"You like this stuff."

"Well...yeah." He rolled his shoulders. "I'm just wondering how I *missed* it, in all the time I've spent on this water."

"You only came out on windy days, when the water's too ruffled to see through? You sensibly stuck to the deep sections?"

"I guess."

She glanced at the sun, rising high and hot, and at the chrono on her wristcom. "I suppose we'd best break off. You want to take the rear seat, going home?"

"Sure."

He slid himself down flat on his back, centered above the keel. She grasped both thwarts and edged over him, stopping to lower herself for a kiss in passing. "Not in a canoe, I suppose," she murmured in regret.

"I think we both would have to be much younger."

"Ha." She grinned into his mouth. Her smile tasted...just fine.

With them both safely upright in their respective seats once more, he dug his paddle into the silken waters and aimed them back toward Penney's Place. "I wonder if I could get one of these glass boats?"

She glanced over her shoulder, her still-lean muscles moving smoothly under her only-slightly-age-softened skin as she swung and dipped her paddle. "Ask Penney. Or his stepson. New Hassadar, didn't he say?"

"Ah, yes."

"I expect you could order a sailing hull, and have both kinds of boat at once."

"Mm, perhaps. All-purpose tends to be no-purpose, sometimes. It would depend on one's primary aim."

"Since when has your primary aim when presented with a lake not been sailing?"

Since about an hour ago? That...was a thought too new to examine closely, lest it pop like one of the soap bubbles the radials were not. "Moot point anyway, till I get more time."

"That is unfortunately true."

Time, yeah. They'd pushed theirs to the limit, and probably past. *Pull up your shorts, Cinderfella, the dance is over...for now.* They matched their strokes and put their backs into a straighter, mid-lake course to the distant dock.

Settling up with Penney took Jole very little time; he added a generous bonus for the extension—and, tacitly, the discretion—which made the man shake his hand, grin, and invite him to bring his guests again. Rykov had already packed their meager belongings into the aircar. Jole and Cordelia slid into the rear compartment together once more, and pressed their faces to the canopy for a last fond look as Lake Serena fell away behind them.

Jole scooted closer and slid his arm around Cordelia's shoulders, and she snuggled into him. She'd caught a rosy touch of sun across her nose and cheeks as well. They were both a little manky in yesterday's clothes, after two days of varied holiday activities and no wash-up but a pitcher and basin and Penney's outdoor showerhead, but it was a good camp-people smell.

"When shall we two meet again?" he inquired lightly.

She blinked. "I'm sure there are a couple of committee meetings on the calendar this week, but I don't think that's what you mean."

"We two, not we ten, yeah."

Her lips sneaked up. "Not unless we want to put on a show, no."

"I think not." But then his smile was swallowed in another thought. "How, uh...I suppose we'd better get our signals straight. How do you want to play this thing, publicly?"

"This new thing? New old thing?"

"New thing." Though he could never wish the old thing away. His mind was drawn sideways despite himself. "Uh...*do* you still have your old Betan sex-toy collection?" Not all of which had been Betan, to be fair, but it was a useful and distancing shorthand.

"Mostly not. In a fit of something—depression, probably—I disposed of it a couple of years ago." She glanced up at him through her eyelashes. "Do you still have yours?"

"Mostly not," he admitted. "Same reason."

"Huh." It was not quite a laugh. "Maybe we can go catalog-shopping together some night."

"Brilliant idea." He kissed her curls, nestled under his nose. "When?"

"My schedule this week is packed."

"On purpose?" he asked quietly.

"Yeah."

He nodded. "Mine, too." Though with the Gridgrad Base project swinging into high gear, he hadn't needed to *look* for extra time-and-thought-absorbing tasks. Well, this was nothing new. Back in the old days, spontaneity had seldom been an option, though it had tended to be memorable when it occurred. "You'd think it easier to schedule a spot of privacy for two people than three."

She frowned, although into space, not at him. "Shouldn't think we'll need *that* much privacy. What do you imagine us to be doing?"

"I...um..."

"If the word you are groping for is *dating*, Oliver, it's not illegal, immoral, or fattening. Unless we go out to a great many meals together, I suppose."

"*Dating* sounds...a bit adolescent, somehow."

"Seeing each other?"

"Vague. Invites... unrestrained speculation."

"Courting?"

"Too Time-of-Isolation."

"Fucking?"

"Don't you dare!"

"Well, screwing, if you want a politer utterance. I wasn't actually planning to write a press release, you know."

"I'm relieved."

She gave him an amused but admonishing poke.

"I'm just trying to figure out how to describe this." Aside from private, nobody's-business judgments such as *joyous* or *astounding*, he supposed.

"Ambushed by your need for categories, again? Most categories are arbitrary, though I admit people do tend to find them reassuring."

"I guess the category I'm groping for here is, what security level are we on?"

"Ah." She rolled out from his arm and frowned, perhaps by chance, at the back of the piloting Rykov's head, distorted through two thankfully sound-blocking canopies.

"I mean to be *done* with such things," she said after a moment. "I grant you there was real need, once. Surely not now. I gave forty-three years to Barrayar, and I'm not asking for a refund, but the next forty-three years are *mine*. After *that*, Barrayar can negotiate."

"You will never not be a public figure, Cordelia."

Her fist swiped the air, a negating gesture. "No, I'm going to escape. They'll all forget soon enough." She settled back once more. "Though if you insist on going all Old-Barrayaran, I suppose we could tell people I'm your mistress."

He snorted involuntarily. "Are you trying to get me strung up? Also, not to channel your nephew Ivan, but that's just wrong."

She raised her chin and considered this. "There's a model for you. Alys and Simon. They weren't, and then one day they'd always been. Very smooth transition, that."

Lady Alys Vorpatril, Cordelia's longtime friend and the Emperor's diplomatic hostess for the better part of three decades, and Simon Illyan, Aral's Chief of Imperial Security for most of that same period, had become a known romantic item very shortly after Illyan's own medical retirement. "*Had* they always been? There was speculation, after." If not, perhaps, unrestrained. Jole had known both of them well, earlier in Vorbarr Sultana in the course of his work for Aral and later on the couple's few holiday visits to Sergyar, and even *he* wasn't sure. That occluded view was nonreciprocal; Simon had certainly known *everything* about Jole. *Once.* They'd all moved on since then.

"Mm, let's say they had valued each other very much for a very long time. But no, alas, they didn't get started on anything worthy of proper salacious gossip—is that an oxymoron?—till after Alys no longer had to compete for Simon's attention with his memory chip and the security of a three-planet empire. *I* thought they'd wasted a heartbreaking amount of potential happiness, but—not my decision, that one. At least they seem to be happy now." Her lips curved in unselfconscious gladness for her old friends. Their old friends, truly.

She added after a little, "Why are you uncomfortable with being open? Just habit?"

"Safety."

"Habit, in other words. Appealing to reason, instead—just for a change, you know—I would point out that open *is* safer. No one can make blackmail or scandal out of something that was never a secret in the first place."

He thought she underestimated the ingenuity of persons determined to be hostile. And the degree to which she could be a target in her own right. Decades of standing next to Aral could do that to a person, he had to concede.

Her brows drew down. "Unless this is your oblique way of hinting that you feel this should be a one-time event? Cold feet?"

"No!" he said, panicked.

"Well, I didn't *think* so..." Her eyes crinkled at him, and he subsided, slightly embarrassed. "To get back to your original question, then, let's both keep an eye out for some coordinated opportunity next weekend, and I will undertake not to climb to the roof of the Viceroy's Palace and shout to all of Kayburg, 'Admiral Jole is a great lay!'"

"Thank you," he said austerely. "I think."

"And I shall in the meanwhile engage to be boringly discreet while we both mull on it."

"I'm not saying you're not *right*," he protested weakly. "It's just..."

"Conditioning. I know, love," she sighed. "I know."

Kayburg was coming up all too soon, rising on the horizon. They might get some snatches of time to talk later in the week, but probably not to kiss. He pulled her to him, and, till the town limits passed below, they used the time more profitably.

The vicereinal aircar dropped him off in front of his base quarters. He made an effort to transit the walkway into the building suitably sternly, like an officer just returned from a mission-critical weekend conference with his boss. As if looking forward to the queue of his duties on his comconsole, not back at the aircar lifting off with his wildest dreams.

Cordelia's first priority upon hitting the Viceroy's Palace was a shower, but after that the pile-up on her comconsole absorbed her attention till dinnertime. Didn't anyone else on Sergyar ever take the bloody weekend *off*? She ordered sandwiches at her desk when the tasks overran the dinner hour; they were brought not by Frieda, but by Ryk. He laid out the plates and her tea with his usual military precision, and then stood back and cleared his throat in the time-honored signal meaning, *I am about to tell you something you don't want to hear.*

"Yes, Ryk?" She bit proactively into her first sandwich.

"Begging your pardon, milady, but I thought you might like to know that the lieutenant of your ImpSec security detail has laid a formal protest before his boss, asserting that Admiral Jole's

ImpSec training is too out-of-date to make him a substitute for a proper perimeter."

"The little twerp!" said Cordelia, spitting a few crumbs. She rounded them up and put them more daintily back on her plate while she chewed this through. Her small crew of ImpSec Palace guards, arriving from home very excited to be guarding the *Vicereine of Sergyar*, were usually disappointed to discover their duties more nearly resembled something that could have been done by any hired commercial security service. Cheaper. The senior-most officers of ImpSec-Sergyar tended to be more focused on the neighbors—Cetaganda, Escobar, and transiting commercial ships of other flags—and upside station and wormhole security, and mostly dealt with Oliver. Who, having been trained on and by Simon Illyan, back in the day, handled it all with his usual unruffled efficiency, and seldom troubled Cordelia with anything but a short and accurate précis.

"I strongly disagree," she said, when she'd sluiced down her bite with a swallow of tea. "And I am seriously annoyed. Oliver was judged fit to be last-man-standing next to Aral when that kid was still in diapers!" Her lower lip stuck out. "And he might say the same of you, for that matter. Does he include you in that . . . assertion?"

"No, milady, but only because he hasn't thought of it. Naturally, I did not point it out."

"I commend your restraint."

He shrugged. "Seemed prudent."

She supposed he was right. For all of Aral's public life, which was nearly all the time she'd been married to him, his score of liveried retainers sworn to him as Count Vorkosigan had needed to work closely with the Imperial security appertaining from his wider duties. Cannily rendered smoother by Aral frequently *recruiting* his armsmen from Dendarii-district-born ImpSec veterans—Ryk was just such a one, who'd retired a twenty-year man and gone on into his Count's personal service almost two decades ago. But ImpSec and the armsmen had always been two separate chains of command, with all the tension and arcane communication protocols that entailed.

Rykov's official—and personal—loyalty was to the Dowager Countess Vorkosigan, not to the Vicereine of Sergyar. Well, now to Count Miles, she supposed, technically. But Ryk, among the armsmen that Aral had hauled along when he was appointed viceroy, had seldom worked with Miles, and barely knew him. Ryk had brought his wife and half-grown children in the baggage train; the four youths had adapted with alacrity to Sergyar, and were now all pursuing their adult lives here. Which was why Ryk and Ma Ryk had petitioned to return with the widowed Cordelia, a boon that Miles had readily granted upon his mother's advice.

Ryk had first arrived at Vorkosigan House in Vorbarr Sultana at about the midpoint of Aral's prime ministership, when Oliver was already a fixture. He had been discreetly introduced to the special security arrangements occasioned by the Vorkosigans' three-sided marriage—because even then, she'd recognized Oliver as her co-spouse in all but name, though neither he nor Aral would ever have used the Betan term—by his armsman-commander and brother-armsmen of the day. Whatever Old-Barrayaran shock Rykov had felt had never been displayed to *her*, at least, and he'd settled into the household's routine quickly. Everyone had had bigger things to worry about, back then.

"About this weekend," Ryk began again, then, "...permission to speak freely, milady?"

"If you haven't been speaking freely these past twenty years, it's a surprise to me." She gave him a nod nonetheless.

"It wouldn't be my business, except that it is. The outward face of things, belike."

She drew a long breath, for patience. "Acknowledged."

"Was this a one-time event, or is it to be ongoing? A resumption of the former, um, system?"

Not quite the same questions Oliver had been asking, but uncomfortably like. *Barrayarans.* "Ongoing, I trust. The former-system part...I'm not sure you can call it a system when the whole benign conspiracy is down to one armsman. Does that make it easier or harder for you?"

"I don't quite know, milady. Ongoing where? To what end?"

"I don't think either of us knows, yet." She added after a somber moment, "Though not another Barrayaran-style marriage, for me. It's not—no reflection on Oliver, mind you—it's just...not."

He gave a short nod, *Fair enough.*

"Look, it's not as if Oliver is, is, I don't know. As if I'm running off with the gardener's boy, or, or, a Cetagandan spy or whatever. He's a loyal and very senior Barrayaran officer who has been a good and kind friend for twenty-three years. What those old Time-of-Isolationists would call *an eligible connection.*"

"Gentleman Jole, the troops call him."

Cordelia laughed. "*Do* they? Well, I have heard him remark, *You must never start a war at a cocktail party by accident.* Lady Alys would doubtless agree."

"Born a prole, though."

"So was I."

He rocked his head in a *can't-disagree-with-the-facts-but* gesture. "Betan...is not the same thing."

"*You* were born a prole, for that matter."

He was beginning to look harassed. "That's not the point I'm trying to make, milady. It's not what *I* think, it's what other people will think. As soon as—if ever—something is known to be going on, some people are going to start wondering how *long* it has been going on."

"Like with poor Simon and Alys? My goings-on have been going on for one weekend, so far." *And a lovely weekend it was.* "And that is true in every sense that most matters."

He drew his own breath for patience. "M'lord was often careless. It gave *us* fits."

Cordelia shook her head. "In the list of all the deadly Barrayaran political secrets we shared over the years, that little bit of—personal privacy—didn't even make the top five." She frowned into the past. "Ten." And, after another moment: "Fifteen."

His brows flicked. "See your fifteen and raise you twenty?"

She shrugged, her lips twitching. "I might have to fold at twenty." She sighed. "All right, Ryk. If any of these nebulous *people* should approach you, it's the same drill as always. Rumors are neither confirmed nor denied nor acknowledged. It's pointless to do otherwise, since people will believe whatever the hell they want anyway, and *damn* it!"

Ryk jumped, or at least flinched.

"This is *not* some crisis, real or manufactured," Cordelia boiled on. "Any widow or widower can date again, or, or whatever, after a decent interval. In general, their friends are *pleased* for them."

"Not everyone is your friend, milady."

Her palms came up, half fending, half accepting. "I decline to give *them* a Betan vote." She placed her hands carefully back on the desk. "This is all very hypothetical, so far. So just keep an ear out as usual, and if you do hear anything substantial that you think I should know, pass it along. Preferably someplace out of earshot, in case I have to scream."

He nodded shortly.

She considered further. Was his palpable unease personal as well as professional? "You do know, since those six embryos have proved viable, I plan to resign the viceroyalty within the year." Armsman Rykov had necessarily been in on that from the time she'd collected the freezer case back on Barrayar. Although she hadn't mentioned Oliver's addendum to him, subsequently. No saying whether that would ever be his business.

Another head-duck.

"You'll have a choice at that point—retirement here on Sergyar, or, always, employment in my private household. Though it will no doubt be smaller and duller than the current circus." *I hope.* "But you will always have a place if you desire it." Ma Ryk as well, although the armsman's wife was presently pursuing an independent vocation as a primary school teacher here in Kareenburg. A readily relocatable career, Cordelia couldn't help reflecting. She could name a dozen outlying schools that would kill to get more teachers, and regularly pelted the Viceroy's Office with petitions to that effect.

His head drew back in mild offense at her implied doubt of his implied doubt. "I never feared for *that*, milady."

"Right-oh, then."

On that somewhat ambiguous note, he withdrew. Cordelia nibbled her sandwich and took up arms against her comconsole once more, trying to remember what she'd been about before Ryk had come in. If she finished her work—hah, now *there* was a fantasy, this work would never be finished, only abandoned, or, all right, *passed on*—she might squeeze out another day off by next weekend. Her lips curved up despite themselves at the memory of Oliver in the crystal canoe, gazing as entranced as a boy at his newly discovered underwater Sergyar. *O brave new world, that has such people in it...!*

"Thank you, Lieutenant Vorinnis," said Jole, settling at his desk and accepting his first morning offering of coffee. "And how was your weekend?"

"Not sure, sir." Kaya wrinkled her nose. "I took your advice, but I don't think it worked quite the way I thought it would."

"My advice?" What had he said, again...?

"About doing something outdoors."

"Ah, yes." *Well, it certainly worked for me...*

"So I invited Lord ghem Soren out to the firing range. He seemed very interested. But not very expert. He picked it up pretty fast, though," she conceded.

"Firing range!" Jole's brows rose. "I would not have thought of that."

"I took a first back in basic in small-arms," Kaya explained. "And my mother always told me not to beat the boys at games and things because then they wouldn't ask you out. So I took him out to the range and trounced him. And a couple of other fellows who were hanging around. Except then he turned around and found some place outside Kareenburg that rents horses, and asked me to go with him *again*."

Jole rubbed any untoward expression from his mouth. "Mm... More of a backfiring-range date, then?"

"I guess."

"Did he seem to show any special interest about any other aspects of the base or our military arrangements?"

"Not as far as I could tell, sir." She seemed more disappointed than otherwise at this failure of her modest venture into counterintelligence.

Lord ghem Soren, Jole gathered, would have proved far more interesting to the lieutenant if he had behaved in a more spylike fashion. Not that this indicated anything one way or another. The good agents, you *didn't* see coming.

She added, in a tone of fairness, "He looked a lot better with his face paint washed off, I have to say."

Someone must have finally advised the attaché on local dress. Or perhaps he'd figured it out for himself. "The ghem—and the haut—are in general very symmetrical in their physical features," Jole allowed.

"How was your weekend, sir?" she asked politely in turn.

"Good. I, ah, had a long conference with the Vicereine. We flew out to inspect Lake Serena."

Vorinnis shook her head in wonder. "Don't you two ever take a day off?" She made her way back to her battlements in the outer office.

Jole bit back a grin and bent to fire up his comconsole and triage the first complaints of the week. A batch of tightbeam memos from Komarr Command came up.

After a few minutes, he spoke aloud, half-consciously. "What the *hell*? This *has* to be a mistake!"

Vorinnis appeared in the doorway. "Sir? Did I make a mistake?" If so, she would be keen to correct it, her posture proclaimed.

"No, not...not really. Though you might have marked it..."

Urgent? No. "For special attention," he finished vaguely. "They're decommissioning the *Prince Serg!*"

"Oh, yes, saw that one, sir." She nodded. "But I thought the mothballing protocols were considered routine...?"

Barrayaran warships tended to be not so much mothballed as hoarded. The eldest members of the General Staff were notorious for an attitude toward ordnance that resembled that of a famine survivor stashing foodstuffs, and perhaps for analogous reasons. Ships that most Nexus militaries would have sent directly to the scrapyards were instead tucked away to age a few more decades like dodgy food in the back of a refrigerator, out of sight, before the Staff—or more likely, its successors—was finally persuaded to give them up. Just such an elephant's graveyard was part of Jole's patch, hidden discreetly out of sight a couple of jumps into the blind wormhole that led nowhere. Someday, the Imperium would finally give in and declare it a museum.

The words were jerked from him nonetheless: "Yes, but the ship—it was the flagship of the Hegen Hub fleet. We still had civilian crews on board *building* it when Aral ordered it out of the space docks at Komarr. We tried to leave some of the crews on Pol, but there was no time. They were still installing and patching when the battle was *over.*" The memories came back in a spate. "It had the longest-range gravitational lance going, up to that time."

"I believe it's considered short nowadays," said Vorinnis cautiously.

"Insanely short, now, certainly. The Cetagandans probably thought we were trying to *ram* them. At the time, it was bleeding edge, and a hell of a surprise to them." He nodded in remembered satisfaction of the wild whoops going up in the tactics room, under the rank-revived-for-the-purpose Admiral Vorkosigan's command. Aral's last military command, as it had proved. *He* would have considered that the best part of the victory.

"But the *Serg* is over twenty years old!" Vorinnis protested blankly.

It was the newest ship to me. Back when he had been a lieu-tenant not that much older than Vorinnis. *We were all agog for it.* And now, for a tiny stretch of time, it would come under his command.

Most of its weapons and minor systems would have been removed, sealed, or shut down in Komarr dock. Whatever scant ceremonies were bestowed upon the event would have also been completed there. A skeleton crew would bring the skeleton ship to Sergyar. There were no formalities left for the Admiral of Sergyar Fleet to observe.

"Mm. Nevertheless...schedule me an upside inspection of the old beast. Just...in passing. Try to slot in a time that won't delay either of us unduly."

"Yes, sir." Vorinnis withdrew, baffled but obedient.

Chapter Eight

On the grim anniversary that week that Jole had not marked on his calendar, he only saw Cordelia at a joint morning meeting between military and civil engineers to discuss Gridgrad infrastructure, or, more accurately, lack of infrastructure, and whose fault it was going to be. It ran long. In the hallway afterward, she touched his hand in passing, looking away; he caught hers and squeezed, and hers spasmed hard before opening again.

"Will you be all right, tonight?" he murmured.

She nodded shortly. "Dinner at the Betan consulate. I expect to be lobbied, and lobby back unmercifully. Immigration issues. You?"

"A queue of tightbeam reports from Ops HQ to read. Some to answer. Desplains and I are arm-wrestling over jump-point station logistics this week."

"Good luck pinning him down. I mean to stop in at the rep center on the way home, after, for a quick visit. Just..." Her throat moved.

"...because."

"Yeah."

In this place, all he could give her was a nod, so he did. Her lips twitched up in silent understanding. As a smile, it was a travesty; as acknowledgement, sufficient unto the day.

Jole was able to organize another jaunt to inspect Lake Serena that weekend, though only a day-trip. To his regret, it was too breezy for the crystal canoe, but to his delight, the breeze sped the little sailboat around to the leeward side of the peninsula, where they found a quiet nook to tie up under some trees that bent to trail curtaining branches in the water. It was almost like a bower woven of wood, and decidedly more inviting for an intimate hour than bobbing around rudderless out in the open. The new radial-repellant spray seemed to work well, its brisk masking perfume more redolent of camp life than ballrooms. Alas for his late fantasy, the boat was notably less comfortable than the old bed, but a determined, if sometimes giggling, cooperation overcame all obstacles. Even a barked elbow failed to impede his blissful post-coital snooze, while his pillowing Cordelia seemed content to drift in quiet meditations of her own.

They shoved off again at length with just time for one tack across the wider part of the lake. As they approached the opposite shore, the sound of power-hammering drifted out over the water.

"Looks like Sergeant Penney's getting a neighbor," Cordelia observed, shading her eyes with the flat of her hand.

"And a mere five kilometers away," Jole agreed. "I wonder if he'll think Lake Serena is becoming too crowded?"

Her lips turned up. "His own fault, then, for renting his place and allowing Kayburg to find out about it."

By Vorbarr Sultana standards, Kareenburg boasted little in the way of fine dining, but midweek they managed to engineer a not-too-working dinner at the same terrace restaurant where Cordelia had so upended his life recently with the gametes offer. They nibbled and talked through a fine fair sunset, and watched the town lights come on below in competition with the stars above. The stars were still winning, but probably not for much longer.

At one point, Cordelia bent forward with laughter at some turn of phrase, reaching out to touch his arm, but then her glance shifted beyond Jole's shoulder toward the nearby table where her ImpSec bodyguard lurked attentively, and she withdrew her hand and straightened with a sigh.

"It's not that the ImpSec duenna-corps that Chief Allegre sends me aren't all nice, earnest boys and girls, but sometimes I wish I could drop them all in an oubliette. Why don't I have an oubliette?" she added, as if suddenly struck by this lack. "I could have designed one into the Viceroy's Palace when we were building it, easily enough. No foresight."

He laughed. "It would go with your moniker."

"I have a moniker?"

"Haven't you heard it? They call you the Red Queen."

She blinked and tossed back her last sip of wine. "Wasn't she the chess piece who went around yelling 'Off with their heads'? Or is it a bio-evolutionary reference?"

"I believe the bloodthirsty queen was a playing card. The chess queen was known for her sprinting."

"You do wonder sometimes what they were ingesting, back on Old Earth. But yes, I certainly do have to run as fast as I can to stay in the same place. Though I suppose I could hope it's for my hair. Is it intended as a compliment, or the reverse?"

"That seems to be malleable according to the tone of voice in which it is delivered." Though he had come down sharply on one grumbler who had used it pejoratively in his hearing.

"Well...there have been worse political nicknames in Barrayaran history."

"Mm," said Jole, not disagreeing. Speaking of security, he was himself the recipient of a painfully polite memo from the local head of ImpSec-Sergyar, Colonel Kosko, pointing out that Jole's own last physical-security short course was many years overdue for a refresher, and would he please not let the Vicereine's notorious carelessness on the subject override his own mature judgment. That Kosko had sent a memo, and not just dropped a word in his ear when they'd seen each other in person, betrayed either a shrewd sense of just how unwelcome such comments were in his superior's hearing, or a nervous desire for documentation. "But you do have to allow that if you were killed on their watch, there'd be nothing for the poor bastards to do, once the forms were filed and the court-martials concluded, but eat their own nerve disruptors. *En masse.*"

She grimaced. "If Aral had been assassinated back in Vorbarr Sultana..." She did not quite complete the thought. She didn't have to.

"Possibly." He shrugged. "My feelings would hardly have been *less* complicated."

She tapped his arm firmly, this time, in a gesture of strong negation. "Sergyar is safer. At least in terms of organized plots. *Disorganized* plots, well..."

"It only takes one nutcase to decide that you, not he, are the reason his life sucks, and set out to even the score. Nutcases are not in short supply here."

She sighed in agreement. "Even though everything else seems to be."

"Indeed. Did you get any reply yet from your son Mark about entrepreneurs we could lure to Gridgrad to set up a materials plant? The offer of land?"

"He says he'll put the word out, but he notes that as the land does not seem to come with streets, buildings, utilities, or a workforce, it's not quite the bait one would hope."

After dinner, they rode back to the Viceroy's Palace in her vicereinal groundcar, driven by the alert bodyguard. They did not shed this appurtenance until they reached the double front doors, where he was smoothly excluded by Armsman Rykov. Cordelia led Jole upstairs to the door of her personal office—her public office was now in the converted barracks across the back garden. It made a short and pretty walk to work.

"I will be in conference with the Admiral, Ryk," she told her seneschal. "Interruption level, mm, three, I think."

Must involve emergency medical teams, Jole recalled, right.

"Yes, milady. Sir." Rykov maintained his usual expressionlessness, for which Jole was grateful. Cordelia closed the door on it with a bright smile.

As Jole's imagination was cycling between actual confidential conferencing for which he'd somehow missed the memo, or rude but riveting visions involving the use of her comconsole desk for purposes its makers had never intended, Cordelia led onward to the far door, which proved to open into a full bathroom and from there into a modest bedroom overlooking the back garden.

"Ah," he said, enlightened. "You moved." If only across the hallway.

"Yes. The big suite"—the one she'd shared with Aral and, now and then, them with him—"was too big. I took a leaf from the Vorkosigan House generational shuffle and converted it into a guest suite."

"I don't believe I've ever been in here." *Entirely unhaunted.*

"You might have, but I redecorated. Alys and Ekaterin advised." That explained the serene style, now overlain with a practical clutter that was more Cordelia. Both aspects comforted him, and he moved into her welcoming arms without delay.

It was after midnight when Rykov let him back out the front doors. His lightflyer was parked across the drive, and so this was why she'd told him to come to the Palace and they'd ride to dinner together—planning ahead. Nicely smooth.

"Cordelia asked me to tell you she didn't expect any more duties for you tonight, and you could turn in."

"Very good, sir." Rykov hesitated. "Do you plan to be having many more conferences with the Vicereine?"

God, I hope so, Jole managed to keep from blurting. He hadn't been drunk even earlier, right after dinner, but he felt a little inebriated still. "Cordelia..." He hesitated in turn. "Has indicated that she would actually prefer something more open, but I think discretion"—*is a hard habit to break*—"might be better advised." *At least for now.*

"I am always," stated Rykov, with a direct stare at him, "in favor of discretion."

Allies of a sort, then? *I'll try not to make your job any harder than it already is* seemed a mildly idiotic thing to say, so Jole returned only an acknowledging nod.

Letting himself into his own base apartment later, he looked around with new eyes. The prior Admiral of Sergyar Fleet had brought a family along and stayed in larger digs, a house off-base. Even after his latest promotion, Jole had contented himself with the same rather Spartan apartment in the senior bachelor officers' building he'd occupied ever since he'd first been assigned to local space. All right, it was on a third-floor corner, and better supplied with windows; otherwise, the living room, single bedroom, bath and kitchenette were standardized and compact. A place to sleep, wash, keep his clothes, and grab breakfast. A base cleaning service and laundry allowed him to dispense with the batman that would otherwise be due his rank. He entertained at the officers' mess, or assorted Kareenburg venues, or occasionally for formal functions jointly with the Vicereine at the Palace. A quarter of his time was spent on upside rotation anyway.

He tried to imagine bringing Cordelia here for a conference— Aral had visited now and again, as their opportunities arose—but, really. Besides, he lacked a Rykov to guard their privacy. And if Cordelia brought her armsman along, where would they stow him? Aral had excluded his own occasional outriders at the door with ruthless and utterly unselfconscious courtesy, sending them off to patrol on their own for imaginary hazards, or read in the downstairs lobby, or whatever they chose until he called them back. It wasn't Vor arrogance, exactly, but whatever it was, prole Jole had never quite caught the knack. And...however misguidedly, Jole suspected his being alone with the Vicereine in his quarters would be seen differently than his being alone with the Viceroy.

After failing to imagine Cordelia here, he was suddenly struck by how much more out-of-place an infant would be. Let alone three of them. Family quarters. He would have to move to the base family quarters, he supposed. How would he—they—Jole and Sons fit in over there? There must be a few single parents in the crowd—how did they manage? Well, there was Fyodor Haines and his fractious Freddie, but Freddie was fifteen, outwardly mobile. The general—not yet a general then, of course, just a mid-grade officer—had not after all attempted to raise his infants himself, from scratch.

Was Cordelia's model any help to Jole? Their two situations did not feel precisely parallel. He wasn't sure what personal funds she held. The jointure of a count's widow was not rigidly set, but constrained by law and custom to a range, never below a certain minimum nor above a certain maximum. Aral would certainly not have chosen the most straitened option for her. He might even have suspected Cordelia's choice of more children, in the event of his premature death, and provided for it consciously.

There could have been no such thought for Jole, no place in Vor tradition or custom for this technological option, though one might perhaps stretch various provisions Vor lords sometimes made for their acknowledged bastards. But Jole's sons would be legal and legitimate, properly fathered even in Barrayaran law, laboriously updated as it was. His lips twisted in dry amusement at that thought.

A Barrayaran admiral's pay, though not generous by civilian or even galactic military standards, was expected to support a family, and normally did. Even an admiral's retirement half-pay was less frugal than that of the prole household Jole had grown up in. His simple tastes had left him with more savings than he'd ever had the time to spend. It was merely a matter for careful management. Making do. *You get what you pay for.* He could choose to pay for this.

It wasn't a father's support this vision was missing, but a mother's labor.

Jole's childhood home had certainly not included servants. Yet even Cordelia, undeniably female, who'd grown up just as middling-prole and servant-less on Beta Colony, wasn't planning to go it alone. *Seventy-six* might have something to do with that, true. Or just good sense.

On the other hand, Cordelia shared that noted Vorkosigan genius for personnel. If finding household help was a new challenge for Jole, Cordelia, forty years a high-Vor lady, even if simulated, certainly knew how by now. The obvious solution was to get her to find someone for him—hah. *Problem solved.* One did not reach Jole's rank without learning how to delegate. He grinned, but his smile faded.

The nature of his work was a subtler problem. By oath, he owed the Emperor his time, his energy, his best efforts, and, if necessary, his life, all on an instant's notice. How did that square with his taking on a twenty-year project of such profound responsibility? On the other hand, any parent, at any time, could be as unexpectedly run over by a groundcar. Maybe this wasn't such a civilian versus military dilemma after all. Maybe it was a fundamental human risk. Which didn't make it less intractable.

It came to Jole, staring around as he began to undress, that this space, however convenient it had been for his recent past, was much too small to hold his future. If he chose the great gamble.

Cordelia walked across the garden to the Vicereine's Office the first morning of the next week in an exceptionally good mood. She and Oliver had managed an overnight at Shack One that past weekend, and found that its rustic delights not only stood up to repetition, but were enhanced by preparedness. They managed one sail devoted to actual sailing, and took out the crystal canoe that evening for a combination of sunset-watching and examination of the local lake fauna—Oliver had acquired a field guide and, while she steered them gently over the quiet shallows, attempted to match the exotic creatures he was seeing below with the images called up on his holo. The database, he informed her indignantly after this exercise, was entirely inadequate. She'd serenely agreed, while wondering how such a detail-oriented mind had managed to avoid the sciences all his life heretofore. Drawn away by all the pains and needs of Barrayar, as she had once been? Perhaps. He'd had the canoe out again alone early the following morning while she blissfully slept in, which she'd counted as a plus for both of them.

"Good morning, Ivy!" she cheerily greeted her executive secretary as she strolled into the outer office.

Ivy looked up from her comconsole, raised her eyebrows, and smiled back. Ivy Utkin also qualified as an old Sergyar hand, having arrived nearly two decades ago with her engineering-officer spouse and stayed on when he'd mustered out here. She'd held this post for about five years, shy and nervous at first but slowly growing into her tasks, and she'd been a life-saver for Cordelia all through the miserable stresses of Aral's death and its aftermaths. Her children were mostly grown, but the experience of raising them while following the drum had endowed her with the brisk efficiency of someone who got everything done *now*, because she could be interrupted by the next emergency at any moment. Which made her an ideal fit for the Viceroy's Office, to be sure. Also, she didn't take her work home with her, which meant she didn't bring more for her boss *back*.

"Your revised morning schedule is on your com," Ivy reported. "First meeting in thirty minutes, the water quality people." Ivy rose to follow her into the inner office. "Blaise is already here."

Cordelia tried not to feel less cheery at this, and gave Blaise Gatti, who was perusing a hand-reader but jumped to his feet as she entered, as good a smile as the one she'd given Ivy. They settled into their usual chairs, three-around by the window overlooking the garden side of the building, and Cordelia braced herself for the morning briefing.

Blaise was new, having held the post of Press Officer for less than a year. And young, barely thirty. And excessively energetic. He had an interesting background as half-Komarran, born in the domes to a Komarran father and a francophone Barrayaran mother, and had arrived here after an early career with assorted Komarran news services upon the recommendation of one of Empress

Laisa's Toscane relatives, proving that nepotism was not solely a Barrayaran way of life. Cordelia wasn't sure if it was because somebody'd thought she'd needed a younger face to represent the young colony, because his half-blood status would be less of an issue here, or because it was assumed that, after a lifetime of dealing with Aral and Miles, she'd know how to handle an adult hyperactive.

Her and Aral's prior press officer had been an older fellow, much in the stodgy mode of the Barrayaran official news services from which he'd been recruited, who'd done exactly as he was told and nothing else, a quality she'd learned to appreciate more after he'd taken his lack of excitement home with him upon retirement. Blaise, well...she was still trying to get across to him that his job for her was not to *create* publicity, but rather, to make it *go away*. She wasn't sure if he regarded his post as a culmination or a stepping stone, but she wouldn't be surprised if Sergyar ended up seducing him as it had so many others. *Including me?*

"First thing to come in over the weekend," Ivy began, "is a petition from something calling itself the Kareenburg Committee of Concerned Parents, asking you to declare deliberate worm scarification a misdemeanor."

Cordelia had heard of the custom only peripherally—the latest local youth-fashion craze. The so-called worms were a Sergyaran parasite that, upon burrowing into the skin of a human host, became confused in its life-cycle by the rich alien biochemistry it encountered there. Instead of producing crops of new baby worms and dying, they settled in, still in their juvenile form, and hypertrophied. Tiny in their natural habitat, they grew in the adipose tissues to, usually, several centimeters long and a few thick, sluggishly twitching, though some whoppers had been recorded, upon surgical removal, at thirty centimeters and nearly a kilo in weight. Their main effects upon their human hosts were general debilitation, some allergic reactions, swelling, and disgust and horror, plus dangerous secondary infections following amateur attempts to dig them out. Old Sergyar hands could be identified by their arrays of faded worm scars. Overseeing the development and distribution of an effective anthelmintic vaccine had been one of Cordelia's early triumphs as vicereine, she'd felt.

Some new young Sergyarans, apparently feeling deprived of their chance at this dramatic frontier debility, were now deliberately introducing the worms into their skins in attempts to grow them into artistic patterns. She'd seen a few pictures of the results. They mainly inspired her to want to invest some money in a plastic surgery clinic, but, all right, one or two human palettes had indeed been dramatic. *And* disgusting, of course. She gathered that was part of the point.

"You know, Aral and I went to a great deal of trouble to *eradicate* the worm plague..." And if she and Aral had made their first grim trek across Sergyar at a later season, they might have been the ones to discover the species themselves, but as it was that dubious distinction had been left for the early Barrayaran military occupation. Poor sods.

Ivy shrugged sympathetically.

"Nevertheless, I decline to get suckered into attempting to promulgate sumptuary regulations. And I'm not calling it cruelty to animals, either. Why is this even on my desk? Shouldn't this have gone to the Kayburg town council?"

"It did, I understand," said Ivy. "They ducked."

"I see." Cordelia frowned. Youth fashions were short-lived by their nature. Surely this would go away on its own by the time, say, Aurelia was Freddie Haines's age...?

Blaise put in, "This could be an opportunity to please a vocal block of active and responsible subjects."

"What, a bunch of parents who want me to do their jobs for them? And have you considered how the devil such a regulation could possibly be *enforced*? What an utterly pointless waste of political capital that would be. No."

Blaise rubbed his chin, and switched tacks obediently. "Alternatively, I suppose refusal could be taken as tacit support of young people's rights of self-determination. That could be popular, too."

"I don't see people, young or otherwise, as having a *right* to be idiots. It's just impractical to try to stop them, unless they're hurting somebody, and this sport—extreme art?—does not appear to be lethal. But it's not my patch, as Oliver would say."

"So . . . what do you want to say to them?"

Cordelia answered literally, and with some passion: "Don't you people have some *real* work to do?"

Blaise looked taken aback. "I . . . are you sure, Vicereine?" And, after another moment, "Er . . . which ones?"

Ivy put her hand over her mouth, mercifully.

"All of them. But that was a joke, Blaise. Although nonetheless true." Cordelia sighed. "Just bounce it back down with the standard *The Viceroy's Office declines to hear,* Ivy. No comments. *Tempted* as I am to make some."

"Yes, Your Excellency." Ivy bent her head and made a note, incidentally hiding her smile. She looked back up. "Second, an invitation for you to speak at the twelfth anniversary of the founding of SWORD."

"What?" asked Blaise.

"The Sex WOrkers' Rights and Dignity association," Cordelia clarified. She smiled in fond reminiscence. "At the time Aral and I first arrived as joint viceroys, a grubby stretch of Kayburg out by the base was having a bit of a crime wave. Some very unpleasant men had taken control of the sex trade, and were making things difficult for everyone. The military wives were complaining, the officers were unhappy with the debasing effects on their subordinates, there were beatings, adulterated drinks and bad drugs, crooked gambling, a couple of murders, the usual. Aral took the base side and I took the civil side. I decided that the quickest and most long-term solution would be to unionize the girls, and the few fellows, of course. It took a little while to get the idea across, but they cottoned on and self-organized very well, once they had some real protection."

"Was it, er, dangerous?" Blaise inquired, staring at her.

"It took me a bit of doing to get some of the stupider pimps to actually make threats in front of witnesses. At *that* point, they had officially committed treason, and they entered a world of hurt of which they'd never before dreamed. ImpSec does have its uses, sometimes. A couple of the smarter ones tried moving directly to action, which, alas, proved fatal. The *very* smartest one rolled over and cooperated, and in fact is still in the trade—he joined the Union, too. Proved to be one of their better organizers, once he'd figured out the new rules.

"Once the initial issues were settled, I was able to import a team of Licensed Practical Sexuality Therapists from Beta Colony on short-term contracts to do some wholesale sex education for the Union and its members. And, obliquely, their customers. Most of the customers really liked the new regime—safer, among other things. And better and nicer in other ways, too, I gather. Certainly healthier. Unsurprisingly. A few soldiers couldn't adjust, and tried complaining up their chain of command. Got some support from enough of the old guard to give them a chip on their shoulders. Aral very kindly undertook to knock it off. Held a meeting. Brief, as he was the only speaker. Very few words. Showed a short vid of his public execution of the very first commander of the Sergyar base, the officer who had permitted the abuses of the Escobaran POWs quartered here, back during that war." Cordelia grimaced in sudden, too-vivid memory. And not of the vid. "He said the room was very quiet when he was done."

"Oh," said Blaise. "Er." After a distracted moment he added, "Shouldn't it be called SHEATH?"

"Hah. *You* try to think of a name to go with that acronym."

Ivy glanced at her chrono. "About the speech?"

Cordelia sighed. "I am so burned out on speaking. They deserve better. See if you can persuade Dr. Tatiana to find something good for them." One of the Betan therapists who had stayed on. The *Tatiana* part was a professional name; the doctorate was real. She was one of Cordelia's favorite Betan ex-pats, whom she frequently invited to Palace social events when she needed someone to enliven the party. Ivy nodded and made another note.

The secretary glanced at her panel and remarked, "The Red Creek murder-case appeals trial has been delayed another week."

Some of the light seemed to drain out of the morning. Cordelia said, "Part of me is glad. Part of me wants to get it over with. I hope they finish it off on that level."

Blaise perked up. "Is it likely to reach the Viceroy's Office, do you think? That could be big news."

By Sergyaran standards only, Cordelia reflected. She shrugged. "Most capital cases eventually do, as we're the last stop for appeals. Petitions for pardon or commutation by that time, usually. Except for Vor charged with treason, which could go to Vorbarr Sultana, but we haven't had any of those, thankfully. The Sergyaran courts do a pretty good job of sorting out the facts. I am so grateful for fast-penta. I can't imagine how horrific these decisions must have been back when there was real uncertainty over whether the perpetrator had been correctly identified." She added after a moment, "Fortunately, our criminal capital cases are few. Aral and I only had to deal with a couple a year. Far more Sergyarans manage to kill each other by accident than by intent. I suppose the numbers will inevitably change as the population grows."

The Red Creek case was especially ugly. And stupid, as these things tended to be. A woman's boyfriend had killed her in a domestic brawl, so far so crime-of-passion. The woman, Cordelia gathered from the reports she'd seen so far, had been in her own scattered way a piece of work herself. But then, in a panic, the man had also pursued her two small witnessing children through the house and murdered them as well, then tried to hide all the bodies by burning the place to the ground. His first trial had been local and short. The appeal didn't look too hopeful for him, either.

Blaise said, cautiously, "Will that also be a *The Viceroy's Office declines to hear*, then?"

"Oh, Aral and I always went over all the material the courts and any other source we could find could supply. First separately, then together. Watched the recordings of the penta-interrogations. Once, we even repeated an interrogation ourselves, to be certain."

Cordelia's lips thinned at the unpleasant memory. "'Declines to hear' is just a shorthand for 'We're not going to reverse the court's decision.' We had some pretty intense debates sometimes, coming as we did from, so to speak, two very different legal traditions.

"The Betans would consider something like this a matter for nonvoluntary sociopath therapy. Up to and including neurological rewiring, if there were underlying physical deficits discovered. Of course, Beta has far fewer such cases to start with, as in"—Cordelia almost said *our culture*, but it hadn't really been hers since the Pretender's War, had it—"that culture, therapies would be supplied at a much earlier stage. Barrayaran legal theory, according to Aral, holds that humans have a natural right to revenge, but that leads to blood-feuds, so subjects cede their natural right to their overlords, who are beyond revenge, in exchange for justice administered on their behalf. Which derails the blood-feuds, but obliges the overlords in turn to actually supply the justice. He took that very seriously."

"Who, uh, won these debates?" Blaise asked.

"'Winning' is a null concept, here. There was never any good prize. We were able to see our way to a few commutations. The rest were declined. Once, I was all set for a test case—I was going to send a convicted man to Beta Colony, paid for out of my own purse, for full-on nonvoluntary therapy. To demonstrate the feasibility of importing that system to Sergyar. Instead, he managed, with some difficulty, to commit suicide a couple of days before he was due to be shipped out. Irrationally terrified, or just being Barrayaran, it was hard to tell." Was there a difference? "So I'm still looking for a test case." She wasn't sure the Red Creek matter was it, though. Or that *I would/wouldn't pull the trigger on this jerk myself* was the right metric. "I've considered offering the next convicted person a choice, death or therapy, but that feels awfully like ducking out of my Imperially mandated responsibility."

Blaise said slowly—slowly was good, in his case—"I suppose I had not thought about it from that vantage. What it must feel like to hold life or death in your hands."

Cordelia drummed her fingers on her chair arm, frowning. "When I was about your age, I earned my first Betan Astronomical Survey ship command. For every blind wormhole jump my ship's probe-pilot made, the final go-or-no-go decision was mine." Jumping into death, or the splendor of scientific discovery? Most often, of course, jumping into nothing much, or just more jumps. No wonder she'd never found gambling for *money* to be interesting. "They were volunteers, of course. We all were, out there. It's...something that comes up on the supervisory level of a lot of professions." The military most of all, she supposed.

She added after a moment, thinking back to Blaise's remark that had triggered this spate of reminiscence, "Nevertheless, this Office will not make theater out of lives." Ah, wasn't that very like something Aral had said, decades ago?

Blaise looked frustrated, but did not argue. Ivy glanced at him and tapped her chrono.

"Press report for the weekend," he dutifully began. One of his jobs—his main job, from Cordelia's point of view—was to watch the local civilian news feeds and filter up anything she needed-to-know. Better him than her, and it entirely suited his ferretlike attention span. ImpSec performed a similar task, behind the scenes, but their focus was different. "Top of the list are the Lake Serena rumors."

Cordelia blinked. Now it was her turn for a cautious tone. "Lake Serena rumors?"

"From your repeated inspection trips out there with Admiral Jole, recently. There are several. First is that it is being planned as a new development site, perhaps for a military installation. It's started a flurry of land speculation out in that sector—you can probably look for a spate of proposals submitted to the Office soon."

"Two of them popped up on my comconsole this morning," Ivy confirmed this. "I wondered where they were coming from." She regarded Cordelia with alert interest.

We were just taking some time off! Cordelia converted this indignant protest into a leading, "Hm, and...?"

"Next, that some new hazard has been discovered out that way. Biological or volcanic. The Kareenburg development community has been denying that one as loudly as they can."

"Ah, well, they would. I think we can leave them to get on with it. Anything else?"

"Oh, that Lake Serena has been discovered to have a carbon dioxide inversion zone, like that weird lake south of Mount Stewart."

Cordelia had managed to get that one named *Lake Lethal* on the map, in hopes of discouraging settlers. An utterly fascinating place, scientifically speaking. Lethal was a deep lake with volcanic gas seepage under it. The weight of the water, above, acted like a cap on a soda water bottle, trapping the gas until, every fifty or a hundred years, some chain reaction of a disturbance released it all at once. The colorless, odorless, heavy gas then erupted from the water and spread through the low places nearby, asphyxiating any animal life that unluckily chanced to be present. It was especially dangerous in windless conditions.

"Good grief, Serena is much too shallow for that!"

"Do you want me to issue a denial to that effect?"

"Lord, no. The conspiracy theorists would go wild, and we'd never hear the end of it. Let the science boffins at the university correct them. Or try to correct them." Sergyar's sole university was, well, not quite as primitive as Penney's Shack One, but it certainly was trying hard to get big education out of tiny budgets. Cordelia slung it what support she could. "Dignified silence, that's the ticket."

Blaise, with a kicked-puppy look, stopped mentally writing a bulletin. "What was it all about, then? Is it secret?"

"Not at all. Admiral Jole very kindly...took me sailing. It's something we used to enjoy with Aral, you know. Because a nice day off outdoors helps keep people sane and happy. So I can come back to a week of *this*"—a vague wave around took in the Viceroy's Office as an entity as well as a building—"and not be driven as mad as Emperor Yuri. Think of it as...nautical therapy, or something." *We were* dating, *dammit!* She wasn't sure whether she was relieved or piqued that this didn't seem to be part of the gossip.

Ivy shot her a curious look, but then it was time to break things up and go tend to the water-fight. Cordelia only wished it could be with real water, and not with words. More words.

Chapter Nine

Dinner at the terrace restaurant followed by a confidential conference at the Viceroy's Palace had worked so well the prior week, they repeated it midweek. *Worked again*, Jole thought, swimming muzzily up out of his sex-stunned haze to find a warm, naked Cordelia tucked up under his arm. He lifted his head to find her eyes slitted open, silvery-gray in the night-gleam, not asleep but just as obviously not going anywhere in particular right now. He squinted past her hair, tickling his nose, at the bedside chrono, and made a faint disgruntled noise.

"Hm?" Cordelia inquired, still not moving.

"Should get up an' go. Doan' wanna."

"Don't, then." She backed a little more firmly into him.

"Mm..." He sighed, thinking of his empty bed back in his base apartment, and how small and cold the place had grown of late. "Should."

"See, there's another advantage to a public relationship. You could stay here all night. Get more sleep. Be fresher for work in the morning."

"Temptress. You know a man's susceptibilities, don't you."

She smiled sleepily. "Only my men."

He grinned into her hair and kissed the top of her head. "Lake Serena again this weekend?"

Her lips pursed in doubt. "It has been brought to my attention that maybe we ought to vary our pattern. Our repeated trips out there seem to have triggered a spate of speculation, and not the sort I would have thought. Apparently, nobody under thirty thinks anyone over fifty has sex, so the explanations, while inventive, are bound to lead people astray."

He returned a disappointed *mm*. Just *having* a pattern seemed a nice change. He could imagine this one repeating for quite a long time before he became bored with it. Months at least. Maybe years. A regular schedule that no one had to fret about. Nevertheless . . .

"We'll have to vary the pattern anyway. My upside rotation starts next week." An utterly routine inspection tour of the wormhole stations guarding the two blank-or-might-as-well-be wormholes. This supervisory task had slipped from exciting to dull with repetition, but not nearly as dull as the station-keeping duty itself. The brief, artificial excitement of their sector commander's personal attention was about the only validation the fellows manning the wormhole forts ever received, and while boring was *good* on a space station, considering the alternatives, there were morale issues to consider. And, once in a great while, a real problem to uncover, preemptively making sure no one literally died of boredom. These inspections were worthwhile on several levels; Jole had never *resented* them before.

It was Cordelia's turn to make a disappointed noise. "Ah, that's right." She rolled over; Jole obligingly turned on his back and let her rearrange herself with her head on his shoulder, her arm draped possessively over his chest. "I suppose vid sex is right out. I can't see how it would work with several light-hours of time delay, anyway."

Jole sniggered. "No. Not that I wouldn't love to see that, mind you."

"You, ImpSec, anyone on the tightbeam repeater-route with the clearance to tap the link..."

"Exactly what I was thinking. Don't want to share." He gave her a hug with his woman-weighted arm. "At least...if anything happened to you while I was out there, this time I could order *myself* home."

She raised her eyebrows at him. "Hm?"

"I was just thinking of that frantic mess during my second trade-fleet escort tour." He had advanced to exec on the *New Athens*, a then-new ship and a plum posting, he'd thought. "We were out halfway past Earth, at about the farthest jump on our route, when the news of the Prime Minister's heart attack came through. I could do *nothing*, stuck where I was. And no one to talk to. Oh, there was plenty of political gossip and speculation, and of course everyone knew I'd been on his staff for years, so people interrogated me, sure. *That* was excruciating, even with the few who realized he wasn't just a figure to me, but a friend. No basis to ask for compassionate leave, no way to get home in much less time than the fleet itself was going to take...I was never closer to deserting."

Cordelia sighed. "I'm sorry my bulletins were so terse. Things were utterly crazy in Vorbarr Sultana, what with Miles missing-presumed-dead, and Mark coming in from the cold, and all the medical anxieties...I won't say it was worse than the Pretender's War, but it gave me flashbacks."

His hug tightened. "Your bulletins were lifesavers, from my point of view. I watched them over and over. Trying to read between the lines, then trying *not* to read between the lines... That last one, after his heart transplant—you looked so exhausted, but it was like the sun had come up in your face." He smiled. "And the next one was from him, and then...it was all right."

All right for then, at least. But that unwanted preview of mortality and loss and helplessness had been part of what had turned his career toward Sergyar space, as soon as he could engineer it.

She'd known what he'd wanted to hear, she'd known what

he'd *needed* to hear...her first private tightbeam had been sped on its way within a day of the disaster, before she'd even slept, as far as he'd been able to discern. For all the assurances, subtle and unsubtle, that he'd received from her before, that message and the ones that soon followed had finally driven home to him that she truly considered him not a Betanly tolerated caprice of her husband's, but an equal partner, *worthy* of all consideration. He'd always been a little bit in love with her, as what men around Aral were not? It wasn't that he was more in love with her after, either. Yet there had flowed in under his feet with those messages, almost unseen, a profound and unshakable *trust* which had given him a new place to stand, when they all met again. And from that had followed...well, the rest of his life, so far.

When I was alone and afraid, you comforted me. He turned up her face and kissed her properly for that, a mere decade-and-a-half late. She looked pleased, if bemused; he did not attempt to explain.

He was dressing before they returned to weekend plans. She rolled over, plucked her wristcom from the bedside table, called up her calendar, and frowned. "Ah, I was afraid of that. I have two afternoon meetings that will put a hole in anything out of town...booked ages ago. I must tell Ivy to guard my weekends better in future."

He sat beside her with his own wristcom, and they compared calendars. The results were disheartening.

"Dinner and a conference here again, that night?" Cordelia suggested at last, pointing. "We could even *have* dinner here. In Ekaterin's garden—that would be nice. As long as we don't let anyone else know where to find us. At least we can leave room at Penney's for his other customers."

Cordelia had expressed some guilt when she'd learned that having Penney's Place to themselves had been no accident, but a security compromise Jole had arranged. His argument that Penney didn't suffer since he was paid for a full occupancy that he and Ma Penney didn't actually have to serve had only made a small dent in this.

"I won't be able to stay very late. I have an early lift-off the next morning."

She nodded understanding and blocked out the time, with a note to her kitchen staff. A mental review of his tomorrow-morning's schedule was not much motivation, consolation, or help for tearing himself away, but with a heroic effort that he suspected wouldn't garner much sympathy even if there *were* someone he could complain to, he decamped into the Kayburg night.

❧ ❧ ❧

Oliver had been gone on his upside rotation for only half a week, and Cordelia wondered how it was that she felt *bored*. Bored and restless. Drumming her fingers on the black glass of the comconsole desk in her personal office, she stared out into the rainy night of the back garden. Low, colored lights among the plantings and walkways made oddly cheerful accents in the dark blur.

It wasn't as if she didn't have plenty to do. Once she'd worked through the top layer of the day's crises, there was always another layer, further down and more detailed. And a third one below that. The best camouflage for work-avoidance was more work? She contemplated the paradox, and decided, in all fairness, that it was just task-avoidance. One particular task, albeit with sub-headings. *Drat it*, as her delightful daughter-in-law would say. She'd been thinking about this for months, years. Decades, in a sense. There was no reason for it to suddenly seem hard, here at the point of final fruition.

She called up her secured-tightbeam recording program and settled more firmly in her chair, straightening her shoulders and fixing a reassuring smile on her face.

"Hello, Gregor. This isn't a crisis-call; I'm merely making it emperor's-eyes-only because it contains personal elements, and also to be sure it gets to you promptly." Because the next message out would go to Miles, and on the not-unlikely chance that her son and foster-son compared notes, Gregor should not be blindsided. "The first thing you should know is that I am planning to hand in my resignation as Vicereine of Sergyar within a year. Or so. So you'll be wanting to keep your eyes open for a possible replacement. Or choice of replacements, since the list of those willing shall likely be a subset of those most able and suitable." She paused the recording to mentally muster her own list of qualities most desirable in the person or persons who would be inheriting responsibility for *her planet*. People who wouldn't screw up all the projects she'd started or had in progress—certainly nothing on Sergyar was *finished*. And yet, wasn't part of *turning over* turning over just such choices of direction, as well? Starting with *turning over* to Gregor, which had first been done almost three decades ago when Aral had laid down the regency, to generally good effect, barring a few shakedown problems. Which she tried not to remember and hold against Gregor, maternally or otherwise. The grinding nightmare with that ugly plot of Vordrozda's and Hessman's had worked out all right in the end, after all. Not to mention the whole Hegen Hub near-disaster, *argh*. Both of which, possibly, might seem longer ago to Gregor than to her.

She shook her head ruefully, jotted down a written list of her bullet-points—thankfully not with real bullets these days—and drew lines through half of them. Then through a few more, till she had winnowed it to her top three concerns. There would be time later to discuss the details, after all. She restarted the recording and delivered them with the clipped efficiency she had honed through decades of reports. Then paused once more. Restarted.

"Which brings me to the reason for my resignation. My health continues excellent, by the way," she added hastily, anticipating and with luck heading off any alarm her emperor might be feeling on that score. She could barely recall what all she had said to Gregor when sending the first message about Aral's death, three years back. She could call it up from the files to refresh her memory, she supposed. If given a choice between that and sticking her hand in a campfire, she'd pick the fire, thanks. *Focus, woman.* "That being the case, I have decided now is the time to pursue a long-delayed wish of mine."

've somewhere, but the weight of the Imperium did a pretty
job of keeping it suppressed, poor boy. "Neither of us have
idea where this will be going in the long run, so there is no
t in asking, but...it's good to know we both can grow a little
alive again after all." *In the midst of death, reaching out for
With all due defiance.* Ekaterin might well offer some lovely
phor about shoots struggling up from a burned-over place.
elia's emotions certainly felt like that, tender and green and
erable. She hoped her parting smile looked happy and not
goofy. Not able to think of what else to add, she signed off.
he reran the message for review, but it all seemed sound;
and succinct. That last smile did indeed look a trifle goofy,
replacement would probably just come out looking strained,
h would be worse. Whatever else Gregor wanted to know,
uld ask. She set the security code to the highest level, and
t on its way. She pictured the data packet traveling from
iceroy's Palace to the orbital relay station, from there to the
hole jump-point on the Komarr route, and onward, stitched
jump to jump at light speed, past Komarr, into the cul-de-sac
to Barrayar itself, to its governmental orbital communica-
station to the Imperial Residence to Gregor's comconsole
in that sober, modern office he kept, also looking out over
len. Would it be day or night when it arrived? She was too
just now to work out the time differentials in her head.

nd now for the next message on her short list. She was, she
ed, glad for the practice on Gregor's. She considered, and
tly rejected, some cheerful opening like *Good news, Miles,
getting a little sister!* For one thing, she suspected it would
to him less *good* than *startling*. For another, any sibling
nship was going to be generationally skewed. Functionally,
would be more like a distant uncle, his children more like
Aunt Aurelia's slightly older cousins. She wondered how
the two dislocated—in both time and space—parts of the
would even meet in person. Tied to his count's duties in
cestral district, Miles traveled off-world less and less now,

In much the same terms as she'd first ex
she went over the history of the sequestered
status, their journey with her to Sergyar, and th
of Aurelia and her five still-frozen sisters. Si
lia now was—Cordelia had visited the rep c
night—two weeks past the time she had prom
this happy announcement. Historically, the sta
had been three months past conception, she
because so many early hopes could be dashe
riages, in part because—what had they called
was it, was the first certain proof of progre:
times before reliable pregnancy tests. She st
strange faint flutter in her lower belly with
forty-four years ago now. For which *quicken*
prescient a term. She smiled a little, then p
to consider the place of Oliver's potential
Miles's half-brothers, technically.

There were a great many people whose b
If there was a short list of others, Gregor p
usual. She sighed and started again.

"What follows is, for the moment, strictly
me and you." She explained about the lefto
bright idea of offering them to Oliver. She
of Barrayaran special custody rights of fath
with that of mothers and daughters. "Whi
legal business not at all, although I expect
in due course, just as a family courtesy.
uncertain about Oliver's future choices, a
premature announcements in that directio
one decision about her next message, mad

"And to close on a still-more-personal, i
probably mention that Oliver and I have st
lips curved up in memory of her debate wi
terminology, but she wasn't sure if she ou
with Gregor. Gregor harbored a sense of l

and without the need to make the annual Viceroy's Report, not to mention an Imperially-supplied jump-pinnace in which to travel, how often would Cordelia make the trek back to Barrayar? Well, time would tell, though as usual it could benefit from a dose of fast-penta. She started the next recording and launched herself into the void once more.

"Hello, Miles, and Ekaterin if you are listening. Miles should play this for you in any case, by the way. First of all, don't be alarmed, the security code on this is just because the message is personal, not because it's a crisis. My health is fine, by the way. But I will be resigning my position here on Sergyar within the year. The reason is..." She paused and backed up over the start of that last sentence. "First, a little history..." The story of the gametes was getting easier to tell with practice. It led up reasonably naturally to the Announcement of Aurelia, Cordelia fancied. Because it was pertinent to district business, Cordelia detailed her scheme of continuing to draw her Dowager's Jointure for her girls' support till they were grown, then cutting it off. "Such arrangements were not made with galactic-style lifespans in mind, after all. But given that I never received a tenth-mark of salary for all the expected—and unexpected—work I ever did as Lady and then Countess Vorkosigan, a pension seems a reasonable recompense. There's something to spring on the Council of Counts, if you're looking for a project, by the way. Salaries for their wives. I'll bet that would set off some *fascinating* debates." She half-suppressed a very dry grin, which she suspected came out looking vulpine.

Oliver's embryos could remain off this table, for now. *The Oliver and I are dating* part could wait a little, as well. She was not, certainly, ashamed—Oliver was a pretty damned remarkable acquisition by any standard, in Cordelia's opinion—she was just... shy, she supposed. Were vicereines allowed to be shy? She could better imagine discussing her renewed love life with Ekaterin than with Miles. *Later.*

She finished with a few brief, amusing anecdotes of the latest chaos on Chaos Colony, and closed.

Her tightbeam to Miles's clone-brother Mark and his partner Kareen Koudelka was shorter, and oddly easier. Mark, certainly, was well up on the complexities of nonstandard family creation. She tried not to let any hint of *And when are you two going to get started on some children?* leak through, although she was not above hitting the *sequester gametes for future contingencies, you could be glad you did* pretty firmly. She was not sure just where in the empire or out of it Mark's far-flung business enterprises had taken him and Kareen this week, but his reliable forwarding service would catch the message up to them.

That left her with Simon Illyan and Alys Vorpatril, among her and Aral's oldest and closest friends on Barrayar. At least the same message, address, and security clearance would do for both recipients.

The resignation news, gametes-tale, and Aurelia-announcement were all much the same, more fluent and confident-sounding for the repetition, Cordelia fancied. She wasn't sure how they'd construe the subtext. She'd suggested years ago to the pair that they weren't too old to be parents, but time had slipped by since then, while Alys's son Ivan had acquired his wife Tej and a start on Alys's long-desired grandchildren. Simon, though, had been married to his job for decades. Did he even have any thwarted desire for genetic offspring? Cordelia had never quite been certain. She decided to let her worked example of *how* sit uncommented-upon. And if Oliver wanted to share his news-in-potential that should probably be Oliver's choice; they were his friends, too.

Cordelia hit *pause* again. This was where her efficiency rose up to bite her, she supposed. She *really* wanted to burble to Alys about Oliver. She really did not want to burble to Simon about Oliver. Simon liked and valued Oliver at his true worth, but it could not be denied that the years of security tensions that Aral's extracurricular relationship had trailed in its wake on Simon's watch had left scars. Furthermore, Simon absolutely *could* be counted upon to note the slight jump in the vid message where Cordelia had paused to think about it all. She sighed in frustration.

She finally settled on, "And in other good news, Oliver and I have started dating. It's been like finding water in the desert. For both of us, I gather."

Of all the people on her short list, Alys and Simon were the most likely to understand just how much complexity that simplicity concealed. She left it at that.

◦◦◦   ◦◦◦   ◦◦◦

This upside rotation, Jole at length decided, was the slowest eight weeks of his life, including the time he'd spent in hospital back in his twenties. Not that there wasn't plenty to do, hitting every wormhole jump-point military station between Sergyar and Nowhere. Although there was a certain useful entertainment to be had by springing different emergency drills at each station en route, occasionally skipping one just to keep the opposition guessing.

Vorinnis trailed in his wake as secretary and aide, because all his usual office tasks followed him by tightbeam. As this counted on her records as space duty, she was remarkably perky about the rotation. She was also, he was pleased to discover, a useful surprise-drill co-conspirator.

"We're not only testing readiness, or even just observing the mechanics and looking for ways to improve them," he told her during one of these exercises. "At this level, I'm just as interested in how each senior officer handles his people. Especially when things go wrong. All part of the, hm, process of earmarking candidates for further promotion."

"Isn't that kind of hard on any officer who gets some duds in his personnel roster?" she inquired. "I mean, the screw-ups might not be his fault."

"We try to weed out the duds early on and send them to less critical downside duties. Unfairly for Fyodor," he reflected. "But any officer can be made to look good by fortunate staffing. Getting the most out of your people when you aren't so lucky is a better test, really." What had that ship of Aral's been nicknamed, way back when? *Vorkosigan's Leper Colony*, that was it.

Granted, Aral's lepers had been as likely to be political screw-ups as military ones, in those fraught days.

Her eyebrows twitched, considering this. "So, this earmarking. How do you...learn how to decide? If it's not just perfect scores on the drills?"

"Practice," he sighed. "Repeated observation. Aral seemed to do it by some sort of Vor instinct, like breathing, but I suppose he'd got all his practice in before I came along." Jole's process still felt conscious, but at least he worked through it a lot faster these days.

His communications with the Vicereine were few, brief, unprivate, and depressingly utilitarian. He did beg her to beam him another popular book on Sergyaran biology when he'd finished the first two that he'd brought along, and was surprised to be told that there weren't any more. She scrounged up a more technical journal from the University, instead—also the only publication on the topic, it appeared. Its ten years—only ten years?—of back issues promised to keep him diverted for a while, at least.

The knowledge of those three frozen embryos in the Kareenburg clinic was an itch in the corner of his mind that he determinedly did not scratch. Except that, somehow, all the articles on reproductive biology in the back issues caught his attention first. The reproductive strategies of Sergyaran fauna—and flora, for that matter, when you could tell them apart—were *weird*. They did put what he was doing—thinking of doing—not-thinking of doing—into perspective, he supposed.

At last this rotation ran out of minutes, even subjectively lengthened ones. He'd been counting. He hadn't proposed to linger upside—even he was due some days off after such stints, though he'd seldom taken them all. His plans were altered when he learned that the Vicereine was away at Gridgrad with Haines, wrestling the locals for infrastructure or, as Cordelia phrased it when he'd dropped in directly from orbit, squeezing stones from blood.

Apart from one brief handclasp and a speaking look, he

was forced to share her the rest of the day with committees. It did catch him up with the Gridgrad base progress, at first hand rather than via the reports he'd still need to read later if only to compare-and-contrast. The suborbital shuttle hop back to Kareenburg was infested with Fyodor's staff and her own; the first group they shed at the base, but the second accompanied them almost to the Vicereine's Palace. She sent them all home firmly. It wasn't till the bloody front *door* had closed behind them that he got his proper welcome-home kiss. He made it a good one, dancing her across the wide entry hall.

"Alone at last," he murmured, and "Finally!" she huffed into his mouth.

"Dinner first?" she asked, drawing back to comb her fingers pleasurably through his hair. "Or a conference?"

"Conference." He dotted tasty kisses across her forehead. "Have Rykov bring dinner on a tray."

"I admire your efficiency, Admiral."

He closed in for more-lingering seconds. Snaked a hand around her butt and pressed her hips inward, which made her grin through the kiss at the implicit, not to mention explicit, promise. He could feel her day's tension start to unwind under his stroking hands. Alas that sweeping her off her feet and carrying her up the stairway was physically impractical, more likely to result in a trip to the emergency clinic than to the bedroom. They slow-danced toward the stairs, instead.

A happy, breathless young voice cried, "Grandma!"

Cordelia's eyes widened as she stared over his shoulder. "Oh, *crap*," she breathed; only Jole heard her. They flinched apart.

He turned, then had to brace her against the impact of two short bodies who'd dashed from the archway and flung their arms possessively around her waist. Leaving no room for him.

The shrieking sprog attack continued in a second wave. A shorter and a more-shorter child galloped in, to compete with their siblings for a turn at the matriarchal torso. A pair of toddlers followed, clearly not quite understanding what all the excitement was about, or who these tall grownups were, but determined not to be left out.

Jole had not seen the Vorkosigan offspring in person for three years, when the squad had been smaller and he had been grimly distracted, but from viewing some of Cordelia's vid messages he had no trouble sorting them out. Alex and Helen, a dark-haired boy and an auburn-haired girl, now about eleven years old; twins only by the shared date that their replicators had been opened. Elizabeth, eight, and Taura, five, more naturally, or at least more traditionally, spaced. Selig and Simone, another set of not-twins of identical ages, two-ish; the pair, the last of the planned family as Jole understood it, had been started very shortly after Aral's funeral. Their father Miles feeling the breath of mortality on his neck, perhaps, or so Cordelia had theorized. They all had eye colors ranging from gray to blue, genetically enough, their parents having gone with the natural roll of the dice on that issue, apparently. Jole's mind darted to those frozen embryos downtown; he jerked it back.

"Where are your Mama and Da?" Cordelia asked the mob. "When did you get here?"

Helen took it upon herself to be spokes-sprog. "Couple of hours ago. Da said we were to be a *surprise*. Were you surprised, Granma?"

Cordelia, recovering quickly, rose to the challenge: "Like Winterfair in midsummer," she told the girl, ruffling her hair fondly with one hand and her brother's with the other. "And here, I take it, is Father Frost."

Jole followed her glance to the archway, where a very short, slightly hunched, dark-haired man in his early forties, swinging a cane, strolled through accompanied by a tall, dark-haired woman of similar age. "We thought you'd like it!" Miles said heartily, although Ekaterin's apologetic expression, unseen by him over his head, didn't exactly endorse this assertion.

"Hello, Mother," continued Miles, making for Cordelia. Any attempt at a familial hug of greeting was blocked by the rioting children, one now hanging off each of her arms. And nor did Cordelia, smiling rather tightly back, seem quite in the mood to return such a gesture.

Mood. Yeah, he could kiss their evening's anticipated mood goodbye, Jole supposed. *Forlorn hope*, wasn't that the term for a doomed struggle? As the blood slowly returned to his brain from warmer regions, it occurred to him what a surprise this surprise was. Was sometimes-Lord Auditor Vorkosigan making some secret inspection on behalf of his master Emperor Gregor? Miles couldn't be engaged in a dangerous investigation on Sergyar, or he'd hardly have brought his family along. Unless he was dropping them here on his way to elsewhere. But if they'd traveled by official, even if unscheduled, government fast courier, Jole should damn well have heard about it from the moment the ship made Sergyar local space, and he hadn't. Could the surprise be for him or his? He still had burning memories of that thrice-damned military theft ring they'd uncovered several years back. "Well, hello, Count Vorkosigan. Countess." He managed a polite nod and smile. "I trust you had an uneventful journey. How did you travel?"

Ekaterin answered, "We came on the regular commercial passenger ship. For a welcome change, this isn't for work, only for family, so it didn't seem right to tap the Imperial Service for a lift." Her smile at him felt more genuine than her spouse's. "The children seemed to enjoy it very much more than being cooped up on a courier. They met rather a lot of interesting prospective colonists."

"Interrogated them to within an inch of their lives," Miles confirmed. "I should rent the team out to ImpSec, I think."

"Oh, *Da*," said Helen, and rolled her eyes. Alex's mouth just tightened a fraction.

So, they'd reached the *Oh-Da* stage. A few years back, both elder twins had clearly thought their Da hung the moons. Puberty must be imminent.

Jole's slightly malicious smile faded, as he considered what *only the family* meant to Cordelia, mother to a key Barrayaran count and foster-mother to an emperor. Could, for example, Emperor Gregor have sent Lord Auditor Vorkosigan to find out if the Vicereine of Sergyar had gone insane?

She's not insane, Jole wanted to protest. *Just Betan!*

Now, there was a reflection to keep to himself.

"Is Nikki with you also?" he inquired politely of Ekaterin. Son of her first marriage, now almost . . . what, twenty? No, more.

She shook her head. "Too caught up with school to tag along, he said. I gather things are getting intense, since he graduates soon."

"Already?" said Jole.

"Yes, I know." She smiled wryly at him, swaying a little as the toddlers kneecapped her. She bent to hoist one up; the other clung to her trouser leg and stared in suspicion at Jole.

"Well. I would seem to be redundant to need here, this evening," he excused himself. "Enjoy the family reunion, Cordelia."

She cast him a strained smile and only a slight eye-widening of anguish. "We'll have to reschedule our conference. I'll try to call you later." She dispatched Armsman Rykov, now hovering unobtrusively, for a car and driver to convey Jole back to the base. No one tried to urge him to stay.

Under the cover of escorting him out, she managed to get the door closed between them and her family.

"You didn't seem all that surprised by this visitation," he observed.

"No, only appalled." She grimaced. "I didn't think they'd just *show up* like that. I'm so sorry."

He read this as a statement of fact rather than an apology; he nodded ruefully.

"I sent them all a vid message the first week you went upside, you see. Told Miles about his sisters. It *was* time."

Jole did a quick time-speed-distance calculation in his head, allowing margin for shifting six kids, a wife, and an entourage. A rapid response in force, it would seem. "And, um . . . about his brothers?"

She shook her head. "Not yet. I did tell Gregor, in strict confidence."

"Yet not Miles?"

"It's not wholly my tale the way the girls are. Have I your permission to mention them? Or would you rather wait and tell him yourself, or what?"

He hesitated, sorely tempted to let her do the hard part. "I doubt you'll have much chance for a private talk tonight with the kids cavorting about. Let's wait a little." He added after a moment, "It's hard to see how one would explain the boys without explaining... more history than Aral saw fit to apprise him of."

"If we had been open from the beginning," she said rather fiercely, "this would be a non-problem right now."

He touched a consoling finger to her lips. "There would doubtless have been other problems."

Her smile twisted. "Conservation of tribulation?"

"There's a law of nature for you." Explaining to Miles how Jole had come to be the father of his three frozen half-brothers had seemed much less daunting when the damned fellow had been a string of wormhole jumps away. "Don't let them exhaust you. You've had a long day."

"You had a longer one."

He could only shrug agreement. Yet half an hour ago, he hadn't been a bit tired. As the Vicereine had so eloquently summed it up, *crap*.

Then the groundcar arrived, and he'd lost his chance even for a kiss goodnight. He squeezed her hand and retreated.

Chapter Ten

A s Cordelia had foreseen, it was quite late by the time six overexcited and overtired children had at last been tied to their beds, or at least kissed goodnight and threatened with dire retribution if they popped up *one more time*. It took teamwork by four adults—Cordelia, Miles, Ekaterin, and the armsman's daughter they'd brought along to help wrangle the kids in exchange for a generous stipend and the chance for an exciting trip offworld.

"We could have stunned them," Cordelia wheezed, as the last door closed. "We have stunners..."

Their fond Da, who had actually been less use in the calming-down part than Cordelia had hoped, said, "Tempting, but Ekaterin would object."

"No, I wouldn't," said Ekaterin faintly.

Indeed, she looked tired. Miles looked...wired, but that was his default mode. Cordelia considered just bagging the smoking remains of the evening and sending them to bed, too.

"Well!" said Miles, with a somewhat rehearsed-sounding cheeriness. "Now the grownups can sit down and talk."

A mental review of all the times a worrisome Miles had been so remarkably elusive to her in his younger days paraded through Cordelia's memory; she suppressed it. *Forgive, forget.* Well, *try*, anyway. She led them out to her favorite nook in the back garden, instead, pausing in the kitchen to snag a bottle of wine and three glasses, because the day staff had all gone home. In the soft shadows and low, colored lights they dragged the padded chairs around a small table, and she let Miles open and pour. His glass got a splash; hers, he filled nearly to the top before handing to her. Ekaterin's glass was delivered half-full, or perhaps half-empty; after a wry hesitation, she topped it up herself.

"I use your garden every day," Cordelia told Ekaterin. "For entertaining, diplomacy, work, and even, occasionally, sitting down and resting. It's been a superb space."

Her smile grew genuine. "Thank you. It will be good to get a chance to review it."

"Actually, now you're here, there's another project I might have you look over. With the Gridgrad base project going live, my next goal is to move the planetary capital, while I still can. Which will, among other things, require a new Viceroy's Palace. With a new garden, in a rather different climatic zone than this semi-desert."

"That sounds interesting," Ekaterin allowed. "I'm not sure how long we'll be staying on this trip, though. And I didn't plan to burden your staff with the children."

Meaning, Cordelia decoded easily, that Ekaterin herself was understaffed for working. "I'll see if I can rustle you up some local help, in that case." Cordelia kicked off her shoes and wriggled her tired toes. "This was a wonderful surprise and I love you all dearly, Miles, but I'm quite tightly scheduled at present. Usually, I have several weeks' notice to clear my time before a family visit." She could see that the few breaks she'd earmarked for private time with Oliver were going to be the first to go on the fire, too. Dammit.

Ekaterin glanced at her husband, who was not-sipping wine

and flexing his feet. She was far too loyal to say, *I told him this was a bad idea*, but Cordelia fancied she could read it in her body language.

Cordelia went on, "While a box of chocolates is a lovely gift, what I really need is a box of *plumbers*. You don't happen to have a building-materials manufacturer up your sleeve, do you, Miles?"

"Sorry, no," replied her son. "Ask Mark?"

"Tried that already. He's not got back to me in any useful way, yet."

"Ah." Miles shifted uncomfortably. Probably looking for an opening to choke out his pitch, whatever it was. Ekaterin sat back and sipped, palpably not helping.

Not having been handed an easy hook, Miles refashioned the one in play. "So, ah ... have you told Mark about this plan to resign the viceroyalty? And the, um, personal scheme?"

That was in reverse order of his chief concern, Cordelia suspected. "Yes, I sent a tightbeam to him and Kareen at the same time I messaged you and Ekaterin. And Gregor and Alys and Simon, for that matter. Don't you people talk to each other anymore?"

"Mark's offworld," he excused this.

Slight, awkward pause, right. Cordelia prodded gently, "And Gregor and Alys and Simon? You didn't bring me any personal greetings? I would almost trade the plumbers for those." *Almost.*

"I talked to Gregor. He said he didn't know any more than I did, and I should talk to you myself."

Good boy, Gregor. Cordelia smiled. She wondered when the adult Gregor had been apprised of the complexities in his greatest supporter's private life. Not during the earlier Vorbarr Sultana days, she would swear. Not later than that period in-between, when Aral had sent Oliver off to build his career, and it was all assumed to have been an anomalous fling—*seven years was not just a fling, boys*—regretfully, gently, and carefully concluded. So who had conducted that briefing, if not her? Simon? Aral? Some tag team? Aral must have endorsed it, certainly. Simon would have been relieved. Gregor, well, who knew what Gregor thought of it all. But the reunion on Sergyar hadn't thrown him.

Miles continued, "I was wondering what brought on this extraordinary decision. About the daughters. I mean, now."

"I thought I explained all that in my tightbeam message."

"Yes, but..."

Miles, at a loss for words? Cordelia leaned her head back against the cushion and observed, "You know, we'll likely all get to bed earlier if you try for a little Betan frankness, here."

"Good idea," murmured Ekaterin. Yes, if Miles had been venting any Betan frankness heretofore, it had probably been to her. Beleaguered woman. Wasn't this spring in Vorbarr Sultana, the busiest season for Ekaterin's garden design business? She could only have been dragged away by a force of nature. Which, Cordelia conceded, Miles on a tear could be.

Miles straightened his shoulders and steeled himself to bluntness. Thankfully. "But you already *have* six grandchildren. Isn't that, like, enough?" And in a somewhat smaller voice—getting down to it, she recognized the style, "Don't you like my work?" And blinked, as if surprised by the words that had fallen out of his own mouth.

Such a raw truth should be handled with care. Cordelia hoped she was up to it. "I adore your work. Consider it my inspiration, if you like."

"It seems like...double dipping, somehow."

She grinned over her wineglass. "That, too." *But I can. And I'm going to.* "Look on the bright side. I'm not nearly as greedy as your Count Vormuir."

Vormuir had tried to help his underpopulated district by a scheme involving a bank of uterine replicators, some dubiously acquired eggs, and a single sperm donor—himself—till he'd been shut down by Imperial order. Not quite directly; he'd merely been ordered to supply his progeny with proper Vor dowries. One-hundred-eighteen of them. Ekaterin, who had originated that solution for the investigating Lord Auditor, made a face, laughing under her breath. Cordelia wondered how the count was doing these days. The first girls must be teenagers by now...

"Then why not when Da was still alive?" Miles's voice, in the shadows, was smaller still.

That was harder. "We talked about it, a few times. He seemed to think he was too old to start such a long-term project." *Maybe he'd been shrewd.* "If he'd lived to make it home, I might have persuaded him to it as, I don't know, a retirement hobby." Or not. Cordelia had been eleven years younger than Aral even without the Betan lifespan. Or maybe he had just been reluctant to give more hostages to fortune. From life came death, inevitably, and then grief. Possibly not something she ought to say to Miles, who had died once already. He might take it personally. He might be right to.

"Are you coming home, then? To retire?"

Hadn't she mentioned that part of her plans? She really needed to review those tightbeam messages. She was losing track of what she'd said to whom. "No, I'm staying on Sergyar. I like everything about it except the name." She wondered if she could fix that, as even the edited version of the late Crown Prince Serg was slowly fading from Barrayaran memory. And good riddance. "Barrayar was home while Aral was there. Now..." She didn't want to say *I'm freer*, although it was true.

Miles's voice grew nearly microscopic. "He still is, sort of."

There was a place reserved for her beside that grave above the long lake at Vorkosigan Surleau. Was she planning to abandon that bed as well? The chill thought came to her that given his health issues, she might well outlive Miles. Thus no later change in her destination could dismay him, and there was no point in troubling him with such now. She settled on, "Of all of Barrayar, which he loved with all the passion, dispassion and anguish of his heart, Aral loved the lake place best. It's so right that he be there." And, experimentally, "But I prefer to build a more living monument to his memory."

"Mm." Miles seemed to take this in as a reconciling thought, suitably Barrayaran-romantic. Making this All About Aral would probably work on him rather well. She hid a grimace in a sip of wine.

"You really think you'll be all right out here? So far away?"

Losing one parent could make a child—of any age—more anxious about the remaining one, true. She'd learned that when she was a lot younger than Miles. Aral had, too, having witnessed his mother's political murder when he was eleven, though survivor Piotr had certainly been in a parental class by himself. So she perfectly understood why her son might suddenly want to put her in a safe box. The safe part she was fine with. The box, less so. "Have you somehow lost track of where I've been for the last thirteen years?"

That got through, a little. "Sorry," he said gruffly, and drank more wine.

"So," she said, changing, or at least spinning, the subject with ruthless cheer, "If I can pry open my schedule tomorrow, shall we take the kids to visit their new Aunt Aurelia down at the rep center? It's actually just a short walk from here. I'll bet I can get them a good behind-the-scenes tour. It could be very educational."

Pitching Kayross as a sort of science museum worked better on Ekaterin than Miles, who was wearing a nonplussed expression. Ekaterin immediately responded, "Yes, really, you never know what experiences will spark a child's interests. I'd love it."

After which Miles, of course, could not refuse.

The wine bottle was empty. Deciding this was the best note she was going to find to stop and get three physically and emotionally exhausted people to bed, Cordelia stood up and firmly led the way.

And she still hadn't got to Oliver, dammit. Well, one wormhole jump at a time.

⚯   ⚯   ⚯

As Jole escorted Freddie Haines purposefully down the street between the Viceroy's Palace, where they had failed to find Cordelia and company, and Kayross, where he hoped to run his quarry to earth, she made one last attempt at escape.

"Really, sir, just because I'm a girl doesn't mean I know anything about babies. I was the *youngest.*"

"Freddie," he said affably, "do you remember how much trouble you got into with the Kayburg guard for filching your da's sidearm?"

She looked confused. "No...?"

"Precisely."

Her face twisted up as she took the point.

"Think of this as the community service that you didn't win from the night court. And I'm sure the Countess will recompense you generously for your services, unlike the night court. So, if you think it through—a good habit to get into, I might note—you see you are coming out ahead." He added as he opened the clinic door for her, "It might even prove to be fun. The Vicereine's grandchildren are a lively bunch."

This was demonstrated as they found their way back to where the Vorkosigan family was being given a suitably modified VIP tour. Even just four of the six offspring managed to give an impression of an explosion of short humanity in the formerly quiet clinic. Their reactions to this excursion were interestingly varied. Helen seemed to be practicing a somewhat precocious studied teen indifference. Alex looked wary. Lizzie was plainly fascinated by the banks of replicators, pelting a tech with questions that sounded, from the snatches Jole caught, startlingly beyond her years. Taurie was busy being five, and had turned the drab tiles into an impromptu hopscotch grid in a complex pattern visible only to her.

Ekaterin's eyes lit with joy when Jole presented her with his prize, and she shook Freddie's hand in a very friendly way when he introduced them. Freddie managed one last gasp of resistance, despite looking considerably more daunted by a countess than by a mere admiral.

"I really don't know much about babies, ma'am..."

"Oh, the two youngest will be looked after by their regular nanny. Alex and Helen"—Jole could sense her edit on the fly as the two drifted over to inspect the newcomer—"are too old for a babysitter as such. They're really more in need of a native guide."

Oh, good job, Ekaterin.

Freddie's spine straightened considerably at this news. Ekaterin made the further introductions all round.

Jole put in, straight-faced, "Now, there will be no going out into the backcountry to blow up vampire balloons unless the Vicereine escorts you."

Freddie winced. The twins both perked up, apparently not having realized that this healthy outdoor activity was among their options. After a thoughtful pause, Jole added, "Be sure she brings her laser pointer."

This won him three extremely blank stares. Jole grinned and moved off in search of the Count. He found Miles standing with his mother by the bank that held, among other pre-persons, his sister Aurelia.

Miles gave up the viewer to Cordelia, and remarked, "Human beings really aren't very prepossessing at this stage of the game."

She peered into the display. "What, I recall you were enchanted with your own blobs."

"Novelty?" he suggested. "It wears off."

She smiled in profile. "*You* looked like a drowned kitten at five months along."

Miles blinked. "You saw me?"

"Just a glimpse, between the time you were lifted out of the incision and the time I passed out from the hemorrhage."

"Wait, you were *awake* during the surgery?"

"Initially. Have I mentioned that this way is better?"

"Repeatedly."

Miles turned with some relief to the new visitor. "Good morning, Admiral Jole. Mother said you'd come through for her. I'm amazed, but gratified."

Good. Cordelia's call to Jole last night had been very late and very brief, but he seemed to have figured out her chief concern correctly. The labor shortage on Sergyar was a challenge at every level. He was nonetheless glad he hadn't had to raid his actual chain of command for her, though he would have if put to it. Fyodor, when approached, had sacrificed Freddie not only without a qualm, but with a certain degree of enthusiasm.

Greeting Miles, Jole wondered for the first time how he had dealt with being the child whose life his mother had famously *decapitated an emperor* to save. Was it the sort of thing a boy was teased about at school? Miles had been twenty when Jole had first encountered him, soon to graduate from the Academy and laser-focused on his upcoming, and certainly hard-won, military career. Awed by the father he adored, he'd seemed to take his mother for granted. Would Cordelia consider that a subtle victory?

Jole led smoothly into his planned olive branch. "I thought you might be interested to know, Count, that the old *Prince Serg* is passing through local space shortly, on its way to cold storage. Decommissioned, you know."

Miles's eyes widened. "Really!" And, after a moment, "Already?"

"My feelings exactly, but there you go. I now have baby officers who are younger than that ship. I'd been planning to pay it a short visit while it's in transit. Because..." Sentiment? Historical wonder? Mourning? He escaped the sentence with a shrug. "I wondered if you might like to go along. Together with whatever family members you deem appropriate." Not, pray God, the toddlers.

Ekaterin had wandered up during this, Freddie and the twins at her elbow; Lizzie followed. It even drew Cordelia away from the scanner.

"Now, there's a remarkable idea," said Cordelia. "History and family history at one go."

"*I'm* not history," said Miles under his breath. "...Am I?"

His eye summing the assembled offspring, Jole could only think, *You are now.*

"What do you think, kids?" said Miles. "Would you like to see your grandfather's old ship?"

"Wow, sure!" said Helen, echoed by Lizzie's "Neat!" Alex looked wary, again. Freddie breathed, "Go upside...?" her babysitting job plainly acquiring an unexpected new glamour. Taurie cast no vote, having apparently abandoned hopscotch as so last-minute in favor of competitive twirling.

"Ekaterin...?" Miles belatedly sought endorsement.

Ekaterin looked to her mother-in-law. "Do you think it would be all right? Safe?"

"Sure," said the Vicereine. "I'd love to go, too. I haven't seen that old ship since I exploded a bottle of champagne on its hull when it was formally commissioned. Several months after its return from the Hegen Hub war, mind you, when they'd finished the repairs. Hugely fun, that. They produce a special break-away safety glass for the bottle, and you have to work in a force bubble to capture the debris. Entirely pointless and insane. Very Barrayaran."

"That one's not *just* a Barrayaran tradition," Jole objected. "Other people's orbital shipyards do things like it, too." He added after a curious moment, "So what's the Betan custom?"

"Splash the hull with water. Which, in a vacuum, is actually more exciting than it sounds." She glanced down at the interested children. "It all goes back to superstitious Old Earth customs of making sacrifices to dangerous gods of fortune and the sea. Like a bribe. Take this wine, not my ship, as it were. Or our lives."

Alex frowned. "But... Old Earthers didn't have *space* gods back then, did they? So why do it now?"

"Because we still have fortune and misfortune, I suppose." Cordelia shrugged. "Remind me to explain symbolism, projection, and displacement to you sometime."

"Much easier than explaining fear, loss, death, and grief," Jole murmured to her ear alone.

"Isn't it, though?" she whispered back. "Why d'you suppose people made this psych stuff up? Distancing, that's another one for you."

Jole thought that asking an ex-Betan-Survey commander for

safety judgments might be going to the wrong store, but after making a few more cautious-mother noises Ekaterin allowed Cordelia to soothe her. Miles was all for the proffered treat, and regarded Jole almost favorably.

His invitation and the teen slave labor delivered, Jole bade everyone farewell and made to decamp, despairing of getting a private word with Cordelia, but she nipped out after him to the corridor. A brief handclasp was all they dared offer each other here.

"Six more children, Cordelia?" he teased her, with a glance back at the doors. "Are you so sure?"

"Not all at *once*," she protested. "And I could stop any time. In theory."

He snorted, then said more seriously, "Did you get any further with Miles this morning?"

"Not yet, no. It was noisy at breakfast. And you have to let me know what you want. I can't..." She didn't seem to know how that sentence should end, either. "I thought taking Miles to the rep center would help him process it all, but so far he seems to be less processing than, than storing it all up in his cheeks. Like a hamster."

Jole tried not to be too distracted by this word-picture. "I had a couple more thoughts last night," he told her. While lying awake for hours. "Until and unless my share of this project goes live, I don't really suppose we *have* to tell Miles anything. Could be years. Decades. And even then, purchased donated eggs would cover it." That had been her very own initial argument, come to think. Miles and his family had seemed a lot more remote, then.

"Mm," she said.

"Or, a perfectly valid half-truth. We could say you donated those eggs to me entire. The boys would still be his half-brothers, same as before." Well... not quite the same.

"Let me think about that." Her expression was unpromising, but he wasn't sure which aspect of these suggestions she was disliking most.

"No rush," he backpedalled slightly.

"No, I suppose not."

A couple of techs came through then, and the Vicereine's bodyguard poked his head around the corner, and they both gave up and wryly parted.

Walking back toward the palace where he'd left his groundcar, Jole wondered how his personal life had grown so tangled in so short a time. Vorkosigans did that to you, though. Flung you off cliffs, expected you to absorb the flying lessons on the way down. And yet, if some—not good, not evil—if some ambiguity fairy suddenly appeared amidst the screams and offered to undo it all, roll back your life to *Go*, you would refuse her. Unsettling insight, that.

If you want a simple life, Adm'ral Oliver, you are making sacrifice to the wrong gods.

Jole detoured to grab lunch in downtown Kayburg before going back to the base. Returning along the main street, he was surprised to see Kaya Vorinnis coming down the steps of the city council building. She also had been due some leave after the long upside tour, and was dressed in civvies: Komarran trousers, sandals, and a halter top. She was waving a hand and talking to a tall, male companion whom Jole belatedly recognized as the Cetagandan cultural attaché, Mikos ghem Soren. Ghem Soren, too, was casually dressed in trousers, shirtsleeves, and sandals, and not only lacked face paint, but had foregone his ghem clan face decal. For a Cetagandan, that was downright going native. His symmetrical features looked younger without the window-dressing.

The pair turned onto the sidewalk, and Kaya glanced up and saw Jole. Her face lit not with the natural distanced courtesy of a subordinate encountering a boss outside of work, but with an alarming *Aha!* expression. She punched ghem Soren on the arm and gestured more vigorously at Jole, talking faster; as they came alongside, Jole caught the tail end of some pitch: "Well, *ask* him! One rebuff doesn't make a defeat!"

"No, but that was the fourth—" Ghem Soren broke off, switching to, "Good afternoon, Admiral Jole. I trust this day finds you well."

"Yes, thank you," responded Jole. He nodded. "Kaya."

"Sir."

Ghem Soren fell awkwardly silent. Another arm-poke failing to goose him into gear, Kaya went on, "Mikos has an interesting idea for a project. A cultural outreach sort of thing. He calls it a Cetagandan discernment garden."

"Although it doesn't actually have to be in a garden." Ghem Soren quickly modified this. "Any publicly accessible venue would do to house the display."

"And that's the problem," Kaya went on. "He hasn't been able to find one. We've tried the library, two business headquarters, and city hall, and no one will give him the time of day. Or, more practically, a room."

"I was told this would be a challenging posting," said ghem Soren. "But surely a simple discernment garden should not inflame Barrayaran historical sensitivities. How can I work to overcome cultural ignorance if cultural prejudice refuses me any platform?"

"It might not be, ah, prejudice," said Jole. "Space in Kayburg is at a premium, with new immigrants coming in every day seeking not only housing, but business sites. Why not just set up this...display, whatever it is, at the Cetagandan consulate?"

"But that fails the educational outreach purpose," said ghem Soren earnestly. "No one goes there except on consulate business. Such persons are *already* willing to talk to us." He added after a moment, "And also, my consul said it would be too childish. But to make a start with people, one must begin where they *are*."

"But what the devil *is*—oh, here." Jole jerked his thumb over his shoulder back to the cafe. "Let's go sit down."

Perhaps taking this as a chink in some imagined armor, rather than as Jole's feet being tired, both Kaya and ghem Soren brightened up. They followed him to the cafe, and a few more minutes were spent securing coffee and finding a table for three. The lunch crowd was tailing off, but that was just the difference between *jammed* and *busy*. When they were settled at last, Jole continued, "So what exactly is a discernment garden, Lord ghem Soren?"

The cultural attaché's spine straightened, perhaps at the prospect of a Barrayaran who actually showed some interest in culture. "It's such a simple thing, really it's not *hard*. You could find one at any children's art museum, or academy, or in private homes, or anywhere there is an interest in cultivating our youth. A training aid, to put it in military terms. A well-designed display offers a carefully curated progression of challenges to each of the five senses, to increase the fine awareness of each. At the end, the student is invited to observe a piece of artwork aesthetically combining, first, a blend appealing to one sense, then a more complex work combining several senses."

Kaya put in, "I guess it's like tasting a string of varietal wines, and then trying some balanced blends and trying to guess what went into each. Except not with wine."

Ghem Soren nodded. "Tastes, sights, sounds, textures, and scents."

"The finer the gradations a person can distinguish, the more... the more points they get, I guess," said Kaya. Ghem Soren looked faintly pained at this athletic metaphor, but Jole suspected she'd hit it square on.

"Your base," said ghem Soren carefully, "is very large, and many people go there..."

Oh, right! thought Jole. *By all means, let us expose as many of our soldiers as possible to the ingestion of untested Cetagandan biochemistry!* And whatever else could be slipped into the audio-visual portion. All right, Jole couldn't exactly see the somewhat feckless ghem Soren as such an agent provocateur, but that didn't mean he wasn't being operated by someone subtler. On the other hand, perhaps the young man was simply trying to do his job, and without much support from his consulate, it sounded like. Or, even more likely, trying to impress a girl.

"Mm, I think using the base would be starting at the most

difficult end of your cultural teaching challenge," Jole said, more diplomatically. "I'd advise some practice in civilian venues, first. Observe, learn, modify, move up."

Ghem Soren's face pinched, trying to decode this; Kaya, sighing, translated, "That means no, Mikos."

Jole thought she knew very well it meant, *Over my dead body*, but the lieutenant wouldn't have been sent to him if she'd been as lacking in nous as some of the rank-and-file.

A little silence fell around the table, as each person followed out his or her not-necessarily-related line of reflection.

"Starting smaller," said Kaya. "There's a thought. What about— what about some temporary, simplified demonstration model, for a first outing? To prove the principle."

"A discernment garden is *already* a simplified model," objected ghem Soren. "It can't get much simpler and still perform its function."

"Yes, but I'm thinking... there's an event coming up which will have base people *and* town people *and* all the consulates, and square *kilometers* of spare space. The Admiral's birthday picnic. They're setting it up a ways outside town. You could plunk in your garden as a sort of kiosk, and anybody could come by and look at it. It could be an advertisement. Then, once you'd worked up some interest, you might have a better chance setting up something more permanent in town."

"You would have to clear it with the officers' committee organizing the picnic," said Jole, thinking, *Wait, how did the consulates get in on this?* He had steadfastly refused to involve himself in any planning for a party he didn't actually want in the first place; perhaps he should have been paying closer attention...?

"Yes, I'm on the committee," said Kaya. "It's, um, it grew a bit while we were on upside rotation. We've got a lot of townies to help, including some of the galactics, and since the Vicereine's coming you can't invite one consulate without inviting them all. And some of the local businesses chipped in a bunch of supplies, so they had to be invited as well, of course."

"Are you keeping the Kayburg municipal guard apprised of this...expansion?"

"Certainly, sir. We've got a couple of their people on the committee, too, now."

He hesitated. "Did that by chance result in a mass invitation to that organization, as well?"

"Um, yeah, sort of. We thought it would be a good idea."

Maybe, maybe not. Off-duty guardsmen weren't quite the same as a scheduled patrol. And Kayburg's on-duty guardsmen had some vigorous history with off-duty soldiers from the base.

General Haines, Jole dimly recalled, had wanted to set up the party on-base to keep it under control. It had been Jole's own bright idea to banish it to the wilderness, for what had seemed sound reasons. Right.

"The Vicereine," Jole seized a straw. "Given that she's coming, any such display would have to be checked by her ImpSec people. In advance. And again on-site."

"But it's only a—" began ghem Soren, only to be poked again.

"That was a *yes*, Mikos. Provisionally. You could get something together for them in time, surely?"

"Yes, but—" he glanced at her firm face, and mustered some manly resolution. "Yes."

Jole was reminded that Cordelia's ImpSec commander, Kosko, had annoyed him more than once, recently. And that if anyone had the resources to examine weird-ass Cetagandan art for hidden toxic properties, ImpSec did. It would be good exercise for them. Even though the absurd display was probably utterly benign, except for whatever hidden slur there might be in presenting a children's show to adults. A prospect that ruffled Jole not at all; he'd met some scarily smart children.

Jole said thoughtfully, "You have had your anthelmintic vaccine, have you not, Lord ghem Soren?"

Ghem Soren nodded. "Yes, all the consulate personnel were required to receive them."

Jole *really* ought not to think, *Oh, too bad.* "My one other suggestion is that you plan to have your display taken down and back to your consulate by dark. Most of the families will be going home then, too."

"Is the Sergyaran wildlife that dangerous?" asked ghem Soren.

"Only if the troops share their booze with the hexapeds. Nightfall will be when the heavy drinking starts."

Vorinnis grinned. "See your point, sir. It's all right, Mikos. I'll even help."

And so it became a done deal, rather against Jole's more conservative judgment. He probably could rely on Kosko to defend them all against Cetagandan art education; defending its earnest preceptor from his audience would be the chore of either the municipal or the base guards. Jole endured both his subordinate's pleased beam and Cetagandan thanks—how *did* a man manage to be both gormless and patronizing simultaneously?—and made his escape.

⚮   ⚮   ⚮

Back at his base apartment, Jole checked his comconsole. His diligent second-in-command, Commodore Bobrik, had gone upside to the orbital transfer station yesterday as Jole came down, smoothly swapping chairs. All communications were routed through his office while Jole was supposedly off-duty; in theory, Bobrik ought to let nothing through this filter but emergencies and personal messages, and any notification of emergencies should come immediately by wristcom. Jole was therefore a little surprised to find a message stamped Ops HQ in Vorbarr Sultana, addressed to him eyes-only.

The figure of Admiral Desplains, Chief of Operations, Barrayaran Imperial Service, formed over the vid plate. Ops was a tall building in downtown Vorbarr Sultana topped with communications equipment and packed from there down to the sub-subbasements with stress addicts and monomaniacal detail-men wearing (because this *was* the Imperial capital) dress greens. The rumor was not actually true that the taps in the lavs were labeled *Hot, Cold,* and *Coffee.* Desplains had been master of this domain and all it surveyed for the past nine years, so it was no wonder that his hair was a lot grayer than it used to be. The glimpse of window behind him suggested it was night outside, which put him at the end of a long day, an impression supported by the fatigue-lines in his face and the date stamp. But he was smiling, so this couldn't be any surprise too horrifying.

"Hello, Oliver," he began in warm tone, and Jole settled back in his chair, relieved, to attend to his distant commander. "I'm sending you this message by way of a private heads-up. There will be an opportunity opening up soon on my end here that I think is in your weight class.

"As you know, I passed my twice-twenty a few years back, but was persuaded to stay on at the helm of Ops by"—he waved a hand—"several people. My wife was not among them, I should add. It's heartening that she thinks she wants me underfoot an extra sixteen hours a day, although that may only be because she's not tried it lately." His smile twisted at this not-quite-a-joke. "Which is to say, I will be mustering out in the near future, God and Gregor willing.

"This gives me the task of scouting for my own replacement. The last three years have made it plain to anyone who didn't already realize it that it was never your formidable mentor propping you up, although I'm sure you miss his comradeship. And God knows anyone who worked with Aral Vorkosigan for so long knows how to survive in a high-pressure and high-political-stakes environment. Chief of Ops has always needed both. I have other candidates with the military depth, but none to match your insider's view of the capital. And I have other insiders, but none who are not Vor." Another little wave of Desplains's hand acknowledged the political slant of *that* comment.

Jole wondered uncomfortably if Desplains realized how out-of-date Jole's Vorbarr Sultana experience was. Never mind; Desplains was going on. Jole leaned forward, frowning.

"With your agreement, I'd like to put you in the queue for Chief of Ops. I may tell you confidentially that you are presently

at the head of that queue. Gregor has mentioned to me on the
q. t. that there may be some administrative changes coming up
on Sergyar. I suspect you may know more about that than I do.
It could be an ideal time for you to make a change as well.

"I might add that if I had dropped dead any time in the last
two years, this might have been an order and not an invitation.
In any case, please get back to me at your convenience. You can
have a little time to think about it, of course, should you need
it. Oh, and give my best to the Vicereine. I must say, I rather
miss her nephew Ivan, speaking of the usefulness of high Vor
insiders, although I'm glad to hear he seems to be coming along
in his new career.

"Desplains out." He cut the com.

Jole sat back and blew out his breath.

A *little time*, in Ops-speak, might mean days, but hours would
not be disdained. Certainly not weeks. Desplains didn't need an
answer instantly, but a prompt reply would be courteous.

All right, admit it, he was stunned. Chief of Ops would be
the crown of any twice-twenty-years man's career. And this was
an offer without the slightest tinge of Vor nepotism, favor, or
privilege.

His first coherent thought was that Aral, were he still alive,
would have been pleased, proud, smug, and have urged him to
take it up. Followed by a darker might-have-been—would Aral
have followed him home, would he have finally retired himself?
Would that have made any difference to the aneurysm or its
medical outcome?

His second was that Chief of Ops was a post that ate its
holder's personal life alive. Desplains had trailed a family when
he'd started, true, but his children had been near-grown, and his
wife had been his executive officer, master sergeant, and troop
combined on the domestic side.

If Jole went back to Barrayar for *this*, the three frozen possibilities would have to stay in cold storage on Sergyar. Any other
choice fell just short of madness. The job wouldn't last forever,

but then, neither would he. And when Ops spit out his cooked remains a decade from now, who would he be then? Besides ten years older.

I could do Desplains's job. The certainty was sure, without false modesty or arrogance. He did not underestimate the task, but he didn't underestimate himself, either.

I could be a father. An entirely different kind of challenge, and he didn't have thirty years of training and career experience with which to approach it. That was a whole new world, without maps or navigation aids.

What he could not do was both at once. The choice was sharp-cut, like a blade.

Cordelia...Barrayar had been the scene of her greatest joys, but also of her greatest horrors and most grinding pain. He could feel that all the way down to his bones. If she would not return there for the sake of her own family and grandchildren, she sure as hell wouldn't climb back down into that gravity well for Jole. However much he delighted her, and she'd left him in no doubt that he did. She was a woman full of mysteries, but there was no mystery about this: she would no more return to Barrayar than she would walk barefoot through a fire.

He reached for his comconsole to call her. Stopped.

What would she, could she, possibly say but *This has to be your decision, Oliver?* He could hear her Betan alto in his head. He could hear the pain lacing her voice.

He sat back.

He had a little time, yet.

Chapter Eleven

This was not the day off that Jole had expected, but if he couldn't flex in the face of tactical setbacks, he was in the wrong line of work. Cordelia had gone out on another fast-flying trip to Gridgrad to show her daughter-in-law the proposed site for the new Viceroy's Palace—and garden—and have a consult with the young city architect brought in to manage the planning.

"I know everyone is leaning on the boy for maximum economic efficiency, but we need to persuade him to leave room for parks and gardens," Cordelia had informed Jole in her hurried morning comconsole call. "Nothing makes a city civil like the injection of some country, paradoxically. I know it *all* looks like country now, but that won't last. You have to plan ahead." She added after a reflective moment, "And parking. And a bubble-car system. With adequate plumbing. Because wherever people are, they always want to get somewhere else, and generally hit the lav on the way."

"With facilities for parents trailing little children," Ekaterin's voice put in from offsides, in a tone of muted passion. Sounds of young Vorkosigans having, apparently, a minor riot penetrated from farther rooms in the Palace. A muffled paternal bellow was either quelling the disorder or fomenting it.

"Yes," said Cordelia. "Some architects' designs look very snazzy, but when you drive down to the details you find they seem to think people are born fully formed out of their own heads at age twenty-two, never to reproduce. And vanish silently away at age seventy, I could add."

"Should you have a more experienced designer?" Jole asked doubtfully.

"Question is, could I *get* a more experienced designer, to which the answer was, alas, no." She sighed, then cheered up. "But this one seems to learn fast. And I don't have to make death threats to get him to listen, unlike some older Barrayaran types more set in their ways, so there's that."

And she had departed in haste trailing, like a billowing banner, fretful staff frantically triaging schedule changes.

This left Jole with a blank day to fill with something that would block his temptation to go back to the office and annoy Bobrik with kibitzing over his shoulder by comconsole. His apartment made a peaceful refuge, although, after about an hour spent perusing more science journals from the Uni, he found himself growing restless. For a man accustomed to the cramped facilities of Barrayaran warships, he could hardly call the place *too small.* Too . . . something. Not enough something? *Not enough Cordelia.* He buried his impulse to replay the message from Desplains for a third time—it wasn't going to *change*—in another half hour of reading, at which point he found an excuse to escape.

The University of Kareenburg was as grandly and deceptively named as the Viceroy's Palace, Jole reflected, as he parked and walked toward the motley collection of buildings clinging to a slope on what had used to be the outskirts of town. The school had been started less than two decades ago in, as usual, a collection of ex-military field shelters. Since then it had acquired three newish buildings in a blocky, utilitarian style, plus a clinic that had grown into Kareenburg's main hospital. Training medtechs locally was a high priority, along with other hands-on technical skills needed by the young colony from and for a population that could not, for the most part, afford to send their children offworld for education. The U. of K. lacked dormitories for backcountry students, who instead lived scattered among local households like soldiers quartered upon an occupied town. The field shelters still lingered, repurposed for the nth time to house departments unable to elbow their way into the newer buildings.

The Department of Biology, being needed to help train aspiring medtechs—and soon, it was hoped, physicians—rated an entire second-floor corridor in one of the newer blocks. Jole flagged down a man dressed in Kayburg-casual trousers, shirtsleeves, and sandals, hurrying along carrying a lavatory plunger.

"Pardon me, but could you tell me where to find—ah." Not the janitor. Recognition kicked in from holos in the articles Jole had been reading. "Dr. Gamelin, I presume?"

The man paused. "Yes, I'm Gamelin." He squinted back in brief puzzlement, as if Jole's was a face he knew but couldn't quite place. If Jole had been in uniform instead of civvies, Gamelin might have hit it. "Can I help you?" He squinted harder. "Parent? Student...? Admissions is in the next building over." His accent was Barrayaran, a hint of South Continent lingering in his voice.

"Neither, at present." Either, ever? There was yet another new train of thought in his crowded station. "Oliver Jole. Admiral, Sergyar Fleet."

"Ah." Gamelin's spine straightened, for whatever atavistic reason—Jole didn't think he was an old Service man—and he switched the plunger over and offered an egalitarian handshake, as if between priests of two dissimilar faiths. "And what can the Department of Biology do for Sergyar Fleet today? Did the Vicereine send you?"

"No, I'm here on my own time, today. Although the Vicereine may be indirectly responsible. I've been reading—"

Jole was interrupted as a taut, tanned, middle-aged woman dressed in shorts and sandals dashed up. "You found it! Thanks!" She plucked the plunger unceremoniously from Gamelin's hand. "Where?"

"Dissection lab."

"Ha. I should have guessed."

Gamelin put in, "Admiral Jole, may I present our bilaterals expert, Dr. Dobryni."

The woman looked Jole up and down with rising eyebrows and a growing smile, and nodded. "You're very bilateral, aren't you? So pleased! Can't stay." Sandals slapping, she continued her gallop up the corridor and swung in at a doorway, calling back, "Welcome to the U! Don't come in!" The door slammed behind her.

With an effort, Jole returned his attention to the department chief. "I've been reading your departmental journal on Sergyaran native biology, and enjoying some of the articles very much." Gamelin himself was one of the more lucid contributors, as well as being listed as supervising editor.

Gamelin brightened right up. "Excellent! I didn't think our journal had much reach beyond a few sister institutions, a small circle of local enthusiasts, and some obscure Nexus xenobiologists."

"I think I'd call myself an interested layperson," Jole said. "Like the Vicereine."

"Oh, the Vicereine is a lot more than a layperson," Gamelin assured him. "Fortunately. She really understands what we're trying to do, here. Such an improvement over some of our prior Imperial administrators." He grimaced in some unfond memory. "Not that she can't be demanding, but at least her requests aren't ludicrous."

"She claims her Betan Astronomical Survey training is very out-of-date."

Gamelin waved a negating hand. "She's structurally very sound. As for the details, we all grow out-of-date practically as fast as we learn. And then we work very hard at helping others to become so, too." A brief grin.

"In fact, that was what I'd been wanting to ask about. I wondered if you had anyone doing more work on the biota in and around Lake Serena."

"Not at present," said Gamelin. "Everyone we could spare has been dispatched to Gridgrad. Trying to get ahead of the builders, you know. No one wants a repeat of something like the worm plague, or worse."

"I can see that." So much for his vague plan of finding the expert and turning him or her upside down to shake out the latest science.

A man popped out of the stairwell, spotted Gamelin, and trotted up, waving his arms. "Ionnas! Julie stole my gene scanner for her damned students again! Make her give it back before they break it—*again*."

Gamelin sighed. "If we're ever to teach them *not* to break our equipment, they need some equipment to practice on. You know that."

"Then give her *your* scanner!"

"Not a chance." Gamelin met the man's glower without embarrassment, then seemed to relent. "But you can use mine this afternoon. I haven't a prayer of getting to it myself. Meetings. Put it back when you've finished."

"Eh." Mollified, the man made off, with a grudging "Thanks!" tossed over his shoulder.

"Defend it from Julie!" Gamelin called after, which won a snigger as the man turned out of sight.

"Equipment wars," sighed Gamelin, turning back to Jole. "Do you have them in your line?"

"Pretty much the same thing, yes," allowed Jole, smiling.

"It will be worse next week, when the Escobaran invasion arrives."

Jole blinked. "That sounds more like my patch. Shouldn't I have had a memo?"

Gamelin was nonplussed for only a moment. "Oh!" he laughed. "Not in force. The City University of Nuovo Valencia sends a party of grad students and related riffraff each year to do some work here. Which would be *fine*, but in order to save freight charges, they try as much as possible to equip themselves on this end. Makes for more-than-scientific competition."

"And scientific jealousy?"

"Oh, hardly that!" said Gamelin fervently. "I'd welcome anyone." He added after a moment of judicious thought, "Well, maybe not Cetagandans. Unless they brought their own equipment." Another contemplative moment. "And left it. Like after their pullout from the Occupation. *That* could be all right."

"Would you like me to drop a hint at the consulate?"

It was Gamelin's turn to snigger, then pause. "Oh, wait. Coming from you, that wasn't a joke."

"Only about half," Jole admitted.

Gamelin shook his head. "I came here to do basic survey science, myself, almost twenty years back. Housekeeping science, but I knew I was never going to be some brilliant hotshot. Do you know when I get to do any? Weekends. Maybe. This little department fully classifies, catalogs, and cross-references about two thousand new species a year."

"That... sounds impressive," Jole hazarded.

"Does it? At this rate, we should have Sergyar's entire biome mapped in about, oh, roughly five thousand years."

"In the course of five thousand years," said Jole, "I expect you'll have a little more help."

"That's certainly the hope." He stared away, as if at some distant vision. "And then there's Sergyaran paleontology. How did it all *get* this way? To say *We've barely scratched the surface* is an understatement. Our rock-hounds break down in tears, regularly. Overwhelmed."

"Do Sergyaran radials even fossilize?" wondered Jole. "It would seem like trying to fossilize jelly."

Gamelin threw his hands up, and exclaimed with barely suppressed anguish, "Who knows? Not us!" He glanced at his chrono. "I would love to show you around, Admiral, but I have a meeting with some students shortly. Meanwhile, what—oh, right, Lake Serena, you said."

"Yes, I've been out there several times lately. The underwater life is very curious stuff, some of it very beautiful, but much of it doesn't match up with anything in the field guide."

"Yes, well, there's a reason for that." Gamelin looked briefly abstracted. "I think I can give you something to help. Follow me."

Gamelin led off down the corridor past a couple of busy-looking lab rooms to what proved, when he flung wide the door, to be a crowded equipment closet. He plunged into its depths to emerge a few minutes later. "Here!" He passed a large, heavily loaded plastic bag into Jole's arms.

Jole looked up, confused. "Hm?"

"Collecting equipment. There's a vid guide in there somewhere, should be, with all the how-to. We developed it last year for an advanced class of some Kayburg city school biology students. Some of them have come back to us with some really helpful prizes, too. Great kids." Gamelin looked up happily. "For your next trip out to Lake Serena."

This was, Jole reflected, a *very* Sergyaran version of assistance. It reminded him of Cordelia, somehow, which made him smile back in turn. "I see."

Gamelin cocked his head. "That said, the Uni has been fielding the damnedest questions from the Kayburg public about Lake Serena, lately. Carbon dioxide inversion layer, really! Serena is *much* too shallow."

"Yes, I know."

"So, um... is there some other reason for your interest in the area? That we ought to know about? On the q.t.? Because if there's a *problem*, we're sure to get thrown into the breach, and while public service is part of the university's mandate, it's a lot easier to supply if we get some advance warning." Gamelin rocked on his heels, as if trying to look inviting and worthy of confidences.

"My interest is purely personal."

"Hm." A disbelieving smile, though not disrespectful. "We

all have our duties, I suppose." He glanced again at his chrono. "And mine are upon me. I really must run. Please do call again, Admiral Jole! I promise you a better tour!"

And he trotted away.

Jole shook his head, readjusted his bundle, and made his way more slowly toward the end stairs. Scientific excitement at the U. of K., it seemed, had edged over into scientific hypomania, and who could blame them? He thought of old metaphors like *kids in a candy store*, but it seemed inadequate. *Kids on a candy planet*, maybe. Had the mood on Cordelia's old Survey ship been as electric as this? He suspected so.

As he passed a half-open doorway, a heartbroken female voice howled in high anguish, *"What have you done to my worms?"*

Jole jerked to a halt. Apparently, he possessed an embedded spinal reflex in response to female screams. Not a *bad* trait, on the whole. But in this case, perhaps he could overrule instinct by the application of higher mental functions? Like prudence. Or maybe cowardice. *Curiosity* threatened to trump the whole set, but he wrestled that down as well. All the way to the end of the corridor, where he turned back.

He eased the door open a bit wider and peeked through. A man and a woman were standing together at a lit lab hood, staring down with dismay into a large tray. As he watched, the man bent to peer more closely at whatever lay within.

"Huh!" he said slowly. *"That's* weird..."

The no-longer-screaming woman, eyes narrowing, echoed his motion. "Hmm...!"

Whatever was going on here, Jole decided, he did not wish to go down in scientific history as the man who had interrupted it. He trod softly away.

⁂ ⁂ ⁂

Dusk was gathering in Kayburg when Cordelia and Ekaterin arrived back from the trip to Gridgrad. As Rykov pulled up the car, Cordelia spotted Oliver just strolling around to the Palace front. The canopy rose, and he paused to courteously help them out: Cordelia, to steal a handclasp, and Ekaterin, because she was burdened with the remains of the day in the form of her portable workstation, a briefcase, and a stack of long rolled flimsies.

"Am I early?" Oliver asked.

"No, we're running late," Cordelia replied. "It was an extremely productive excursion, though."

Rykov drove the car away as Frieda opened the doors to let them all in.

"Do I still have six children and a husband?" Ekaterin inquired of her, and she smiled back.

"I believe so, milady. They're all out on the back patio. I wouldn't let them bring all those dirty rocks inside."

"It never hurts to do a headcount..." She offloaded her supplies, and they trooped through to the patio, where all the lights were on. "Hm. We seem to have added some."

Cordelia's six grandchildren were spread out all over the space, accompanied not only by Freddie, but half-a-dozen other Kayburg young teens, intently looking over piles of broken slate and geodes. Miles was sitting back in a padded chair with a master-of-all-he-surveys air, occasionally directing events with his cane. That he was actually sitting, rather than hunkering down on the floor with them, suggested that her advised plan of *take them all out to the country and run them around till they're tired* had worked across the board, good.

"Who are the spares?" Ekaterin asked.

"I believe they are friends of Freddie's," said Cordelia, recognizing the crew from the brush-fire incident. Yes, there was even Bean Plant No. 3, shining a hand light across a piece of slate and squinting. "I'm not quite sure how they got added, though."

"Fyodor Haines calls them the human hexaped," Oliver supplied. "Six heads, twelve legs, and moving as one body, although... that doesn't exactly work out even if they were two hexapeds. Still an apt metaphor."

"Perhaps xeno-anatomy is not the general's strong suit," said

Cordelia, as Miles spotted them, hoisted himself up, and came over, smiling. He was actually using his cane as more than a conductor's baton, which told its own tale to an experienced maternal eye. She reminded herself that she knew better than to comment on this. He exchanged a satisfying uxorial kiss with Ekaterin, which he managed to make look smooth despite their height differential. Cordelia experienced a moment of envy. She would have *liked* to have kissed Oliver hello...

"Successful day?" Ekaterin asked Miles.

"Brilliant," he assured her. He added to Cordelia, "That geology teacher you recommended led us to an excellent spot. The whole crew ran up and down the ravine banging rocks together for *hours*. Helen and Alex were a little standoffish at first, but then Selig and Simone, in the course of trying to brain each other, discovered what Miss Hanno assured us was an entirely new fossil species. Very excited, she was. After that, the competition was on. It took some negotiating to get their special rock away from them, but we managed to trade off some sparkly purple geodes, and the crisis was averted. Sharp dealers, for age two. I wonder if they're going to take after Mark and Kareen?"

"Any damages?" asked Ekaterin.

"Nothing permanent. Scrapes, a few banged fingers and bruises, some blood and sweat, but, as the medkit seemed an object of almost equal interest, surprisingly few tears. Lizzie now not only wants to be a paleontologist, she knows how to spell it."

"Good!" said Cordelia. "It's about time we got some scientists in the family."

"She wanted to be a medtech, yesterday," Ekaterin pointed out.

"And a jump pilot last week," said Miles. "Perhaps she'll be a Barrayaran Renaissance-woman."

"Sounds more like Betan Astronomical Survey to me," said Cordelia, a bit smugly.

Ekaterin stared around uneasily at all the piles of detritus with rapt heads bent over them. "Are they going to want to take all those rocks home on the jumpship?"

"Probably," sighed Miles. "Or maybe they could be persuaded to leave them as a museum exhibit at Grandmama's house."

"Oh, thanks," muttered Cordelia, which made him smirk.

"They're not wanted for a real museum?" said Ekaterin.

"Miss Hanno took possession of the three new specimens," Miles assured her. "The rest are apparently common."

"Three! In one afternoon?"

"It's Sergyar," Cordelia told her. "Where you literally can't turn over a rock without discovering something new. Have I mentioned that I love this place?" Except for its politics, but those were a human import.

Adult conversation was then interrupted by a general rush to show the two arriving women all the best new prizes, and collect praise for their discoverers' cleverness. At length, with some regret, Cordelia broke up the party in favor of dinner—the Kayburg locals sent home, the resident Vorkosigans dispatched upstairs to wash. She told Frieda to supply Oliver with a real drink of his choice and, leaving the tidying of her grandchildren to the parent who had allowed them to get untidy, galloped back downstairs in record time. *This* round, she managed to grab a hello kiss.

"And how was your trip, Your Excellentness?" Oliver asked her.

"Also brilliant, I must say. And exhausting. I worked Ekaterin ruthlessly, but she seemed to enjoy a whole day with wall-to-wall grownups to talk to, so I hope she isn't feeling too exploited. Although she was."

"And, ah . . . did you get any of that personal girl-gab you were hoping for?"

She made a face. "I *meant* to. There just wasn't time." She added after a moment, "I'm thinking I might get a chance to bring up the subject later tonight. Of us, I mean. Do you mind?"

His fortifying intake of breath did not sound like enthusiastic endorsement. "Miles is your chain-of-command. To state the thuddingly obvious, you know him better than I ever will. Your judgment call on this one."

"Ha. He can be remarkably opaque at times, even to me."

"And Ekaterin?"

"Ekaterin . . . has more distance." And, Cordelia reflected, also the experience of having been a Barrayaran widow, though spared the public speeches. "I don't see a problem there."

"So even you don't know which way your son will jump?"

"I'm not giving him a Betan vote, love." She added, as he failed to look anything but wary, "Any imagined disloyalty to Aral could be thwarted by telling him the whole story, you realize."

Which only made him look even more closed. "I'm . . . not ready for that. I don't . . . I have never wanted to get between you and your family. Between Aral and you, and your family."

"Which consisted, in the early days, of Miles alone." Well, and Ivan, more distantly. And Gregor. All right, Oliver had a point, there. Poor outsider stepchild that he obviously thought he was, in that context.

His brows went up. "Are you listening to yourself? Miles, the Army of One?"

She had to laugh. "All right, all right. Well, I'll wing it, then."

"Just don't put me to the blush."

She brushed her fingertips across his face. "Hey, I like your blushes."

"I know." He caught and kissed the fingertips in passing. "And I would cheerfully hold my breath till I turned scarlet to make you smile. Or snicker, as the case may be. But still."

It was his privacy, too, that he was placing in her hands. She nodded understanding. "May I just point out, the trip to the *Prince Serg* is going to be an overnight excursion. The viceregal jump-pinnace is more spacious than a fast courier, but it would be handy if we could bunk together, don't you think?"

This won a smile at last. "Very efficient, yes."

They *still* jerked a little apart, by whatever accursed ridiculous reflex, as Miles wandered in. "Ah," he said, looking curiously at Oliver. "You're still here. Anything going on?"

"I invited Oliver to join us for dinner."

"You sure? I don't think you'll be able to get much business in."

"I plan to *forbid* business at the table tonight," said Cordelia, widening her eyes for emphasis.

Miles laughed and opened his hand in concession. "Understood."

In the event, between exchanging tales of Chaos Colony and of the latest activities back in the Vorkosigans' home district, the dinner conversation was quite lively. Cordelia wasn't sure if Oliver was being unusually quiet, or if he just couldn't get a word in edgewise. He did spend time coaxing actual speech from some of the younger members of the party, with the same even-handed ease he might have applied to a diplomatic soiree. And listening with the same multi-leveled attention, Cordelia thought.

Another excursion upstairs oversaw the younger children put to bed and the older ones occupied, and Cordelia, trailed in a bit by Miles and Ekaterin, was at last able to rejoin Oliver back downstairs in one of the cozier public rooms for grownup after-dinner drinks. She plunked herself down next to him on the couch where he'd been waiting, thinking, *You could put your arm around me now, Oliver,* but he didn't take the telepathic hint. Miles and Ekaterin sat together on the couch across the low table; Frieda served them, and then, at Cordelia's nod and wave, discreetly retreated.

Oliver continued to be rather reserved, even by Oliver-standards. It couldn't be something brewing at work that was on his mind; he was supposed to have taken the day off. Cordelia would be peeved if she found out that had not been the case. She tried, "And so what did you do all day, Oliver?"

This, happily, triggered an amusing anecdote from him about a trip out to the Uni, where things sounded to be proceeding as usual for the Uni. Ekaterin seemed very interested, though Miles might have preferred to swap tales about Sergyar Fleet. But it was Miles, spinning his emptied glass in his fingertips, who asked, "Why the interest in Lake Serena?"

"I took your mother out to sail."

"Ah. Da used to like that."

"Yes, he taught me how, back when."

"Me, too. Though I confess I preferred grandfather's horses, when I was younger."

Cordelia perked up in the hope that this might lead into some more personal revelations, but instead Oliver went off into an enthusiastic description of the Serena lake life as observed through the crystal canoe. The flash of self-forgetfulness brought his considerable charm to the fore, and Ekaterin smiled.

"But you can't be planning development out that way," said Miles. "Mother is trying to get people to move *away* from the local tectonics."

Cordelia abandoned patience as unrewarding. "Actually, Oliver and I are dating."

Miles stared. The silence stretched just a little too long, though Ekaterin raised her eyebrows, looked back and forth between Cordelia and Jole, and ventured, "Congratulations!" Miles closed his mouth.

In another moment, he opened it again. "Er...what exactly do you mean by dating? In this context."

"Screwing, dear," Cordelia replied, in her flattest Betan tones.

"...Ah." He added after a moment, "Thank you for the clarification." *I think*, said his expression, though not his mouth.

Ekaterin, glancing aside at her spouse, suppressed what sounded suspiciously like a snicker. Oliver was still lying low, metaphorically, but a slight smile twitched his lips. And no blush. To Cordelia's delight, he *finally* leaned back and stretched an arm around her shoulders along the top of the sofa, in a claiming gesture. His chin came up, and he regarded Miles blandly.

"Is this...publicly known? Around here?" Miles asked cautiously.

"I haven't sent out a press release, no. I did tell Gregor, when I messaged him about Aurelia. And Alys and Simon, of course."

"They *all three* knew? And didn't tell me? When did *I* become a security risk?" Miles sounded indignant. He added after a moment, "Though that explains why Gregor kept saying that if

I wanted to know any more, I needed to ask you. I thought he was hinting that he wanted me to investigate ... something."

Perhaps he was. Cordelia didn't say *that* out loud.

Miles's brows drew down. More. "Aren't you worried about political fallout? Locally? Or even further afield." He hesitated. "I could see some enemy getting up charges of conflict of interest, if the two top people in Sergyar space were known to, er, be in bed with one another."

"The ..." With a glance at Oliver, who had gone inexpressive again, Cordelia regretfully edited out the word she wanted, *three*. "The two top people in Sergyar space were in bed together for a decade. I'd think people would be used to it. I wasn't just Vicereine because I was your father's wife; it was always a co-appointment."

Miles made an impatient *Yes, I know*, hand wave.

"That sort of complaint is usually made when one partner is seen to be illegitimately parasitizing the other's power base. It would take some very convoluted thinking to see Oliver and me as anything other than a working team."

"That wouldn't stop them, if they were determined to be hostile."

"Neither, in my experience, would anything else I did or didn't do."

Oliver put in, unexpectedly, "One of your father's aphorisms was *Don't let your enemy choose your ground*. He didn't mean it only militarily."

"Still less a hypothetical enemy," said Cordelia dryly. "On hypothetical ground. Anyway, what could they do? Pressure for my resignation?" She considered this not-unlikely scenario. "That actually could infuriate me, come to think. Getting stuck in this job for extra time just to prove to some wastes-of-oxygen that they weren't running the show. Gah."

Miles played with his empty glass. Still trying to think up a logical reason that he could slide in under his floating unease and justify his emotions? Cordelia wasn't sure whether to let him or not. He *was* an experienced tactical pathfinder. A good thing—as long as he was on your side.

"If my family is happy for me," stated Cordelia, hanging the challenge in air, "the Sergyaran public, or any other, can go hang."

Ekaterin still looked concerned. Given her natural reserve bordering on shyness, this wasn't a surprise. Not for the first time, Cordelia wondered how such a woman had managed to marry a man so far outside her comfort zone. *Though I'm so glad she did.* "My aunt Vorthys once remarked to me that the first attack on any woman who is a public figure is usually sexual slander."

Cordelia shrugged. "The Professora is a wise woman and an excellent historian, but that's old news from my point of view. If there was any slander, sexual or otherwise, *not* whispered about us when Aral was regent, or even later when he was prime minister, it's beyond my imagination. I don't know how they thought we could find all that *time*."

"That . . . is true," said Miles reluctantly. "It was your Betan connection that mostly got them excited. And Da was always a target. I suppose he thought words weren't as bad as grenades."

We weren't too fond of either one. "My old Betan Survey science training didn't really fit me for Vorbarr Sultana politics, I admit. I'd always thought the very worst thing one could do was say or repeat anything that one hadn't made sure was true. People's *lives* could depend on one's accuracy. To me, the rumor mill seemed not just cruel, but *deranged*."

"It's odd," said Ekaterin. "The standard Barrayaran view of Betans is that they're sex-obsessed, but when you go there, you discover they're not."

"Of course not. They don't have to be," said Cordelia.

Miles's lips twisted up, but he did not pursue whatever objection he was entertaining to that.

Cordelia, frowning, said to him, "I'm sorry that you were disturbed by the slanders. You never said much . . ."

"It happened at school, mostly. Boys trying to get me going, when the mutie insults stopped working. I eventually taught them . . . not to. Ivan had it easier. He could just slug them. I couldn't get him to slug them for me very often, except for the one time some twit accused Aunt Alys of sleeping with *you*. That . . . went off well. In a sense." A vicious grin.

"Alys came in for a lot of criticism in her own right for not remarrying," said Cordelia. "Still, at least that one credited me with *good taste*. I was flattered."

"Grandfather once said to me, when I was upset about, God, I don't even remember which one, 'We're Vorkosigans. If the charge isn't at *least* murder or treason, it's not worth rolling over in bed for.' Then he thought a moment and changed it to, 'Treason, anyway.' And after another, 'And sometimes not even then.'"

Cordelia chuckled darkly. "That was old Piotr. I can just hear him. That was pretty much Aral's perspective, too. Probably where he got it from. The only one that really made him angry was the Butcher-of-Komarr slur. The rest just made him tired."

"They made *me* angry," Oliver muttered.

Miles glanced up at him. "Yeah, I suppose you were dropped right in it, during his prime ministership."

"I wasn't allowed to slug anyone, either." After a glum moment of who-knew-what memories, Oliver added, "Very trying."

In his era, there had been rumors about the prime minister's handsome aide as well, in every imaginable combination of sexuality and/or dis/loyalty. Even, on the same principle of a stopped clock being right twice a day, a dark distorted imitation of the real story. Miles must have heard that one, too, and presumably dismissed it with the rest. Or given that Miles was mostly off-world by then, maybe not? Cordelia wasn't sure how to ask. She glanced aside at Oliver, who showed no sign of wanting to seize the cue.

"It tailed off by the time I got to the Academy," said Miles. "Well, mostly. Less of it, uglier when it popped up."

"The regency was over by then. But it tailed off generally, over time," said Cordelia. "Thankfully."

Ekaterin said cautiously, "What about social reactions here? To the new children, too. Or do you care?"

"Not greatly, though I see no reason to *invite* harassment." Cordelia shrugged. "Given Sergyar's mixed population, that one is really hard to guess. In the Barrayaran Time of Isolation, widows still of fertile age were not only encouraged but pressured to remarry, to keep their contributions in the gene pool."

A wry look crossed Ekaterin's face. "Not just in the Time of Isolation, I'm sorry to say."

Cordelia nodded, and continued, "Widows *beyond* childbearing age were not, presumably so they didn't tie up a man ditto. They didn't *phrase* it that way, of course, but that was the cumulative effect of all those weird social shibboleths, if you analyze them."

"Mm," said Miles, who, Cordelia guessed, had never before stopped to analyze them.

"We are not on Barrayar, it isn't the Time of Isolation, and *childbearing age* is an exploded concept. A person can not only sequester gametes for decades, there's the recombination of somatic cells at any age. Including posthumously, if someone thinks to freeze a tissue sample. One could in theory even draw eggs from a female infant, for that matter. Closer to home, there's your clone-brother Mark."

Miles made a random gesture of theoretical surrender at that last point. "True, but... won't some people think Oliver is a bit, er, young for you?" The look on his face suggested that he was already imagining the jokes, and not being much amused in prospect.

"Thank you for not asking if I were too old for Oliver, at least," said Cordelia tartly.

"Thank you twice," Oliver observed from her side, his voice faintly amused. "I'll be fifty shortly. You're all invited to the birthday picnic, if you're still here, by the way."

Ekaterin said, "That sounds delightful."

"I'm not sure about delightful, but it promises to be lively," said Oliver ruefully. "A lot of the base families will be there. So there will be lots of other children."

"Oh, good."

Miles, outnumbered and edging toward capitulation, tried,

"Though I suppose, if you do the math, it makes sense. Betan versus Barrayaran lifespans and all that."

Ekaterin winced, but smiled valiantly.

Well, somebody had to say it. Cordelia turned to Oliver in a sudden resolve that had nothing to do with the amusement of tweaking Miles. Fiercely, she said, "Yes. If you only promise me one thing, Oliver, I want you to *promise* that you will *outlive* me."

Oliver looked taken aback. "I'll...try?" he hazarded. He rubbed his free hand across his mouth, and understanding grew in his eyes. The arm draped so tentatively across her shoulders tightened in silent support.

Miles took a minute to process that, but he got there eventually, Cordelia thought. "Oh," he said. Ekaterin didn't seem to have any trouble following at all; she gave her mother-in-law a somber, sororal nod.

᨝ ᨝ ᨝

The party broke up shortly thereafter, three members being very tired and the fourth...looking as though he had a lot to digest. At least Cordelia suffered no tag-alongs when she saw Oliver out. They shared an insufficient goodnight kiss.

He let out a pent breath. "Whew. That went..."

Well? Badly...?

"—more politically than I expected."

"Miles is growing very countly these days."

"I'm still not sure how he reacted, and I sat there and watched him."

"At a guess...I think he'll express any further doubts to our faces—although more likely to Ekaterin, poor girl—and present a solid front to outsiders." Or so she fervently hoped.

"Me against my brother, my brother and me against the world?"

"That certainly sums up Miles and Mark in a nutshell. So he's had the practice."

"I'd say I couldn't wait to see that," he sighed, "but I really think I could."

Cordelia snickered.

"Will I see you before tomorrow evening at the base?"

Where they would all depart for her jump-pinnace, and thence for the *Prince Serg.* "Afraid not. My staff has a long list of things for me to attend to before I escape them for one whole day, with only a mere three dozen tightbeam channels to reach me." A day bracketed by two onboard nights, by whatever happy accident of efficient orbital calculations. Though considering that Oliver had used to schedule the most overworked man in Vorbarr Sultana, perhaps she should drop the *accident* from that.

He departed for his groundcar, and she turned back inside, thinking, *So, that was the second wormhole jump survived.* How many more, to navigate them all safely home?

Chapter Twelve

Cordelia rose in the night to pee, then found, to her familiar frustration, that she couldn't get back to sleep. She stepped over to her private office to find a boring report to read. Spoiled for choice, she settled on something financial, and herself into the comfy chair. Half an hour into this, not bored enough yet, she looked up as a soft knock sounded on her door.

"You awake in there?" Miles's voice called quietly.

"I am for you. Enter."

He slid around the door. He was wearing an old T-shirt and loose ship-knit skivvies by way of pajamas, and, as he moved across the room to the chair she waved at, used his cane without any attempt to disguise his need for it. He sat with a small *oof*.

"You look...fried." Face lined, eyes shadowed, gray-flecked hair in disarray.

"Eh. Seizure." He shrugged dismissively.

"Induced, or, er, natural?" His idiosyncratic seizure disorder still lingered from his episode of cryofreezing that had also bounced him out of his military career, over a decade ago. Almost a decade-and-a-half, now, wasn't it? He could control it with a some-what alarming stimulator cooked up by his ImpMil neurology team, which triggered the fits in a selected time and place, rather than allowing them to occur as a random and dangerous inconvenience. This worked—as long as he used the device in a timely fashion.

"Induced. I hate the hangover, but my levels were getting high, and I didn't want to risk spoiling the trip out to the *Serg.*"

"I'm glad you've grown some sense."

His lips tweaked. "Ekaterin insisted. Actually."

"Sensible of you to marry her, then."

"Oh, yes."

"I thought you slept like a brick, after those."

"They upwhack my brain sleep chemistry. Sometimes it's out like a light, other times it's insomnia central."

"Ah. Welcome to my club."

"Yeah, but I'm not, what is it, seventy-six?"

"Bang on. Very good."

"You did have a birthday recently. I remember, because we sent vids of the kids."

"Best present, that."

He smiled a little, and tapped his cane against the floor. "While not sleeping, I got to thinking about our conversation earlier tonight."

"Ah?" She set her reader aside and sat back, concealing her anxiety. *Don't lead the witness.*

"Some of those old slanders back in Vorbarr Sultana."

"That does not exactly narrow the field, love."

He inclined his head. "I suppose not." He took a breath. "In particular, the ones about Ges Vorrutyer. And Da. When they were younger."

Huh. Not the one she'd just braced for, then. This was much older news than Oliver.

"Thing is, I didn't get this one just from people who were obviously trying to wind me up." A longer hesitation. "So... were they, er, lovers, or not? I mean, they were *brothers-in-law.*"

"This...isn't something Aral ever saw fit to confirm or deny to you?"

He looked extremely uncomfortable. "I never asked." And after a moment, "But he never volunteered a denial, either. He did sometimes. The Komarr massacre, for example. He never stopped being enraged about that one."

"There was a hell of a lot there to be enraged about."

"Oh, yeah."

Cordelia sighed. "So...do you think I have either a right or a duty to tell you something Aral never saw fit to? Do you think you have a right to know?" It was not, she hoped he understood, a rhetorical question.

He flung his hands wide. "A right? Or a need? But I'd think if it wasn't true, several people could have just said so. And if it is...there might be a couple of people I owe an apology to. You can't slander the dead, they say."

"Rubbish. Of course you can. You just can't be successfully prosecuted for it in a court of law."

His lips twisted in dry concession of the point.

"The short answer could be misleading," she said. "The longer one...requires a little context."

He leaned his head back in the chair. "I'm not in a hurry."

"It doesn't make a very restful bedtime story."

"Not much from that era on Barrayar does."

A laugh puffed through her lips. "Really." She drew a longer breath. "I know you're aware that after most of their family was slaughtered by Mad Emperor Yuri's death squad—God, Aral would have been just about Alex's age, wouldn't he?—General Count Piotr the Emperor-Unmaker kept him pretty much bolted to his hip for the whole civil war. You can now understand why, I expect."

Miles's eyes flickered, as he perhaps pictured himself in Piotr's place and Alex in Aral's. His face went rather grim.

"After his resultant extraordinarily high-level military apprenticeship had ended with the Dismemberment, Aral was dumped out into that generation's version of your officers' academy. Still a half-formed institution at that time. Ges and Aral were both second cousins and friends at that stage, and probably neither of them anything a Betan would call sane. Even without the adolescence."

"I . . . can't actually argue with that."

"Apparently, same-sex sexual experimentation by male youth was tolerated in that context—well, it was never illegal on Barrayar, just socially disapproved, which I'm not sure is better or worse, since there wouldn't have been any legal protections, either—but anyway, still expected to be kept out of sight. Exactly what old Piotr thought he was about, to arrange Aral's marriage to Ges's sister, I cannot fathom. His own mother was a Vorrutyer, so maybe it seemed, I don't know, an unexceptionably traditional family alliance. Or maybe he had some more complex scheme, trying to use the marriage to detach Ges. He—quite correctly—seems to have pegged young Ges as toxic, by that time. But I can't imagine that Piotr expected to engineer the bloody disaster that he did."

"*Was* there a secret duel? About her fidelity?"

"Two of them. Aral told me this himself, and I've no doubt it was true."

Miles whistled. "Illegal as hell . . ."

"Wildly. But they seem to have led directly to her mysterious suicide."

"Da told me once . . ." Miles hesitated. "Back that time when, in the court of capital gossip, I was rumored to have made away with Ekaterin's first husband. *God* that was annoying. But anyway. He said that he was never totally certain that *Piotr* hadn't murdered her. Fixing his mistake, as it were. What a hellish thing to suspect about your da. And never any way to be sure . . . He said he couldn't ask."

"Not talking to each other seems to have been a Vorkosigan family tradition."

"I . . . kinda had to give Da that one."

"Mm." Cordelia drew breath in through her nose. "In any case, for two or three years after her death Aral and Ges conducted what sounds to have been an extremely lurid, alcohol-soaked, and blatantly public affair." A match made in some special Barrayaran hell, between a proto-sadist and a man bent on self-destruction. Eh, maybe Miles didn't need that many details. "I don't gather it was *aimed* at Piotr, but he certainly would have been in the crossfire. The final breakup-fight drew blood. Aral pulled up, and put his career back together. Ges continued his descent. Although not, alas, militarily. His subsequent positions of authority...did the Imperial Service much harm."

"Da told you all this?"

"Some, plus I put things together from other sources. It was amazing how many people thought I should be told all about it, when I first came to Barrayar, even though it had been two decades ago by then. Even Admiral Ges, in the twenty minutes before his, er, fortunate demise. The results invariably disappointed them." Ges most of all, perhaps...she set her teeth and avoided smiling. "I should perhaps make clear that, as old flames go, my objections to Ges were to his *personality*, not his *gender*."

Miles's shrug conceded, *Betan standards, sure.* "So is it still a slander if it's true?"

"The same set of facts...can be presented neutrally, can be spun up into hype, or can be deployed in a way that is damaging and hurtful, depending on the agenda of the person recounting them. Although I do think the fact that the episode was never a secret—at least, not to the generation that was there at the time—pulled its teeth significantly."

"It bit me." Miles scowled. "Da told me most everything about that bad period himself, except he left out Ges. I mean... I'm half-Betan, aren't I? I wasn't even a kid when we had that conversation, of course you wouldn't tell a kid, but I was *thirty*." He wrinkled his nose in a complicated species of dismay. "Instead, I was left to be...wrong."

Cordelia rubbed her neck, which was beginning to ache. "That happens, when two people are so profoundly important to each other. Consider the possibility...that he cared just as desperately how you judged him, as you ever cared about how he judged you."

"Hm."

"Try this." Cordelia bit her lip. "Think of the three most boneheaded, regrettable things you ever did."

"Only three? I can think of more."

"Overachievement is not needed for this exercise," she said dryly. "The top three will do."

"Still spoilt for choice, but...all right." He settled back, rolling his cane in his hands, his lips thinning at some passing memory.

"So, how old will Selig and Simone need to be before you tell them all about it? Ten?"

"Of course not! That's way too young for moral horrors." He added after a moment, "Or any other horrors, if I can help it."

"Twenty?"

"Twenty...is a very distracted age," he ventured, obviously seeing where she was going with this and not much caring for the view.

"Thirty?"

"...maybe." That shifty look, so familiar from his adolescence, flickered over his features.

"Forty?"

"Forty might do," he conceded, wryly.

"Aral should have gone for thirty-nine, apparently."

"Eh." The pained grunt was a small noise, rather like the ones he made when he was getting up and down, these days.

"Turning it around, how old would you have to be to feel comfortable telling me those top three?"

He looked vaguely alarmed. "Two you know. The other one... is pretty obsolete by now."

"I'm not asking you to confess, love. Just asking you to make an effort to see your da as human, not superhuman. That's too high a pedestal to fall from."

"I guess so. Huh." He bent forward and rested his chin on his cane. "I know so. I do know." A longer hesitation. "I wonder what I'm doing to drive *my* kids crazy?"

"Isn't teenagery on the horizon? They may start to tell you, soon. Or you could observe for yourself."

He winced. Sighed. "Any other advice, O Seeress?"

"Since you ask directly?" She shrugged. "Nothing very original, I'm afraid. Forgive as you would be forgiven, and whatever you want to say, don't leave it for too late."

A dry laugh. "That last was one of my top three, actually."

"It is for many people."

Miles sat back, silent for a while. "I...he always seemed so self-sufficient. So strong. I missed the heart-attack uproar, being cryofrozen. Hearing about it so much later, when everything was on the mend...maybe I didn't..."

"Strong, yes. The other...nobody can sustain that much strength, that long, all by themselves. But I think you know that by now."

He tipped his head in concession, smiling slightly. Thinking of Ekaterin?

A few of Miles's silver hairs gleamed in the lamplight, and Cordelia blinked, bemused. "Next year, you will be the same age Aral was when I first met him. Your hair has just about the same amount of gray in it."

"Does it?" He frowned and plucked at it, making a futile attempt to see up. "Maybe it'll be all white by the time I'm eighty, too."

I hope so, Cordelia thought, and her breath caught sharp. *No, do not let your fears eat the happiness in front of you.* Or your grief consume your future? That was harder.

Despite herself, Cordelia yawned. "Think you could sleep now?"

He stretched, rolling his shoulders. "Yeah, maybe."

"You can sleep in as long as you like, tomorrow morning."

"But you can't, I am reminded." He took his cane and levered himself to his feet, and made his way to the door. "G'night, then."

"Good night. Sleep well, kiddo."

"Good luck on yours, too." He made a hand-wave of acknowledgment, and wandered out. No *Thank you,* no *I'm so glad we had this little chat.* Unsurprising, all things considered.

But a moment later, he stuck his head back inside the door. "So when are you going to tell Aurelia all these lurid tales?"

The boy bites back!

. . . Good.

"When she's old enough to ask. I suppose." *Or never.* Let the future be freed of the heavy hand of the past through the power of selective amnesia? It wasn't the worst approach, in Cordelia's lengthening experience.

Miles vented a short laugh and withdrew. Cordelia sighed unease and turned out the light.

The morning meetings in the Offices of the Viceroyalty went reasonably briskly, Cordelia being fatigued from her disrupted night's sleep and disinclined to suffer diversions, and already starting to fantasize about an early escape that afternoon. Back at her comconsole, she found that the usual virtual mountain of items flagged for her attention had been reduced to a virtual hillock, *Thank you, Ivy*. And not even any hidden volcanoes, till she came to the last item on the list.

"Those *smarmy sons-of-bitches*," she snarled when she'd taken her first survey-scan, apparently less under her breath than she thought, because Ivy called cautiously through the open door between their respective domains, "You, ah . . . get down to the Plas-Dan proposal, did you?"

"Yes." Cordelia unset her teeth, and wondered if there was space in her budget to slip in another raise for her executive secretary. If this had been placed first on the list, she wouldn't have had the concentration to get through the rest nearly as quickly.

An outside eye would have found the proposal unexceptionable, certainly. Plas-Dan wanted to set up a second materials manufacturing plant at Gridgrad. Gridgrad certainly needed one. Plas-Dan, smugly sure of their current monopoly, made a list of demands for support in this enterprise that . . . weren't actually impossible, though they were certainly stiff. It was rather like a man holding *himself* for ransom. Well, that ploy had worked for them once, hadn't it?

And, for lack of another option, Cordelia might just have to roll over and give it all to them. Or else watch her plan to shift the capital grind to, if not a halt, a glacial pace. "Gah."

She read through it again. None of the details changed the broad outline. The most she could do was mark it *Received, hold pending review.* Not that reading it for a third time would alter anything. She couldn't pull a competing bid out of her ear.

She composed and sent off a reminder tightbeam message on the subject to Mark, and another to certain friends back in Vorbarr Sultana, and even one to Komarr, but if the first set she'd dispatched had failed to stir up anything, she wasn't sure how the reprise could. Holding an answer till she returned from the *Prince Serg* the day after tomorrow was unlikely to give her industrial nemesis any sleepless nights in the interim, as they could do the same tactical calculations she could. It didn't even yield the satisfaction of *petty* revenge. She held it all the same.

A little while later, as she was beginning to imagine she would make that early escape after all, and wondering how and what the kids and grandkids were doing on the other side of the garden, Ivy buzzed her desk. She could have just stuck her head around the door; Cordelia realized why not when she said, formally, "Vicereine, Mayor Kuznetsov is here to see you."

Making it easier to brush the man off, if Cordelia was so inclined. She was entirely inclined, but she couldn't really justify it. She needed to establish bridges with him, now that Yerkes was out. Yerkes had been fairly obstreperous at times, but at least *broken in.* Personally, Cordelia had voted for Moreau. The disappointment was not a new experience; back in her younger days as a Betan citizen, it had seemed to Cordelia that she was usually outvoted. *I mean, Steady Freddie, really!* It had taken *years* for the Betan electorate to finally get rid of the clot.

Cordelia sighed, and said, "Send him in."

Kuznetsov was flanked by an older woman, whom Cordelia recognized as one of the town council members. But they did the work of running Kayburg so the Imperial government didn't have to, always a point in their favor. They exchanged greetings;

Cordelia fixed a friendly smile on her face and waved them to the comfy chairs on the opposite side of her comconsole desk. The pair looked determined and nervous. Cordelia canned her usual easy opening of *And what can His Imperial Majesty's government do for Kareenburg today?* with a more neutral—if still inviting, because she wanted to move this along—"And what do you wish me to hear today, Mayor, Councilor?"

Kuznetsov leaned forward to place a somewhat battered readpad atop the black glass of her comconsole desk. "This," he said portentously, "is a formal petition protesting the proposed removal of the Imperial planetary capital from historic Kareenburg to a lesser provincial town. We have so far collected over five thousand signatures, and can certainly obtain more. If they are in fact needed, to give a louder voice to those we serve."

"Very good practice for you in democratic procedures," Cordelia observed, not touching it. Some older Barrayaran immigrants didn't trust such galactic doings; others took to it with alacrity, reinventing every possible method of cooking a vote with dizzying speed. The electorally experienced Komarrans had an edge, there. The cadre of more-ethical local election volunteers was keeping up with the arms race, but only just.

"As a Betan," said the councilwoman, Madame Noyes, "you surely cannot turn this aside."

Cordelia leaned back in her chair and crossed her arms. "I haven't been a Betan for over four decades, but yes, I do understand. Your procedure is good. Your issue, however, is bad."

"Stealing the capital from us will strangle Kareenburg's growth," argued Kuznetsov. "Extinguish its chance at glory!"

Precisely, Cordelia thought, but said aloud, "No one is suggesting knocking the place down. Everything that's here will still be here. Including the base and the civilian shuttleport, which are growth taps that will not be shut off." Anyway, not soon enough. She pursed her lips. "Consider also that size isn't the only driver of fame. What's the population here today, around forty thousand? Same as Florence, Italy, at the height of the Renaissance.

So where's our Leonardo da Vinci? Our Michelangelo?" She did not add, *Where's our Brunelleschi?*, Aral's very favorite lunatic creator of Old Earth, because planting brilliant architecture in doomed Kayburg would be tragic.

"We were the first—and foremost—colonial settlement on Sergyar," said Kuznetsov. "Our history is central to this world."

"Yes, I was there," said Cordelia, a little dryly. Kuznetsov had been in nappies, somewhere back on Barrayar, she estimated. Noyes could have been his elder cousin. "History, yes; glorious, no. Kayburg, or rather, the base, started as a concealed military supplies depot and, soon after, a shuttle tarmac and an ugly POW camp. And some really ugly events. The abortive invasion of Escobar was not Barrayar's most shining hour, you know. No one involved was thinking about rational settlement plans at the time, because they were all caught up in the old War Party's schemes. The peaceful settlement of one of the best Earthlike planets discovered in two generations barely ticked their meters, probably because it offered too high a ratio of hard work to glory grabbing. Not to mention slow returns."

Kuznetsov, no Vor, at least had to shrug his shoulders in agreement at this one. He was not allergic to work, either, as far as Cordelia had been able to discern; he was, after all, doing the job he was paid for right now. Alas.

"Mount Thera has not erupted for thousands of years," argued Noyes. "It could be thousands more before it does it again."

"Hundreds of years," Cordelia corrected. "The big blowout that took off its top was a thousand years back, but there have been minor eruptions since. The event-survey timeline for the past several thousand years is publicly posted." Still being revised as new data arrived, not fast enough. *Need more people.* "It's not dead, just dormant, and as the rift continues to shift and widen under it, long-term predictions are tricky. No, it's not going off in the next ten years, or I really would be trying to evacuate Kayburg. The next hundred? Maybe. The next two hundred? Almost certainly."

"There are cities on Old Earth that have lived for thousands of years beside volcanoes more active than this one," said Kuznetsov. "They rebuild and go on."

"Yes, but they were originally sited before plate tectonics was discovered. People back then thought such geologic catastrophes were punishments from their gods, having no better explanation. After that conceptual breakthrough, it was just inertia. And short-sightedness. And the sunk-cost fallacy. *We* don't have the excuse of ignorance. The sunk-cost will never be smaller than now. And inertia is in part a product of mass which, yes, I am trying to reduce."

"By crippling the future of Kareenburg!" objected Kuznetsov.

Cordelia stifled the urge to tear her hair. "The future of Kareenburg is a *lava flow*." She frowned. "If the earthquakes don't get it first. Although Aral once remarked to me, when we were discussing the subject, 'Earthquakes don't kill people; *contractors* kill people.' I thought he had a point, but still."

"The earthquakes we get here barely rattle my dishes," said Noyes. "Once or twice a year!"

Hadn't she been here for the ground-cracker a decade ago? "No, the seismic activity in the rift is nearly continuous. People just don't notice the deep or minor ones. I know my volcanology team feeds the raw data onto the government net in real-time. Anyone can look at it." She laid her palm out flat on the cool black glass of her desktop. Because clenching her fist might be construed as hostile.

Noyes sniffed. "Obscure scientific gobbledygook! Any lie could be hidden in it, and who could tell?"

Cordelia stared. "On the contrary, all our posted explanations are written in language a ten-year-old could understand. And that's not a figure of speech. I have Blaise Gatti go find a classroom of ten-year-olds to test them on. Their reading comprehension is surprisingly good." Gatti had at first been taken aback by his assignment, but had quickly got into the spirit of the thing. The classrooms now quite looked forward to his visits, she understood. "There's even a tutorial post on interpreting the charts and graphs, *right there*."

"So," said Noyes coldly. "Your much-lauded progressivism is

a sham, isn't it, Vicereine? Five thousand voices, swept aside at a Vor word."

"Look." Cordelia leaned forward, clasping her hands on the desktop. "There is no political solution to this, because it's not a political problem. Asteroids—Admiral Jole's people can fix asteroids, bless them. Not volcanoes. It's a different order of magnitude." Well, unless the asteroid were near-planet-sized, but Cordelia had learned not to undercut her own arguments with excessive precision. "Gregor grants the office of Viceroy many powers, but not superpowers. I can't stop continental drift." She added reflectively, "Which would be a supremely bad idea for the long-term health of the Sergyaran biosphere even if I could, actually."

"But you *could* stop the capital from shifting away from us," said Kuznetsov.

If I were shortsighted, vicious, or stupid, sure. She sighed, and shoved the signature recorder back toward its presenters. "I suggest you take your petition up to the lip of the old caldera and present it to the mountain. It, not I, will determine the long-term outcome, here. Though if you get an answer, *run.*"

"Very funny," said Kuznetsov, with understandable bitterness. "I'm sorry that you see the economic hardships you plan to visit upon the residents of Kareenburg as a joke."

"*Hardship* is an exaggeration. A significant number of people aren't going to make as much profit out of Kayburg as they thought they would, this is true. This is not the same thing as starvation."

Looking equally indignant, Noyes grabbed the pad back. "You haven't heard the end of this, Vicereine."

I should be so lucky. "There is much about Kayburg that I have loved, myself. The Viceroy's Palace is a home that I built, and it and its gardens contain some of the happiest memories of my life." As well as the most devastating one ever, but that was no business of theirs. "It will be more than a little heartbreaking to leave it behind. Aral and I always did our best for the place in the time we had. But if I want to do my best for its *people*, they need to learn to shift ground."

Her petitioners, recognizing that the stalemate wasn't going to be broken today, finally shifted themselves out, still grumbling. But at least they *left*, so that Cordelia could, too.

⚬ঞ   ⚬ঞ   ⚬ঞ

Exiting her office a short time later, Cordelia found Blaise chatting over Ivy's desk, and no other petitioners waiting.

Ivy looked up. "On your way? Have a safe trip!"

"Thanks! It should be extremely interesting."

"I don't suppose you need a press officer along?" Blaise asked in faint hope.

"Sorry, I'm full up with family. Not everything needs to be a PR opportunity, you know." She took pity on his doleful look, which he had deployed at her to his benefit more than once. "You can write up a small squib. Run it past me before you release it."

Accepting this consolation prize, he nodded. It would likely be a large article by the time he was done, but the subject seemed safe and the history lesson useful. Although she'd have to cross-check any mention of the mothballing procedures with the military censors, so that it didn't work out to be a notice to the Nexus at large, *Here, come steal our stuff! Let me show you how!*

About to make for the outer door, Cordelia hesitated, recognizing an opportunity. *Waste not, want not.* "By the way, I should probably mention a recent development to you both. Admiral Jole and I have started dating. This isn't secret, but it is private, so treat it accordingly. But Blaise, if you run across anything, er, pertinent to the subject in your scans, do let me know." *There. Blindsiding averted.* Virtue of a sort, or at least a duty discharged. Like a visit to the dentist.

Blaise looked pole-axed. "Er...?" he managed. "Really?"

Ivy sat up in equal astonishment, and more open curiosity. "Gentleman Jole, the dog who does nothing in the nighttime, *really*? How did that happen?"

Cordelia wasn't sure if Ivy's uncertain smile was salacious or just bemused. In any case, it seemed to indicate that if Cordelia wanted someone with whom to discuss Oliver's fine points, rather the way old Count Piotr had gone on and on with certain cronies about his horses, she would find a willing volunteer ready to hand. This had considerably more appeal than trying to expound on Oliver to Miles, certainly. And Ivy could keep her counsel.

"We'll do lunch about that sometime," Cordelia promised. Which would be sandwiches at her desk, probably. "Have your people call my people."

Ivy mock-saluted, her smile growing firmer.

"You don't think there will be any...any issues?" Blaise tried. "The late Viceroy..." Cordelia wasn't sure what he saw in her face that stopped that sentence, but at least it did.

I will eviscerate anyone who tries to make an issue out of this wasn't something Cordelia could say. Or do either, she supposed glumly. "I have no idea. Hence your heads-up on a subject that would otherwise be no one else's business." *Including yours* hung implied. "You might spend some thought on how to turn it into old, boring, uninteresting non-news, though, just in case."

A faint professional whimper.

Cordelia grinned and blew out.

Getting her family into orbit turned out not to be such a circus as Cordelia had feared. Miles, after all, had also had experience moving small armies. The exercise was aided by the decision to leave the two toddlers and Taurie back at the Palace with their nanny, the phalanx of regular staff, ImpSec, and Rykov as experienced seneschal. The older three who came along, plus Freddie, were seriously outnumbered and surrounded by the adults. As long as Miles stayed on the grownups' side, Cordelia figured they were safe. The military crew manning her pinnace and its shadowing courier vessel were all cheery to be racking up more space-duty hours on their logs, not to mention as excited to be visiting the historic vessel as their seniors. With both the Vicereine *and* their Fleet Admiral aboard, their service grew alarmingly keen.

After the miniature convoy had broken orbit, dinner was laid on in the ship's compact observation lounge. It was split between two tables; the four kids had their own, plus a couple of sacrificial junior officers and senior techs for them to interrogate, leaving the other table—of the elder Vorkosigans, Oliver, those senior officers who weren't on duty, and the Vicereine's personal physician—to get on with boring grownup talk. Which wasn't so boring as all that, although tomorrow night Cordelia promised herself that she would jump tables.

The talk, unsurprisingly, turned to their destination. Oliver stuck to the official versions of his war stories, very practiced by now; Miles kept a straight face, mostly, though he coughed wine once. The heroic role of the free mercenary fleet in holding the Vervain wormhole till the *Prince Serg* and the ships of the extremely *ad hoc* Hegen Hub Alliance could arrive to relieve them in the victory-snatched-from-debacle was, of course, known to all the military folk here.

"So what *were* you doing during the lead-up to the Cetagandan invasion of Vervain, Count Vorkosigan?" asked Captain Aucoin. "You were a very junior officer then, I believe? ImpSec, wasn't it?"

Miles cleared his throat. "I can say that I was working as an ImpSec intelligence pathfinder in the Hub at the time. Further details must wait another three years, I'm afraid. At least any coming from me." When one of the interim marker-dates, which generally ran in five-year increments, for sensitive information to age out of classification was passed at a quarter-century. Was Miles counting down the days? Probably. Although there were some aspects that would have to wait the full fifty, Cordelia was certain. Fifty years seemed a shorter time than it had used to.

"Your reticence is fairly pointless," observed Aucoin. "Given all those Vervani holodramas."

And Cordelia had seen them all; Miles had a collection, which he had insisted on sharing with his family—sometimes including Gregor, or, lately, his historian friend ImpSec Commodore Galeni, who *did* have the clearance—and critiquing the errors in excruciating detail. Aral had not been above helping, in a rumbling sort of way, or sometimes critiquing the critique.

"I know," sighed Miles. "Three more years nonetheless."

Aucoin came off-point like a disappointed bird dog. Before he could evolve another probe that wasn't actually in violation of security regs, Oliver shifted the subject smoothly: "But since you are here, Miles, would you like to repeat your war-gaming exercise that you did a few years back about repelling theft attempts from our mothballing yards?"

Which was how Miles had capped his Auditorial investigation of the busted theft ring, back when, incidentally giving him an excuse to extend his family stay, and to terrorize a select group of Sergyar Fleet's baby officers.

Miles sat up with all the glistening enthusiasm of a trout striking a lure. "Can we do it live-action? It would take me some prep time, but I'll bet I could surprise—"

"Sims," said Oliver. "You can run through more scenarios in less time, that way."

And at much less cost, compared to letting Miles play toy soldiers with real soldiers, Cordelia reflected.

Miles tried, "Sims are good, too, but there's nothing like removing the virtual from the reality to uncover all those snags *nobody* thought of."

"While I agree with you in principle," said Admiral Jole firmly, "sims."

The military half of the table then fell into a vigorous discussion of various ways to set up this valuable training exercise, which diverted them all handily till the end of the meal. Ekaterin, Cordelia, and her staff physician didn't have to endure too long, though, as the kids finished their own meal and grew restive and the junior officers had to go do some actual work. And Oliver, she thought, had as much motivation as she did to seek an early bedtime.

His time alone—at last!—with Cordelia was everything Jole had pictured during those long weeks on his upside tour, if not where and when he'd pictured. The unregulation double bed in her regulation cabin was all the world they needed, for an hour or so. She charitably let him go first to the lav, not sized for two, after. When she came out later, she looked surprised to find him not snoring in a post-coital coma, as she'd obviously anticipated when she'd kissed him goodnight on her way to wash up, but lying on his back with one arm flung behind his neck, staring up into the dimness.

"You're quiet tonight," she said, snuggling in under the covers and arranging her head on his chest, ear to his heart. "Thinking about the past?"

"No. The future." He bent his neck to kiss her hair, then finally said, "Something came up at work."

She raised her head and gave him an admonitory scowl, sideways. "You were supposed to be taking your week off. A balanced life for health and all that."

He snorted.

"Anything that affects my patch?"

"Mm... Yes. No. Maybe."

She appeared to consider this disordered ambiguity. "Would it help to talk it out? Aral used to use me for a sounding board all the time. Or an oubliette to rant into, as needed. If you tell me which parts are confidential, they'll stay that way."

He had no doubt of that. "I had a private message from Admiral Desplains. He's headhunting his replacement at Ops HQ. He says he thinks I'm in the weight class for it, if I want to put my name in the hat."

She went still, except for a careful blink. "So... have you sent your reply?"

"Not yet."

Her brows twitched. "Haven't decided? Or decided but delaying?"

No yes maybe. "Haven't decided."

She rolled away from him, up on her elbow. Long familiarity made her bare body no distraction, if still a delight. It was the concern in her face that locked his eye. "If it were an enthusiastic yes, surely you'd be packing for Barrayar right now."

"Well, not *right* now..." His lips tweaked despite his unsettled mood. "There are in any case a few intervening steps. Such as finding my own replacement. Though Bobrik could be ready to move up." Had to be, in an emergency. "D'you think you could work with him?"

"Yes," she said slowly. "Not as easily—or as pleasurably—as with you, but I could adjust. It wouldn't be for much longer in any case." She did not say, *But what about us?* She did say, "What would you do with your embryos?"

"Just so." *As Aral used to remark, when caught in some fork.* He bit his lip, not happily.

"I—" She stopped herself. Went on, "Shall I have a go at helping you sort it out? Or would you rather I didn't?"

If he hadn't wanted this offer, he could have kept his mouth shut, right? "Are you an unbiased adjudicator?"

"No, but I could pretend to be one for a short stretch." As if in preparation, she moved slightly away from him, leaving a cool space down the edge of his body.

"I've been spinning my wheels for two days on my own," he sighed. "Poke away."

"Well..." Her mouth scrunched in thought. "Try a hypothetical. If Desplains had offered you this five months ago—at Winterfair, say—what would you have done?"

He thought back to those barren days of worn mourning. They seemed improbably long ago, from this vantage. Mourning could be buried in work, he knew, trapped alive in its coffin. "I'd have said yes," he replied, surprised at his certainty. "Despite—no, *because* of the challenge. It would have been—not a decision of despair—it would have seemed a chance to break out of a kind of dry stasis. Move forward into...something. An unknown." Might there have been new people on that road as well? A new lover, maybe even a spouse? In that milieu, he'd no doubt that he'd have been targeted, and could have chosen from propinquity. He recalled Cordelia's laughing voice, once, misquoting, *It is a truth universally acknowledged that a man in possession of a high rank must be in want of a partner.*

Although any man who would trade a Cordelia in the hand for any number of birds in the bush would have to be insanely stupid. Granted, there was no accounting for taste. But then, five months ago, she'd not been in his hand, had she? Because he had not yet lifted it out for her. Or grasped her hand lifted out to him, whichever it had been. It was a bit of a blur now. *Hold on, hold on, we have to stop this falling business, it can't end well...*

He took a breath. "And then you offered me a completely different unknown future. So now I have two mysterious paths and only one pair of feet."

She moved back a little more, as if primly trying to be unseductive and fair. It didn't quite work, given the naked and all, but he respected the effort.

"I keep thinking," he went on, "that Aral would have encouraged me to take this. Ops, that is. I'm not sure he envisioned... the other." Might he have intended Jole and Cordelia to inherit each other? Hoped, even? But the embryos part, no. He suppressed an amused and painful pang at the thought that he would never get to watch Aral's face while Cordelia proposed it to him.

She shrugged. "We all had other plans. Which went the way of most plans. But, yes, I'm sure you're right. He'd have been delighted for your promotion. We might even have gone back to the district, then."

Jole nodded, having had just that vision himself. "He was always concerned about my career. Sometimes even more than I was. Leaving Vorbarr Sultana felt like being sent away, almost discarded, despite the visits on leave, but he was right—I needed that new space to grow into. And not just for career development."

"He was always good at personnel," Cordelia agreed. Dryly? Sadly? Or just a statement of fact? "Though in this case, I always suspected him of a touch of magical thinking—protecting your career as a proxy for protecting you."

"Hm." Jole could understand that better now than he had all those years ago, certainly.

"For what it's worth, even then he was muttering about that

job for you in the district someday. Like trying to put down a book yet keeping your finger on your place in it. A bit contorted."

Jole had to smile a little. "I made a sooner someday by coming to Sergyar."

"Thankfully." She twitched, as if to move to kiss him, but seemed to remember her assumed neutrality just in time. "So—are you setting this up in your head as some sort of self-arm-wrestling, right hand against left, between pleasing him and pleasing me?"

Jole hunched under that too-shrewd observation. "Might be. Some. I know it makes no sense, you don't have to say that—"

She gave a pensive wave of her free hand. "Not that, it's just... Miles and his grandfather Piotr had a, call it a conflicted relationship, when he was younger. Credit to Piotr, even at his age, and however painfully, he grew into the challenge. Aral didn't give him any other choice, true. It was the mutie heir or none. When Piotr died when Miles was seventeen, Miles spent, well, quite a few years thereafter bending his life in knots still trying to please the old man. Miles being Miles, he managed to twist it around to please himself as well. But it was heartbreaking to watch."

"Multitasking, a Vorkosigan family trait?"

That won a smirk. She went on, "It seems to have worn off, lately. Or maybe just been assimilated. He doesn't flinch anymore when someone calls him *Count*. Or look around for the real count." She paused, and lifted her hand to brush his face. "Or the real admiral."

He took her point, but... "Is that supposed to clarify anything?"

She sighed. "Maybe not. Except to say, I've watched someone dear to me work through these issues before. Burning his life as an offering to the dead. We all survived somehow, but sometimes—only just barely." She smiled. "Fortunately, you are not so inventive in getting yourself killed as Miles was. I'm pretty sure you'd survive Ops. And vice versa. Desplains is not wrong."

He nodded shortly. They both knew that wasn't the real question. "Wasn't there some folk tale about a horse starving to death, equidistant between two bales of hay?"

She scrubbed at her hair. "So, which bale is bigger? Or closer? One must calibrate for distance, after all."

"Ops is closer. Oddly. *Easier*, though it seems absurd to say so. But I can't really know, can I? It's more like...two bales of unknown size each behind a closed door." *The lady or the tiger?* "I don't think this metaphor is helping, either." He tried another, more direct assault. "Duty, or happiness? Selfishness," he corrected. "And how could a man be happy knowing he'd left a duty abandoned?"

"Ah," said Cordelia. Her smile grew sad.

"I should answer Desplains soon."

"Ah."

"It's not the sort of offer a man gets twice. There are other officers waiting to move up."

"Ah."

"Though retiring as Admiral of Sergyar Fleet—that's already much farther than I'd ever dreamed of advancing in my lifetime."

"Ah."

"And what does *ah* mean?" he asked, slightly exasperated.

"It's sort of like biting my tongue, but less painful."

"Ah," he returned, which did at least make her laugh.

"Thank you for confiding in me," she said, rather formally considering their state of undress. "It will keep me from making up dire alternate explanations for your distraction."

"Do I seem distracted?"

"Only to someone who knows you very well."

Did anyone in his life know him better, more intimately? *You can't make new old friends,* they said. Well, you *could*, but it took a very long time. And time ran out, eventually. "The embryos could not go with me to Vorbarr Sultana."

"Probably not."

"And you would not."

"...No. I've made my choices. It's Sergyar for me."

"So, unlike your Miles, I can't have it both ways. There might be other rewards in that other future, but not...these." This bed was not exactly the most unbiased place to pick for this conversation, he realized belatedly. Although he couldn't picture having it in either of their offices.

"The embryos would stay safely frozen for a decade. More," she offered, in her adjudicator-voice. "Barring volcanoes, and none are predicted that soon. And I would—" She cut herself off. Shook her head. Closed her lips.

"Would?" he prodded.

"I was about to say, I would still be here. But not frozen in time like the embryos. The most I can say is that I *plan* to be here."

Nor could he ask her to wait, locking herself in cold stasis for him. *Now or never* seemed overly dramatic, but *now or no guarantees* was only justice. Realistic. Sensible. And other depressing, grownup adjectives.

So back around they came to Square One. "Any further thoughts?"

"I'm afraid I've come to the end of my capacity for neutral adjudication. Sorry."

No, she was not going to release him from responsibility for his own decision. It was much as he'd figured this conversation would go. Did he want her to passionately beg him to stay? Demand that he throw it all over for love and life? It was not the Vorkosigan style, and yet . . . she'd done exactly that, once—career, family, roots all discarded when she'd left Beta Colony for Barrayar. *No—for Aral.* Without a backward glance? Maybe not.

"If you could have known *everything*, back then, before you came to Barrayar, would you still have chosen?" he asked her suddenly.

She fell silent a moment, considering this. "Then? Maybe not. I'd have been too much of a coward. Now? Yes. There's a paradox for you. Although really it's no more than saying that I'm satisfied with my life. Changing anything would wish people I've loved out of existence, and yet . . . there would have been other people, I suppose. Who now will never be."

And there was Cordelia, summed. Not *the empire would have fallen*, but people, just people, called into existence or erased by the chances of her life. He did not know if she thought more simply, or more deeply, than anyone else he'd ever known. Maybe both.

He gathered her to him, and reached over her to turn off the light. He did not quite know when their breathing synchronized in sleep.

Chapter Thirteen

Ghost ship, was all Jole could think, strolling through the echoing, deserted corridors of the *Prince Serg* the next day. They glinted in the corners of his vision like fatigue hallucinations, those shades of anxious men. Some of them, he supposed, were dead for real by now; all were gone, scattered away from what had at the time seemed—been—their overwhelming purpose. From the pensive look on Miles's face, Jole wondered if he was seeing similar specters.

So many crewmembers on the Vicereine's expedition had wanted to see the *Serg*, the tour had been broken up into two groups. Hers, naturally, was led by the skeleton crew's captain himself, and escorted by the chief engineer. Extra work for them all, but it did cast a validating few hours of importance across an otherwise boring routine voyage. And it never hurt to get the house cleaned up for guests.

Jole gazed around with almost as much curiosity as everyone else when they reached Engineering. He'd seldom been down here on his own long-ago months aboard. The kids were portioned out among the adults—Cordelia held Alex's hand, Miles Helen's, and Ekaterin Lizzie's, to keep them from straying onto any unfortunate live controls. At a few points Cordelia looked as if she half wanted to pass off her charge to Jole and hold Miles's hand instead, but he did manage to restrain himself and set a good example. His disturbingly expert lecture on the several ways one might go about hijacking the ship right from here was limited to a strictly verbal version, though he looked back wistfully over his shoulder as they left.

The bridge brought them to more-familiar old territory, from Jole's point of view; and then the tactics room, doubly so. The old tactical computer had not been torn out or shut down with the weaponry, though its software had been sanitized of anything currently still classified. The hardware was too obsolete to recycle. It was plain that the skeleton crew, whiling away their voyage, had been using it to play war games, a skill-building leisure activity Jole could only approve. Here, at last, the visitors were allowed to push all the buttons their hearts desired. Miles led his children and Freddie into virtual battle with great enthusiasm.

Jole smiled and shook his head at an invitation to join the fray. "I've seen it in operation before," he murmured, which, recalling where and when, daunted their hosts sufficiently not to press him. Cordelia also seemed to find the temptation resistible, sauntering up to companionably take his arm and watch.

"I've often wondered what it is the officers have left to do, when the tactical computer does so much," Ekaterin, also observing, remarked after a time. "And so fast."

"There are some classes of decisions it can't make," said Jole. "Mainly political ones. Also, rarely, an officer may know something it doesn't. Even so, I only saw Aral override it a few times during the hot part of the Hegen Hub fight. Three instances out of four he was correctly guessing the psychology of the enemy's next moves, when they were overriding *their* tac comps."

And a hellish few hours the battle had been, but not nearly as hellish as the strained weeks leading up to it.

The official version was that young Emperor Gregor had secretly left the economics conference that he'd been attending with his Prime Minister on Komarr to go on an urgent personal diplomatic mission to the Hegen Hub, to try to pull its disparate polities together in the face of an imminent Cetagandan invasion of the planet Vervain. Since the Vervain system bordered the Hegen Hub, the expectation was that the Cetagandans would hopscotch the planet itself to seize the Hub and its vital multiple wormhole-nexus connections; and, if their momentum proved sufficient, perhaps move on to snap up the Pol system as well, which would have brought them right to the Barrayaran empire's Komarran doorstep.

A hastily recruited double of Gregor had been sent back to Barrayar on the pretext of illness, to cover for the Emperor's sudden absence. Another layer of supposed deception was that the Emperor had *disappeared* from Komarr, kidnapped or worse. This was supported by a frantic, if tightly closed-mouthed, ImpSec sweep of the domes and the system for the missing man. To this day, the confusion about which of the tales was true had been carefully maintained in the face of all commentary, well fogged. Every possible permutation had its variously fanatical supporters as the questions slowly segued from current events into history.

Jole and Cordelia were among the few who knew that the real answer was *all of the above,* and not necessarily in the order one would imagine. Evidently musing along similar lines, Cordelia pressed Jole's arm and murmured, "I am *so thankful* that Aral had you with him, when I had to escort that poor boy we had playing emperor back to Barrayar. I had never seen Aral so mutely terrified as when we thought we'd lost Gregor, just when it had all seemed completed, Barrayar safely delivered to its future."

"Not even during the Pretendership?"

"Not the same thing at all, no. And not just because he'd been twenty years younger then, I don't think. This was a qualitatively different crisis, somehow. For a while there, he feared he might be looking down the throat of the third civil war on Barrayar in his lifetime, and it almost broke his heart. Finding himself facing Cetagandans instead was practically a *joy,* by contrast."

That was almost too true to be funny. Fortunately, Aral's usual stern and decisive facade had never cracked in public. Even Jole had only been treated to the occasional alarming flash of Aral's doubts, like vivid filaments of lava seen through a surface one had thought safe stone. He'd done all he could to support the man, whether in his roles as aide, confidante, or lover, not that there'd been much time, energy, or attention left over for that last. Apparently, it had been enough, because they'd all won through alive somehow.

But when they'd received the confirmation that Gregor was at last coming aboard, Aral had smiled, snapped out the necessary orders, walked to his cabin, locked the door, sat down on his bunk with his face buried in his hands, and wept for the relief of it. Not for long; there'd been a wormhole to defend, coming right up. The maniacally cheerful edge with which the aging admiral had approached this task had been a big morale boost to the men, many of whom had never faced live fire before. That its source was far, far more complicated than a native enthusiasm for war was not something Jole had been able to explain to people, then or later. Except, perhaps, to Cordelia, who already understood. He covered the present Cordelia's hand with his own, and pressed it in an unmoored gratitude.

The skeleton crew had offered a lunch of standard rations in the *Serg*'s mess as an authentic military experience, attempting to make a virtue of necessity; they were happily spared this charade by the Vicereine's own chef, who provided for all. Scarfing it down, and discussing the vicissitudes of military chow generally, the engineer sighed to Jole, "I suppose at least the Admiral ate better, on board here."

No, worse. During the lead-up, Aral had barely been able to eat at all, with his old stress-related stomach issues resurfacing, and he hadn't dared start drinking. Jole edited this to, "Only during the diplomatic phases. During the crunch times, he hardly paid attention to what was shoved in front of him." And Jole had quietly added *badger him to eat* to his growing list of key-man-maintenance tasks.

Following lunch, at Cordelia's suggestion, the kids were sent to the ship's gym with some of the younger crewmembers for a modified introduction to onboard military fitness routines. After a brief, surreal peek into what had been Aral's quarters and his adjoining own, now stripped bare, gray and hollow, Jole rejoined the senior Vorkosigans in the corridor for a last slow stroll around.

"It seems so wasteful of resources," Cordelia sighed. "All this short-lived military buildup."

"Till it's suddenly needed, and then it's everyone wailing, Why didn't we *prepare?*" Jole countered amiably.

Miles nodded. "And then you're up to your asses in ghem. Again."

Ekaterin said thoughtfully, "I do sometimes wonder what the purpose of the ghem brotherhood really is, with all their militant cultural traditions. I mean, from the Cetagandan haut viewpoint. Lately, I've started to think their main function is camouflage."

Cordelia's eyebrows went up. "For what, do you figure?"

"Cetagandan haut bioweapons. And very long-range agendas." She extended a hand, turned it over. "I really gathered the impression, on my own trip behind the scenes on Rho Ceta, that the haut could destroy us at any time. The only reason why not is that they haven't *chosen* to."

Miles said reluctantly, "I'm afraid that's true. The haut ladies of the Star Crèche have some biological agents that can melt your *bones.* Literally." He shuddered in memory. "The crew of a ship like this one could all be dead in an hour."

"How do you defend against something like that?" said Ekaterin.

Jole wasn't sure if that was a real or a rhetorical question. He answered it anyway. "Current plans call for fully automated and drone ships. I can't give you operational details, but I promise you, a large number of people both in and out of the military are working on the issues."

"We used to call the biowar intelligence and analysis section at ImpSec HQ the Nightmare Barn," Miles reminisced. "In a large building full of pale, overcaffeinated men, they had a reputation as being the pastiest and the twitchiest."

Ekaterin shrugged. "There are organisms that attack plastics and metals. I can't imagine that the haut haven't thought of hyping them up as well."

"They still have to be delivered," Jole pointed out. "This is— fortunately—a nontrivial problem." But he suspected the gentle gardener knew more than she was saying. *As do we all, here.*

"It's a haunting image, though. Automated warships forever defending a world that has already died, with no one left alive to turn them off." She stared away through the walls, in her mind's eye seeing...what?

Cordelia, ever practical, broke the spell. "If you can find me a manufacturer of any machinery that will last forever, I want their address. Some of our stuff doesn't last a *week*."

Miles laughed blackly, and Ekaterin smiled a little. Cordelia had not, Jole noted, addressed the dead-world half of that scenario.

But then Miles bit his lip, his face scrunching down in some decision. Making it, he looked up. "There's a thing coming along that Gregor's been sitting on, which I should probably apprise you two of. Has to do with that goldmine of old Occupation data that was uncovered when they found that buried lab bunker. And why some of it hasn't been declassified yet, despite the howls from the academic community. Duv Galeni's been overseeing the work on it for ages, and even he agrees with Gregor. Though he'd love to publish—he's actually written the book, which is sitting in his ImpSec secure files waiting for the go-ahead. He let me read the first draft."

Jole had the utmost respect for Commodore Galeni, one of the more overworked men in Vorbarr Sultana, simultaneously holding down the ImpSec Komarran Affairs chief's desk because of his background as a Komarran, and, because of his background as a trained historian, given oversight of the examination of an enormous cache of abandoned Cetagandan military and other data, left behind at the century-past pullout and not found until seven years ago. Jole wondered if his own high classification status would allow him to put himself forward as a peer reviewer for Galeni's manuscript...

Miles was going on: "Anyway, he's solved certain mysteries

about the last days of the war and the pullout from the Occupation that we didn't even know *were* mysteries, although, when the clues are laid out, you wonder how we missed them. I have some theories on that, too. The ghem only used lightweight chemical warfare on Barrayar, back then, and almost no biologicals, even when they were losing ground."

The people they'd been used *on* might have a different opinion of that "light" classification, Jole reflected, but this was more-or-less true. "Because the haut wouldn't let them use the good stuff, I've always understood. Which is part of how an apparently effete, apparently unmilitary genetic aristocracy keeps control of their own warrior class. Apparently."

Miles's grin flickered at the string of ironic *apparentlys*. He'd had more direct experience of the haut than even Jole had, and was quite alive to the depths those elegant, deceptive surfaces hid.

"A cabal in the ghem junta running the Occupation had an operational plan for stepping up the game, it turns out, after their nasty foray into nuclears backfired so thoroughly. Seems that wasn't their last-ditch effort after all. The existence of the abandoned bunker itself was actually a fat clue, once you step back and squint—they wouldn't have packed that much wealth and data into it if they hadn't imagined they'd be coming back to collect it. Plus Galeni was also given some unique contemporaneous eyewitness testimony by Moira ghem Estif, though it was typically haut-oblique—even he took a while to decode her pointers.

"The *real* pullout plan called for the use of stolen haut bioweapons—some kind of virulent plague, as I understand it, rekeyed to Barrayaran genetics. Picture it. Pull all your people out, release this hell-brew, seal the wormholes behind you and let it work in tidy isolation. A planet-sized culture dish. Come back in a year or two to a neatly depopulated landscape freed of that pesky native crowd who kept irrationally refusing to be culturally uplifted, and move in. There would be galactic outcry, sure, but—too bad, so sad, too late."

"How close to operational did this plan *get*?" asked Jole, chilled.

"They'd got as far as actually stealing the base material and trying to set up a crew of biochemists—with at least one suborned haut among them—for the modifications and replication. They were figuring on getting away with a *fait accompli*. But then their central Imperial—in other words, haut—government caught up with them. Remember all those famous executions when the junta returned to Eta Ceta? Everyone thought the ghem were being punished for *losing*, for losing the war, for losing face. Which made a handy dual duty for the exercise. But there was a second lesson for stroppy ghem embedded under the more public one."

Cordelia blew out her breath. Jole's brows couldn't climb any higher. He observed slowly, "That . . . certainly puts a different spin on all our military self-congratulations for throwing the ghem off our world, back then."

"*Oh*, yes."

"No wonder Gregor's been delaying this," said Cordelia. "It must feel like brooding a bomb."

"Yes, he keeps wondering and waiting for the right diplomatic time to let it hatch. Most useful or least destructive moment, whichever. Given haut lifespans, all the principals aren't dead even yet. So is it history, or is it politics? I keep thinking such secrets should be out on the table, and then . . . I think some more."

"So, Ekaterin is right," murmured Cordelia. "We continue to exist at the discretion of the haut."

"Yeah, that's the problem," said Miles. "Anybody got a solution?"

"Out of my own head? No," said his mother. "Except to continue to improve our broad scientific and bio expertise, and not just at the top. Which is a process that has to start at the primary school education level." She sighed. "When *everything* is a priority, *nothing* is, but at least that one underlies all others. Thus, you would think people could agree on it, but. People."

"It seems the haut aren't interested in real estate alone—ah." Miles broke off, as the herd of his children and their escorts appeared around the corner, finding their way back to the parental home base. Jole supposed that to Cordelia, the younger crewmen looked like children as well. He only had to squint a bit to see them that way himself.

In light of the conversation just interrupted, he didn't have to work too hard to interpret the introspective, disquieted looks on the adults' faces, regarding their offspring's approach. *Terror, once removed.* He stared around one last time at the creaky old warship as they all started to make their way to the flex tubes.

If his life's calling had been to defend Barrayar, and he did not think that notion was wholly self-delusion, had he been in the wrong line of work for the past thirty years?

The Vorkosigan family was safely delivered back to the base in the Kareenburg dawn. Oliver stopped by his apartment; Cordelia shepherded the rest on to the Viceroy's Palace. She then spent the rest of the morning playing catch-up with all the duties that could not be accomplished by comconsole, mostly meeting with people petitioning her to provide them with goods or services, generally for free. It made her feel wearily maternal. She tried to extract as many chores as possible in return.

Such tasks were pleasant enough when she could actually supply their wants; less so when, more commonly, she couldn't; and least of all when she was presented with multiple irreconcilably conflicting agendas. She wondered if being the parent of an only child had unfitted her for such situations. On the other hand, maybe all the practice at being vicereine would ready her for her rematch with motherhood. It was a consoling notion.

As she made her way back across the garden for the planned family lunch, she spotted Alex sitting alone on a secluded bench, kicking his heels—metaphorically as well as literally? Alex's quiet demeanor was usually camouflaged by the uproar of his siblings, but when one saw him alone like this, it sprang out. She angled amiably over to him.

"Hey, kiddo."

He looked up. "Hi, Granma." As she continued to loom, he obligingly scooted over on the bench, and she sat down beside him.

They both looked out into the variegated foliage and a winding path that might have gone on for kilometers, rather than meters.

"What's everyone up to?" she asked, as a less-invasive version of *Why are you all alone out here?*

Alex gave a defensive kid-shrug nonetheless. But he answered, "Mama's working on the garden project for you. Da went off to the base to see Admiral Jole about that war-gaming thing they were talking about. Helen and the rest of the girls are inside playing with Freddie."

Leaving Alex odd-male-out? It was unfortunate that Selig was too young to be a companion for him. Miles's idea of starting all his children as one fell squadron seemed a little less insane, in this retrospect.

"Did you enjoy the trip out to the old flagship?"

"Yeah, it was pretty interesting." Perhaps worried that this sounded flat, he offered, "I liked the parts when Admiral Jole talked about Granda the best."

"Those were my favorite bits, too." She hesitated, then tried, "So why the long face today? Tuckered out?"

His nose wrinkled, but he waved this explanation-sparing notion away. Either not yet adept at personal subterfuge, or too honest, he sighed, "Not that. It's just Da."

Cordelia groped for neutral-yet-inviting wording. "What's he up to now?"

"Nothing new. He was just going on about the Academy, again. He does that."

Interesting description. At least Alex recognized that this family obsession was as much about Miles as it was about himself. Cordelia detected Ekaterin's hand, there.

"He wants to encourage you, you know. He had so much trouble gaining entry himself due to his soltoxin damage, and went to such, really, *extraordinary* lengths to get around the barriers in his path that, well...he wants it to be easier for you."

"I get that, it's just..." Alex trailed off. "He makes it seem as much a, a thing as being count."

"An unavoidable historical necessity?"

Alex's brows scrunched down. "I guess. I mean, all the counts' heirs went there, like, back since forever."

"This is not technically true. The Imperial Service Academy didn't actually exist till after the end of the Time of Isolation. Before that, officers were trained by an apprenticeship system. Including your great-grandfather Piotr." Granted, Piotr's apprenticeship had been during a real war, as a sort of genius-autodidact with very few seniors able to advise him in that beleaguered new Barrayar. Piotr had made it up as he went along, and his world had perforce followed. There was a *lot* of Piotr in Miles, Cordelia reflected, not for the first time.

"But Granda went there. And Da. And Uncle Ivan. And Uncle Gregor, and Uncle Duv Galeni, who isn't even Vor, and everybody."

"Not your Uncle Mark," Cordelia offered. She perhaps deserved the Look she received in return.

"Uncle Mark's different."

"Very different," she conceded, "yet genetically identical to your da. Biology isn't destiny, you know."

"He even looks different."

"Yes, he goes to some trouble about that." Mark worked to keep his formidable weight up as consciously as some people worked to keep theirs down, if more pleasurably. That this somatic choice disturbed the hell out of his progenitor-brother was more feature than bug, Cordelia gathered.

Alex focused on some unseen vision, apparently between his feet. "Not Great-uncle Vorthys, though."

The Professor, as everyone called Dr. Vorthys, was Ekaterin's late mother's brother, and a galactic-class engineer in his own right. Perhaps Alex's world was not as devoid of nonmilitary male role models as all that? Cordelia suddenly smiled. "Come into the house with me. I have something to show you. Just you."

Alex followed her dutifully, but looking curious.

She led him up to her private office, closed the door, and cleared the small conference table. She then unlocked a tall cabinet stacked with wide, flat drawers. *I haven't had this open for over three years.* She hesitated, then began pulling out sheet after sheet, some plastic flimsies but most real fiber-paper, all sizes from torn scraps to wide folios that half covered the table. Alex watched, then drifted up to tentatively finger them.

"These are your Granda Aral's drawings," she told him.

"I knew he drew pictures," Alex offered. "He drew some of Helen and me once, I remember, when you were visiting for Winterfair." That must have been on their last joint trip home, Cordelia calculated. "I didn't know he drew so *many.*"

"For a long time, he didn't," said Cordelia. "He told me once he started when he was very young—younger even than you. But those were all lost. And some in his teens—those were mostly lost, too, but he kept a few hidden away. He didn't really take it up again, as a hobby, till after the regency. More after we came to Sergyar."

"Did he paint, too?"

"A little. I tried once to interest him in vid imaging, but he seemed to want that direct tactile connection. Something he did with his own hands and eye and brain and nothing else." Belonging to no one else? Aral had spent so much of his life as a wholly-owned servant of the Imperium, perhaps it was natural to want to keep some tiny reserve sequestered.

Alex leaned his elbows on the table, staring more closely. "Why didn't he show them to anybody? Or give them away? There's so many. Didn't anybody want them?"

"He showed them to a few people. Me, Oliver, Simon sometimes. I'm sure quite a few people would have wanted them, but not...not for the drawings themselves. They'd have wanted them because the Lord Regent or the Admiral or the Count had made them, or worse, to sell for money." She paused. "He said it would be like that bicycle-riding bear someone was parading around the district, once. It wasn't that the bear was *good* at bicycling, it was just the novelty of a bear riding at all."

"They look pretty good to *me.*"

"You're . . . not wrong." Even for age eleven.

Alex sorted down through the stacks, handling the paper with reassuring care. "There's lots of buildings. Is that Hassadar Square? Oh, look, here's your Viceroy's Palace! That's good."

Cordelia looked over his shoulder. "Especially considering it hadn't been built yet, yes." She swallowed, and launched her pitch. "Your granda never went to war, you know. War came to him. And he learned to deal with it because he had to. If his older brother hadn't been killed, if he'd never become the heir, if Mad Yuri's war had never happened, I suspect he might have gone on to be . . . possibly not an artist, but I'd bet an architect. Probably one of those men who takes on vast public projects, as complicated and demanding as commanding an army, because all that Vorkosigan energy would have found its path somehow." Like a river running in flood down from his own Dendarii mountains, bursting its banks. "Building Barrayar in another way."

Alex's face had gone still. "But I am the heir."

"But living, now, in the Barrayar your granda remade, which is not like the one he inherited. *You* have more choices. You have all the choices you can imagine. It would have pleased him very much to know that was a gift he gave you. That your life *didn't* need to be like his." She hesitated. "Nor like your da's, or his granda's, or like anyone's but your own. To the top of your bent. Whatever that bent turns out to be."

It was hard to tell how he processed that. The boy was almost as reserved as his mother. Miles's mobile young face had revealed all his urgent soul, usually; this had spoiled her as a parent, Cordelia suspected. But Alex's hand crept to the papers, and he said cautiously, "Can I have some of these?"

"In due course, you will inherit all of them. I'm so glad to know you're interested. But if you would like a few to take with you now, you could pick out the ones you like best and I could have them made up into a kind of scrapbook for you, to protect them along the way." Archival-grade backing and what-not—someone on staff would have a clue.

"I'd like that," he said, in a voice so soft she had to bend her head to hear.

"Then it shall be so. Take your time." She retreated to her comconsole to give him room to explore unhurried. Watching him covertly over the vid display, she tried to guess if this had been a good idea or not. Probably so, because they had to break off for lunch before he'd finished. Curiously, he did not mention the project over the dining table, not that he could much get a word in once the whole clan was gathered.

Surrounded by them all, she was reminded of the old parental curse—*May you have six children just like you.* Except that this curse seemed to have gone awry. Miles would have reveled at six children just like himself; he'd have known exactly what to do. Instead, he seemed to have received six children, none in the least like himself, and furthermore, each one different from all the others. As parental revenges went, this was actually *much better.*

Back in her personal office, she took up her reader and started on the next report, trying to make herself as unobtrusive as possible while Alex continued his quiet survey. She kept her ears pricked for his occasional noises of surprise or interest, or his undervoiced commentary. They were close to the time she would have to break this off and go back across the garden, when he said, "Oh, here's you, Granma! Why aren't you wearing any clothes? Were you swimming?"

Cordelia just kept herself from bolting up out of her chair, converting it into a casual approach. She should probably have locked *that* drawer, except there was no way to secure them individually, just the whole cabinet at once. "Artists are encouraged to draw nudes," she said. "The human body is supposed to be the hardest thing to get really right. I posed for Aral when he wanted to practice."

"It looks pretty good. I mean, it looks like you. And here's Admiral Jole, too. I suppose you'd have to practice drawing both men and women."

"That's right." The erotic edge to the portraits clearly escaped him. There were a few more down in that stack, she recalled, the tenor of which no one could mistake; she confiscated the pile under the pretext of picking it up to look through.

"Are there any herms, then? There ought to be herms, too. And maybe quaddies. And those water people. And heavy-worlders."

"I think Aral lacked a live model. Consul Vermillion wasn't here yet." Would Vermillion have volunteered to pose if she'd hinted for it? Maybe so. Too late, as were so many things.

The next sheet down had a sketch of her and Oliver together, clearly in bed. That would have been harder to explain. She plucked out a couple of her, Oliver, and a few other people unexceptionably dressed, and set them down to distract Alex while she whisked the remainder out of sight. He would inherit them someday—she could never bear to destroy them—but not yet.

"Can I keep this one of you on the sailboat?"

She glanced over at it. "That's one of a pair." The sketch of Oliver, shirtless at the tiller, peeked out underneath. "They ought to be kept together." *Indeed.* "How about this one, instead?"

"Are you in Mama's garden here? All right." He seemed satisfied with the substitution. She blew out a furtive breath of relief.

If he'd been raised a Betan child, would she have had to hide any of them? Well... maybe a few, yeah. Aral had been in a puckish humor when he'd done some of the caricatures, and in a serious one for a few more, some from memory, some from imagination, and a few as an aid to imagination. *Those* had proved useful. She wasn't sure whether she was suppressing a grin or tears, but she kept her face turned away from Alex till she could smooth it once more, and restore the stack to its cave of fragile memories. Let it rest there in the dark till the edges no longer cut.

"No pictures of Granda, though," Alex remarked.

"That is unavoidably true. Except... in a strange way, they all are. A view of him very few people ever had."

"Huh." His brows drew down, not so much puzzled as contemplative.

"Which is your favorite?" she asked, turning back to his selected treasures.

To her surprise, he pointed not to one of the portraits, but to a large, elaborate, and immensely detailed architectural drawing of the imposing facades of Vorkosigan House.

"Interesting. Why?" Was he homesick?

His hands worked, as if groping for an unknown tool. "It's got the most... everything."

She looked again. This was an unexpectedly recent piece, drawn here on Sergyar, presumably from some combination of memory and visual references. One would need a magnifying glass to take in all its features—if she recalled aright, Aral had used one in its composition—yet it didn't feel in the least mechanical. Not Alex homesick, but someone else, perhaps?

"I do believe you are right, kiddo."

Chapter Fourteen

Diverting Miles via the targeted application of war game sims seemed to Jole to go well that morning. He pulled Kaya off her leave to set up the show in one of the base tactics rooms, a skill-building task she seemed to resent not at all, which incidentally also assured she couldn't be elbowed out of a front-row seat. On the theory that some opportunities should be less optional than others, he made sure to tap a few officers he judged needed to be waked up from sleepy habits in a military backwater that could become a frontwater on very short notice. The remaining slots filled in quickly as word got around, if only from a curiosity to meet Admiral Vorkosigan's son.

Thus Jole not only entertained his VIP guest, but escaped having to actually converse with him, until, breaking for lunch, Miles said, "So, show me that dodgy plascrete you and Mother were complaining about."

So, once again, Jole led a Vorkosigan on a trudge out to the mesas of stacked pallets, moldering gently in the tropical sun. The maze, he observed from the tell-tale bits of detritus scattered about in some nooks, seemed to have been attracting other denizens of the base looking for a private talk, tryst, or party. He made a mental note to make sure base security was keeping an eye on it. Yet another reason to shift the damned crap, if only he could figure out an economically favorable place or person to shift it to.

To Jole's faint alarm, Miles, clutching his cane, insisted on climbing a stack to look around. He seemed to have the same curiosity and instinct for the high ground as a cat, without a cat's supple ability to land on its feet. Jole breathed a little easier when Miles sat down on the edge, dangling his legs and scooting into a comfortable position that put him just slightly higher than eye-to-eye with his host. Not exactly subtle, but Jole was willing to spot him the point. He leaned back on the stack opposite, crossed his arms, and waited.

In a close simulation of casual, Miles began, "So, did this posthumous-children scheme of my mother's come as a surprise to you? I mean, what with the dating and all."

So much for the plascrete as a conversational barrier, then. Or any other kind. "Yes," Jole admitted. "I had no idea it was possible. Although we weren't dating yet, when she arrived back from her Winterfair trip with the samples." He hesitated. Where was Miles wanting to go with this? And did he really want to go along? "Ah—and you? Were you surprised?"

Miles tilted his hand back and forth in a no-yes-no gesture. "I always knew she'd wanted a daughter. Not *instead* of me, mind you, it wasn't like that. In addition. She seemed content to take out that maternal mania on assorted Barrayaran girls she mentored over the years. I thought she'd given up the idea decades ago. I knew about the samples—they went past in the stream when I was doing executor duties for Da—but I had a million other things to attend to and that one, at least, was her problem not mine. And then I didn't think anything more about it, and she didn't *say* anything more about it." He frowned at this last.

"She didn't say anything to me, either, until after she'd ascertained their viability," Jole offered. "That might have been what she was waiting for." And if the samples had proved dead, would she have kept that grief locked silently in her own heart, never to be shared and thus halved? Sad but likely. It was his turn to frown.

"The real surprise is Sergyar," Miles went on. "I thought she'd be coming home. And doing—I don't know what. Something. Grandmothering, maybe. The kids are a little shortchanged in that department, with Da gone, and Ekaterin's mother long gone, and her da ensconced down in South Continent. Although I suppose there's her Aunt and Uncle Vorthys, in town. And her brothers, and their wives and kids, and Nikki, and Alys and Simon, and... well, I guess they aren't as lacking in relatives as I was. I had old Count Piotr. And cousin Ivan, sometimes." His brows drew down as he reflected on this generational disparity.

"I had the impression your district is Ekaterin's patch, now," said Jole mildly. "Are two countesses in one district anything like two women in one house?"

"My mother's not *evicted*, dammit," said Miles. "Surely she doesn't think she is—does she?" Genuine dismay flashed in his glance down at Jole. "That's not what this is about, is it?"

"I don't think she feels that way, no," said Jole. "I think it's a more positive choice. She's just getting back in touch with her old Betan Survey roots. She joined up to explore new worlds—so, Sergyar's a new world—it'll do."

Miles's grin flickered. "Like Barrayar before it? Could be."

"You don't mention your Betan relatives in that roster," Jole observed curiously, shifting his back against his support-stack. "I know Cordelia keeps in some touch with her brother. And you have cousins there, yes?"

Miles, taken aback, shrugged. "Three of 'em. Though I never really met them till I went there for my school year at age fifteen. And they were all rather different ages than me which, at fifteen, matters. I've given up trying to keep track of their partners and sprogs, although Mother gets bulletins on them all from *her* mother that she feels obliged to pass along."

Jole, the occasional victim of similar maternal reports on relatives he'd barely met and wouldn't have recognized in the street,
nodded understanding. Obituary column and all, as the extended
family aged. It was only in recent years that he'd become able to
recognize that as a clumsy expression of her sense of loss, and
not a long-distance attempt to depress him. He'd grown better
at writing back.

Miles frowned. "Maybe you have to be the right age to imprint
on your relatives. If you're not actually around each other enough
when you're young and feckless together, you miss the ship. The
most you can become after that is adult acquaintances. With
maybe extra emergency docking privileges," he conceded. "If I
were somehow stranded on Beta, say. Or if any of them were
stranded on Barrayar—I suppose that's reciprocal."

Jole's rural home district had been a place he couldn't wait
to escape, at age eighteen, and little about his rare visits back
there had altered that view. It wasn't as if his relationship with
Aral or, later, with Aral and Cordelia had cut him off from his
family much more than distance and his career had already done.
And yet...to maintain the necessary political reticence, silences
had always seemed safer than lies. And it was much easier to
maintain silences when one didn't engage in a conversation in
the first place.

Would his sons, if he chose to have them on Sergyar, end
up enjoying much the same untroubled distance to Jole's prole
family back on Barrayar as Miles had with his Betan cousins?
Even more so with their Vor nieces and nephews, especially if
knowledge of their relationship was suppressed? But what about
their half-sisters, much closer in time and space? Silence could
divide the siblings from each other as surely as light-years. But no,
if Jole stayed on Sergyar, he'd want to make household arrangements as close to Cordelia as she would permit, throwing their
offspring together as well. They'd be the girls next door, perhaps.

Which led to a fresh and more alarming reflection—given
propinquity, Vorkosigan charisma, and the odds, when they grew

to be teenagers, would some of them want to *date*? Now, there was a hazard of convenient silence that hadn't crossed Jole's mind before. He swallowed a horrified laugh that he had no desire to explain to Miles. Cordelia had a point about starting as you meant to go on. The anonymous-egg ploy was looking less tenable all the time.

Miles cleared his throat. Stared down at the dirt. Looked up. "So, ah—do you think you two will ever marry?"

If she asked me, I'd say yes, Jole thought without hesitation, startling himself. Which made it different from anything else Cordelia might ask of him, how? She could roll him out like a pastry—he resisted the sexual innuendo with only a slight twitch of his lips. The woman didn't know her own strength, fortunately. But all his prior *yesses* had been so fabulously rewarded... He managed, "We haven't discussed it."

"Yet? Or ever?" He swung his heels in an absent rhythm against his sack-seat, a physical tic that ought to have looked juvenile, yet didn't.

Jole couldn't figure out if Miles was more concerned for his mother's future or his father's past, in this line of... interrogation, yes. At least the former ImpSec operative didn't have a hypospray of fast-penta on him at the moment, as far as Jole knew. He stifled an urge to move farther out of reach. "Not any time soon, certainly. She's been very definite about wanting to keep her daughters well clear of certain Barrayaran legal and custody issues. I doubt she'd even consider it till her youngest daughter comes of age, by which time whatever... arrangements we end up with will have been in place for decades, and the question will be pretty moot."

Miles cocked his head. "Decades, huh? You thinking that long-term?"

"*She* certainly has to be, to embark on all this." He allowed, "Although decades do seem to be passing faster than they used to. Maybe more so for her."

Another twitch of a grin from Miles, who was not, after all, *that* much younger than Jole. He half-lidded his eyes, and ventured, "So...do you think you two would ever have a child together? By whatever technical intervention. Given how enchanted she seems with the idea of personally populating Sergyar. Possibly on the theory that if you want something done right, you need to do it yourself."

Jole blinked, blindsided by this new notion. His imagination had been filled with his three potential sons. Might there be a daughter, too, in some more distant someday? It was an oddly mind-melting vision. "I'd think those slots are filled by what she has on ice already. You don't imagine I could talk her into more, surely?"

Miles snorted. "Have you ever heard the phrase, like shooting fish in a barrel?" A reminiscent look came over his face. "Except, actually, that turns out not to be as easy as it sounds. I tried it once, when I was a kid down at Vorkosigan Surleau."

"With what?" Jole couldn't help asking, diverted by this vision of the young Miles. Would his half-brothers be anything like him? Minus the soltoxin damage, thankfully.

"I started with an old bow and arrows I'd found in a shed, but the results weren't too satisfactory. Refraction in the water, plus the bow was too big for me and I was pretty awkward—I'm not sure I could have hit a real target at that age. Plus the fish were slippery buggers. The stunner that I filched from one of the armsmen didn't work all that well, either—the water absorbed the charge. The fish just sort of...grew confused. Swam very oddly. I was just set to try a third test run with a plasma arc stolen ditto when they caught up with me. Sadly. I'll bet that would have been *spectacular*."

Jole choked a laugh. "Or lethal!" Betan science crossed with Barrayaran militarism made an appalling hybrid at age, what, six or seven, maybe?

Miles's lips tweaked back. "Certainly for the fish. But, yes, steam burns and barrel shrapnel for anyone within range, I'm sure. Which would have certainly included me, though in my defense, I had also secured a dustbin lid." He mimed this shield with a sweep of his arm.

Was this a good opening to confess to his frozen sons? Jole, with an effort, pushed himself as far as, "Do you like being a da?" Because nothing said this impromptu grilling had to go in only one direction.

Miles leaned back atop his stack, as if surprised in turn. "It's had its hair-tearing moments, but—yeah, so far I like it a lot. Although it's still a bit scary if I stop to think about it, which happily I don't often have time to. My scope for really screwing up seems hugely expanded. Thank God for Ekaterin."

It occurred to Jole that Miles, too, must once have undergone something like Jole's venture to the rep center. Or maybe he'd had some sort of at-home arrangement—Vorkosigan House's basement-level infirmary, made top-grade during Aral's regency, was presumably kept up-to-date. Perhaps his bride had helped out, rendering the enterprise less lonesome. He wasn't about to ask.

"I can't imagine going it alone as a parent," Miles went on, "although come to think I suppose old Piotr was forced to, when Yuri's War left him with only my da. Half-grown by then, but still. It seems to have been rough sailing for both of them. Disturbing to think that, by the time I came along, Piotr was said to have *mellowed*. Though it might have just been exhaustion." The edge to his faint smile reminded Jole of knives. "They both did all right in the end, though. I guess people do, somehow."

Cordelia's mother had been a widowed parent, too, Jole recalled. He wondered why Miles didn't trot her out as a counterexample as well. The Betan bereaved-family experience seemed to have been much smoother than the Barrayaran, and not only for the absence of a bloody civil war. *There's Cordelia's model*, he realized. *Her mother.* Consciously or unconsciously internalized? Either way, it had left her remarkably confident.

Miles's expression grew more introspective. "My one regret was that I didn't start my kids sooner. Couldn't, I suppose, but... Lizzie and Taurie won't remember Granda Aral, and of course

Selig and Simone never had the chance to meet him at all. Well, he did come to look at the cryofreezer, soon after our marriage when Ekaterin and I had sequestered the six embryos, but that's hardly the same thing."

Jole tried to picture the scene. It must have fallen early in the joint Viceroy and Vicereine's sojourn on Sergyar, during one of their trips home. He would have been left helping hold the fort here in what was now Bobrik's seat. "How did he, er, seem to process it? All the technology?"

Miles wrinkled his nose. "Bemused. I guess. Pleased for us, really pleased, though with my mother standing right there he could hardly have expressed any doubts about the tech. For all that he had worked all his life to drag Barrayar up to galactic standards, medically and otherwise, I'm not sure he expected what that was really going to feel like to him personally. What it would mean to his House, to that central Vor...thing." A ragged wave of Miles's hands, as if futilely trying to encompass the complexity of his history. "He adored the kids when they finally arrived, of course." He glanced away, over the sunlit tarmac. "I thought we'd have more time."

Jole swallowed and, cravenly, said, "Speaking of time, if we want any for lunch..."

"Ah. Yes, I suppose." Miles managed to wriggle down off the stack of sacks without breaking anything, and Jole managed not to annoy him by grabbing for him, a dual victory of sorts.

As they paced back toward the mess hall, Jole trying not to be obvious about shortening his steps, a strange ripple of feeling coursed through him, deep and confounding. *Sunstroke*, he tried to tell himself, but instead it came out, *Please, be born soon. I want to meet you.*

While there is still time.

Shaken, he walked on.

✿   ✿   ✿

Miles arrived back at the Palace late for dinner after his war games; Cordelia ruthlessly carried off Ekaterin right afterward to steal a few more hours of civic garden planning, leaving Miles to deal with his offspring. They suffered no interruptions from explosions, fire alarms, or panicked people pounding on her office door, so she gathered his child-minding went smoothly. She'd readied herself for bed and was doing one last comconsole check—although really, if there was another task waiting, she didn't want to know—when he stuck his head around her door, grunted a greeting, sloped in, and thumped down into a chair.

She sat back and regarded him doubtfully. "And so?" she prodded.

"Eh." He did that thing with his feet; she wondered if he ought to be checked for restless leg syndrome. But they stilled, as if they had wound him up sufficiently for another whirr around the room, and he said, "Had a talk with your Oliver today."

She noted the possessive. A good sign? Or was it more of a rejective, *your* Oliver, *your* problem . . . "Oh?"

"I grant you, he seems a nice fellow—always did—"

"I certainly think so."

"But he's not very *forthcoming*."

She cast him a glinty-eyed maternal scowl across her desk. "Were you *interrogating* the poor man?"

"It wasn't like that!"

Which she construed as, *It was exactly like that.*

"We just had a talk. Perfectly civil. Aired a few concerns. Well, I did, anyway. He listened. You could see he was thinking, but I'm damned if I know what."

"He has a lot on his mind at the moment." She smiled at a sudden memory. "Although it used to be fairly amusing to eavesdrop on him when he was cornered by Nexus diplomats at official functions. He grew very adept at getting more than he gave, to their dismay."

Glumly, Miles rubbed his nose. "I certainly ended up talking more than listening."

Cordelia's lips twitched. "Well, that would be the problem then, wouldn't it?"

He jerked up his chin and bared his teeth back at her.

"So what were you interrogating him about, that it proved so unsatisfactory?"

"Oh, just...plans for the future. His. Yours..."

"Miles—were you actually *demanding to know his intentions?*"

He scrunched a bit, looking shifty. "Not precisely. Well, sort of."

"I think you'd best save those impulses for Helen's suitors. They'll doubtless be coming along any minute now."

Miles gave a theatrical shudder. "Surely not yet."

"You could be surprised. Anyway, Oliver's plans are Oliver's business."

"But if he won't talk about anything that involves you, and you won't talk about anything that involves him, how the hell do I find out about...anything?" he protested.

"Maybe you don't."

He gave an offended snort. "You can't feign that what you do doesn't affect me. I don't expect to have a Betan vote, but some basic information would be nice. At least enough for going on with!"

"I haven't made a secret of my plans. I mean to move the capital, resign the viceroyship, build a home, and raise my girls. That should take me to my century. After that, who knows? Maybe I'll revive my science career. Or retire for real. Or engage a harem to entertain me in my declining years. Foot rubs, lots of foot rubs."

He was startled into a laugh. "Male or female harem?"

"I was thinking male, but I could be flexible."

He appeared to be briefly distracted by this vision, but then, alas, came back on track. "But then what are Oliver's plans?"

"He's still working on them, and I'll thank you to leave him alone while he does it. He's a smart man. He'll figure it out."

"Figure what out? He seems to think you don't want to marry him."

"I don't want to marry anyone, till the girls are launched. After that...will be a new world. Another new world." Her, what...fifth? Sixth?

"Yeah, that's what he said. So how come he knows that, and I don't?"

"He's not hard-of-listening?"

Miles drummed his fingers on the chair arms. The feet started up again.

Obviously, Oliver had not mentioned his boys yet, or this would be a much different and possibly more explosive conversation. Well, she'd registered her views about that; the rest was up to Oliver.

"Gregor said, if I wanted to know more, I should ask you. This implies that there's more to know, or he wouldn't have said any such thing, right?"

Cordelia was more inclined to interpret it as Gregor saying, sensibly, *I'm not touching this with a stick.* But the trouble with handing Miles a stick was that he'd take it and head straight to the nearest wasp nest, and what idiot had ever decided that importing Earth wasps to Barrayar would be a valuable addition to the ecosystem? Speaking of fellow invasive species. Little Miles, who had gritted his teeth through any number of broken bones, had actually cried for that encounter. Screamed, actually. It had taken a couple of hours and some scary drugs to get him settled down. After which Cordelia had taken a military stunner and a poison sprayer and made damn sure it would never happen again. *Speak softly, and carry the right tool for the job.*

But that same attitude was part of what had made the grownup Miles one of Gregor's best Imperial investigators, later in life. He'd plumbed the depths of mysteries and drains with equal tenacity. She was beginning to get an inkling of why his suspects had so often tried to sting him.

"I am under no obligation to gratify your salacious curiosity," she told him. "Just...channel your inner Betan and try to relax, all right? I expect all things to resolve themselves shortly." *One way or another, thank-you-I-think Admiral Desplains.*

"So where *does* Oliver fit into all this?" The corner of his mouth tucked up. "Besides heading the harem, I suppose."

Indeed, Oliver is diligent in all tasks he takes on. Cordelia quashed a smirk, and answered forthrightly, "Where he chooses. He has a certain career decision to make, which is not mine to discuss with you, after which...we'll all know more."

Miles pursed his lips. "Career decision? What career decision? He's Admiral of Sergyar Fleet, for pity's sake!" His eyes narrowed in rapid thought. "They wouldn't move him out of the line at this stage of his career. Resign and go into diplomacy, like Ivan? He'd be good at that. Or—no. Has to be...Komarr Fleet, Home Fleet, Chief of Ops? Thibault is solid on Komarr, Kuprin just got promoted to Home Fleet last year, Desplains is...good grief, has he been offered *Chief of Ops*?"

Argh. She'd forgotten how quick Miles could be, and how eclectically informed. "Miles! I promised confidentiality! I had need-to-know as Vicereine. You don't."

"I need to know—wait, what? That would take him back to Vorbarr Sultana! What is this, hit-and-run love?" He sat up, suddenly seething with indignation. "He seduces you and takes off, and you're not even trying to trip him on the way out the door?"

"First, we seduced each other, and second, he hasn't made it to the door yet. And third, it is all much more complicated than that."

"Which brings us back around to why is that?"

"A few days ago, you were glaring like a suspicious guard dog at him when we so much as snuggled. Have you switched sides?"

"I'm on your side," he grumbled. "If I could figure out what it is."

"I know, love," she sighed. *I just wish you'd be on my side more quietly, somewhere else.*

"Chief of Ops," he mused on, unhelpfully. "Wow. You do know, turning *down* a plum offer like that is something of a career-killer. They think you aren't committed."

"I am aware of the psychology of the high command, yes."

"Not that Oliver's career isn't pretty...pretty mature as it stands."

"That it is."

A wistful look stole over his face—envy for the Imperial military life he'd once aspired to? Frankly, Cordelia thought Miles had been much better placed in ImpSec, where his erratic genius had found its full scope. Sticking him in the regulars would have been a disaster—*had* been, she recalled from the results of just such an early experiment. *We all have our might-have-beens.*

He rolled his cane in his hands, and conceded, "All right. Yeah. That is some serious decision for a working officer. Especially for a prole of his generation who came up out of nowhere."

"If you were in his place, how would you make it?" she asked curiously.

"My life would have to have been radically different, for me to be in his place."

"Granting that. But a speculative scenario. Say, you were courting Ekaterin, and she could not or would not leave Sergyar."

"That...doesn't quite work. Because any woman engaging herself to a senior Imperial officer would know she was taking on the package, presumably. It would be her choice to follow or stay, not his to stay or go. I mean, if he were under orders. Which isn't quite the case here, yeah, true. The only decision I ever made that put my heart on the line like that..." He stopped rather abruptly.

"Mm?"

"Wasn't about a woman," he finished. He added after a meditative silence, "It was about ambition, though. Um. Yeah. I don't think I envy Oliver his dilemma."

Oh, kiddo. You have no idea.

He was watching her face, she realized. He offered, not quite facetiously enough, "I could help trip him if you *want*..."

Eee. "What I *want* is for Oliver to make a decision he won't regret. I don't think either of us can help him with that." She managed to add, "Though I appreciate the thought. It was well-meant." *Potentially disastrous, but well-meant.* "But if you really want to be helpful, go to *bed*, so I can."

He snorted. "Yeah, yeah. I can take a hint." To her relief, he clambered up and limped out, with a backward wave.

The best way to avoid another uncomfortable tête-à-tête with Cordelia's inquisitive son, Jole decided, was to not let himself get caught alone with him. In pursuit of this plan, he invited Kaya and Fyodor along to the next day's lunch in the upstairs dining room of the officers' mess. Between fiendish hijacking sim schemes—Kaya was with Miles's team on the attack side this afternoon—and Gridgrad gripes, avoiding the personal seemed easy, and Jole relaxed back in his chair and let his guests go at each other with his good will.

Until Kaya, after a brief lull while people remembered to chew and swallow, came out with, "What do you most want for your birthday picnic, Admiral?"

Taken by surprise, he answered honestly: "No casualties."

"Amen," Fyodor endorsed this, in a heartfelt growl. He had not yet said, out loud, *I told you so* in Jole's hearing as the event had ballooned, but he had managed a few expressive silences along the way. An appreciative grin flicked over Miles's face.

"The committee has a safety officer assigned," Kaya assured him earnestly. "He's liaising with the Kayburg Guard and everything. But no, seriously."

The committee had obviously detailed Kaya as scout on this burning question, logically enough. Jole dragged his brain into gear. His first pick would be a day alone with Cordelia in Penney's Shack One, obviously not on. His next would be a day alone, period, ensconced somewhere quiet and comfortable, feet up, perhaps with the next issue of the Uni's bio journal and its endlessly strange explorations. A hike, preferably with Cordelia, in the backcountry might be fine, too—packing a picnic for two, not two thousand. He could go on, but probably shouldn't.

Kaya plainly hoped for something simple and manageable, such as a bottle of his favorite liquor—a null set, alas—a pony ride, whatever. And if he didn't come up with an answer, or at least a direction, he risked being lumbered with God-knew-what.

He'd hesitated a little too long. Fyodor, himself a veteran of a career's worth of promotion parties and change-of-command ceremonies, and thus doubtless having no trouble figuring out his dilemma, snorted in amused fellow feeling. "Whatever happened to that lunatic scheme of yours of having a son for your fiftieth, Oliver? Although I suppose that's not something the committee could supply. Unless you adopt one of the junior ensigns, which, let me tell you, could save you a world of steps."

Miles went still, then blinked like a lizard. "Really? Did my mother get to you, Oliver?"

In so many ways. "She pitches the virtues of the new rep center to anyone who will listen. She gets very Betan about it." Two perfectly true statements.

"But how would that square with..." He trailed off, giving Jole that disturbing laser-scanner look he could sometimes come out with, just when you thought he was squirreling off in some other direction or three.

We need to talk, thought Jole, and *No, we don't*. In any case, not here, obviously. "Remember," he said to Kaya, instead, "I have very limited storage space." In his apartment at any rate, though he could probably tap odd corners of the base for stowing anything up to the size of a combat drop shuttle. Fyodor, to his relief, did not point this out.

"If you want to surprise him, try asking my mother for ideas," Miles suggested helpfully.

Kaya took this in with a considering look. "I guess you two have known each other for a long time."

"And so well," Miles murmured. "One gathers." Evaluating, again? Jole shot him a quelling frown.

Fyodor put in, "Right, you do know Oliver will be escorting the Vicereine to this shindig? Don't leave her out of your ceremonies."

"Yes, sir, knew that," said Kaya. "We've asked her to award the prizes for the boot polo tournament."

Boot polo was a prole infantry version of the old Vor cavalry polo, which had used, in its traditional incarnation, to be dubbed "Capture the Cetagandan's Head." Early in Cordelia's service here as Vicereine, someone had once tried to redub it "Capture the Pretender's Head" in her honor, but she had shut that down in a hurry. It involved three opposing teams of men in combat boots, armed with sticks, huffing after a beleaguered ball over a patch of marked-out but ungroomed terrain chosen for its maximum roughness. As were the men, Jole supposed.

"We will be having a medical tent, I trust?" he inquired mildly.

"Oh, yes, sir. With that many people, there's bound to be something come up. We'll have a full field team, set to handle anything from radial bites to indigestion to broken legs to heart attacks." She cast Fyodor a special reassuring smile at that last, which Jole did not think he entirely appreciated.

Kaya and Fyodor mooted a few more bits of news about the picnic which, while it was not Jole's favorite topic, at least beat *More fun with uterine replicators* with Miles sitting right there sucking everything in. The meal drew to a close without further awkward revelations.

Or almost. Jole hit the mess lav along with Fyodor before heading back to help referee the war game sims. As they were washing their hands Fyodor glanced around, ascertained they were alone, and said, "You likely ought to be told—there's a rumor going around you're not just escorting the Vicereine, you're *dating* the Vicereine. Don't know what you want to do to quash it, but, in your ear and all that."

Already? Jole thought, but said only, "Really?"

Fyodor grunted. "Well, it was a more direct term than that. Doesn't alter the heads-up."

So, Cordelia. I guess we're going to test your social theories. "For a change, rumor has it right."

Fyodor's eyebrows climbed. He was silent for a long moment, then said, "That's flying high, prole boy. Don't let your wings get singed."

A brief smile turned Jole's lips. *I had my flying lessons long ago from Aral, who never let me fall.* Had this altitude really become his home country? Perhaps not quite, and a little caution could make all the difference. Knowing when to stop was not exactly a Vorkosigan talent; maybe a Jole must supply. *I am not drunk enough for these thoughts.*

He said only, "I'm hoping for a soft landing." *But where?*

Fyodor did not ask for further elaboration, and Jole did not volunteer it. He dried his hands and led out.

Chapter Fifteen

On the day of the picnic Jole woke at his usual time, wasted half an hour trying to get back to sleep, failed, gave up, and arose to seek coffee. He should have spent last night at the Palace despite the thundering herd of Miles's family and entourage that filled it, tromping freely through Cordelia's privacy—two-year-olds especially being not clear on respecting boundaries, closed doors, or the possibility that someone might have an agenda not including them. Some forty-three-year-olds, as well? Surely they all had to go home soon. Wasn't there a district back on Barrayar missing its count? As it was, he wouldn't see Cordelia today till she picked him up at noon.

He took his mug and went up on the roof to look out over the base, a favored and relatively private viewing spot, not yet baking in the morning air. The weather seemed to be auspicious for the day. People had been trickling back and forth to the picnic site, some twenty kilometers out in the country, for a couple of days, including a convoy last night of teams to set up the pit roasts—real carcasses, not vat meat, *sorry, Cordelia*—and portable latrines. As he watched, another small caravan departed out the front gate, military and private vehicles mixed.

The base would nevertheless not be stripped of its preparedness—Haines had made sure there were plenty of short straws to go around. And then there was Jole's entire working upside fleet, from Sergyar orbit to the wormhole jump-point stations, out of luck except for the rota of personnel on downside leaves or duties. He wondered how Bobrik was getting along up there. Now, if there had been no party, there could have been no such unfairness—ha, there was a counterargument that came too late.

I am fifty.

It was the first, though it probably wouldn't be the last, time that realization had come to him today. *How strange. I used to think fifty was* old.

His eye was drawn to Kareenburg in the distance, spilling out of the broken side of the mountain and onto the red plain. This place had been his home for the last dozen years—but one way or another, not for much longer. The building boom was getting a grip in Gridgrad, despite the fierce starved competition for materials and labor. He realized he had been looking forward to that move as a fresh start, and not just for the region's more attractive environs, water-braided, gray-green and alive after its own peculiar Sergyaran fashion.

Back in his apartment, he found the call light blinking on his comconsole. He sat down to find a message from Ops Vorbarr Sultana, stamped eyes-only but without an urgent flag. He eyed it with a faint and entirely futile dread, albeit not dread of surprise.

Sure enough, the image of Admiral Desplains formed over his vid plate. The Ops chief smiled affably.

"Good day, Oliver. If I have this calculated right, this should reach you just in time to congratulate you on your birthday. Welcome to your next decade. Looking back on my own fifties, it wasn't too bad. Looking ahead—well, who knows.

"I trust my prior message reached you—the pingback said so. If it has somehow gone astray, a copy is attached hereunder.

"I thought I would have heard from you by now, but a check shows that you're having your week's downside leave. I imagine you're out sailing somewhere suitably flat and wet, and that this will find you promptly on your return from the wilds."

His leave, Jole realized gloomily, had so far included no sailing at all, and only two nights with Cordelia. Between the inspection tour out to the *Serg* and the war-game/theft-prevention training exercises, it had all been pretty un-leavelike, so far.

"Again, best wishes on the day. Desplains out."

It was a perfectly cordial-sounding reminder, camouflaged under the birthday greeting, except that they were both keenly aware it shouldn't have required a reminder at all. *Jole, answer your damned mail!* scarcely needed to be said more explicitly.

Desplains wouldn't expect an answer today. Nor tonight, assumed correctly to be devoted to some celebration or another, though Jole doubted Desplains pictured the scope of the field maneuvers so unstoppably in progress. Nor even tomorrow morning, command being fairly tolerant of traditional Barrayaran hangovers as long as they didn't occur during some crunch. But by tomorrow afternoon . . .

Desplains needed his answer; if *yes*, to start making plans, if *no*, to resume his headhunt. Jole *couldn't* let this decision drag out past noon tomorrow.

He blew out his breath and pushed up to head for the shower.

The canopy of the vicereinal aircar closed over them as Oliver slid into his seat beside Cordelia. Rykov—with Ma Rykov beside him in the driver's compartment—glanced back over his shoulder to assure that all was secure, and slipped them into the air.

Cordelia took in Oliver's summer-weight undress greens, standard downside office wear. "Goodness, you look a tad formal for a picnic."

He touched his chest. "The jacket comes off as soon as the opening ceremonies are concluded. It'll be shirtsleeves after that, I promise you." He added after a moment, "Besides, I had a message to record before I left."

Her heart lurched. Had he finally replied to Desplains? And what has his answer been? Nothing about his face or posture conveyed a clue.

He did make a vaguely dissatisfied gesture. "I wanted to say something to all my people out on space duty. Took a bit of thinking so it didn't come out like one of those dire vacation greetings, *Having a fine time, wish you were here.*"

"That seems a reversal, for someone's birthday. Aren't you the one supposed to be getting the greetings?"

"Yes, I spent a good bit of time this morning fielding those. But I thought my troops and techs manning all our—God spare us—budget-built Imperial equipment out there deserved some kind of *well done* acknowledgement from me this day. They get little enough, in peacetime." His mouth twisted. "Usually, the more effusive lip service from on high was a preamble to attempts to cut our supplies and personnel and make it harder to do our actual jobs. We learned to be suspicious of floating praise."

Cordelia snorted appreciation. "Did you at least bring sandals?" She extended her own semi-bare foot, and wriggled it.

"You may risk plague worms, fire radials, and sand rashes in the name of fashion if you choose. I'll stick to my nice regulation shoes, thanks."

And so well polished, but perhaps that wouldn't last the day. At least, she hoped he would eventually relax. This wasn't an Imperial military review, for pity's sake.

He went on, "You, on the other hand, look just like a picnic. Makes me want to open the basket right here." Finally remembering to kiss her hello, he trailed a friendly hand down over her sage-green tank top and rusty-red trousers, floppy in the legs after the Komarran fashion and therefore, she hoped, cool enough while still providing protection. "Did you mean to look like you're planning camouflage?"

"I was thinking about Alys Vorpatril's stern lectures on color coordination, mostly." She flipped at her gauzy swing coat, pretty but delicate—she would probably abandon it about the same time Oliver peeled down.

"You're dressing to match your planet?"

She chuckled. "Maybe that's it."

"So, where are Miles and Ekaterin and the horde?"

"Went on ahead in more cars. They'll meet us there. The kids are really excited. There has been much speculation about cake." Seizing what she figured would be their last opportunity today, she kissed him back, and all too soon, *there* became *here.*

"Happy birthday, by the way," she said as the aircar descended and they broke off.

"We'll see," he said, in a tone of foreboding. Or perhaps forbearing; he was being pretty amiable about all this.

She glanced out. "Oh, my! It looks like a cross between a nomadic tribal camp and Hassadar Fairgrounds. *How* many people did you say were going to show up for this?"

"*Originally*, I thought it was only supposed to be a couple hundred base people, max. That was before half of Kayburg invited itself along."

"I suppose someone will have a head-count..."

The picnic area was spread out on a slight rise along a trickling watercourse, well supplied with spindly trees, though it would be inaccurate to call it a shady grove. An irregular tent-and-booth village was laid out near the center, banks of latrines backing it, with what Cordelia recognized as a brigade-sized military medical tent at the near end and a viewing stand and open area at the far end. Aromatic smoke rose from dozens of widely scattered fire pits, with clusters of people and their picnic supplies defending each, divided by what rationale Cordelia was not sure—by unit? Garrison versus townie? Spacer versus ground-pounder? Half-a-dozen improvised parking areas were filling with a motley assortment of civilian lightflyers, aircars, and lift vans mixed with sturdier-looking military transport vehicles, float-bikes, ground rovers, and possibly wheelbarrows. And, no joke, some horse-drawn wagons and carts, though they seemed to have been unloaded from parked lift vans.

A length of the rise, some outcrops of rocks, and a portion

of the watercourse about two hundred meters on a side were marked off, surrounded by cheering people; a scrum of red, yellow, and blue T-shirted figures heaved across it. The boot-polo team elimination rounds had been going on since midmorning, she understood.

The aircar oozed down to a patented Rykov landing that would not have spilled her champagne had she been blessed with any, followed at close range by the ImpSec car that had been shadowing them. Dutifully, she waited until Kosko's boys and girls had first got out, had their look-round, and opened the canopy for her. A large public venue and, in a bit, public speeches meant that she couldn't legitimately arm-wrestle them into backing off.

A subcommittee of Oliver's officers hurried up to greet them and pass on the final, no really, these are the last changes, schedule of events. By whatever persuasion—broad hints through Kaya?—Oliver had managed to get them to front-load the congratulatory ceremonies, rather than having them fall more naturally between dinner and the fireworks. Thus the last half of the picnic might simulate a day off for its principal. Plotting an early getaway with her? Cordelia hoped so.

Being early for a gig that was running typically late, they seized the chance for a stroll up what Cordelia mentally dubbed the midway. Several open-sided tents housed branches from Kayburg eateries, plus two bars, not yet very busy. At this time of the day, with people's children running all over, their adults gamely trailing, the smaller booths that offered ice cream, cold snacks, and gimcrack toys were a shrewder sell.

SWORD, she was amused to see, really had put up the free kissing booth that Dr. Tatiana had threatened, staffed at the moment by two attractive women and a striking young man. Unlike the restaurants, they were not selling any of their regular services today—Haines had discouraged this with an eye to objections from the base spouses, and Cordelia had softened the economic blow by hinting that really, *everyone* deserved a day off sometime. Stacks of Dr. T's educational book-discs sat at the ready, one being handed out gratis with every kiss, which Cordelia hoped might help with some people's—and not just the younger ones—tangled lives, provided that what was tangling them was lack of accurate information.

Showing support, Cordelia pressed Oliver's arm and they turned in to collect a kiss each, to the applause of a few onlooking picnickers of both sexes, which made Oliver blush quite fetchingly. Oliver only aimed for one of the women, but the other wouldn't let him get away without giving her a turn. Cordelia tried the cute fellow, who grinned bashfully through the kiss, though really, he was much too young for her tastes—thirty, probably. Her lips quirked as Oliver tried not to turn his head at the kid, though their eyes tracked each other briefly.

"Dare you to kiss that one," she whispered in his ear as they turned away, and "Choose your ground," he murmured back.

Music from an amateur band spilled out of another tent, where they also found Cordelia's family. Up front, a gaggle of children were dancing to steps of their own devising, while their elders perched on chairs resting in the shade. Miles, gravely attentive, was being hung off two-handed by his daughter Simone, stomping happily to the beat. Ekaterin sat in the front row holding his cane. Cordelia slid in beside her.

"Is he going to be all right without that?" she asked her daughter-in-law.

"Lots of painkillers tonight," Ekaterin murmured back, "but would you stop them?"

"Not for worlds."

Taurie, brimming with energy and, as far as Cordelia had yet been able to tell, entirely devoid of social fear—or any other sort— bee-lined for Oliver and demanded him as a partner, too. *Ah, the old Oliver-magic, still working.* Given her athleticism and his practiced skills they actually turned in a quite dancelike performance, as he guided her neatly through turns and twirls, if under his elbow rather than in his arms. The morning's odd tension in his face gave way to amusement as she bounced and giggled.

The band, who knew very well who they were, swung promptly into another old backcountry jig, playing even faster.

Cordelia looked around. "Where are Helen and Alex?"

"They went off with Freddie—she and her friends are helping Lon ghem Navitt who is helping that cultural attaché fellow with something or another."

"Ah, Oliver told me about that. We'll have to go check it out."

When Oliver's shoes were no longer quite so shiny, and his face was pleasingly flushed, she mercifully extracted him from her granddaughter's clutches. They made their way slowly along the makeshift promenade, receiving cheery greetings from garrison and town alike; Oliver seemed to remember an astonishing number of his people's names. Cordelia, too, did her best to recognize people back, though years of practice had made faking it no stretch.

Oliver's hand brushed the back of her neck, and she prepared to emit an encouraging purr, but he flicked his fingers down.

"Radial," he explained, trying to squash the hazard with his shoe, but the thumbnail-sized creature evaded death and bobbed erratically away. "As windless as today is, I'll bet they'll come out in force from around that creek at dusk."

"Ah, yes. We'll have to slather the kids with repellent before then." There was a supply in the boot of the vicereinal aircar; she hoped she'd brought enough to coat the whole clan.

Beyond the open area, tucked up under some trees, stood what appeared to be a small, panel-walled maze, its entrance made fetching with flowers in pots, leaves drooping in the still heat. *Discernment Garden*, read the hand-calligraphed sign, and *Test your perceptions! Sight, sound, smell, touch, taste—which is your strength?* Mikos ghem Soren waited hopefully by the entrance to shepherd visitors inside. Nowhere about it did the word *Cetaganda* appear, by which Cordelia detected Kaya Vorinnis's shrewder sense of marketing, though ghem Soren, dressed appropriately enough for a picnic in shirtsleeves, trousers, and sandals, still defiantly sported his clan's colorful face decal. Kaya's hand, too, might be behind the shift in the come-on's tone from vaguely patronizing to cheerful challenge.

Lon drooped rather like the flowers at ghem Soren's elbow, drafted minion—the others, Cordelia discovered upon inquiry, had helped finish setting up the display and then gone off to explore the creek. A quick cross-check on her wristcom assured her that their ImpSec minder had them all in sight, so Cordelia turned her attention back to this earnest effort at cultural outreach.

Diplomatically concealing his lack of enthusiasm, Oliver permitted them to be escorted within, though Cordelia's ImpSec bodyguard went first. "Sight" offered a display of colored cards that reminded Cordelia of optical illusion demos, "touch" a like array of concealed textures that one felt without being able to see. For "sound" ghem Soren presented a row of chimes—no electronics allowed, she gathered. Would that be considered cheating? "Scent" was supplied by a queue of saturated sponges in little bowls, "taste" by apparently identical colorless liquids in, necessarily, tiny disposable plastic cups evidently scavenged from the medical tent—that last compromise plainly pained their host, who explained that the proper presentation involved dedicated hand-made porcelain vessels. To her relief, it turned out that she was not expected to drink the stuff, merely to dip in her tongue and let the flavors seep around her mouth. Ghem Soren was taken aback when Oliver made no errors in his sorting-out, but cheered up visibly when Cordelia did and he could gently correct her in, she gathered, a style copied from some long-ago Cetagandan kindergarten teacher. The kids probably would like this, she decided, and regarded ghem Soren more favorably. Alas, the piece of Cetagandan artwork that they were invited to contemplate at the end of all this perceptual fitness training remained as baffling as ever.

"At least we didn't have to lick it," Oliver muttered to her ear as they exited again. "I'd have drawn the line at that."

She snorfled, covertly.

Ghem Soren, engaged in one last follow-up bit of lecture,

interrupted himself to stare in surprise at his left arm, where a grape-sized radial had stealthily attached itself. To Cordelia and Lon's unified chorus of *"Don't slap it!"* he slapped it.

He did not emit anything so undignified as a yelp, but his mouth did open on a huff of hurting surprise.

"Don't scratch it, either!" Cordelia restrained his right hand, maternally, as it made to do just that. "The remains stick to everything like gum"—though the more usual description was *snot*—"and the acid keeps right on eating away into the skin underneath. Your choices are either to go to the creek and wash it off immediately, or go to the med tent, where they have a concoction to neutralize all that interesting biochemistry. On the whole, I recommend the med tent."

So authoritatively directed, the attaché jogged off, though not without pausing to give Lon a string of last-minute instructions on holding the fort till his return, which Lon, to Cordelia's eye, took in with all the responsiveness of any other fifteen-year-old boy presented with an unwanted chore. *Just like pushing pudding uphill.* And then Oliver's wristcom chimed with the news that they were finally ready for them at the music tent, if you could come over now, sir?

With a call over her shoulder to Lon of, "And do water those plants you're holding prisoner. Their lives depend on you, you know," they headed for the next event.

The crowd at the temporarily repurposed music tent, Cordelia estimated, was just about that core two hundred or so of space officers, dates, and families who had started this whole thing off, back when. The picnic and outdoor atmosphere would at least keep the formalities from being too formal, she trusted. In the background, Blaise Gatti dodged around taking the official vids—she'd had to browbeat him a few times to train him to be *unobtrusive* about those duties, but the lesson seemed finally to have stuck.

The cheery officer acting as birthday master of ceremonies was a lieutenant commander from Orbital Traffic Control, apparently just as much of an organizer out of uniform as in it. He guided the pair of them to seats on the dais behind a comfortingly defendable table, and launched into a suitable opening spiel to welcome the guest of honor, the military cadre, the Vicereine, and the Vicereine's visiting family, who now occupied the whole of the front row, only squirming a little. She was surprised that Alex and Helen had returned for the boring bits—maybe she'd underestimated the draw of cake. Beside her, Oliver braced himself to be fêted with whatever Barrayaran military humor ruled the day.

The first birthday offering, carted up to the table by a grinning lieutenant from the shuttle pilot pool, was a two-liter beer mug, frosty but not filled with beer—the contents were a clear faint green, and clinked with ice. Cordelia had never been sure whether those mugs were a joke, a challenge, or a sign of someone too lazy to reach for refills. The crowd applauded as Oliver dutifully lifted it to his lips and swallowed. His eyes widened, but he set it calmly back on the table and called back, "What, are we having an ice shortage out here today?" which won about the chuckle it merited.

"What?" whispered Cordelia, to which he responded by shoving it a few centimeters her way in invitation to sample.

"Frieda didn't mix this one."

She tasted it, nearly choked on the lethal potency, and hastily shoved it back. "Your patch, I think."

"Are they trying to render me legless before we even start?"

"You don't know your reputation?"

"Which one?"

"You think no one ever noticed you knocking back drinks at Palace receptions? You're widely believed to have the hardest head in the Sergyaran Service."

"It was generally hot. I was *thirsty*," he muttered plaintively. He toasted the crowd and took another sip, sensibly ignoring the calls to chug it. "At least it beats Cetagandan art."

The next foray into military humor was the presentation of a fake campaign medal about the size of a saucer, hung on a colorful ribbon, "for surviving Admiral Jole's inspections." This Oliver received with bemused good will, though then a puckish glint came into his eyes and he capped the moment by turning around and re-presenting it to Cordelia, slipping the ribbon over her head. By the slightly stuffed looks that came over Miles's and Ekaterin's faces, they caught the personal subtext; she hoped no one else here did.

"Is this anything like when the young ladies compete to get their fellows' old dog tags off them?" she asked, resisting the urge to kiss him right there in front of them all.

"You win," he said simply.

There followed a few obligatory retrospectives from some of his senior officers, occasionally dipping into roast but not, to her relief, into tastelessness. And then it was her turn to stand up and deliver her own short speech, to be followed, she understood, by the Serious Gift. She had to take care not to let any of the too-practiced stock phrases from most of the past three years slip out, not least because Oliver would recognize them—*We come to praise Caesar, not to bury him*, thankfully. Appreciation, not eulogy.

Though if Oliver left for Vorbarr Sultana, it occurred to her, there would be a change-of-command ceremony entailed. Military ceremonies, like all ceremonies, tended to echo each other. *Eulogies then, perhaps.*

Cordelia wondered what his officers had finally decided on for the gift. A subcommittee spearheaded by Kaya Vorinnis had tackled her in her office the other day for a short but intense exploration of the possibilities, and gone away looking thoughtful. They had given no hint of their budget, though considering the size of the group and its heavy loading with senior personnel, it probably wasn't going to be like a typical impoverished-junior-officers whip-round.

A stir came from the front of the tent, people making way. "Stand back, Admiral's birthday present coming through...!" An aisle opened up, and down it came two officers hauling, to Cordelia's intense surprise—was it the crystal canoe from Penney's?

No, not quite. It was longer and wider, and the stern was cut off square, suitable for attaching a propulsion unit. Shallow draft, flat bottom, perfect for detailed underwater viewing. Call it a crystal bateau, perhaps. A large red ribbon was wrapped around its midsection, tied in a quite passable bow.

Oliver's mouth dropped open in astonishment; his face lit up, and it was only then that one realized how reserved it had been heretofore. "Woah!"

"We *got* 'im," chortled a happy voice from the mob. "Ha!" Laughter and applause at the success of their surprise.

Oliver, stirring to get up and come down, turned to her. "Was this your doing?"

"No!"

He cocked his head in disbelief.

"It wasn't me. I did point them in Penney's direction, but I thought they were going to go for, I don't know, a gift certificate for a weekend out there or something." In part because she'd hinted around, without ever being able to say it outright, that perhaps they had better pick something that was either immediately consumable, or could be packed up to take back by jump-ship to Vorbarr Sultana. Someone must have researched further. And had a better idea.

She followed him as he stepped eagerly down off the dais for a closer look, and touch, as if he didn't quite believe his eyes. The lines of the craft were enchantingly elegant—it seemed to promise to slip over the water like a dragonfly.

She asked the grinning—yes, engineering officer, "Was it expensive?"

"Naw. We fabricated it ourselves. A vat of canopy plastic and a night in the shop with the big printer, easy."

Oliver, she was reminded, rode herd on a cadre of people who routinely repaired spaceships. She should not have underestimated them, or their resources, or their design skills, even though it appeared some of those resources were borrowed from Imperial supplies.

She murmured to the officer, "If anyone questions the use of equipment or material, you can tell them the Vicereine authorized it."

His eyes twinkled. "Thank you, Your Excellency."

"Does it float?" Oliver asked, a bit breathlessly.

"Yep, we had it out for field trials this morning," another officer told him smugly, watching him run loving hands over the smooth thwarts. Instant infatuation, it appeared, wasn't just for romance anymore. "It floats in any attitude you put it, including upside down, longitudinally, or full of water."

All right, any well-liked officer might get a birthday whip-round in his honor. But this had taken real time and thought, and a shrewd awareness that could not be plucked off the shelves in the base exchange. More—he'd invited plenty of his colleagues out on the water with him over the years, they all knew about that interest; she'd have guessed they would have presented him with a sailing hull, not something so, so *on-top* of his latest changes. *Yeah.* Oliver's command style was not much like Aral's, and he'd always imagined it as inferior therefore. But in this, she thought, they were alike; each had won loyalty by first giving it. *How can he abandon this life?*

After some more of the attendees milling around and taking turns crowding up to get a better look at the Serious Gift, she quietly recommended to their emcee to move it forward or face a cake riot from the front row. *Yeah, let them eat cake.* He took the directive to heart, and shortly the group was transmuted into people standing around trying to balance their portions of carbohydrates, grease and sugar on the inevitable too-flimsy disposable plates. Or smearing same on their faces, depending on their ages and/or degree of inebriation. The base mess had supplied cake abundantly.

She and Oliver recaptured their chairs, which came with the only usable table in the tent. With the thoroughness that distinguished him, Oliver ate his piece, alternating with sips from the giant drink, which must have been a horrifying taste combination. Cordelia took advantage and slipped her portion to the nearest frosting-smeared grandchild doing an unconvincing impersonation of a famine victim.

"You don't have to drink all that," she advised Oliver, who was still valiantly sipping. "No hapless potted plants in here, but outside you'll have an entire desert to slip it into, and no one the wiser."

"But they gave me the expensive stuff," he protested, by which she concluded that the alcohol was already gaining on him. Although Oliver's weirder frugal impulses while drunk weren't only from his early prole upbringing—space duty reinforced parsimony. Like gilding the lily in reverse.

Making a Viceregal decision, she took it away from him, which he did not protest, and no one else dared object to. At long last, he divested his uniform jacket and opened the round collar of his shirt, looking vastly more comfortable and, oddly, more himself thereby. And then, after a short conference to assure that the crystal bateau would be safely delivered to temporary storage back at the base—for which, of course! it appeared the techs had already made provision—it was time to decamp for the boot polo field.

⚬⚬⚬   ⚬⚬⚬   ⚬⚬⚬

"Have you ever played boot polo, Oliver?" Ekaterin asked in curiosity as they were ushered to a row of canvas seats under an awning, reserved for the honored guests. Lesser watchers had taken to ground sheets laid out on the slope overlooking the playing field.

Jole shook his head. "Not me. I'm an officer."

She looked surprised. "Is it against regs, then?"

He chuckled. "There are no regulations for boot polo. The game started back in the Time of Isolation as a camp and garrison pastime for bored soldiers. They made it up themselves for themselves out of what they had on hand, including the rules, such as they are—of which the first was *no officers allowed*. That's part of why there's no set number of players to a team, either, though in play they do try to keep the teams near-even."

The Admiral and Vicereine's party had arrived in time for

the deciding match of the day, between the surviving teams of
the prior rounds. As a result, the sides were more varied than
usual, with the winners of the base men's, the ISWA women's,
and the Kayburg town sets pitted against each other. Upholding
Kayburg's honor was the team from the municipal guard, mixed
in gender, but salted with a few Service veterans who had obviously provided expertise. The base men, in the red T-shirts, were
considered stronger but tireder, the ISWA women in blue lighter
but smarter, and the yellow-shirted Kayburg team featured a pair
of players, a large guard sergeant and a skinny female secretary,
who had shown a killer knack for hooking. The secretary, Jole
understood, was the more vicious, with a fiendish skill at rolling
opposing players through the fire-radial mounds, of which today's
field boasted four, all rather flattened by now.

Cordelia leaned over to confide to Ekaterin, "Aral was the
first Barrayaran to discover that underground species of radial,
you know. On our opening hike here."

Ekaterin looked suitably impressed; Jole tried not to laugh.
He'd heard that story.

Miles escorted Taurie and Lizzie off for a look around; after a
bit his voice floated back: "No, darling, you can't pet the hexaped.
It would bite your hand off, and then your Grandmama would
execute it, which wouldn't be fair to the poor beast, now would
it?" A surly hiss underscored this.

Jole craned his neck; Ekaterin turned anxiously in her seat.
Down on the sidelines stood a large cage containing one of the
region's iconic native creatures. It was about the mass of a pig,
though with longer legs ending in clawed feet: six-limbed, flat-
faced and neckless, with a sharp and heavy parrotlike beak. Its
rust-red fur, Jole considered, was about the only attractive part
of it, assuming you ignored the smell.

The mini-zoo expedition returned shortly, all hands still
accounted for, Miles grinning. Jole watched him as he sat with an
oof. "So why do we have a hexaped today? Did someone decide
they needed a mascot?"

"I'm told there are a number of local rules here for wildlife hazards on the playing field."

"This is true."

"Trouble is, every creature able to move has evidently fled far from your noisy occupation. So a hunting party went out last night and *caught* some, so as to be able to release one per game onto the field. Keeping it fair and even, y'see."

Jole made an amused face. "All right, the players are all armed with their sticks, but what about the innocent bystanders?"

"All the refs are carrying stunners. Though whether for obstreperous hexapeds or argumentative players, my informant didn't quite make clear."

"And, ah . . . how has this worked out so far?"

"Disappointingly, I was told. Almost all of them dashed straight through the crowd and ran off, except for one that went to ground in a hole in the creek bank and still hasn't come out."

"I see." Jole grinned and took a swig of his hard cider. A float-pallet load of cases had been bestowed on them a bit ago by one of his officers from B&L, whose sister-in-law owned an orchard and cidery north of New Hassadar. After a long start-up, this was the first year of production, but only enough for the extended family—commercial amounts were hoped for next year, when they would also have to start pasteurizing. The brew was smooth and tasty, he had to admit, if also cloudy and a peculiar color—full of vitamins and animals, certainly. The Vicereine, always a supporter of colonial enterprise, had accepted the offering with pleasure, and the B&L officer had gone off to com his relatives and brag about it.

The crowd stirred as the players filed onto the field and a ref carried out the wooden ball, about the size of a cantaloupe and brightly painted. The original balls had often been cannon balls, readily found lying about in rusting stacks in old forts, but wood and even solid plastic was preferred these days because players could get a better loft and more distance with them. The painting was a tradition that had started during the Occupation.

"Hm," said Jole.

Cordelia glanced at him.

"That's the ghem Navitt clan face paint today, I see." Very recognizable, even at a distance. "Any, ah, diplomatic concerns about that, Vicereine?"

Cordelia stared thoughtfully. "On the whole...no."

"Right-oh, then." Jole settled back and drank more cider.

A familiar, but surprising, voice hailed him from the side, "Admiral Jole!"

He turned and waved a welcome. "Dr. Gamelin, Dr. Dobryni! Glad you could make it." The Uni bio department was the only outside group Jole himself had personally invited, after it had become clear that there was no keeping this blow-out from proliferating. The two professors were trailed by four others—from their ages, students; from their gawking, newbie visitors. He encouraged introductions, and indeed, they turned out to be those Escobaran grad students Gamelin had threatened, quite startled to find themselves meeting the Vicereine. From their expressions, this smiling, tousled woman in picnic clothes toasting them with local cider was not what they had expected. Cordelia was an effect Jole never tired of watching.

"We heard you had a hexaped!" said Dr. Dobryni.

"Yes, and very bilateral it is, too. Right over there." Jole pointed cordially. "Help yourselves."

Ciders in hand—one student was looking *very* hard at the murk, clearly wishing for a bioscanner—they shuffled off to marvel at the biota, and soon Jole heard Dobryni's voice drifting back, "No, don't try to pet it..."

Thwacks and cries drew their attention back to the field.

"What odds d'you give today?" Miles asked him.

"Well, the base boys are bigger and rougher, but they also have more standing issues with the Kayburg guard. The ISWA girls are smaller—which may be an advantage in this heat—can you speak to that?"

"Sometimes true. No doubt why high command sent me to the arctic, on my first assignment."

Jole chuckled. "And they've probably been drinking less all

day. And the women's teams are generally better at keeping their attention on getting the ball in their basket, instead of disabling opposing players. So I wouldn't count them out."

Miles explained aside to Ekaterin: "With three teams, the obvious strategy is to hang back and let the other two wear each other down, then swoop in. Everybody knows this, so they pay attention to not letting each other slack off. For a game so devoted to bashing each other, it's remarkably cooperative." Though such cooperation could shift around suddenly and rapidly.

"Are they allowed to hit each other with those sticks?" A clatter echoed from the field. The sticks resembled field hockey sticks, but with a larger, curved blade, the better for scooping up the cranium-sized ball and lobbing it.

"Well, there's no hitting, grabbing, or tackling. Or bludgeoning. But tripping—hooking—is permitted. If a player's stick breaks, they're not allowed to replace it till the next goal change, so there's some motive not to get too carried away."

The goals were three baskets sited around the field according the evil ingenuity of the crew laying it out. Today, one was out on the far side of the field, one was fastened to the highest point of the rocky outcrop, and one was stuck down in the creek bed, under water. With each point scored the teams rotated baskets, to keep the playing field even.

Taurie, watching the players shift and run, bounced with excitement. Lizzie went off to covet her neighbor's hexaped and pelt the biologists with questions. Could they be tamed to ride? Pull a cart...? The disappointing scientific consensus was not, but human attempts to domesticate Sergyaran creatures were barely begun, so what might the future bring...?

"Where are all the twins?" Jole asked, finally noticing that Ekaterin was actually sitting down for a change, and that the cloud of chaos surrounding the Vorkosigans was oddly reduced.

"Gone off with their nanny and two ImpSec minders to that swimming hole upstream. I hope they're all right." She glanced uneasily at her wristcom.

The organizers had dammed the creek with rocks three days ago and allowed it to fill up to provide a pool for the picnickers—cleared of skatagators and other aquatic biohazards—and, not secondarily, to provide a water reservoir for the fireworks tonight, just in case.

Jole had glimpsed it earlier. He sighed. "I suppose it really doesn't have enough scope to try out the bateau." Cordelia smiled and drank more cider. That trial would have to wait for another day. *There will be time*, Jole told himself, and then, *Will there?*

Miles studied him sideways. "Nice boat, that."

"Gorgeous."

"Be kind of hard to fit in a space officer's luggage allotment, though."

His mother frowned at him. "At Oliver's rank, I'm sure his allotment could be expanded to include anything up to and including his lightflyer."

"Eh, I suppose." Miles subsided.

It's not my biggest possessions that are the hitch, Jole reflected. *It's the three smallest.*

Cries of triumph and outrage sounded from the field as the ersatz head was lobbed into a goal basket, and he returned his attention to the game.

In due course, the boot polo slammed to its close-fought close, and Cordelia handed out the award ribbons and the donated cases of beer. The blue shirts won today, to the applause of their dates, spouses, and kids, who carried them off in triumph to, probably, fix dinner. The losing teams glumped away, a good portion of them to the med tent. If they'd kept their minds more on the game in front of them and less on old outside grudges, Jole thought the final results might have been different, but so it went.

There had been a wail of protest midgame from Lizzie at the waste of a perfectly good hexaped, bought off with a consoling paternal murmur of, *It's all right, honey, it's just run off home to all its brother and sister hexapeds*, which seemed to suffice. Jole found himself taking mental notes on the spin-doctoring technique.

Then it was time to gather up their party and go to their designated roasting pit node and eating area. Jole was just as glad to be strolling in late. Their dinner group was loaded with the same senior tech officers responsible for the crystal bateau, whose idea of setting up a campsite ran to such suggestions as, "Hey, let's try speed-starting the fire with an infusion of pure oxygen!" Because inside every senior tech officer was a junior tech officer who'd been on a short leash for a long time.

However, everything had settled down by the time Jole, Cordelia, and the Vorkosigan clan arrived to be distributed among a couple of dozen portable tables. The side dishes were a pleasant mix of contributions from family potlucks and the base mess. The roast was about half a cow, resurrected from the fire pit to either a divine culinary apotheosis, or a gruesome field dissection, depending on one's point of view—Lizzie's was right at the servers' elbows, asking questions. Since that crew included two ship's surgeons and three medtechs, the resemblance to a teaching autopsy grew marked.

Special vat-meat briskets were provided for the moderns, headed by but not limited to Cordelia. She sighed at her Barrayaran family's unselfconscious carnivory, but passed no censure. In due course, Alex and Helen were cleaned of their coating of grease and sauce and, trailed by their ImpSec minder, a female sergeant named Katsaros, allowed to go find Freddie.

The level rays of evening, throwing long shadows through the slender trees, shifted toward sunset and the swift twilight of the tropics. Unlike in higher latitudes, no one here was going to have to wait till going-on-midnight for the final official treat of the day. Which suggested to Jole that a midevening getaway with Cordelia might actually gift them with some real private time before their well-earned exhaustion set in. Was this too ambitious a fantasy for a man of—he barely winced anymore—fifty? Around the picnic area, the fizz of sparklers and snap and squeal of bottle rockets and other small private fireworks enlivened the air, foretastes of the booming pleasures to come.

Jole was mellowing out with his umpteenth bottle of cold

cider—it wasn't that high in alcohol, but people kept *handing* them to him—when Cordelia's wristcom chimed with the ImpSec code.

By her side, Jole came uneasily alert as she raised the comlink to her lips. "Vorkosigan here."

"Vicereine? Sergeant Katsaros here. We're having a bit of a situation over by that Cetagandan attaché's, um, art installation. It's under control now, but I think we need you. Neither of the kids were hurt, really."

That last fetched her; she was on her feet and moving in an instant. Jole lumbered up to pursue her, more for intense curiosity than any belief that Cordelia was going to need his slightly inebriated help. Miles and Ekaterin were delayed by their scramble to make sure the other four children were still present and accounted for at the dinner, and covered, before they could follow on. Cordelia waved them back with a, "I'll call you if you're wanted!"

Cordelia and Jole headed at a jog-trot out of the picnic grove and across the open area in front of the viewing stand, now undergoing its final decorations for the upcoming fireworks. Beyond the clearing, he could see the roped-off staging area where the official display was being prepared under the supervision of a volunteer crew of base explosives experts. The evening crowd was thickening rather than thinning down, as a lot of not-necessarily-invited Kayburgers streamed in for the promise of a show pushed right up to the borderline between *fireworks* and *munitions*.

The Discernment Garden hove into sight—or its remains. The wall panels had been flattened, the tables overturned, the flowers kicked out of their pots, and the most repulsive stink rose from the ruins, apparently the effect of smashing all the bottles of scents and flavors together on the ground. Half-a-dozen each of uniformed base security personnel and Kayburg guards held at stunner-point what looked like most of the base men's losing boot-polo team, cross-legged on the ground with their hands behind their heads—some looking sheepish, some scared, some surly, and all drunk. A few red-shirted bodies lay in silent, stunned heaps. One man was stretched out on his back, moaning.

Alex, Helen, and Freddie were clustered around Sergeant Katsaros, who stood boots apart, stunner drawn, scowling at the guardsmen's catch. Lon ghem Navitt hovered anxiously over Mikos ghem Soren, sitting bent over clutching his stomach, some fist-sized red marks showing on his face, his nose leaking blood. Apparently attracted by the stench, a smattering of radials bobbed about, making tentative passes on the just and the unjust alike or mustering in little gleaming phalanxes around the puddles.

Cordelia drew in a very long breath. Jole, prudently, stepped back a pace to give her room to swing. Her glance took in the clues, assembling the probable course of events, hardly mysterious. However much force the uniformed guards were presenting now, it was plain they must have turned, if not a blind eye, a very nearsighted one in this direction when the altercation had first commenced, or the vandalism could not have reached this stage.

Alex looked shaken, Helen was seething with fury, and Freddie had retreated into that sturdy stolidity he'd last seen her assume when standing next to a hard-to-explain burnt-out aircar. Cordelia's first words were mild and directed at the juniors. "You kiddos all right, here?"

"Yes, Grandmama," Alex mumbled, but Helen burst out, "They were breaking down the stuff we helped put up! And they knocked down Lon! We *had* to do something!"

"I *told* her we were too outnumbered to mix in!" said Alex. "But then that guy picked her up, so I had to go in after her!"

A hand stemmed the spate. She asked the dirt-smeared Freddie, "Did you get banged around any in all this?"

"Eh." She shrugged. "Maybe a little."

By which Jole gathered she was in the *No arterial blood or broken bones, no foul,* camp. Fyodor, he was sure, was going to take a very different view—that she had not yet called him was self-evident. It would be *wrong* to look forward to that...

Cordelia was continuing her initial assessment. "Sergeant, report?"

"I'm sorry, Your Excellency. The kids got ahead of me. I shot the jerk who was shaking Helen, and shouted *ImpSec, halt!* but some of them were too stupid-drunk to hear, or listen."

"I kicked him, first," Helen offered. She sniffed in satisfaction.

"Backup arrived"—Katsaros glowered at the security teams— "eventually. And here we are."

"So we are." That flat, unfriendly tone reminded Jole that Cordelia *had* been a ship captain, once.

She walked in among the late boot-polo team, who scrunched and exchanged mutters of *Crap, the Vicereine!* and *You morons!* Reaching down, she jerked the supine moaner half up by his T-shirt, and growled, "Are you the man who laid hands on Aral Vorkosigan's granddaughter?"

"If I'da known who she was," he gasped out, "I wouldn'ta touched her!"

"You know," said Cordelia after a reflective moment, "that argument doesn't help your cause nearly as much as you think."

"...she hit me first...?"

For all his stubble, muscle, and stink, the fellow couldn't have been much more than twenty, Jole estimated. Cordelia, he suspected, was making a like evaluation, for the next thing she said was, "Do you have sisters?"

"Yes?"

"How many?"

"Three?"

"Older or younger?"

"Both?"

"I see." She let go of his shirt, and he thumped abruptly back to the ground. She stood up and sighed.

"All right. I rule that this is not an ImpSec matter." Not treason, in other words, or treasonlike, or in any case an order of magnitude more hurt than any of these goons on the ground had ever imagined coming down on them before. "Base Security can take them in hand." Base Security braced; the Kayburg people stepped back, looking relieved to unload this mess onto their military colleagues. "Put them all in the base tank for tonight. I'm sure you can work out suitable charges. Don't forget *unprovoked attack on a diplomatic guest.* And you can let your chain-of-command know that I *will* be following up personally tomorrow."

"As will I," said Jole. It was hard to make out which, the arresters or the arrestees, looked more apprehensive.

A couple of medics finally turned up, and Cordelia directed them on to Lon and Mikos. Brushing off a few more radials that tried to bumble into her hair, she added, "Oliver, could you escort Helen and Alex back to the grove for me? I'll be along soon."

"Certainly." He gestured the kids away. Freddie, perhaps out of some dim sense of standing by her troops, went to help Lon.

"Is Grandmama very mad at us?" Alex whispered as they turned to make their way back across the parade ground.

"Angry, certainly, but not at you," Jole reassured him. "Of all the people involved here, you two have the best excuses for acting like eleven-year-olds."

Helen frowned, apparently scorning this defense.

Alex looked up and stared. "What is *that*?"

Jole followed his gaze, then stopped and scrunched his eyes a few times for focus. A vast cloud of blur was spiraling in toward them—ah. Yes. "That's a radial swarm." Just like the one he'd had to have scrubbed off his lightflyer a few months ago, followed by a refinishing job. "You don't usually see them gathered in those numbers at this altitude. Good grief!"

Other people, across the grounds and in the stands, had spotted the swarm, and were yelling and pointing in dismay.

"They're coming this way," said Helen uneasily.

"They certainly are." As he hesitated, wondering whether to hurry the kids back to the trees—no, definitely not—or forward to the bleachers, better, an enthusiastic soldier holding a large-sized bottle rocket, its fuse burning, came charging out of a cluster of his friends to position himself beneath the cloud.

"This'll drive them off!" he yelled.

From behind him, Jole heard Cordelia scream at the top of

her lungs, *"No, don't!"* just as the trail of red sparks began to streak upward in the gathering dusk. Too late...

Time seemed to stretch, but not very far. Jole reached deep into himself and found a parade-ground voice the like of which he'd seldom used before, a reverberating bellow: *"COVER THE KIDS!"*

An instant later, the firework burst in a brilliant flare of blue and gold, spreading out like a flower. An instant after *that*, the sparks struck the myriad of floating radials.

The firestorm was astounding. With a vast bass *whoomp*, it spread out through the mass of creatures; as each exploded, the incendiary fragments of its demise spread in turn, in a chain reaction of chemical conflagration, to ignite any that had escaped the first bombardment, which exploded in turn. The heat and light and sound pulsed in waves. There was nowhere to run. There was no *time* to run.

Jole ripped off his shirt, flung it around the twins, clutched them to his torso, and bent over them. "Stay tight!" he yelled into their hair as they tried to bolt, or maybe just to see out. "Keep your faces down!"

And then his world turned into a pelting rain of flaming snot.

Chapter Sixteen

The patter of firedrops trailed off around them, and Jole dared to look up and around. He blinked against the kaleidoscope combination of neon afterimages, and fragments of radial on the ground burning out yellow-orange-red, then dark. A few last splats sounded as those bits that had exploded upward, and therefore had farther to fall, hit late but hard.

The twins squirmed in protest of his grip, but he seized them tighter as his head swiveled around to check the *ohdearGOD!* fireworks staging area on the far side of the parade ground. The adrenaline surge of purified terror that he had experienced only a few times in his life sluiced through his body, and he froze, unsure whether to run, dragging the kids along, or throw them on the ground with himself on top. After a second, his dazzled eyes made out that the frantic activity over there was not people sprinting away in all directions, just figures grabbing up assorted fire-dousing equipment, raised at the ready against this unexpected assault from the skies. The incendiary shower had fallen just short of them. And therefore mostly around him, but in that instant he was willing to consider it a fair trade.

Then the pain cut in, a spatter of echoing fire all over his back as if he had been bombarded by a squadron of the nastiest wasps ever bioengineered. *Cetagandan assault wasps!* and the image struck him as so funny that he shook with laughter. Alex and Helen, finally squirreling out of his slackening grip, stared at him in new alarm. He peered back, relaxing as it came clear by their lack of screams that he'd succeeded in sheltering them.

People who hadn't been blobbed were running up; those who had been were running more *around*. Nearby cries were undercut by distant applause, and a general sense of movement toward the parade ground as more-remote witnesses imagined that the fireworks were starting early.

Sergeant Katsaros was the first to arrive, holstering the stunner that, Jole had a fractured impression, she had been firing futilely into the air. If she'd had a plasma arc, that ploy might have helped, reducing the burning bits to ash before they'd reached the ground. *Right reflexes, wrong weapon,* Jole's spinning mind analyzed. Automatically, his eye checked her for burns, but she seemed to have evaded the worst of it.

"Sir, you're hurt!" cried Katsaros.

"That's all right, Lieutenant," Jole chirped. "The enemy couldn't hit an elephant at this dist—" and bent over again, laughing helplessly. This reassured neither the sergeant nor the twins, who edged away from him as their grandmother galloped up. So sad when people didn't get his jokes. *Cordelia* would get his jokes... He tried to tell it to her again, but he lost the thread, and his sentence ended in word salad. He did manage to add, "For God's sake watch where you step, in those sandals."

She gripped his shoulders, avoiding the throbbing wasp stings and turning him to face her—oh, good, no burns in her hair or on her face—"Oliver, are you in shock?"

He squinted, considering this question seriously. His hands were shaking, his belly shuddering as if cold. Triage, an officer had to do proper triage..."I think so...?" *Ow. Ow.* He quaked again with laughter, trailing into giggles that he choked off because they sounded disconcerting even to him.

"Get him to the med tent," Cordelia ordered someone urgently.

He had not the faintest desire to protest. He gestured the twins into her charge, redundantly, as they had both glued themselves to her waist, and let the medtechs hustle him off the field.

He considered the score. *Sergyar One, Oliver . . . Everything. Yes.*

So, that's what an epiphany feels like. I'd no idea they were so painful . . .

After one of the most aggravating hours of her life, Cordelia finally made it to the med tent, Miles limping at her elbow. He'd been dispatched by Ekaterin from the grove to follow them up, and had made it to the parade ground in time to witness, but fortunately not to experience, the radial blast. He'd taken the shaken twins in charge as she'd dealt with the immediate on-site aftermath, which had helped; they were now passed back to their mother, temporarily.

The intake area to the med tent had been filtered down to only mild chaos by the time they arrived. She demanded Oliver, but received instead his physician, a medical colonel and burn specialist, whom she did not savage because he guided her inside promptly. She had to give the Service credit: however weak they were on, say, gynecology, they were right on top of trauma.

"Fortunately, we were well set up to handle burns this evening," he told her, far too cheerily. "Having twenty people hit us at once was a bit of a challenge, but let me tell you, we didn't jump the Admiral to the head of the queue because of his *rank*. In here."

It wasn't exactly a private room, but it was blocked off with a better grade of canvas. An array of specialized medical equipment and a spent IV were shoved to one side, footed by a daunting mound of rolled-up soiled linens spilling over damply from some kind of catch-basin. Oliver, shirtless, lay on his stomach on a treatment table, head pillowed on his crossed arms. He raised his face as they entered, and smiled. "Ah. There you are."

"Are you in much pain?"

"Not since the drugs cut in." His smile widened. In context, it was not all that comforting.

Miles stumped around to stare at his back, and whistled.

"What does it look like?" asked Oliver, attempting and failing to crane his neck. "I haven't seen a mirror."

"You look like some horribly diseased leopard," said Miles, ever frank. He added after a contemplative moment, "Or leopard frog."

"That would be the burn ointment," said Oliver. "Probably."

"Well, and the blisters and bleeding ooze. They seem to have done a good job cleaning out all the radial bits. Somehow."

"Painfully. They were playing around back there with surgical hand tractors, and some kind of cold slop, for a couple of hours."

Twenty minutes, mouthed the doctor to Cordelia.

"Yeah," breathed Miles. "I owe you big, Oliver. If not for you, those burns would be all over Alex and Helen."

Oliver shrugged. "You'd have done the same."

"No," said Miles simply, "I couldn't have. I'm too short. I'd damn well have *tried*, certainly."

"I was going to ask you this," said Cordelia to Oliver, "but you're pharmaceutically impaired." She turned to the physician. "They're holding the fireworks for him. They sent me in to see if he could make it or not."

Oliver lifted his head again. "While they might make me flinch, just now, I *was* looking forward to them."

"If you can sit up for an hour, I think it would be a good idea to reassure your people. There's, well...not quite a panic out there, but certainly a good deal of anxiety for you." Which she had entirely shared. And they absolutely did not need rumors of his death, however greatly exaggerated, to start circulating.

Oliver's brows twitched up. "That's touching, when you think about it. Though they could just be anxious for the fireworks, you know. Been a lot of anticipation for them."

A medtech entered carrying more supplies, and the colonel temporized, "Let's finish getting the dressing on those burns, first."

The two collaborated on fitting a permeable thinbrane and a protective gauze over his back, with an annex to the back of his neck. Cordelia helped him sit up, sock feet dangling over the side of the table. He squinted a bit woozily.

The physician frowned. "While I would prefer to admit him to the base hospital for overnight observation, we've done all we can for him for now. Such severity of burns over"—an assessing glance—"that percentage of your body is *not* a trivial injury, and if you try to treat it as such, I'll put you on the lesser painkillers without hesitation."

Oliver grinned. "So sit me up on a bench for an hour—I'm definitely not sitting back in any chair—whisk me off to my nice quiet apartment in the luxury of the vicereinal aircar. I don't see a problem here."

"I thought I'd take you back to the Palace," said Cordelia. "I have a perfectly good on-call physician who's had nothing more exciting to do for weeks than treat skinned knees, and the infirmary there could handle anything this place could. And I agree, I don't think you should be alone tonight."

"I could endorse that," agreed the physician. He gave her a special approving smile, which she had no trouble interpreting as, *By all means, let's put this patient into the hands of the one person who* outranks *him.*

"I wanted to get back to my apartment to—no." Oliver turned his head and frowned at Miles. "I need to talk to you, first. Later. Tonight. This might do."

"Oh?" Miles looked for enlightenment to Cordelia, who shrugged, *No clue.*

Oliver's shirt proved ruined, so there followed a short delay to seek an alternative—"*I'm not going out there in one of those damned things that flaps open in the back!*"—which was found in the tunic of a set of surgical scrubs, loose fitting and clean. That its blue brought out the color of his slightly glazed eyes was a personal bonus that Cordelia kept to herself. Miles knelt and helped him with his shoes, which, after one abortive attempt to bend down and do them himself, he bemusedly permitted.

"Five days' medical leave at the minimum," said the physician firmly, "and you don't go near a shuttle until I clear you personally, understood? Sir." With a stream of further instructions about liquids, electrolytes, and when to call on his direct comcode, all documentation sensibly copied to the Palace medico and Cordelia's wristcom, the physician released him on parole to the Vicereine.

The cheers and applause as they made their way to their reserved seats in the stands assured Cordelia that she'd judged the mood, and needs, of the crowd correctly. The cheers turned to hoots and whistles as Ekaterin, waiting with the restive children, stood up and gave Oliver a smacking kiss. Not to be outdone, the rest of the Vorkosigan girls insisted on following suit, including Simone—*Ah, my granddaughters have good taste—hope it survives puberty*—Helen last and a bit self-consciously. Sheepish, Oliver waved thanks and sat.

"You were a hero," Ekaterin told him. "Certainly to me."

Oliver studied the parade ground from this vantage. "I looked a damned fool, I imagine."

"It did make for a memorable birthday," sighed Cordelia.

Oliver shook with quiet laughter. "Yeah. I'm sure the scars will heal in time."

Cordelia's hand stole down between them and gripped his, which gripped back. And then the first whistle, boom, and blaze of the show began, drowning both further speech, and any need for it.

Miles came to Jole in the dark garden, bearing the bottle of cider he'd requested and a liter of oral electrolytes that he hadn't. He didn't refuse either one. Lining them up on the little table, he waved at the wicker chair. "Pull up a seat." Jole had appropriated the bench, a bit hard on the butt, but—backless.

The garden was all shadowed leaves and mysterious vegetative shapes above the colored lights that outlined the pathways, the air cool and soft after the heat of the day. A faint organic night music from the little creatures that lurked unseen, Sergyar on another scale, overlay a more distant human hum and haze of light from the town beyond. Miles sat, his features faintly limned by the path lights, red and green and blue, and laid aside his cane. His posture was relaxed but his eyes were very attentive. The Emperor's key investigator, facing off all unbeknownst with one of the most willing informants of his career.

Willing, of course, was not the same thing as *easy*.

Jole covered his last hesitation with a swallow of cider, dutifully followed up with a swallow of the electrolyte solution, *gah!*, then hastily chased the latter with another swig of cider. Maybe a shot of gin would improve it, the way Old Earthers had used to lace their quinine medications? Not an experiment for tonight, no. The painkillers were still working, but on some deep level his body knew how much it was injured, and was not really cooperating with command central. Best move this along.

Miles took a swig of his own drink—at this hour something mixed by Frieda, Jole suspected—and chose to help out. Maybe he wanted to go to bed, too. "So, ah . . . what did you want to talk to me about?"

"Too many things, probably. The past. The present. The future . . ."

"Sounds comprehensive, yeah." Miles tilted his head. "Let me guess. You are trying to work up to explaining to me that my mother has offered you an egg or eggs. Which is a deeply weird bribe, but that's my mother. Am I right?"

"Yeee . . . no. Yes and no. Not quite. It's more complex."

"You know, people keep telling me that, and then not telling me *what*. Makes me ready to bite." Since he didn't even look ready to stand up again, Jole figured the threat for empty.

Where to begin? *Somewhere, anywhere, just start and it will all unravel.* "You did know your father was bisexual, yes?"

A slight eyebrow lift. "My awareness of that has shifted over the years. I have a pretty good handle on it now. I think."

"Well"—Jole took a breath—"so am I."

A much longer silence. Miles's voice came again, carefully ironic: "So, how long has my mother had this questionable fetish for bisexual Barrayaran admirals? I don't think even the Betans have earrings for that one."

Jole barked a laugh. "I expect not. Well, the bisexual part, no problem for them. The Barrayaran-admirals part might land her in involuntary therapy."

"That . . . may actually be less a joke than you think. If some of what she's told me about how she broke from Beta after the Escobar war is true."

Jole had heard a little—he'd have to follow up and extract the full tale from Cordelia, at some easier time. "To answer your question, I imagine it dates from when she first met your father."

"Is she trying to collect the whole set, or what?"

"I don't know if there are any more. She's surely collected me." More cider. More electrolyte. More cider. More oxygen.

"Aral collected me first."

More stillness. Miles's under-reaction was a bit worrying. Hard to read. Perhaps it was one of his old professional skills? But then he came out with, "How long ago?"

"What would you guess?" Because it never hurt to cross-check, or maybe it was just morbid curiosity.

Miles angled his chin up. "During the prime ministership, had to be. That was . . . risky. Did Illyan—no, of course Illyan knew. Who else? Besides not-me."

"Quite a few people, really. It was all more discreet than secret. But you weren't there much, during that period."

"You were very self-effacing when I was." Miles frowned. "Which I totally failed to notice. Huh. Logical, I guess."

"Give yourself credit, half the time you were home you were on some very serious medical leaves. That does tend to concentrate the attention upon the self."

Miles lifted his glass in toast to him. Ambiguously. "So when did my mother first collect you?"

"How much detail do you want?"

"Not...much. Just enough to understand."

"Shortly after I followed Aral to Sergyar. It started as a birthday present for him, that first year."

"Ah, yeah, that's probably enough." He drained his glass. "The Betans *do* have earrings for that one, you know."

"Your mother pointed this out to us. Many times."

"I'll bet. Twenty years. Hell. That's not a dalliance, that's a damned marriage. You do realize that, Oliver?"

"By the end, I think we all did. Till death do us..." He broke off. Cleared his suddenly tight throat with another swig. His bottle was running low.

"And you went through that whole state funeral circus without ever letting on. Ran command on the cortege convoy...ye gods." It was Miles's turn to stop short. "At his funeral, I barely noticed you. I'm...sorry."

"We were all walking around in shock. If there was ever a better occasion for charity, I can't think of it. For oneself as well."

Miles nodded jerkily. "So, I gather this thing has continued to date? Triped become biped?"

"No, in fact. There was a three-year hiatus. As we...lost our ways for a time. We've renewed on entirely new terms."

"I see. I guess." His brow wrinkled. "Although I don't see why you should have stopped."

"Grief does odd things to a person. And both our jobs were demanding. And...maybe we both needed time to become our new selves, before we could start over. It's hard to explain. It makes sense to us, anyway."

"If you say so."

"So. Back to the eggs."

"Oh. There really are eggs?"

"*Not quite* is a literal answer, though if you want technical details you'll have to apply to Dr. Tan at Kayross. After her six girls were"—engendered? conceived?—"created, a scant handful of what Cordelia dubs eggshells were left over. Enucleated ova.

Which she offered to me along with gametes from Aral to make crosses. She suggested I stick to sons, for legal reasons."

Miles took a rather longer breath, this time. "All right. *That* I would not have guessed, I'll grant you." And, a little through his teeth, *"My mother..."*

After a moment he went on, "So is that what this is all about? You're trying to decide whether to take her up on this?"

"No, that's a done deal. Three male embryos are in the Kayross freezers with my name on them. Been there for a few months. My sons. Your half-brothers."

Miles made an inarticulate noise, then swiped his hands through his hair in a gesture reminiscent of Cordelia at her more harassed. Sitting up straighter, he looked Jole in the eye. "So are you asking me for a vote? A veto?"

"Neither," said Jole. The firmness of his voice surprised himself. "I'm telling you what I'm doing because..." He broke off. *Try to get it right. Or at the very least, try to get it true.* "I've been watching you since you were twenty years old, in snapshots. You've made a long journey since then."

A jerk of Miles's hand, starting with denial but ending in concession.

"Cordelia and Aral between them raised a good man, which I find encouraging."

"I always imagined I was my own invention, you know. Although that's because I was young and stupid. In my defense, I've got better."

"Yes, it's been fascinating to see you grow into a father. If you can do it..."

"Anybody can?" Miles finished for him.

"I was going to say, maybe I can, too," said Jole.

"That's only because you're terminally diplomatic. Or maybe you just never let your ego get between yourself and your goals, I dunno. Scary trait, that."

"Nonetheless, the results so far are pretty impressive. You have some good kids there, Miles."

"*I* think so, but I don't know if it's because of or despite me. But I can tell you, it wasn't my doing. Everybody has it wrong way round. Parents don't make children—children make parents. They shape our behavior from the first wail. Mold us into what they need. It can be a pretty rough process, too."

Jole's eyebrows went up. "I'd not thought of it that way." It seemed a strangely hopeful notion.

"Well, believe it. Though my whole life has been on-the-job training—I don't know why I thought this should be any different." He hesitated. "If earlier this evening was a demonstration, you do have the right reflexes for going on with."

Jole's turn for a head tilt. *If,* he began, but that word no longer applied. "When I have my children, I don't want them to be cut off from their real family by unnecessary silences." He amended after a moment, "Aral's children. Even though he didn't get a vote or a veto either."

"He left his vote on that matter very explicitly to my mother. I see now why that clause of his will was made so clear. I could recognize his voice, cutting through the legalese."

"And—if you are seen to accept them, others will fall in line." Likely not all others, but enough, as Miles had put it, for going on with.

Miles took this in. "And if I don't, ditto?"

"That as well."

"I suppose that would grieve my mother," Miles sighed.

"It would grieve me, as well." And not just on Cordelia's behalf, Jole was sobered to realize.

"Huh."

Jole, with a grimace, finished off his electrolytes. His painkillers were beginning to fade.

"So, ah..." said Miles. His look Jole's way grew coolly probing. "How does any of this square with your going back to Vorbarr Sultana to take over Ops? Which my mother didn't tell me," he hastened to add. "She didn't break confidentiality; I guessed. Pissed her off, too."

"Huh. That's the one thing in all this that's become easy. I'm not going."

Miles's eyes widened. "When did you decide this?"

"About four hours ago."

Miles wrinkled his nose. "If my mother had known that was all it would take, I'm sure she'd have been willing to, I don't know, set marshmallows on fire and fling them at you before now."

Jole vented an involuntary chuckle. "Frighteningly, I can picture that. Though it wasn't quite that sharp-cut a decision. Except that—this morning, I didn't know, and tonight I do." He added, "I prefer to tell Cordelia myself, by the way. If you don't mind. I have a few duties to discharge first."

Miles waved understanding. "Right-oh." He added, "Can I tell Ekaterin? Because if I can't, my head is going to explode."

"Sergyar's had enough explosions for one day. Go ahead. Caution her to—not secrecy, just discretion. I don't plan to launch this till I've supported Cordelia through moving the capital and the base, and she stands down as Vicereine. The vagaries of the Service permitting, I'll send in my resignation then as well."

"And other people in Vorbarr Sultana? Key people, not a news bulletin."

"That, I leave to your discretion. Count Vorkosigan. You have to live there, I don't." *Thankfully.* He wondered how much of this Miles would pass back to Desplains; it was bliss to not need to care.

Miles scratched his nose. "So . . . *does* Gregor know all this?"

"I believe your mother sent him a complete précis, yes."

"Your side of things, too?"

"Yes."

"Sonuvabitch."

Jole wasn't sure if that was a general comment or a specific description.

Miles went on plaintively, "So if Gregor *knew,* why did he all-but-dispatch me to investigate?"

"Why does he usually send you to investigate anything?"

"To poke into things. Find out what's going on. Fix what I can. Report back."

"Answered your own question?"

"You copied that rhetorical trick from my mother," Miles grumbled.

"Did it work?"

"Yes."

"Well then."

Miles leaned back, recrossed his legs, tapped his fingers on his chair arm. Looked up. "So, ah...what are you planning to name them?"

Despite his weariness, a smile tugged up Jole's lips.

I win.

We all do.

Chapter Seventeen

Cordelia walked across the garden to the Viceregal offices at midmorning, after sending Oliver off to the base hospital to see his burn specialist and get his dressings changed, pick up some clothes from his apartment, and come back without any detours allowed to *his* office. She'd sent Rykov to drive him with strict instructions to see that he both got there, and got back. She wondered if she could persuade him to start keeping a few changes of clothes over here, for their mutual convenience. Speaking of public declarations of private matters.

He'd come in last night from the garden unsurprisingly exhausted—trust Miles to wear a tired person altogether out, and what *had* they been saying to each other?—had a cat wash, and fallen into bed with a groan. There, thanks to the wonders of military pharmaceuticals, he had slept, rather than tossing in the wakeful agony his burns would otherwise have incurred. His start this morning had been...slow. Not quite the walking dead—his sleepy smile had seemed too contented for that—but she hoped he would be moving less stiffly by the time he returned.

Blaise and Ivy had both had big days at the picnic yesterday, Blaise by way of work and Ivy having invited all of her family she could round up. A fine time without serious injuries had apparently been had by all. Despite everything they were ready as usual with the morning agenda.

"I have a preliminary edit of the official vids from the picnic for you to approve," Blaise reported. "There are a lot of private vids of the, er, unfortunate incendiary incident circulating on the planetary net this morning. I think it might be wise to include our own, with a more controlled spin, so to speak."

"Do we *have* our own?"

"Yes, I happened to be in the area taking location shots of the parade ground, and of the fireworks staging process. I got some great angles on the action!"

Cordelia hadn't guessed him for a thwarted war correspondent. "I don't think Oliver would be too thrilled."

"Oh, Admiral Jole came off *very* well. My surveys show that the shots of him protecting your grandchildren are the most popular of any, this morning."

"Yes, they're quite fine," Ivy chimed in. "I captured the best ones in a file to keep."

Cordelia couldn't help herself. "Let's see."

Indeed, Oliver with his shirt off being quick-witted and heroic did make for some fine images. Cordelia contemplated them.

"You're married, Ivy," she said at last.

"Hey, I can *look*."

"Yeh. Copy me that file, eh?"

Ivy gave her a sunny smile. "Certainly, Vicereine."

Blaise's expression had grown a bit confused. The two older women looked at each other, and did not enlighten him.

Cordelia said to Blaise, "Include them, but focus on the fireworks crew, and what a fine job they did in safely controlling the crisis. Sergyar's military preparedness, yes, it works! and so on."

"None of the fire actually fell inside the staging area, though."

"And thank heavens for it. Spin, Blaise."

He grinned and made notes.

She added, "And when you have a moment, round up all the raw shots you can collect of the cloud of radials, before, during, and after, and send them off to Dr. Gamelin at the Uni. He was all over me last night—previously unobserved animal behavior, apparently. Very excited, he was. Some theory about why those species always go to ground in electrical storms, and if they can be used for predictions. He's not a man to waste a good natural experiment, I gather." Cordelia approved. The Escobaran grad students the professor had been towing had been more appalled, and had needed to be reassured that this was not an everyday event. *Wait'll they get to our temblors*, Cordelia thought, and, *The Sergyaran ecosystem. Not for sissies.*

Although by far the most dangerous animal on the planet was an invasive species of ape. She might have to point that out.

She settled at her desk for the morning correspondence queue. About three down, her mood was dimmed by finding a follow-up message from Plas-Dan, being ingenuous about the nonreturn of their proposal, and prodding for a reply. *Haven't any of you people studied game theory?* Defaulting on the Prisoner's Dilemma, i.e., double-crossing your partner, only worked when the game consisted of *one* round. Life was not a set of discrete rounds in a game, but a continuous-flow process. Which they had no excuse for not understanding, because they had some procedures like that in their very own plant, no? Alas, she was dealing with management, not the engineers.

But they *needed* materials in Gridgrad...she permitted herself a small snarl, and set the message aside to fester a bit more. Though she really couldn't hold it much longer.

A not-unwelcome interruption from Ivy, on the com and therefore signaled as refusable: "Vicereine? Attaché ghem Soren from the Cetagandan consulate is here to see you. No appointment, but he seems to feel it's urgent."

Well, maybe a little unwelcome. She had no idea what the

fallout at his consulate had been from yesterday's art debacle, as they'd been silent so far, but she supposed she needed to find out. "Send him in."

Ghem Soren was washed up and in clean clothes, but looked decidedly underslept. His nose was swollen, and his bruised face missing his clan decal, curiously. He came to attention in front of her desk with the beaten air of miscreant soldier on discipline parade.

"Vicereine Vorkosigan. I am here to ask—no, *beg*—you to give me asylum on Sergyar."

Cordelia blinked. She said cautiously, "Ah . . . why?"

"My consul is very angry with me. He is maintaining that he never gave me permission to set up my Discernment Garden, but in fact, he never *forbade* it. I am to be sent home on the next ship, where I will almost certainly be discharged from the diplomatic corps. There will be no future for me there except employment in my family's business." From his tone, he considered this a fate worse than, if not death, at least a serious hospitalization. "Nothing awaits me but disgrace!"

Cordelia, possessor of a longer view, made an effort of memory. When your young life offered its first disaster, naturally it loomed large. After you'd survived dozens, you basically just told the next one to take a number and get in line. In his current distracted state, she suspected ghem Soren would not appreciate this observation.

"Asylum seems an extreme step. You'd be renouncing your own citizenship, for one thing. Can't you just apply for immigration status through normal channels?"

"I understand the legalities, Vicereine. But I'm being shipped out *tonight*. And I can't afford to come back. My family would never give me the money."

Were they poor ghem, clinging by their fingernails to their status like some poor Vor? Had they sacrificed to give their son his chance at helping reestablish the family's place in the sun? "What does your family do?"

He reddened, and cleared his throat. Looked away. And mumbled, "My father and his brothers run a large plumbing supply company on Sigma Ceta."

Cordelia took this in, revising her mental picture. It sounded more as if the older generation, making no headway in the standard roles apportioned to their class, had unified to say, *Screw the ghem game, we're going for the money.* In which case Mikos was the throwback in the clutch, his role as a culture hero entirely self-appointed. She could understand the lack of appeal to him of going back to a rousing family chorus of *We told you so.*

"I did try another route first," ghem Soren told her. "I asked Kaya Vorinnis to marry me, which would have given me a blood right to stay. But she said no."

And I thought my morning couldn't get any weirder ... "And, ah, how emphatically did she say no?"

He cleared his throat again. "Very ... very emphatically, Your Excellency."

Good for you, Kaya. "Lieutenant Vorinnis seems very devoted to her career at this stage of her life."

"She ... indicated that, yes."

Told you a refugee Cetagandan husband would be a bloody sheet-anchor to her promotion schedule, did she? And so he'd turned to the next woman in line to try to get her to solve his problems for him? *You should be fixing your own life, kid, Cetagandan or not you're thirty years old—*

A chime from the comconsole desk, Ivy in the outer office passing through—what? Something more important than this, presumably. "Yes, Ivy?"

"Vid call for you, Vicereine—you'll want to take this one. It's Kareen Koudelka."

Cordelia sat up, suddenly energized. *My favorite almost-daughter-in-law, here?* What *was* it with these surprise family visits this month, couldn't anyone figure out how to send a tightbeam anymore, but this wasn't a tightbeam—"Where's she calling from?"

"Orbit. Commercial ship from Escobar, just arrived."

"Put her through." She swiveled her head to ghem Soren. "You . . ." *can go back to Sigma Ceta?* If she was ever going to be the evil queen around here that her detractors hypothesized, she really needed to upgrade her puppy-kicking skills. "—can wait in the outer office."

He hunched out; as the door slid shut behind him, Kareen's smiling face appeared over her vid plate, a decided improvement. Still as blond, blue-eyed, and all-girl's-commando-team incisive as ever. *Sometimes, Mark-love, the universe does make restitution to us.* But he knew that.

"Kareen! Delighted to see you! Is Mark with you?"

"He's following on." Her grin widened. "He sent me ahead to find out where you want him to put your factory."

Cordelia's mouth opened in astonishment. "He's found a competing bid? Where? I thought I'd turned every contact I had on both Komarr and Barrayar inside out, looking. He actually has something in view?"

"Better—in hand. It's an Escobaran company, specializes in industrial construction."

"Escobar! I hadn't thought of trying—oh, my. Oh, this is going to make their consulate happy with us."

"Good, because we'll be wanting them to expedite the documentation. So, if that land offer at Gridgrad is still open, I have the company's site engineer with me to do the prelim surveys."

"Outstanding. How soon can they have things together?"

"Their designs are pre-fab. They build most of it in their own factories, then more-or-less drop the pieces from orbit. Snap them together like a set of blocks for really *big* kids. Once the site is leveled and plumbed, they could have the core structure in place in a week, and starting to run in two, depending on how fast they can source local raw materials."

She'd meant how soon could they have the *bid* . . . "You can tell them they can count on every cooperation from *this* office. Getting anyone else to come through will be the usual struggle. But, oh my goodness, this could certainly blast open a bottleneck for us."

Kareen nodded cheerfully.

It was a long shot, but... "You don't suppose—find out if they can use a small mountain of plascrete mixer, can you?"

Her brows went up. "Why? Do you have a spare mountain of plascrete?"

"Not the 'crete, just the mixer. High-tech innovation for high-impact uses. Such as military shuttleports. Long story."

Kareen frowned in new thought. "Not sure. It sounds like it may be a proprietary mix, in which case it might not be compatible with our stuff. Shoot me a copy of the tech specs, and I'll run it past the engineers."

Cordelia nodded, and sighed. She'd got the pony; it was perhaps unrealistic to expect it to come with the cherry on top as well. It looked more and more as if the final fate of that crap mixer was going to be as sandbags against future lava flows. "Will do. Send your man on down to Gridgrad and find my city planner—I'll give you all his contact info in a moment. He'll be *so* glad to see you. Him, rather. *You* are requested and required to come to the Viceroy's Palace for dinner tonight. Miles and Ekaterin and the kids are all here, did you know?"

"Mark said something. Not sure where he got it from—it was either Miles or Ivan or Tante Alys."

"You just caught them—they'll be leaving again tomorrow. And there's someone else...well, you've met Oliver Jole before."

Kareen expression grew shrewdly interested. "I may have heard something about that, too. I'll be interested to see how well family rumor matches fact."

"Ah. So will I. From the other direction."

"Wouldn't miss it. Now I've got to dash—they'll be unloading us shortly."

"Give me a call when you get down to the civilian shuttleport. I'll send Rykov for you."

"Right. Love and kisses, Tante C. 'Bye." Suiting actions to words, she blew a kiss and cut the com.

Cordelia let out a whoosh of breath. *And sometimes, Barrayaran nepotism works* for *you.* She sat back in a warm glow of creative revenge, already mentally composing an oh-so-polite go-to-hell memo for those Plas-Dan bastards. Oliver would be so *pleased*...

Her office door slid open; with careful trepidation, ghem Soren poked his head through. "Uh, Vicereine? My asylum...?"

He entered at her impatient gesture. She stared at him in a more benign mood than a few minutes ago. Perhaps...

Finally, she spoke. "Ever work in your family business?"

"Some. When I was young."

"Are you willing to take work on Sergyar as a plumber? Because while we will certainly want artists in the future, we need plumbers right now."

His eyes widened in a compound of dismay and hope. "Uh... yes?"

"All right!" She slapped her hand down on her comconsole desk, making him jump. "You pass the Vicereine Vorkosigan test for determination of purpose and flexibility of method. Sergyar wants you. This way."

She breezed past him into the outer office and said, "Ivy, take this young man in hand and fix him up with the most innocuous grant of asylum you can make sound plausible." Because she'd undoubtedly be dealing with his overlings tomorrow. It sounded as if his consulate was already on their back foot over this, though. Good. Because then she could hold off putting them there by trotting out bogus counteraccusations of deep-laid conspiracies involving bioweaponized attacks upon the Admiral of Sergyar Fleet and the Vicereine's Own Family which, if she knew her people, someone was already floating out there in the rumor-net, right along with "Lake Serena is a carbon dioxide inversion zone and the government is concealing it!" And the dozens of other exotic fantasies that had so often made her morning briefing an exercise in the surreal.

Chaos Colony. We really don't need to make it up...

She was reaching the end of the morning queue Ivy had rationed out for her, and beginning to imagine escaping the office on time, when a bustle in the outer chamber heralded yet another unscheduled visitor, *blast*. Her annoyance flipped to delight as Oliver's voice resonated, and Ivy's returned, "I'm sure she's available to you, sir. Go right in."

She was on her feet to seize a hello kiss by the time he'd closed the door behind him, though she thoughtfully forewent the hug. Somewhere in his morning's travels he'd washed up and changed into a loose civilian shirt and old fatigue trousers, looking just as off-duty as he had been instructed. The medicinal scent of fresh burn ointment and new dressings clung to him, and he still moved stiffly, but his face was relaxed and his eyes were smiling.

"We're getting a plascrete factory!" she told him, and excitedly detailed Kareen's call as he found a straight chair, flipped it around, and sat athwart it. She perched on the edge of her desk within touching distance.

He grinned up at her. "You know, I'd expect a woman to get all swoony about, I don't know, gifts of clothes and jewels."

"Piffle, I'm a *way* more expensive date than that. You are warned. But better still, Kareen will be downside for dinner."

"Oh, very fine. I've always enjoyed Kareen."

"Everybody enjoys Kareen. It seems to be her personal superpower. Fortunately, she uses it for good."

He crossed his arms on the chair back. "I have news as well. Following up on the arrests from yesterday—"

"Ack! I lost that in the shuffle this morning, and I said I'd—"

He held up a stemming hand. "Freddie Haines is getting a stern lecture, a mandatory trip through the self-defense course run by those bored commandoes out at the base, and a stunner permit."

"Well...all right, that seems well balanced, but—"

"The late boot polo team is getting—Fyodor. I wasn't sure if the angry father or the embarrassed commander was uppermost, but if I were them I'd be more frightened of the first."

"Ah." She smiled. It probably wasn't her nice smile. A Red Queen smile, maybe.

"Consider the follow-up effectively delegated."

She nodded, then said more hesitantly, "How, ah, did you get on with Miles last night? He didn't say much this morning."

That relaxed look returned. "You know the feeling of a clean, solid docking, space or sail, when it all clicks and you know you've brought your ship in safe? And you can finally stand down?"

"That good, huh?"

"I think so." He shifted in his chair, stretched his back, only winced a little. "I told him about the boys. Which entailed telling him everything, in outline."

The relief was unexpectedly profound. "Oh, *thank* you."

His mouth softened as he studied her. "You carried that burden of silence, too. And never bent under it."

She made a vague, fending wave. "Goes with the job, sometimes."

He eyed her, seemed about to say something else, but then went on: "I wasn't sure if I'd find myself talking to the Old Barrayaran Miles or the Galactic Miles, but fortunately last night he came down on his Betan side."

"I had a spoke or two prepared to stick in his wheel if he started channeling old Piotr," she confessed. Starting with that pair of great-something-grandmothers up her own family tree—had anyone ever mentioned them to him?

"Does he?"

"Now and then. This countship thing, it goes to their heads sometimes. Cultural reinforcement, you know." She fell silent, waiting comfortably now. Soon, it came.

"When I stopped by my apartment, I sent a tightbeam to Desplains. Offering my thanks and regrets."

"You're very sure?" she said quietly.

A short nod. "I knew the moment I hit send. I'm not sure I can call it a weight off my shoulders, since none had yet been placed there. More of a sense of space, as if my world had unfolded, opened out, leaving me standing there all amazed. Very strange sensation. I don't think it was the pain meds." He studied her. "You don't look altogether surprised. How could you know when I didn't?"

"I didn't, but I thought it was a fat clue when you went for the fertilizations and not just freezing gametes. It seemed to me you were making it harder for yourself to abandon the project. Perhaps not consciously."

He considered this. "In another era, you could have been burned for a witch."

"Oh, rubbish," she said, pleased.

⚭   ⚭   ⚭

Unusually for Miles, the departure the next morning was not for a dedicated fast courier that awaited the Lord Auditor's pleasure, but for a scheduled passenger ship that would undock on time. Ekaterin, marshaling the exodus, seemed more conscious of this fact than her husband, but in due course all the principals, support staff, and luggage were assembled in the general vicinity of the front portico to load into the convoy of groundcars. Getting to overhear Miles negotiating the personal weight allotments of the souvenir scientific rocks with his children had been the highlight of Cordelia's day so far. Well, he could afford the fees.

Oliver had said his goodbyes at breakfast, and gone off to keep his next appointment with his burn colonel. Kareen had left to catch the earliest of the new three-flights-a-day shuttles to Gridgrad where, Cordelia was fairly sure, she would shortly have engineers following her around like entranced ducklings. Nothing had yet tackled Ivy to the ground and leapt through her comconsole to displace the Vicereine's precious allotment of time for sendoffs. *Life is good.*

Miles stumped up to Cordelia on the front walkway, a little out of breath, and surveyed the scene. At least it was *organized* chaos. After a moment, he spoke.

"I know I had issues with being an only child, but really, Mother, *nine* siblings?"

"Don't forget to count Mark," she replied. "Although whether you should be defined as his brother or his parent is an arguable point."

"Brother," said Miles. "We definitely decided on brother. It's all legal and everything."

"So, you go from a lonely only to one of eleven. A bit late, but I did my best. Life is full of ambushes like that."

"Not like that, ordinarily."

She cocked an ironic eyebrow at him. "And when have you ever aspired to be ordinary?"

He shrugged, *Point.*

"Look on the bright side—situated as we are, you won't be forced to share your toys."

Ekaterin, going past with her arms full in time to catch this, threw in, "At least not until they're much older."

"That doesn't even make *sense,*" Miles complained under his breath. He looked away, into the bright Sergyaran morning. "I keep wondering what Da would have thought of it all."

"Dubious at the method, delighted with the results, I expect," said Cordelia. "It's a circular sort of hypothetical." *Or maybe a corkscrew.* "If a thousand things had been different, if I could have dragged his head all the way out of the Time of Isolation instead of just half, if he'd never been lumbered with the regency, or the countship for that matter, if we could have been a quiet private family somewhere, if, if, if... Once you start making up might-have-beens, there's no end to them."

"Mm." He shifted his weight on his cane, and she wondered if she should let him keep standing, or make him sit. But then he'd just have to clamber up again in a minute. *Hands off, hands off.* Or be bitten for her pains. Could his half-brothers possibly turn out to be as maniacally independent as he'd been, and should she warn Oliver? *Too late.*

"I like Oliver," he said after a minute. "Always did. Although I didn't actually know him nearly as well as I'd imagined. I, um... won't mind getting to fix that, as our chances permit."

"I would like that," she said quietly, and he gave a quick chin-duck.

He added, "Just don't abuse the poor sucker. You have him

totally under your thumb, I trust you realize." In the balance of his tone between being offended for his gender and smug for his mother, she fancied the smug was winning.

Ekaterin went past again, going the other way, and Miles's glance followed her.

"You would know something about that, I think. Is it worth it?"

"*Oh* yes," he breathed. "It's plain he'd take a bullet for you in a heartbeat."

"Which would be the stupidest waste of his talents I could imagine." She grimaced. *Let's avoid that necessity, this time around.* "I have *much* more interesting things in mind for him to do for me."

"Can't argue with that." And, more quietly, "I hope you'll be happy."

"Oliver has a knack for happiness." At least compared to the average Vorkosigan, if that juxtaposition of words wasn't a contradiction in terms. It was perhaps the subtlest reason Aral had grown addicted to having him around. Given his early life, Aral had nearly feared happiness, as if daring to reach for it tempted some sadistic Barrayaran god. But he could safely enjoy it at one remove, delegating the task like a shrewd senior officer. This seemed too complicated a thing to explain on a doorstep. She said only, "What is love but delight in another human being? He delights me daily."

A gruff nod. "That's all right, then."

Ekaterin hove to. "I'll send you the final designs for the six municipal gardens and the new Palace grounds after I get back to my office and have a chance to run them through my programs there. Or rather, final for the basic layouts. I still have a lot of fiddling to do with the plant selections. I'm still weak on Sergyaran botany, especially in the new Gridgrad ecocline, and I don't want to miss any opportunities to bring in as much local flora as I can."

"Everyone's still weak on Sergyaran botany," Cordelia assured her. "We're working on it, though."

"I'll probably have to make at least one more personal visit, before turning them over to local follow-up," Ekaterin warned.

"Make it as soon as you like." Cordelia embraced her. "And as often."

"I'm afraid they'd have to clone me," said Ekaterin ruefully.

Miles, clearly thinking of Mark, bit his tongue on whatever tart quip had mustered in his mouth. Indeed, he was growing into his new mature roles—when he remembered. Cordelia supposed it would be as pointless to beg him to slow down as it had ever been.

Doors slammed, voices called, hugs were exchanged all around, some of them startlingly sticky; this necessitated a last-moment foray for wipes. A certain thick and well-secured portfolio was taken under the personal supervision of the Heir. Persons short and tall were loaded, unloaded, rearranged, and loaded again.

"Goodbye!" Cordelia called. "Travel safe! And remember, tightbeams—they're not just for emergencies, dammit!" She semaphored to Ekaterin. "Send me more pictures of the kids along with those plans!"

A last acknowledging wave, and the caravan pulled out. It grew a bit blurry, turning away into the street. She watched it out of sight, and a while longer.

O loves, take delight in one another.
While you can, take delight.

Epilogue

The day after the day after the joint formal openings of the Gridgrad shuttleport base, and the almost-finished, already-occupied Viceregal palace in what was rapidly becoming West Gridgrad's city center, Jole and Cordelia took some time off together. It would have been the prior day but, as Cordelia sighed in one of her mantras, *There's Always Something.*

The ceremonies had gone quite smoothly, entirely devoid of explosions or fires and with only the normal attrition of persons to the base infirmary for minor complaints or, much later in the day and thankfully off-duty, drunken accidents. General Haines had been puffed and pleased and almost over his lingering grudges against Sergyaran contractors.

Fyodor had been joined at last by Madame Haines, who'd proved dumpy and frumpy and quietly decisive. A hint of their more complex inner world was supplied only by the fact that Fyodor kept her hand locked through his arm whenever he had the excuse, as if to anchor her there, and that he could be spotted cordially massaging the back of her neck when he thought no one was looking.

Chief of Imperial Service Engineers General Otto shared the ceremonial platform, in one of his periodic rechecks of their progress. Cordelia, who had known him back in Vorbarr Sultana in both their younger days, had hailed his initial arrival last year with nearly the ecstatic squeals of a teen girl crushing on a musician. As Jole shortly figured out, it was Otto's energy, efficiency and calm good sense that beguiled her, not his sex appeal. Although even that was not lacking, for a certain mature taste, though it was clear that for him *physical* was the first half of a compound word followed by *plant. Hey, I can* look. After watching him get things done, by hook or crook, Jole had come to see Cordelia's point, and joined her fandom.

West Gridgrad actually looked more like a war zone than the base did just now, but things were coming along. Cordelia assured him that her daughter-in-law's civic gardens were *supposed* to look like that at this stage; they had great bones, which everyone would see when they were draped in their living cloaks of green and gray-green, with a touch of Barrayaran red-brown here and there for contrast. Jole had to take her word.

Kareenburg was still complaining bitterly of its abandonment; even a strong series of temblors six months ago that had cracked pavements all over town had not quelled the chorus. Cordelia had gripped her hair but, since she was getting her way after all, refrained from tearing any out.

There had been, in the inevitable course of events, some quite imaginative slanders circulated about the Vicereine's and the Admiral's new private life. The contents had ranged from risible to enraging. Cordelia had ignored them. Jole had tried to. She wasn't *wrong.* As the lack of angry, or indeed any, reaction failed to reward their detractors with the attention they desired, they moved on to other less-wise and more-profitable targets. *Poor stupid sods,* Cordelia had muttered, but made no move to rescue these sacrifices. She hadn't always loved her Vorbarr Sultana experiences, but no one could say she hadn't learned from them.

As their suborbital shuttle lifted off, Jole had to admit that his strongest emotion at leaving the new capital and all its local uproars in their wake was *relief*.

Cordelia glanced out the window at the ImpSec shuttle pacing them. "I don't suppose ImpSec and I will ever be entirely shut of each other," she sighed.

"No," Jole agreed. "Even when you're done being Vicereine"— he'd seen the calendar on her bathroom wall, days marked down with a broad red flow-pen—"you will never stop being Gregor's foster-mother."

"And therefore a potential handle on the Emperor, I know, I know." She frowned. "Gregor knows how to stand his ground, if he has to."

"But it would be cruel to make him." Cordelia's ImpSec coverage, however much it made her itch, shielded Jole's heart as well, and at no added cost to the Imperium. Not to mention her property and her progeny. She might have his sympathy on this issue, but they both knew she'd never get his accord.

"Well—I just hope Allegre's boys and girls can learn to like the backcountry." Her eyes narrowed in calculation. "Maybe I can find some chores for them, in their down times."

The small shuttle had been borrowed from the base, and was fast and utilitarian rather than luxurious. The seats had been rearranged into four groupings, one held by Jole and Cordelia, with Aurelia's seat strapped in across, the other by Rykov, Ma Rykov, and the young nanny expensively imported from the Vorkosigan's District, another armsman's daughter who had grown up on Sergyar and had hankered to return. The third held a trio of Palace servants in charge of the picnic, and the fourth housed their secured supplies. Not exactly solitude, but in the ambient noise of the flight two people with their heads together could converse in reasonable privacy.

"I started my resignation process yesterday," Jole told her.

She nodded, trying not to smile too much. "How long till your replacement arrives?"

"Two to six months, I was given to understand." He'd found

himself hoping for the lower figure. "And then I called Dr. Tan and told him to start Everard Xav."

The grin this time escaped and took over her face. She squeezed his arm in silent enthusiasm. "He and Nile will be almost age-mates, then." Aurelia's next younger sister, now brewing blobbily in her replicator.

Jole's third piece of news had to wait as Aurelia woke up and began burbling at her mother, who promptly rescued her from her seat, and Jole was treated to the always-fascinating sight of Cordelia playing with her daughter.

Aurelia had escaped from her uterine replicator some eighteen months ago, and promptly embarked on, as nearly as Jole could tell, a course of world domination. She'd certainly captured the government on the first day.

"You're such a big, strong girl!" Cordelia told her. "So good! Such a sturdy baby!" Aurelia chortled back and with Cordelia's aid began dance-marching on her mother's lap. These observations had been repeated about five hundred times since her birth, by Jole's count.

Cordelia had been fiercely protective at first, scarcely letting anyone else touch the baby and reducing the nanny to tears more than once. Jole had finally taken the poor girl aside and explained about Miles's infancy. Undersized, bones nearly friable, subjected to endless medical procedures and in constant pain, frustrated by hampering pads and braces, he'd reportedly let the world know, but the world had not responded at all satisfactorily. It was easy to see how his medicalized start might have traumatized Miles; less obvious till now that it had also left Cordelia a trifle crazed. The nanny had caught on, and, slowly, Cordelia had started to relax as Aurelia plainly thrived. Maybe after Miles, a perfectly normal infant *would* seem like a super-baby to her. Jole hoped that by six repetitions she would get used to it.

"If only she would start talking in complete sentences," Cordelia added aside to Jole, her new worry. Language acquisition had been young Miles's only early accomplishment, Jole understood, blasting through words to sentences to paragraphs with alarming speed in his drive to gain some control of his bewildering universe.

Aurelia was currently doing quite well at operating her adults to her satisfaction with a combination of body language, facial expressions, and weirdly strung-together vocabulary. Plus built-in siren, for emergencies. At length Cordelia, showing a trust Jole felt obliged to support, handed her over, and then it was his turn to be reduced to apparent idiocy in their strange transactional dance of communication. His performance today seemed to be up to her exacting standards, anyway.

At last the shuttle dropped toward their destination. Jole strapped Aurelia back into her seat for the landing, to her futile annoyance. The coastline was visible first, a forbidding line of red cliffs with a ruff of surf below. Then the harbor mouth disclosed itself, and the astonishing sheltered waters beyond.

The harbor wound its way inland through the surrounding hills for nearly twenty kilometers. Promontories and points alternated with deeply involuted coves to create a lavish length of shoreline. The site lay on the borderline between the sub-tropic and the temperate, moderated still further by the sea and the deep, translucent waters of the bay, almost a warm-water fjord. Jole had visited the place several times with Cordelia, and it still seemed a dream of clarity and light.

A hamlet-growing-to-village was sited about halfway in, taking advantage of an optimum combination of fresh water coming down from the low hills and a steep marine drop-off to place a quay. Port Nightingale's small fusion plant produced a hundred-fold more power than the present thousand or so inhabitants could use, but Jole suspected it would be running to capacity in far less time than Cordelia projected. Flatter lands behind the first range of hills were already peppered with small farms and sapling orchards and vineyards.

Instead of the village shuttlepad, their vessel and its outrider aimed for a promontory thrusting out into the bay about two kilometers closer to the sea. A decade past, Cordelia had purchased it and its entire backing cove, all the way around, her one personal Sergyaran speculation. Jole could see why.

Cordelia had set her new home toward the mouth of the cove on the hillside facing roughly east, toward the sea. As the party disembarked and set up for the afternoon, Jole and she took a stroll around the building site. The rectangular foundation had been cut into the slope about fifty meters above the shoreline and, they discovered, plumbed since their last visit, the well drilled and septic system in place. No actual facilities yet, the necessities being supplied by a builders' privy downslope, but one could see their promissory shapes. Cordelia was thrilled.

No builders present today. In the evolutionary struggle for local resources, they'd all gone off to work on the hamlet's first clinic. She would get them back eventually, she supposed with a sigh. Today, she was full of her plans for an underwater steel net to be strung across the mouth of the cove to create a safe swimming and diving zone for future residents and guests. The colonists had scarcely begun to explore their new seas, but their wild array of interlocking ecosystems had already been discovered to include larger predators than any yet found on land.

"Have you decided where you want your section?" she asked Jole, as she gazed around the somewhat scrubby gray-green amphitheater embracing the cove.

"I'm thinking directly across. I like the view back up the bay and the sunsets. It will make a nice healthy walk around the cove to you, or a short kayak ride across, weather depending." He wondered how much time his future kayak would spend parked in her future dock. Lots, he trusted. "Or a swim, if I'm feeling energetic."

She grinned. "I like that picture."

The eastward promontory itself, they'd agreed, they would save for the future.

They shared their picnic lunch with the small ImpSec crew, whose most diligent efforts had failed to discover anything remotely resembling a human hazard out here. Biological ones, well, everyone was still working on that. Afterward, while Aurelia and Armsman Rykov both took naps on blankets, Jole and Cordelia walked around the perimeter of the cove where a path had already been cut and beaten into the undergrowth, and climbed the promontory for its fabulous view up and down the bay. To the east, the harbor mouth gave a glimpse of an unimpeded horizon stretching across the rim of the world, sea and sky imperceptibly blending in a hazy line of blue and violet.

"That," said Jole, catching his breath after the scramble to the top, "is one great big lake."

Cordelia laughed softly.

"I wanted to tell you," he confided almost shyly. "Gamelin tells me that if I pick up one more biochem course, and pull together all those field notes I've been sending him for the journal the past two years into a coherent paper, he wants to roll my bachelor's and master's into one, and shove me directly into his grad program."

Even Jole had stopped pretending *this is only a hobby* some months ago. Cordelia had been entirely unsurprised.

She replied lightly, "A student who can already write and think, who could organize any sized field expedition to the most exotic locale, safely, with one hand tied behind his barely scarred back, who could probably run an academic department or an entire university in his sleep if he wanted to—"

"Field work," Jole put in firmly. "I want field work. Outdoors."

"Of course Gamelin is panting." She laced her arm through his. "I predict your future students will adore you, Professor Jole, and sooner than you think. You even already know how to teach."

"Well, sure. The peacetime military is almost nothing but teaching. Processing newbies all the time, bringing them up to speed. Getting people to do things they've never done before." He added reflectively, "The wartime military too, only faster. Outsiders... don't always recognize that function." The good officers and noncoms modeled the military virtues, and sometimes a few more besides; the bad modeled rot that could linger for several short generations of personnel turnover. Jole wondered what model of officer he'd been, and how long his wake would last.

"Geophysically, the Sergyaran seas are mapped to the millimeter."

"I know," said Jole. "We did a lot of it from orbit."

"Their biosphere needs someone to go take a closer look."

"More than one someone. Five thousand years, Gamelin once guessed, and it took me a while to realize that wasn't a joke. This bay alone could keep an explorer busy for half a lifetime." And close to home—right out the researcher's front door, perhaps. "Beyond the harbor mouth—well, a man would run out of breath long before he ran out of questions." The extensive and intricate reeflike structures along the northerly coast of this very continent were already getting some attention, but practical needs were still drawing most resources to the land. "Finding funding for a proper research vessel could be a stretch."

"Mm, I might know a couple of people who are adept at finding funding. Don't give up on that idea too soon."

"Hadn't planned to. It's a grand buffet, but no one could eat it all at once."

Cordelia's grin widened. "*God* I've missed the sound of scientific greed. You could almost be—"

"Betan?"

"I was going to say, Betan Survey. We lot were always, mm, not as good a fit back in the home tunnels as some."

Her hand stole into his, and he gripped it back.

After a little, she said, "I know where you might find a navigator for that boat, for cheap. She'd probably work for foot rubs. And lab access."

"It's a deal," he said, and they stood a while longer, looking to the horizon line where a new sun would rise tomorrow.

Miles Vorkosigan/Naismith: His Universe and Times

CHRONOLOGY	EVENTS	CHRONICLE
Approx. 200 years before Miles's birth	Quaddies are created by genetic engineering.	*Falling Free*
During Beta-Barrayaran War	Cordelia Naismith meets Lord Aral Vorkosigan while on opposite sides of a war. Despite difficulties, they fall in love and are married.	*Shards of Honor*
The Vordarian Pretendership	While Cordelia is pregnant, an attempt to assassinate Aral by poison gas fails, but Cordelia is affected; Miles Vorkosigan is born with bones that will always be brittle and other medical problems. His growth will be stunted.	*Barrayar*
Miles is 17	Miles fails to pass a physical test to get into the Service Academy. On a trip, necessities force him to improvise the Free Dendarii Mercenaries into existence; he has unintended but unavoidable adventures for four months. He	*The Warrior's Apprentice*

CHRONOLOGY	EVENTS	CHRONICLE
	leaves the Dendarii in Ky Tung's competent hands and takes Elli Quinn to Beta for rebuilding of her damaged face; returns to Barrayar to thwart plot against his father. Emperor pulls strings to get Miles into the Academy.	
Miles is 20	Ensign Miles graduates and immediately has to take on one of the duties of the Barrayaran nobility and act as detective and judge in a murder case. Shortly afterward, his first military assignment ends with his arrest. Miles has to rejoin the Dendarii to rescue the young Barrayaran emperor. Emperor accepts Dendarii as his personal secret service force.	"The Mountains of Mourning" in *Borders of Infinity* *The Vor Game*
Miles is 22	Miles and his cousin Ivan attend a Cetagandan state funeral and are caught up in Cetagandan internal politics.	*Cetaganda*
	Miles sends Commander Elli Quinn, who's been given a new face on Beta, on a solo mission to Kline Station.	*Ethan of Athos*
Miles is 23	Now a Barrayaran Lieutenant, Miles goes with the Dendarii to smuggle a scientist out of Jackson's Whole. Miles's fragile leg bones have been replaced by synthetics.	"Labyrinth" in *Borders of Infinity*

CHRONOLOGY	EVENTS	CHRONICLE
Miles is 24	Miles plots from within a Cetagandan prison camp on Dagoola IV to free the prisoners. The Dendarii fleet is pursued by the Cetagandans and finally reaches Earth for repairs. Miles has to juggle both his identities at once, raise money for repairs, and defeat a plot to replace him with a double. Ky Tung stays on Earth. Commander Elli Quinn is now Miles's right-hand officer. Miles and the Dendarii depart for Sector IV on a rescue mission.	"The Borders of Infinity" in *Borders of Infinity* *Brothers in Arms*
Miles is 25	Hospitalized after previous mission, Miles's broken arms are replaced by synthetic bones. With Simon Illyan, Miles undoes yet another plot against his father while flat on his back.	*Borders of Infinity* interstitial material
Miles is 28	Miles meets his clone brother Mark again, this time on Jackson's Whole.	*Mirror Dance*
Miles is 29	Miles hits thirty; thirty hits back.	*Memory*
Miles is 30	Emperor Gregor dispatches Miles to Komarr to investigate a space accident, where he finds old politics and new technology make a deadly mix.	*Komarr*
	The Emperor's wedding sparks romance and intrigue on Barrayar, and Miles plunges up to his neck in both.	*A Civil Campaign*

CHRONOLOGY	EVENTS	CHRONICLE
Miles is 31	Armsman Roic and Sergeant Taura defeat a plot to unhinge Miles and Ekaterin's midwinter wedding.	"Winterfair Gifts" in *Irresistible Forces*
Miles is 32	Miles and Ekaterin's honeymoon journey is interrupted by an Auditorial mission to Quaddiespace, where they encounter old friends, new enemies, and a double handful of intrigue.	*Diplomatic Immunity*
Ivan turns 35	ImpSec Headquarters suffers a problem with moles.	*Captain Vorpatril's Alliance*
Miles is 39	Miles and Roic go to Kibou-daini to investigate cryo-corporation chicanery.	*Cryoburn*
Cordelia is 76	On Sergyar, Cordelia Vorkosigan and Oliver Jole work together to reconcile the past, the present, and the future.	*Gentleman Jole and the Red Queen*